UNTIL THE END OF THE WORLD

also by Michael Summerleigh
from Dancing Wolf Press

⁂

Tales of the City
The Unfading Flower
Arabella
A Skulk of Foxes
Ere Ever the City Sang
The Witch of the Westvales
The Adventures of Roddy & Dante
The Further Adventure of Roddy & Dante
Farewell Thou Fair Day

⁂

coming in 2025 from Jackanapes Press

⁂

The Exile & other Tales of Carcosa
The Black Wolf
Light From a Gibbous Moon
Fantasy & Nightmare

UNTIL THE END OF THE WORLD

& OTHER QUESTS FOR PEACE

MICHAEL SUMMERLEIGH

Dancing Wolf Press
Tamworth Ontario
2024

for Peggi S

Copyright © 2024 by Michael Summerleigh
Cover "Spacehunter" by Larry Dickison (1984)
Dancing Wolf logo by L.S. Madden - SeeShell Graphics
with inspiration from a design by DansuDragon (UK)
Music credit from *Sanctuary*
"...If I gave you everything you wanted...would I be the one who'd have t'cry..."
McKendree Spring (Dreyfuss-Slutsky) IF I GAVE YOU EVERYTHING

MIRANDA MOON appeared on the **Scarlet Leaf Review** website (April-July 2021)
IN TRANSIT appeared on the **Literary Yard** website (16 April 2020)
THE CHEWING GUM GOD appeared on the ***cc&d*** (**Scars.tv**) website (Volume 296 – April 2020)
AU 'VOIR appeared on the **Scarlet Leaf Review** website (October 2019)
LOST & FOUND appeared on the **Literary Yard** website (10 August 2019)
UNDER THE GUNS appeared on the ***cc&d*** (**Scars.tv**) website (Volume 297 – May 2020)
A DREAM OF NATALIE appeared on the **Literary Yard** website (16 July 2019)
COMFORTABLY NUMB appeared on the ***cc&d*** (**Scars.tv**) website (Volume 302 – October 2020)
FORTY YEARS & FIFTEEN MINUTES appeared on the ***cc&d*** (**Scars.tv**) website
(Volume 308 – April 2021)
PAST DUE appeared on the **Literary Yard** website (11 July 2020)
DIANE appeared on the **MONO** website (October 2021)
CHELSEA appeared on the ***cc&d*** (**Scars.tv**) website in three parts
(Volumes 299-301, July-September 2020)

THE YOUNG GIRL & THE SEA appeared on the **Lamplit Underground** website (Volume 7 – July 2022)
HEART'S-EASE appeared on the **MONO** website (11 June 2021)

Dancing Wolf Press
P.O. Box 194
Tamworth, Ontario
Canada K0K 3G0

UNTIL THE END OF THE WORLD

(& OTHER QUESTS FOR PEACE)

Until the End of the World (*Jusqu'a la fin du monde*)
Dancing with Shadows
Miranda Moon
The Chewing Gum God
In Transit
Under the Guns
Au 'voir
Lost & Found
A Dream of Natalie
Sun Going Down
Comfortably Numb
Forty Years & Fifteen Minutes
Haunted
Past Due
A Song for Catherine
Sanctuary
Diane
Chelsea
The Young Girl & the Sea

Dreaming of Damascus
Heart's-Ease
l'Ombre de rien (The Shadow of Nothing)

UNTIL THE END OF THE WORLD

& OTHER QUESTS FOR PEACE

UNTIL THE END OF THE WORLD (Jusqu'a la fin du monde)

PROLOGUE: A CONVERSATION BY CANDLELIGHT IN THE HOUSE NORTHWEST OF KINGSTON ONTARIO - SUMMER 2010

"Rosie was so sweet today. This afternoon when I was helping get her stuff together for her sleepover at Caitlin's she said it was about time you and me had some alone-time together."

Christina seemed startled...put her head down, a shower of midnight hair falling over her face.

"I said that once...it was a long time ago...it doesn't feel that way..."

"Oh Tina I didn't mean t'make you cry."

"It's okay, honey. It's just that it feels like they're still here. Sometimes I look out back and I think I can see them sitting in Pooh's Garden together feeding him treats and I hear little bits of Beethoven and Jimi Hendrix or Janis or Laura Nyro. Holy shit it's like my whole life was nothing but all this wonderful music watching them so in love with each other that it just kept spilling out over me...and he wasn't even my real father."

"What?!?!?!"

"I never told you. I was four months on the way when they met each other."

"No way! The three of you could have been brothers and sisters…"

Christina nodded.

"Mom told me right before I graduated high school, and the day I decided I wanted to come back here he was driving me into Mesa and stopped to tell me himself. I just said I didn't care, nobody could have ever been better than him…

"We went to have some breakfast and we both started crying it was one of the last times I can really remember when he put his arms around me and I ducked under his hair where I knew I was safe."

"You did that a lot."

"He did it all the time whenever he got freaked out. He'd put his head down and try to disappear but he was *always* there when *I* got scared, whenever *I* was worried or sad. He tried so hard for everything to be perfect for me and mom all the time."

"Tina they wouldn't want you t'be hurting so much."

"I know I know…I just miss them so much…the sound of their voices…watching them always reaching for each other and the way he made fun of her whenever she messed up with her English."

"I remember that."

"They were so funny."

"Yeah they were."

"My *Anglais* poophead lover boy daddy."

UNTIL THE END OF THE WORLD

"And your hot French girl mama."

The candles made dancing shadows across the walls lined with records and compact discs and books about the music, a few photographs, a poster over fifty years old—a rickety old wooden Jefferson Airplane with cartoon propellers...

"We need some music, girl! We need to get crazy. Your daughter said we should."

Christina wiped her eyes...

"*Our* daughter, Sophie. Ours. You pick I'm gonna roll one."

She got a thumbs-up from across the room.

"I talked to my mom the night before it happened, told her I knew we were gonna be sharing an apartment someday soon. She said she knew something had been there all along from long before even that night when we were on our holiday...in San Diego... she said she could tell and that she was so excited she couldn't wait to get here to see us again."

"I'm pretty sure your dad knew too."

"Did he?"

"I think so. I was feeling left out when you and your mom hit the bathtub together. I think that was when we were in Sedona. Remember that...? And he said I belonged with you guys...that I was family..."

"And you just waltzed in and took off your clothes."

"Well you guys were already bare-ass!"

"Having a bubble-bath fight."

"Your mom was so cool."

"Yeah...she was. Whattaya got for us it's time for tunes..."

"This one. Roxy Music. *Avalon*."

"Remember when you'd sleep over in Ottawa?"

"Your bed was right up against their bedroom wall."

"We'd be up half the night!"

"Your mom made all these neat yummy sounds and talked dirty in French. I couldn't believe some of the things she said but the way she said them was so sweet, and your dad never even knew half of what she was saying but he'd like growl or purr or something at the same time and—"

"Yeah...come over and cuddle. I love you so much."

Sophie walked across the room in the candlelight, held a lit match to the joint Christina held up to her lips.

Christina whispered "The only time my dad would play *Avalon* was when they made love."

Sophie inhaled...smiled...exhaled and said: "I know."

PART ONE - OUT IN THE COUNTRY

1.

She was folding laundry in the bedroom when she heard the front door slam. Somebody went thudding down the stairs to the basement. Then silence...and more silence that went on for a while before she walked to the door, called out down the empty hallway:

"Rosalie? Rosie May is that you?"

She looked back over her shoulder at the clock on the nightstand, unconsciously registering it was a little bit too early for Sophie to be home...just about right for Rosie...but the quiet was unsettling. Usually she said something when she got home, even on the days when they were *having issues*...

She tossed a pillowcase back onto the bed behind her, walked out into the living room and found a scatter of mail on the floor beside the sofa, heard some scratching at the back door and stopped long enough to slide the screen open for a large grey-and-white cat to slip through, happily with nothing dead in its mouth. She turned back to the basement stairs, unconsciously counting eleven down then two more down and to the right. The door to her daughter's room was closed and she was staring at (oh god!) someone from not-quite-too-far-below-the-waist up...showing off tattoos and a truly impressive six-pack...

She flashed on a poster image of Jim Morrison from fifty years earlier...over a decade before she had ever drawn a breath yet still so vividly alive in the CDs...the bootleg computer files...the books...the ancient issue of Rolling Stone from only days after he had died...all having belonged to her father...still listened to or safely stored away. Somehow, when they were small, he had managed to magic Sophie into his music too. They listened to it all the time. His collection was like a digital treasure map bestowed upon them by Long John Silver masquerading as a hippie-freak refugee from the Sixties. Sometimes what they found was utter garbage; sometimes it was wonderful beyond words.

She stood in front of her daughter's door and allowed things could always be worse than whoever this guy might be, at the same time grateful for not enough knowledge of what passed for music these days to accurately say just how much worse. She scuffed across the carpet in her bare feet, knocked on his chest as gently as she could, resisting the temptation to bounce one off the smug look on his face.

"Rosie can I come in?"

Something muffled and ambiguous came from the other side of the door. Christina took it as a yes and slipped into her daughter's room, closing the door again behind her. There were no windows in this part of the basement. Rosie sourced light with floor and table lamps re-wired and restored after rescue from the landfill three miles down County Road 4. Old wrought-iron standards topped with hand-painted or brocaded shades, they, along with most of her Victorian-seeming thrift-store decor, all stood in stark contrast to the far corner where she had banked keyboards, brushed aluminum synthesizers, a mixing board, multiple computers and a trio of widescreen monitors. Tucked carefully in amongst all of it was a six-by-eight inch black powder-coat steel case holding a two terabyte standalone hard drive—a digital copy of her grandfather's entire music collection in Windows Media, mp3, wav and flac files.

A three-foot wide bookcase rose from floor to dropped-ceiling in the other corner, filled with books that also had belonged to Christina's father...the old romances in ornate cloth bindings...fairy tales and fantasies...Alice in Wonderland...and modern fiction that was so eclectic as to hold neither rhyme nor reason for anyone looking for a pattern in what had so enchanted him...all of it in some way speaking to his grand-daughter... inspiring the music she was learning to make on her own along with the inspirations bequeathed to her...

UNTIL THE END OF THE WORLD

Rosie sat in a wash of amber light from the small lamp on the vanity against the wall on the other side of the bed...looked up with a face that was very nearly mirror-imaged by the worried one in the three-foot round silvered glass of the antique that had been treasured by the grandmother she had never known.

The most obvious difference between mother and daughter was the length of their hair—longer than waist-length and pony-tailed for Christina, as she had worn it from the time she was in diapers; Rosie's shagged down around her shoulders *a la* Joan Jett—and then the large assortment of studs, buckles and accoutrements that leaned Rosie's clothing preferences in a decidedly Steampunk direction. She appeared ready to cast off the mooring lines on her zeppelin at a moment's notice.

"Honey are you okay?"

Rosie sagged back against the carved wooden headboard of her bed, kicked off her boots and brought her knees up to her chin. Gold light glinted off the brass goggles with blue- tinted lenses that nested down on the brim of her vintage stovepipe topper.

"I got a ride home today...stopped in the village for the mail," she said, looking down at a small letter-size envelope. "It's addressed to Rosalie Maeve Drouin at our street address, but somebody in the post office knew we don't get mail delivered here so it ended up in our box in the village. Tammi asked if this was me...

She held the envelope up for inspection.

"It's from my dad."

"Oh..."

"I told her it was from my father, but we don't use his name at all."

"We never got married, Rosie. I'm sorry...."

"I know Mom I don't care about that...at all..." she said, holding the envelope now in both hands she looked five years old again.

Christina was glad to have the door at her back, could feel her heart-rate spiking... recognising the scrawl on the envelope. The last time she'd seen it had been almost six years ago...a brief note she had tossed into the fireplace after reading...another farewell from Camille Christophe Drouin before he had walked out of their lives for the second time...almost like clockwork...six years...just after her father had died...

"What does he want now, Rosie?"

"I don't know Mom I'm afraid to open it."

"D'you want me t'leave you alone, honey?"

Rosie pulled a long paisley handkerchief from the pocket of her coat...stared at it as if unsure why it was there. She dropped the envelope into her lap.

"No please stay Mom," she said, now sounding like a little girl again. "Just wait a minute okay?"

Christina crawled up onto the bed alongside her daughter, propped pillows for herself as Rosie doffed her top hat and sank down to where she could rest her head on her mother's chest. Together they stared at the sprawl of script on the envelope.

"I didn't mean t'sound angry," Christina said. "He's your father..."

UNTIL THE END OF THE WORLD

"You don't have to apologise, Mom. I know how it feels..."

"He just wanders in and out of our lives whenever it pleases him."

"I know it seems that way," she laughed, "but actually it's only been maybe seven or eight times if you count when he'd get drunk and call in the middle of the night to tell us how much he missed us."

"What a jerk."

"Yeah. What a jerk."

"He's your father, Rosie."

"I guess I better open it then."

She reached for the envelope, in the same motion somehow magicking a slim ivory-handled pen-knife from her coat pocket and slicing it open...unfolding two sheets of lined loose-leaf paper...

"God! Who writes letters anymore! What was wrong with an email?"

"Stop it Mom it's okay. I'm glad he doesn't have my email address. Let me read it..."

A couple of minutes later she refolded them...shaking her head...

"He wants t'know if I wanna spend the summer in Montreal so I can have my sweet sixteen birthday with him. Do I look like a freakin' Neil Sedaka record...?"

"You're gonna be sixteen next year!"

"Well he thinks it's this year...and...he got married in January, but it seems he's been practising for years and I've got a small boatload of baby brothers and sisters that he's been working on since the last time we saw him."

She tossed letter and envelope down to the foot of her bed where they hung for moment before disappearing onto the floor...burrowed herself deeper into her mother's arms.

"I could call him t'say he's a year early. There's an email address and a phone number, but he's probably got caller ID so if I phoned him he'd have our number...start calling us again..."

Her speculations trailed off into silence. Christina stroked her hair.

"I'm sorry, Rosalie."

"It's not your fault, Mom."

"I know that...but he's not a complete jerk, honey. You turned out just fine, even if everything else turned out crappy."

"Aren't you lucky."

"I *am* lucky, Rosie May. I had two parents who loved me and never forgot t'tell me...and then I fell in love with my best friend from when I was five years old...and in between along the way I had a beautiful baby girl who grew up to be you."

"I'm gonna think about it some more, Mom..."

Christina kissed her face. "Whatever you decide t'do is okay with me, honey...I promise... okay...?"

It didn't seem to make either of them any happier.

"...She got a letter from Cam today."

"Who?!?!?"

"Yeah. Exactly."

UNTIL THE END OF THE WORLD

In the dark Sophie found her face in both hands and put their foreheads together.

"How is she doing with that?"

"She said she was just gonna leave it alone for now...until after her birthday, He thought this one was her sweet sixteen."

Sophie growled in her throat...said something rude...wriggled until Christina was cradled against her breasts where she could stroke her hair and kiss the top of her head at the same time.

"How are you?"

Christina licked twice at something soft and salty in the dark...sighed...

"Scared."

"*Pourquoi...?*"

"Because maybe she'll go to Montreal to live with him—"

"That will never happen, Tina."

"He wants her to meet her little brothers and sisters and have holidays with them and he's so sorry about before but now he's making a pile of money and she can have her own room and her own car and—"

"Stop it, baby," Sophie whispered. "She's not gonna fall for being bought like that."

"But she hardly knows him and all her friends have fathers...most of them anyway..."

"Some fathers are over-rated. And out of all the kids I've ever had in a classroom Rosie's the smartest one I've ever known. It's gonna be okay, honey. Let your girl go with her instincts and you'll see it will be fine..."

"She's our girl, Sophie. She belongs t'you too."

"Well then that's how I know she'll be okay, Tina. Don't be upset over stuff that hasn't even happened."

"Je t'aime..."

Christina dipped her head and licked again...heard Sophie sigh. She put her lips around one nipple and felt it grow hard against her tongue...

"D'you remember our first day in kindergarten?"

Christina nodded a little bit, not letting go.

"I had seen you one or two times after we moved onto Fisher Avenue...but that first day... the very first time I saw you in school...when I knew we could be together every day I fell in love with you from that minute...the sound of you always laughing... always trying to make everyone happy all the time...sharing everything...stories of Pooh...

"Tina when I went t'sleep at night I prayed you would pick me, that you would want me as much as I wanted you. The first time you hugged me and kissed me and said Mister Pooh wanted to meet me it was like God was giving me all the Christmas presents I would ever have in my life all at once..."

Christina traced fingertips along the curve of Sophie's hip...down into the smooth warm place growing wet between her thighs.

"She'll be fine, baby. You're the best please don't worry..."

"Did Grimsby come back inside after dinner? I don't like it when he's out too long after dark."

"Go to sleep, honey. I let him in an hour ago he's downstairs with Rosie..."

UNTIL THE END OF THE WORLD

2.

After a summer of circus masquerading as a U.S. presidential election campaign, Rosie hit the *Off* buttons on the remotes and shook her head.

"Wow. That was scary....way worse than reading about any of it online. It was like watching children pretending to be grown-ups...and one of them is gonna be in charge of the United States...!"

They looked at each other, still somewhat dazed at the final flurries of insult and innuendo, only a little bit amused by Rosie's reaction. In the wake of over a year watching Republicans compromise every last one of what they called their principles... and the Democrats openly manipulating primary results in order to ensure the old guy from Vermont didn't get their nomination... Rosie had shown no interest in the first two debates, dismissing them as bad comedy.

"...I mean he really doesn't have any idea what comes out of his mouth from one minute t'the next...and you can almost see her trying t'decide whether it's time to smile or take a shit. Mom...Sophie...am I missing something? I was a kid when Obama got in. Is this how elections in the States are supposed t'go...?"

Over the next three weeks at breakfast before school Rosie came upstairs goggle-eyed and struggling to express the magnitude of her feelings...

"...Every day it's something else," she said incredulously. "Mom, if even a tenth of what they're sayin' these two have done is true, both of them should have been in jail years ago. All you have to do is look at Clinton and you know she's reading from a script...that she'll say anything so she can win...and him! Tapes of him sayin' stuff and then sayin' he didn't say any of it...or that's not what he meant...? What's goin' on? Both of them must think we're idiots."

With the election less than a week away, Christina was concerned that Rosie was so concerned. They had a brief respite chewing their fingernails as the Chicago Cubs clawed their way to their first World Series championship in 108 years...

Laughing at Sophie and Rosie's looks of open-mouthed astonishment when she announced deluxe munchies and a baseball game in the TV room, Christina explained:

"We have to, guys," she said. "My best friend Rosa from Arizona has been living in Chicago for the last ten years and now she's this crazy Cubbies fan. She made me promise to watch."

"I thought I was your best friend," Sophie pouted.

Christina stuck out her tongue and then purred, "That doesn't count because you've moved on to bigger and better things."

Sophie looked thoughtful, crunched the end of a sourdough pretzel stick and dropped her voice an octave.

"Can we try some of 'em now please...instead of the baseball game?"

Rosie shook her head in mock disgust. "Ohmygod turn on the TV or get a room!"

She managed to duck most of the pillows.

"I promised," said Christina. "I named you after her, kitten, remember I told you?"

Rosie nodded.

"You guys don't have t'watch," sniffed Christina woefully; then she crowed "But I get all the treats...!"

Four hours later they all were ready to stagger off to bed having done their part to make Rosa in Chicago happy, hoarse from shouting at the television, and feeling not at all guilty about having said derogatory things about most of the players.

"They're all really chunky-looking and why're they playin' in pyjama pants?" Rosie had said distastefully. "And what's with all the whiskers, anyway? Some of 'em look like they just got off the boat from Old Testament Bible Land...'cept for the tats of course, so now they look like gangsta rappers from Israel."

Sophie said, "I wouldn't kiss the scratchy ones..."

Christina gave her an incredulous look that said *I hope not!* and disdainfully added "Their hair is too short."

"Nobody has long hair anymore, Mom."

"That's why things are so messed up," said Christina sadly.

Fifteen minutes later the rain in Chicago had stopped and the Cubbies were three outs away from history.

───※───

The next morning, before everyone went off to work and school, Rosie brought her mother's last comment up over breakfast, expressed concern over the state of affairs in the US of A.

"...It's not just the stupid election, Mom," she frowned. "It's cops shooting people left and right for doing nothing at all...and the pipeline thing in North Dakota...beating on peaceful protesters who have every right to protect their homes and stuff...setting dogs on them...it's like the whole country has gone totally wacko. Was it like this when you lived there...?"

Christina finished scrambling eggs, onions and mushrooms as Sophie buttered their toast. They had breakfast standing around the island in the kitchen.

"I'm really not sure, kitten, I guess I wasn't really paying that much attention," she said, "and I was feeling so out of place until I finally bumped into Rosa and Dolores and all their friends...but my dad was talking about how things felt different from when he lived in the States... and exactly the same...that nothing had really changed."

"He'd been gone for over twenty years. Things had to be different."

Christina nodded. "Of course...but at the start, even before Bill Clinton started sticking cigars in places they didn't belong and lying about it in the bargain, he was kind of wary...like he thought something was going on under the surface that we weren't supposed t'know about...stuff that had begun before even he was born."

"Conspiracies? You're kidding, right?"

"Yes and no. Rosie, all the things you're worried about now were things he was worried about when we lived in Arizona. He said America's collective consciousness needed to wake up to the fact that the government was conducting business for its friends, not them..."

Rosie backed up. "Sorry. Don't wanna be talking trash about Grandpa."

UNTIL THE END OF THE WORLD

Sophie looked at her...ominously...shook her head. Rosie put her fork down and started for the door.

"I should get goin' I'm gonna miss my bus..."

On the Sunday before the election Rosie came upstairs for lunch, goggle-eyed, with the news that a new poll had Clinton and Trump entirely even in Florida and Ohio—two states that could make or break either of the candidates overnight.

Early Wednesday morning she came charging up from the basement.

"Mom! Sophie! Holy shit the fat-fuck douche-bag won! Trump won the election! And both houses in Congress went Republican with him!"

Sophie said, "Watch your mouth, honey."

Christina shook her head in disbelief, looked at Sophie as if she might have the means of making sense out of something that made no sense at all.

"That can't be right," she said. "He doesn't even know to speak in real sentences..."

Rosie went on. "They're sayin' she got more regular votes but he won with the electoral college thing...thirty states...*merde*! I gotta get goin' or I'm gonna be late again."

She slung a backpack over one shoulder, grabbed toast and a chunk of cheddar off her mom's breakfast plate and was out the door in a flurry of scarves and a clatter of boot-heels on the front porch.

"Wow," whispered Sophie. "That changes a few things, doesn't it?"

"Yeah," said Christina slowly. "I mean...Clinton would have just been a smooth-talking business-as-usual sort of crooked politician, but Trump is a pig...brags about assaulting women and lies about everything else. What the hell is gonna happen once he's in charge...?"

"You mean after he pays off all his rich business friends?"

Christina looked worried. "More than that, Sophie. Rosie has her heart set on going to that music school in Boston, but Trump makes Bush look like a Rhodes scholar and if that many people actually thought he was the answer to their problems, the States could be in the process of becoming a pretty nasty place for anybody who's not an ignorant white racist asshole."

Sophie poured coffee for them both and sat down beside her.

"Rosie'll be okay."

"Maybe. Maybe not. She doesn't care what colour anybody is or who they're sleeping with...and she's got no filters when she gets riled up. All she's gotta do is run into one of those douche-bags and stuff could happen..."

"Are you still gonna go t'Ottawa today?"

"I guess so," said Christina. "I've got an appointment at the embassy for after lunch, but I didn't think I'd be applying for passports to a U.S. being run by that halfwit."

"At least you'll have them, Tina. You don't have t'use them."

"I just want Rosie to have as many options to choose from as we can give her...and I wanna go back to Arizona for my reunion...so bad...all of us..."

"*Moi aussi*," agreed Sophie, "But your Mom made sure Joshua was listed as your father on your birth certificate...born in New York City...so that makes you and Rosie entitled to U.S. citizenship. Getting a passport should be a piece of cake, just a lot of hoops and paperwork. It can't hurt to have them along with our Canadian ones."

"It would make it easier for her going to Boston if she gets accepted there."

"Exactly...and now I gotta go too...my third graders are waiting. You've got everything at the clinic covered for today?"

Christina nodded.

"I set up all of today's appointments for basic dog and cat stuff... vaccinations and blood tests and whatever...Josee and Matthew can manage that with their eyes closed. They'll forward anything serious to the vet service."

Sophie finished her coffee, grabbed her purse and a light jacket off the back of her chair, bent over to kiss her.

"Take the Jeep today and drive careful, my love," she said. "If it goes too long just stay overnight with my Mom and Dad, they'll be happy t'see you..."

"'Kay," said Christina. "I love you Sophie have a good day. I'm pretty sure I left the keys in the truck..."

MICHAEL SUMMERLEIGH

She listened to the garage door go up and down...the slow rumble of the truck down the driveway and then a diesel roar as Sophie headed up onto County Road 4. She sipped her coffee and looked down at the remains of her scrambled eggs, put the plate on the floor by the back door where Grimsby would be sure to find it when he got back from his morning foray into the wilds of their four acres.

3.

It felt funny "celebrating" her dad's birthday. The sun went down slanting liquid orange fire across the front lawn as she lit the candle in the hexagonal lantern that hung in the middle of the big picture window... arabesqued amber glass and pewter...she whispered:

" G'night Uncle Parry. G'night Mom. G'night Mister Pooh. G'night Daddy happy birthday... and everyone else...sweet dreaming...safe and warm...I love you..."

Every night. A tea-light candle in the window on the off chance the earth had given up its dead and somebody was coming home...needed a light to guide them back to someone who missed them so much that lighting the candle hurt as much as it brought comfort. She waited for the tears to stop. Wiped her eyes. Turned back to where Sophie and their daughter were putting plates on the table and a honking big American Thanksgiving turkey with dressing and gravy and veggies and the promise of curry for at least the next week.

She said: "That smells so good. I'm sorry I've been so useless..."

Rosie looked at her funny.

"You cook all the time."

"I'll wash up everything after, okay?"

"Mom, just chill. Have some more wine we got it covered..."

4.

"...Whatever that is it sure doesn't sound much like Christmas music."

A small fire filled the ground floor of the house with the smell of new pine and old cedar, danced shadows across the ornaments suspended from the rod above the picture window. They sat at opposite ends of the couch...reading...with supper in the oven and Rosalie downstairs in her bedroom bending synth notes to fit into a new composition she'd begun at school that afternoon. Grimsby finished up his chunky chicken Friskies in special sauce and stretched out along the back of the sofa for a wash, curling one paw up to where he could make disgusting chewing sounds over each claw. A discordant sustain from downstairs startled him in mid-chew, his eyes going from sleepy bright green to buggy all black while Rosie rearranged the note back into the proper key.

"No Tina, listen again...it is...sort of...like the Irish stuff Loreena McKennitt does...with some of that other English band that did the same kind of music as the Moody Blues..."

Christina cocked her head and listened again. "You're right...it's Magna Carta! There's a riff in there that sounds like something from *Lord of the Ages*..."

"*Oui...c'est celui auquel je pensais...et maintenant il y a un peu de Pere Noel arrive ce soir*! Remember when we went to my cousins in Gatineau...?"

"I remember your mom and my mom dressed t'kill and all the guys in your family getting stiffies just looking at them!"

"Your dad never even paid attention to them."

Christina nodded and laughed softly. "He knew no matter what my mom did or said she was always gonna be there to hold on to him. He stopped being jealous 'cause he stopped being afraid...for a little while anyway..."

The soft laughter went away and the wistful note at the end made Sophie look up.

"Tina...?"

Christina shook her head, brushed something off the page of her book that left a thin streak of darkened paper before it went white again as it dried.

"I'm not getting any better, Sophie," she said miserably. "Every year it just seems to get harder and harder....and Christmas is the worst."

Sophie put down her book, reached forward... dragged her into her arms... surrounded her and held on.

"Don't you ever feel bad about crying for them, Tina. I miss them as much as you do. Sometimes worse, remembering how often they were the ones who always explained stuff to me...how your dad always seemed to know all the things that made *me* scared...

"My folks would get into it sometimes, and then all of a sudden they'd just stop and one of them would say something like *Let's let it go for a while*...and you could almost hear them thinking ...*Josh and Dani have a lot more fun making up than fighting*..."

UNTIL THE END OF THE WORLD

"A cup of tea...or a glass of wine...a joint...and then off to bed," said Christina.

"And *quiet* talking," agreed Sophie, "until whatever it was that had started them seemed stupid or silly compared to what was really important."

Downstairs the muffled strains of music seemed to come together all at once, resembling the kind you heard in Hollywood movies when the audience was supposed to feel uplifted or sad or whatever seemed appropriate to the hackneyed script...except in Rosie's case it was something you knew was coming from her heart.

"I'm not going anywhere, Tina. *Je t'aime pour toujours*...and Christmas is gonna be great with my mom and dad here."

They all sat in a semi-circle round the tree, Grimsby royally perched behind on one of the love-seats, overseeing the ritual opening of presents whilst gnawing on a chew-stick treat with less than his usual ferocity. Christmas breakfast had been sumptuous and he'd gotten more than his share, Rosie totally unaware that both Christina and Sophie knew full well she was slipping him bits of bacon and scrambled egg and small chunks of buttered toast.

Now sleepy green-eyed he glanced up occasionally, peering over his girl's shoulder, just to make sure he wasn't missing out on anything else that might be of interest to him.

Christina conjured up visions of Christmases past...in Ottawa when both she and Sophie were small, with both their parents and Sophie's endlessly extended family; then in Arizona when it was mostly just with her folks and Pooh, because they had been content to keep to themselves, happy in each other's company, and it had been Christina who brought the world to them only now and again.

As her daughter eyed an envelope and three brightly-wrapped packages that were her portion of this year's Yuletide swag, she remembered the holidays when Rosie was growing up, and how she always had seemed afraid to get too excited over her presents because *Grampa is sad today, Mama*...saw some of that wariness still there, now evidenced by quick cautious glances in her direction she said:

"Go ahead, *minou*, you can open one before Sophie's mom and dad get here."

Rosie stopped looking so anxious.

"Are you sure...I can wait, y'know...?"

"Of course you can," laughed Sophie. "Your mom is gonna open one of hers too so it's okay."

Christina said, "I am?"

"Oh yes most definitely, Hot Pants," said Sophie. She smiled devilishly for good measure.

"Which one should I open?" Rosie asked.

"Small ones are good," offered Christina. "How 'bout that fancy envelope?"

Rosie didn't need more encouragement. Having arrived ready for business, her ivory-handled pen-knife materialised in an instant and her eyes went wide and shiny at the heavy-stock gift certificate stamped in Victorian splendour.

"It's from the new vintage store downtown off Princess Street," offered her mom. "The shop looks like a way-station between wherever they've gotten their stuff and your closet."

"It's too much," breathed Rosie. She launched herself at them. "Thank you... *merci merci beaucoup* ...bigly...Caitlin's gonna be so jealous."

"*Joyeux Noel*, Rosalie," breathed Sophie, and then, "You're up next, Tina...and put some hustle in it Mom and Dad are due any minute."

She handed over a package the size of a loaf of bread, wrapped in an elegant almost cloth-like paper embossed with silver-scaled winged dragons breathing crimson and gold flames. Christina undid the taped ends slowly, trying not to tear it...opened the hinged mahogany box...said *Oh!* and blushed before she reached for Sophie.

Rosie said *What?*...on her knees as she leaned for a closer look..."What is it, Mom?"... and her eyes went really wide all over again.

"*Joyeux Noel, mon amour*," Sophie whispered with another mischievous smile. "*Tres joyeux* very soon..."

Rosie continued to stare.

"Wow," she said softly. "This one's a really pretty colour...but where does that little pink one with the tail go...?"

She thought about it for a moment and then looked shocked. Sophie started laughing.

"Oh look! Here's my folks coming up the driveway right now ..."

5.

"...I don't know what it's about, Rosie," she said. "I just got a phone call and they said they needed to talk to your parents at our earliest convenience so here we are and now we're on our way..."

"Did they want me t'be there?"

"No they specifically said they didn't want you t'be there, honey. Is there something maybe you wanna tell me before we go?"

Rosie ducked her head down and took all the wind out of Christina's sails...an instant of breathless ache in her heart when it was her father...the same quick dip to the right...hair falling forward over her face...

"I got into a fight, Mom," she said.

"You? You got into a fight?!?!?!"

"It wasn't really a fight and it wasn't my fault..."

Five minutes later with most of the story told, Christina and Sophie climbed into the Jeep and headed for Napanee.

A couple of hours later they came home. Rosie was half-frantic as they came through the door from the garage...stopped dead at the top of the basement stairs and stared at them bug-eyed with terror and the threat of imminent disaster. Sophie ditched her coat on the sofa and bear-hugged her.

"You mom was amazing!" she said.

Rosie looked dazed.

"What happened?"

Christina slipped out of her coat, picked up Sophie's...hung them both on the hooks beside the front door...

"Mom...?!?!?!"

...Turned back to Rosie and pulled her into another hug.

"It wasn't the brightest thing you've ever done," she whispered, "but I'm proud of you."

They sat around the dining room table come all the way from Arizona that had been stained and polished before Rosalie Maeve Haller had ever been born. On the underside where the unfinished wood had not been touched by her grandfather were fat Magic Marker letters that read: *Joshua loves Danielle & Christina forever*... and then underneath...*also Rosie May*. Christina had shown it to her when she was ten years old...a secret...sliding her across the floor until she was underneath looking up to see it...there was even something that looked like a cat's paw-print. Mister Pooh...

"...Your grandma told me he wrote the last part as soon as he heard you were born..."

There was a pot of tea...green jasmine...according to a much-younger Rosie it was good for you with all sorts of *anti-accidents*...

...Just in case, Mama...

She'd heard the story of Grandma being bonked by the car. Sophie blew across the top of her mug.

"...So we get there and everybody is super serious and your principal introduces us to Mr and Mrs..."

"Lockwood," said Rosie.

"Yeah. The Lockwoods," grinned Sophie. She tossed her own shagged hair back over her shoulders. "Your principal Mr Storring looks at both of us and says something like he'd hoped both your parents would have come to this meeting so your mom says *Well we're lesbians and this is the best you're gonna get...you guys can choose who you want t'be her father*."

Neither of them heard a sound come from Rosie's lips but there was no mistaking the *Holy shit!!!* that would've come out if she'd actually been able to speak.

"Then Storring goes into this big long thing about how you attacked the Lockwood boy and broke his nose and we really need to get you under control because unless we can guarantee your behaviour from here on in you're going to be suspended from school and maybe even charged as an adult with assault because you're old enough to know better..."

"What happened then?" squeaked Rosie.

"Then your mom said *Really?* and after that things definitely got more interesting."

Rosie did another soundless OMGHS and Christina took up the narrative.

"It seems your classmate Brandon—all six-foot hundred and seventy pounds of him—neglected to mention to his parents that the reason you nailed him in the balls and then busted his face with your math textbook was because he reached down the front of your blouse during lunch break...after he'd done it on numerous occasions...and had been asked by you at least twice to please stop doing it...and had failed to stop doing it even after you complained to your homeroom teacher and had been told by that paragon of male chauvinist stupid that he didn't mean any harm he was just being a boy."

"What did you guys do?"

Sophie took a long sip of her tea and went on.

"I was just sitting there tryin' t'be helpful...but your mom was on her feet and she was doing this really quiet wolf-stalk thing around behind all of us. Only your principal could see her but she was making the Lockwoods really nervous....

"Then she walks over to the window behind Storring's desk and stared at the parking lot...the football field...I don't know...

"Anyway...she does that for a couple of minutes...not saying anything... and then she turns around and drops her hand into his crotch..."

"Mom you grabbed Mr Storring in the dick?!?!"

Christina nodded.

"And then she walked around the desk looking like she was gonna sit down again...but on the way she put her hand down Mrs Lockwood's front and kissed her on the mouth..."

Rosie's eyes got big as flying saucers. Sophie finished the story:

"Then she sat down next to me and grabbed my hand...looked at all three of them and said *See how much fun that was? If anything like that happens to my daughter ever again and you fuckheads do nothing about it, I'll make sure you all get to go on unemployment or go to jail as accomplices to sexual assault and then I will sue your ignorant asses into the ground just because.* And then we came home..."

Sophie smiled.

Christina said, "I vote for margaritas all around. Have you got any problems with tequila, baby? Tonight you can have as many as you want until we all get sick together."

They didn't get sick but things got crazy. Sweats and t-shirts and socks. Rosie got over Absolute Terror and began to appreciate what had happened. In typical teenager fashion for the time being she went with:

"Can we do the movie thing with the margaritas...?"

"From *Practical Magic*," said Sophie.

Rosie May nodded. "Yeah. I read Grandpa's book... but the song...I don't even know who that is..."

Christina emptied her glass, surrendered it to Sophie for a refill, leaned her head against her hip and closed her eyes.

"*Nilsson Schmilsson*," she said.

"Mom you're drunk."

"I am, Rosie May...most definitely...but the stupid Lockwood boy isn't ever gonna touch you again and if you go downstairs and look at all the CDs that Grandpa left us, in the Ns there's Nilsson and the song you remember from the movie is on the album *Nilsson Schmilsson* and if you bring the CD upstairs we can have more tequila and dance around the table..."

⁂

"...You did so good today Tina..."

"No I didn't, Sophie. It was terrible. I don't care about that stupid principal, but Mrs Lockwood...who knows what she's put up with her whole life? I used t'talk t'my mom about stuff like this and she said when she was growing up girls didn't really have any choices. Like with that asshole Trump...he was the boss what could any of those girls have done when he decided to walk in and stick his hand between their legs or kiss them or whatever...

"It was wrong then and it's wrong now and if they hurt my Rosie I'll kill them..."

"Baby stop you did okay. You fixed it. She's probably gonna take a world of crap about her gay lesbian parents, but nobody's gonna be grabbin' Rosie anywhere from now on unless she's in on it, and that's because of you and the all the stuff you taught her..."

"All the stuff *we* taught her."

"Yeah."

Sophie brushed the hair from her face and kissed her in the dark, drawing a comforter up around them, warm against each other. Outside, a cold January wind whistled through the skeleton of the tall maple that towered over the east end of the house, flinging ice pellets against the bedroom windows.

6.

"...Grimsby where the hell did you get this?"

Given the nature of the object under scrutiny, it was at best a rhetorical question. The cat hunkered down over the little body between his front paws and looked up at her with something easily identified as feline dismay. She could hear him:

I do this all the time. I always bring them home. What's the problem?

"It's not a problem, Grimsby," she said patiently. "It hasn't been a problem since you took up where Mister Pooh left off...but there's a lot of snow on the ground and mostly it's still frozen solid and this poor thing should have been asleep someplace where you couldn't possibly have gotten to him."

The cat replied with what passed for a shrug.

It's not my fault he woke up early...and if you think I enjoyed chasing his little ass through the snow you can guess again.

Christina sighed. Grimsby hated the snow. His normal winter occupation was to simply hang out on the back deck on the days when it wasn't bone-chillingly cold and it had been shoveled clear to his satisfaction. Otherwise it was big long snoozes safely indoors. It was the way he had come to them, late September three years before, bumping his head against the sliding glass door, trying to get a better look at what was going on inside while a cold autumn rain outside gradually soaked him to the skin.

It was Rosie who had noticed him first, still just young enough to get excited by the prospect of a new cat. She remembered Pooh. Cried out *Mom, look!* and was at the door in a flash, sliding the screen back to admit a bedraggled dripping creature who instantly started casing the joint, looking for food. Well-fed and finally dry, he spent the night curled up against Rosie, rumbling loud enough to keep her awake and thoroughly delighted...heartbroken when he dashed outdoors into sunshine the next morning and didn't come back for three days.

Sophie had tried to console her...said: "He'll be back, honey, don't you worry. He's just making sure this is where he wants to be."

And that was how it had turned out. He came back to stay and became Rosalie's great lumbering terror Grimsby. He wasn't happy with his visit to the clinic for what Christina called "the basics", but bore it stoically and never seemed to miss the parts he'd left behind. The downside to his residency came in the form of his uncanny ability to channel Pooh by bringing lots of little dead rodents home in order to convince them of his devotion and gratitude.

"Are we gonna fight over him now?" asked Christina.

The cat stood up slowly and took a couple of steps backward. She scooped up the little corpse with a paper towel and shuddered.

"Now I have t'go outside and play pitch'n'toss in the snow."

There was a tree-sheltered enclosed area on the west lawn that her father had christened the Rookery...and a free-standing sculpture made from a trio of twelve-foot elm trunks crowned with a dump-scored metal serving platter. All the squirrels, chipmunks, birds and lizards that had ever succumbed to the tender ministrations of Grimsby and his predecessor ended up on top of the tower, snacks for the ravens and crows and red-tailed hawks that lived in the area.

When Rosie got off the bus from school her mother was halfway to her knees in snow and apologising to the poor dead little striped creature she had, for the last fifteen minutes, been hoisting up into the air trying to calibrate a trajectory that would bring it to rest on the metal platter atop the Raven Tower.

Rosie called out *Mom...?* as the wee thing plummeted back into the snow at her feet for the thirtieth time. Christina turned, looking desolate and tired.

"Mom stop I'm gonna get the ladder okay? Just wait for me I gotta put some real boots on first..."

Christina nodded, saying nothing. She picked up the chipmunk, dusted him off some, cradled him in gloved hands as if maybe she could infuse the body with some kind of life-giving warmth...resurrect him before he became a metaphorical Meals-on-Wheels for the crows. After a few minutes she heard the garage door groaning itself open and Rosie shouldering the fibreglas stepladder as she high-stepped through the drifts...A-framed it beside the Tower and reached for the chipmunk.

"Rosie, there's blood," she said. "Grimsby got him real good."

"It's okay Mom just let me have him. I'll put him up there..."

"Be careful with him, honey—"

"Mom he's dead. Grimsby didn't mean it...it"s just the way he is..."

UNTIL THE END OF THE WORLD

"I know, Rosie. Pooh was the same. I just wish..."

She handed the little corpse over, held on to the ladder as Rosie swarmed up the six seven rungs...not knowing just what she would wish given one or a hundred of them. She remembered a fairy tale her father once had told her...about a feral boy raised in the forest by wolves...and three wishes granted by the Earth Mother who had taken pity on him when his wolf family had been killed by humans...

"Mom are you okay?"

It was like looking in a mirror....Rosie's face...her own...the one that had belonged to her mother...all three of them somehow locked into one archetypal mold...Lariviere becoming Desjardins becoming Haller...as if cast in some unending Pilgrim's Progress where the role of each of them was to survive long enough into the future to reach some sort of epiphany or enlightenment.

"Mom...?"

She felt Rosie's kiss on her cheek, the urgency and concern in her voice.

"I'm okay for now, sweetheart," she said.

"Promise?"

"Promise."

"I'm gonna put the ladder away and I'll make you a cup o' tea."

Christina smiled cautiously, put her arms around her daughter.

"Have you got time for a walk first?"

Rosie hugged back. Sometimes it was like they were the same person. When the ladder was stowed back in the garage and a remote button in the shed had creaked and groaned the door closed again, they slipped and shrieked on patches of ice on the long driveway down to the road, started clumping down the hill arm in arm.

"He was really sorry," said Rosie.

"No he wasn't," said Christina.

Rosie laughed. "Actually he looked like he was disappointed you were the one who found him with the chipper instead of me."

"That sounds like Grimsby."

"You're not angry at him, are you, Mom?"

"Of course not he's just bein' himself. Pooh was just as bad..."

They kept as far left off the road as they could manage, more gravel shoulder showing than usual as the township snowplows had taken advantage of a February thaw and no real snowfall in over a week. Late afternoon sunlight grew weak and watery with encroaching clouds, snow-covered fields to their left showing small bare patches of sodden earth before the houses of their nearest neighbours keeked through tree skeletons and new shrouds of mist waiting to become rain...

"Rosie, is everything okay with you? School and stuff. Are you planning on getting pregnant in the next few weeks?"

Rosie sputtered over whatever it was in her mind that had been intended as words...thoughts scheduled to be spoken aloud...

"Mom I'm not doin' it with anybody how'm I s'posed t'get pregnant?"

"But you've been doin' it?"

"Mom!"

"Rosie."

"Not so much lately. Ever since I whacked Brandon in the nuts and you guys did the cavalry thing with Storring I haven't really been a hottie of choice for the male inmate population at my school."

"Well *that's* a relief..."

Rosie started laughing, a sound Christina knew very well because like everything else about her daughter it was like looking and listening to herself except for the fact that she hadn't done much laughing lately.

"What's goin' on with you, anyway?"

Christina didn't answer right away...leaned herself over a bit to where she could rest her head on Rosie's shoulder.

"I don't know, honey," she said. "I feel like I'm getting' freaked out by just about everything these days. I'm makin' Sophie crazy, and even Grimsby looks like he'd rather freeze his butt off in the snow than listen to half the stuff I say at him."

"You worry about everything, Mom...even the stuff you don't have t'worry about."

"I do. I know it."

"Well you gotta stop then," Rosie said gently, "cause most of my friends just think you're a little bit crazy in a good way, but it wouldn't be good if it turned out you were for real..."

Christina picked her head up and daggered her daughter with the look...

"And I don't like seein' you so unhappy."

...That turned soft as she turned...two pairs of Wellies clomping in gravel going toe-to-toe as she buried her fingers in Rosie's hair, drew her face close to return her kiss.

"I love you, Rosie May. I love you forever. Until the end of the world."

"I know, Mom. Me too you."

"Let's go back okay? Sophie's gonna be home soon and I feel bad I got huffy with the cat."

They started back up the hill rapidly disappearing in a deepening fog, arms around each other's waist.

"You were home early today."

"Yeah...it was slow one," Christina said. "It took a whole pouch of those Temptation treats but we finally managed to corral the big black tom that's been hanging around the last few weeks.

"We ponked him out, fixed him and took the tip off that frostbitten ear. After that we didn't have anything else booked but some shots and things that the kids could look after on their own."

"Mom...Josee and Matt are older than me."

"Yeah but you're just a brat."

"Thanks."

"*De rien*, cute-face."

"Can we have pizza for supper tonight?"

"Sure why not."

"Cool. I'll phone down t'the store. Onions and olives and mushrooms?"

"No pepperoni?"

"Thems is dead animals disguised."

"That's true. You're a vegetarian now?"

Rosie made frowning faces.

"I think I'm still okay with fish and stuff...I mean I've never had any really meaningful conversations with a shrimp...but lately I been thinkin' about all the critters that've come to your clinic...and the chickens whenever you took me along for house calls. I think I should try..."

"I stopped in to see the Robertson calf on the way home."

"The sweet little Guernsey I helped with?"

"Yep. She's doin' swell. They called her Daisy straight out so I'm hoping she's gonna be a keeper for them."

"That would be so neat!"

At the foot of the driveway Rosie went back across the street for the postbox junk mail. As they crunched up through the soggy gravel of the drive there was a sudden squall and squawk from the Rookery—a pair of ravens perched atop the tower making a quick snack of Grimsby's chipmunk. Christina grew wistful...

"Back into the soup," she whispered.

※

Rosie called down to the general store to order their pizza, reassured Grimsby his efforts had not been in vain. Then they climbed into the truck, fog crowding in around them as they seemed to swim through it in the places where the spaces on either side of County Road 4 opened onto fallow farmland.

"I could drive you into school tomorrow if you like," Christina offered. "I wanna take our newly-neutered fellow in to the shelter."

MICHAEL SUMMERLEIGH

Rosie said she'd do the bus with her friends so she wouldn't have to make the trip into Napanee that early. In the village she volunteered to pick up the mail while Christina picked up the pizza. Rosie crossed the street, tasseled scarf and long coat-tails flapping, her hair going mist-sodden under her top hat. Christina went inside, waved at one of Rosie's classmates already at one of the cash registers behind the counter, and inched her way through the handful of people queued up to pay for milk, gas and lottery tickets.

She turned right at the glassed-in refrigerators and bumped into a silver-haired guy turning away from them with a carton of milk in hand....offered an apology and then realised who it was she was talking to.

"Oh...hi...you really do live here."

He grinned and his eyes sparkled behind round wire-rimmed spectacles.

"Occasionally. Mostly Vancouver now, but I keep the place here...stash all my stuff there..."

"How's your little girl?"

"She's good...gonna be six in November."

"I saw a photograph of her somewhere I can't remember where, but she's a little beauty."

"Well she keeps us on our toes," he nodded. "Sometimes she's a little bit too smart for her own good."

"Mine too," Christina said, "but Rosie's older... sixteen in the summer. She loves your music, especially the acoustic album you did a few years ago...but she's really keen on a lot of your older stuff too..."

UNTIL THE END OF THE WORLD

He cocked his head to one side, suddenly staring at her as if a light had gone on somewhere inside his head.

"She's kind of young to know those. So are you, for that matter."

He continued to stare she could see him puzzling over something...perhaps a memory of some sort. Christina explained:

"My father played your CDs all the time, even when we lived in Arizona. I've got all the music he ever owned on a big standalone drive. Rosie made me a copy from the one that belonged to him. She's a musician too..."

He seemed pleased and embarrassed at the same time, but still puzzled.

"I feel like I should know who you are. Your face is so familiar..."

Christina said, "I've taken Rosie t'see you at the Grand Theatre a couple of times. I think you even signed a CD for her once."

"Maybe...but no...it's older than that...your father you look just like your father..."

Christina felt a small shiver run up and down her spine.

"I'm like a carbon copy of my mom," she said softly, "but I remember both of them telling me my dad was mistaken for her brother a lot, because they both had really long dark hair and—"

"Did he ever live in Toronto?"

Christina nodded. "Yes he did! Of course. He used t'go see you at the Riverboat and all those places when he lived there in the Seventies...he told us stories..."

41

MICHAEL SUMMERLEIGH

He smiled to himself, adding the tidbit of information to a hazy memory until it seemed to crystallise behind his eyes.

"I remember him. He'd watch me like a hawk when I was playing, but he always closed his eyes with the words."

"Rosie's exactly the same!"

"How are they...your mom and your dad?"

The shiver got sad.

"My mom was killed in Arizona in '02, just before they were supposed to move into the house up the road here. My dad...he died too...six seven years ago...I don't—"

"I'm so sorry..."

"No it's okay. I'm gonna tell Rosie I met you she's off gettin' the mail. She's gonna be green."

She held out her hand and he took hers.

"I'm Christina Haller. Local veterinarian. Mother of Rosie May..."

He grinned again, another twinkle in his eyes... someone much younger... timeless...his smile felt like someone had wrapped her heart up in warm...an essence of something gentle that simply didn't exist in enough quantity in the world.

"The next time I'm in town call the Grand up and tell them you have two tickets waiting for you."

"Could I maybe have three? Sophie loves you too...she's...she's my girl...she takes care of me..."

"Sure," he said, and gave her a thumbs up. "It's been a pleasure, Christina."

"Me too."

UNTIL THE END OF THE WORLD

"I never got t'talk to him, but I remember your father...I do...for sure..."

※

Sophie and the Jeep were in the garage when they got home and there was the usual frenzy of plates and glasses, crushed peppers and grated parmesan, a brace of beers and a ginger ale for Rosie before they all sat down inhaling square slice #1 for each of them. Rosie said:

"You guys are never gonna believe who I met in the parking lot while you were inside, Mom."

Mom said a name and Rosie made google-eyes.

"I met him inside, honey. We talked for a while and I told him you were a musician too."

"He just walked right up to me and said if I had a demo tape or somethin' to make sure he got a copy...that I could leave it in his box at the post office."

"He's a nice man, Rosie. I've talked to him a couple of times too," said Sophie.

"D'you think he meant it about doing a demo tape for him?"

"From everything I've ever heard about him he never says anything like that unless he means it..."

"Charlie and Sam are gonna shit..."

"He knew your grandfather too," said Christina. "Sort of, anyway...back in Toronto... before he met Mom....he used t'go to the coffee-houses and he noticed him... remembered how he used t'watch him play the same way you watch other people play, honey...and when there were words he closed his eyes too...just like you..."

She closed her own eyes trying not to cry over her pizza.

"He wants to hear my music—"

"They never even spoke to each other, but he remembers him..."

"Mom do you ever stop and listen to me? He said we should make a demo tape for him! How come anytime we have a conversation about anything we always end up talkin' about Gramma and Grandpa?"

"Rosie!" said Sophie sharply.

"I'm just sick and tired of hearing how damn perfect he was...how damn perfect *they* were..."

"Rosie don't swear please you don't have to talk like that."

"Why can't there be anything normal in our lives, Mom? Jesus, I've spent my whole life out here fielding questions. Don't you have a father? Who's that with your mom? And why can't you like live here with us instead of always looking backwards... Grandpa did this and Gramma said that...?"

"Rosie you tell me what's normal and I'll see what I can do to make it that way.

"Sure my father was a suicide...to use your special way of making it better for me, *He fuckin' killed himself, Mom...took a walk into a snowstorm and never came back...*

"Just because you know what's going wrong doesn't mean you can make it all right again.

"I'm sorry you feel that way, but you never saw the look in his eyes when I was scared or hurt or just didn't understand something. There'd be this look of panic...

terror... I could see him struggling not to run away from whatever it was...desperate to find the right things to say so I wouldn't have t'go through the same shit he did... and your grandma just tried to give him everything he needed t'get by...she just loved him...with no conditions...gave him back the same kind of total devotion he gave to her. I hope you get lucky and find somebody like that..."

She dropped a half-eaten slice of pizza with onions and olives and mushrooms and no pepperoni onto her plate and ran down the hall into the bedroom...slammed the door behind her. Sophie said:

"How would you feel if somebody just decided t'take her away from you, Rosalie? No reasons. No kind of explanations. Suddenly she's gone..."

"She's always goin' on and on—"

"Rosie for God sakes I saw how good it was for your mom and her mom and dad and the crazy cat. I love my parents but whatever the hell was going on in the family that made you was a million times better than anyone ever had a right to expect from being alive, never mind being loved...

"She cries for them, Rosie. Every goddamn night. Not because she can't live without them but because it was just so good *with* them. Your mom was the happiest little girl on the planet...and then some dumb-ass stupid gangbanger shot her mama...and her father slowly faded away from the heartbreak of it...

"She's afraid to be too happy, Rosie...to love you or me too hard. It's all she wants to do but she's so fucking afraid of losing us. Please, honey...please...stop thinking all the miraculous and horrible things that have happened so we could be here together are just water under a bridge..."

7.

There were a lot of silences over the next week. Christina went about her everyday like it was just another day, but she stopped looking at her daughter and at night it was all Sophie could do to fight her way into her arms...to ease the tense set of her shoulders or the stubborn clench of her thighs when she tried to sneak passion through the unspoken misery of her grief.

Christina always apologised and Sophie, who long ago had been a poster child for Unlimited Patience and Understanding, would simply be there...always...waiting for the moment when the love of her life would relent... give up...let herself be led away from edge of the abyss that had swallowed her parents.

"I'm so sorry..."

"Not to me, Tina...not ever...I love you and if you're hurting I just wanna make it stop..."

She rolled over under the blankets and wrapped her arms around Christina's hips, wriggled down between her legs, nuzzled her nose and then her tongue into her navel and made for damn sure there was no escape...that her Tina knew for a fact she was a prisoner of Love and had best remember it...especially after all the years spent waiting, and then the ones where they finally had come back together again.

"Dammit, Sophie...Rosie's not wrong. It seems like everything in my life always comes back to them. Like just now what you said...Mom said she was crying on a bench in Sandy Hill and the only reason Daddy ever gave for stopping that day was that he could see she was hurting and all he wanted t'do was make it stop."

"Baby you gotta talk t'somebody about this."

"I don't wanna talk t'anybody about it, Sophie. I have you. I have Rosie. The two of you are so good t'me I can't even breathe when I think what my life would be like without you ...even that great lumbering thing masquerading as our cat...he never leaves dead things for Rosie...I mean am I like Mrs Mengele? Should I pat him on the head and say *Zonk yoo pussykaht*..? But I love him anyway...all of you...so much...why can't I be happy...?"

Sophie took her time...thought about it...marveled at how little it took to make herself happy just hanging on to her beloved girl...her face up against the warmth of her belly...the perfume trapped in her pubic hair. She steadfastly refused to do the razour thing like everybody else...just like her Mom...

"Tina, you said it yourself. Just because y'know what's gone wrong doesn't mean you can automatically make it right again. I'll always be here if you wanna talk, baby, but I love you so much I might say anything I think will make you feel better, instead of maybe saying a Truth that could really help."

Christina's hands came up through her hair and drew her into a deep kiss that went on forever until she let herself be drawn back down again with her head against her breasts...

"Deep down I think she despises me for being so weak."

"You're the one who taught her t'be so strong, Tina. She doesn't despise you. I think when she gets angry like she did tonight it's because she's not been through your life or mine. Rosie gets angry because she gets frustrated...not getting her way....and not getting her way with this means that she can't seem t'stop you from hurting, and that's what pisses her off, because she's still young enough t'think she can have everything the way she wants it t'be."

"I'm just so tired, Sophie...so tired. Like I'm fighting something that will never get tired the way I do...of fighting back...will never let me stop fighting..."

"I got something for that..."

"Sophie no..."

"Tina yes...for now anyway. I shared your bed when we were small and mostly we both really had no idea what was going on in the bedroom on the other side of the wall...but it was what they did all the time...for any reason...especially when they were down or freaked out over something."

"Sophie..."

"*Mon amour, ce n'est pas pour faire disparaître le mal, mais pour le rendre plus facile à supporter*...it's not to make the hurt go away, only to make it easier to bear..."

"Stop, Sophie...please..."

"No, Tina. Hush and let me make love to you. You smell so good..."

8.

She'd come home from the clinic and talk to the cat. Too often she'd have to lug the stepladder out to the Raven Tower and deposit another little body in the Airborne Automat, but she found that Grimsby...grey-and-white like

UNTIL THE END OF THE WORLD

Mister Pooh and Grumblegrey before him...was a pretty good listener once she understood that he rarely offered an opinion and more than anything was just waiting for kitchen deadfall.

Her two interns brought her joy...and every problem that entered their lives, perhaps because they sensed an imminence of being cast out into the world on their own and, knowing Rosalie who was only a few years younger then both of them, found her mother maternally cool enough as a source of information and advice, somebody still not too old to understand their own special brand of young adult angst.

"...Josee said her boyfriend wants her to move in with him," she told Grimsby over her shoulder, "but she's pretty sure it's just so he can get into her panties every night instead of just whenever she can come over without her parents knowing about it."

The cat blinked once in some late afternoon early spring sunlight streaming through the sliding screen door in the dining area, before stretching his length on the scrap of carpet in front of it and turning himself upside down as a means of improving his listening capacity. Christina poured oatmeal into a big aluminum mixing bowl, added two eggs, ground black pepper and a big dash of hot pepper sauce, Dijon mustard and a ton of ground beef...her mom's meat loaf for dinner, and more of them down the road once they were frozen into individual easy-prep dinner-size portions.

Rosie stopped being a vegetarian on meat-loaf days.

"I asked her if that was okay and she got really embarrassed. Turned out she loves making out with him, but moving in with this guy feels like it would be like handing over the title of her little car...he'd take ownership...and then the sex would be an expectation instead of a gift and it would go downhill from there..."

Grimsby seemed to agree.

"...Matthew on the other hand thinks his girlfriend is too anxious t'get naked with him... like maybe she's running and so far he's the first thing she's bumped into..."

Grimsby wagged his head disapprovingly.

"Yeah. Not so good. Not somethin' t'overlook just so you can get your ashes hauled, eh?"

Elbows-deep in a bowl full of awful-looking dead animal and things meant to flavour it into something palatable, she failed to see the Grimsby's look of *Who gives a shit I'm a cat...*

Nevertheless Christina continued:

"Personally I think they should just hook up with each other, don't you? I mean...they both love working with each other at the clinic...and I saw Josee sharing some poutine with Matt. She even let him lick her fingers for extra gravy. That's gotta count for something, right?"

Grimsby had fallen asleep in the sunlight. She could hear him snoring softly, now just a three-foot long grey-and-white doormat sort of thing who no doubt would come wide awake the minute he heard a can opener, or his girl coming through the front door.

"I'm gonna buy plane tickets tomorrow," she told him. "That means while me and Rosie and Sophie are away this summer somebody is gonna stay here with you…and you're not allowed t'kill them. Y'have t'promise t'be good, Grimsby, otherwise next time we're gonna let total strangers stay with you…"

She listened to herself say that.

"We can find someone you like this time, okay? Maybe Matt…or Josee…?"

Grimsby chose to remain noncommittal. Christina heard the garage door creaking its way open for Sophie in the ancient Jeep, and the hydraulic farts from Rosie's school-bus at the end of the driveway. Grimsby opened one eye.

"She's home, Noodlehead. Thanks for listening…"

Coming through the garage door Sophie's smile was better than sunlight. Rosie was still tippy-toeing past her mom whenever their paths crossed. Grimsby wriggled himself upright and tried to convince her he'd had nothing to eat since St Paddy's Day.

9.

Late in the previous summer, someone named Hanna Erikssen had called the clinic, left a message with the kids. She'd heard from a bunch of people that Christina Haller DVM had magic when there was nobody else even trying to think out of the box. Christina called her back that night… could hear the catch in her voice…the intimation of unbearable loss impending…

"…She's this beautiful eight-month-old buckskin filly and she put a hoof down a gopher hole in May…"

Had limped all summer. Cost her a fortune in vet chiropractics. Was still limping across her paddock and seemed to beg for babies except she couldn't walk right and was hurting...

"...If I have t'put her down I think I'm just gonna go with her..."

Christina got into the truck in twilight, drive four miles down County Road 4 and turned left...found Hanna Erikssen was friendly and desperate...and then there was the little buckskin girl...Scout...

"*To Kill A Mockingbird*. It's my favourite movie... that's how I named her..."

It was one of Christina's favourite books too, thanks to her father. Rosie had his first edition on her shelf downstairs probably oblivious to the fact it was worth a fortune. Christina gentled Scout for half an hour and went back to Hanna's kitchen for a Molson... listened...

"I don't know what else t'do. Nothing's worked..."

Christina thought she had a hole card in her deck of tricks...had sipped her beer and thought all the while she and Hanna had talked...two country neighbours finally connecting. Hanna was grateful, but tired and grey in her late fifties...her husband gone seven years...had nobody and nothing but her ponies. Christina said:

"Scout's gonna be okay."

Not so much a lie or something said to win a new client...more just an expression of Hope... Faith...a crusade against her own sense of the world getting away from her.

"I'm gonna try something silly," she said. "Simple. I think it will work."

Maybe it had been her own frantic need to stop somebody else from hurting, but after two hours and way too many Molsons, Christina pointed the truck back up the dark country highway and hoped the OPP were busy elsewhere.

In the morning she'd gone into their own medicine cabinet and come away with an extra tube of arnica gel that got mixed into a base of alcohol and some THC oil courtesy of a stoner friend belonging to Rosie. That afternoon she massaged the goop into Scout's left rear haunch—had another quick beer and left instructions to keep on doing it through the winter—before heading back to the clinic...

They'd not seen each other except in passing once or twice at the landfill, not done anythingmlre than wave at each other since then, but with winter's grip on the township growing loose and soggy with spring rain, one afternoon there was a message on the answering machine when she got home. Hanna Erikssen...excited...like it was good news...

Christina rang her up immediately.

"Hanna it's me...Christina..."

"I couldn't tell with her indoors most of the time."

"Couldn't tell what?"

"Scout...she's running around outside in the muck, kicking up her heels and dancing! It's a miracle... whatever that stuff was, Christina, it worked..."

She left a note for Sophie and Rosalie, climbed back into her truck and headed down to Dewey Road...pulled into the big half-circle of a driveway in time to meet Hanna on her way back to Scout's paddock, laughing and pointing to where the filly did indeed seem to be dancing in the mud, stopping only long enough to race around the perimeter a couple of times before she stopped...saw them coming...moved towards them smooth as silk with no trace of the painful hitch in her stride that she'd had back the previous August. The filly put her head down on Hanna's shoulder, whickering softly as she stroked her mane and shoulders. Christina whispered a thank you to no one in particular...

10.

Nobody ever really knew when Springtime would start in Ontario. It was a flexible thing. Just when you figured it had arrived to stay it would snow a foot...or there would be a week and a half of weather that was like a caravan in the Sahara. Nobody knew. Everybody always complained one way or the other.

For Christina it was a crazy time, all the cows belonging to all the beef farmers in the area all popping little moo-cows out all at once she was out at all hours of the day and night running around in Wellies that all too often filled up with muck and rainwater no matter how much high-stepping she did...got left in the fields until she could stop by two days later to pick them up, rinse them out, leave them somewhere else in the middle of the night...

Somewhere close to midnight Sophie looked up from something she was reading and Christina could see it had been a long day for her too....clambered into bed after a quick rinse-off in the shower and got as silly as she could manage finally wrestling her down into the dozen pillows on their bed to kiss or lick as many places as she could find in the dark that she knew would make her feel good...

She said, "I missed you, Sophie. I missed you a ton. A cow almost stepped on my foot."

"And you thought of me."

"I did!"

"A cow."

"I didn't think of you like that! I got my foot out of the way in the nick of time and fell on my ass in the shit in her stall."

"And that's when you thought of me."

"Well...yes...I wished I was doing this with you instead of sitting in the shit."

She could hear Sophie smile. And then she didn't have to be the grown-up anymore, could let her be the one...and she could drowse away in all the deep soft beautiful safeness of being in love with her oldest friend who knew her longer and loved her better than anyone else alive.

11.

She heard stockinged feet sprinting up the basement stairs echoed by some lead-footed thunder on cat's paws...the brief wash of a water bowl being filled, a can of Friskies being pop-topped, crunchies scooped and dumped into another bowl...then more rustling around the kitchen.

Christina stretched out in four directions under the bedclothes, taking something good-if-not-great from waking up alone there on a Saturday morning. Sunshine streamed over the arch of the four-poster's headboard, sneaking in through the window behind it, still not really spring but with more than enough warm now to keep the furnace from rumbling to life.

She stretched again, this time out from under the blankets, kicking off the comforter letting the light and the heat soak into her skin closing her eyes in no hurry to get out of bed she heard Rosie padding down the hallway and smelled fresh coffee...heard her tentative knock on the bedroom door...made awake noises and watched her daughter bump her way backwards into the room with a mug in each hand.

"G'morning, Mom," she said slowly. "I made coffee."

"I know...I could smell it all the way from the kitchen, thank you, honey," she said, sitting up to take the mug in both hands.

Rosie did likewise with hers, lifted it to her lips for a tentative sip...stood beside the bed looking slightly uncomfortable. Her hair was all spiky, her face still a bit pillow-creased with sleep, knees keeking out below the hem of the long t-shirt she wore to bed at night.

"You could've gone with, y'know," she said, without actually looking at Christina. "Me an' Grimsby can manage fine on our own...and I wasn't planning any weekend parties, if that's what you were worryin' about..."

More than three weeks had gone by since their words over supper, almost a month spent by both of them tippy-toeing around each other, at a loss for words, or even how to re-open the subject for conversation. Christina inhaled the aroma of Kenya double-A steaming off the top of her mug.

"Rosie I know you can get by without me," she said, "and I'm not worried at all you're gonna do anything dumb or crazy just because I'm not here.

UNTIL THE END OF THE WORLD

"I thought Sophie might like to have a weekend in Ottawa with her family without me around…her mom and dad fussing over me the way they do when I show up…

"I told her I'd go with if she wanted me to and she said only if I wanted to and then we got into that thing from *Islandia*…you know…*unmeeting wishes*…each of us trying to please the other and neither one of us saying what we really want…"

Islandia was the monster 1000-plus-page novel that had been one of her father's favourite books…a dust-wrapped first edition downstairs on Rosie's bookshelf, though she had opted to read the much lighter (and safer) Signet mass-market-sized paperback. Rosie nodded, smiled tentatively.

"So I finally just told her to go ahead and have a good time…and that I wanted t'get a chance to talk t'you while she was gone… "

Christina got around to her coffee, waiting for Rosie to say something…watched her fidget…sip at her own mug…turn towards the big sliding door into the back yard finally she whispered:

"I wanna say I'm sorry. I've said a lot of things that were cruel and I didn't mean to say them."

Christina let a breath out…slowly.

"Come sit with me, Rosie," she said softly. "I'm not mad. I know it's tough for you. I don't mean to make it tougher… "

"Mom I was bein' a brat…really crappy, t'you *and* Sophie. She said some stuff and I listened more this time, instead of gettin' huffy."

She put her mug on the end table and pulled the topsheet up over them, put her arms around Christina's waist and her head down between her breasts the way she used to do when she was small...the way she always did when she needed to be closer. Christina sank back onto her pillows, sipping coffee, smoothing Rosie's hair, a vast sense of relief replacing the small misery of distance that had come between them. Soft footfalls came closer down the hallway and Grimsby vaulted onto the bed beside them...curious...unwilling to be left out. He used them both for climbing practise and then found a patch of sunlight at their feet, made circles a few times and settled in for an after-breakfast snooze.

"It's gonna be real warm today," Rosie said. "Fifteen and sunny all day maybe we can put the screens into the doors? D'you have t'go to the clinic?"

Christina shook her head, dropped her chin down onto the top of Rosie's head.

"I didn't make any plans for the weekend, honey. I was hoping we could hang out, maybe go into town, go shopping or something, like lunch at the Chinese buffet or the Thai place at Bay Ridge..."

"That would be swell. Big yummies somewhere..."

Christina stuck a finger into her ribs.

"Not that kind of yummy, scamp."

"I'm just teasing..."

Rosie got quiet again, hugged them a bit deeper under the bedsheet.

"Tell me somethin' good about Gramma and Grampa," she said quietly. "Once when we were here I remember

UNTIL THE END OF THE WORLD

I asked him if we could go see the moo-cows down the road...that you were takin' a bath and talkin' to Gramma because you were worried about him. I knew how it was 'cause you'd explained it to me—you talked t'your mom because it made you feel like a little bit of her was still here with you—but Grampa just sort of nodded, as if *Sure that's okay*...

"And then the last Christmas we were here to visit I was like eight years old and he was just staring out through the doors here in the bedroom...he'd forget who we were...and then there were the times when he knew...

"Right before we left he like woke up and he said *I'm so sorry Rosie. Your mom is gonna think I don't care anymore...but it's so hard...I don't know how to live without your Grandma. I keep getting lost at night when she's not anywhere to hold on to and I know it's stupid but I don't think I can do it anymore...*"

Rosie stopped...heard her mother's sharp intake of breath, could feel her starting to shiver.

"I didn't really understand what he was saying, Mom. I kinda knew he was hurting so much because he started crying and then I didn't know what t'do so I just bumped up against him sitting on the bed and I told him whatever it was it was okay I knew you would understand and not to worry. I said *Grampa don't be sad me and Mom and Sophie are here...we're gonna take care of you...*

"And then...well...you know...a couple of months later..."

Christina put her mug down next to Rosie's, could feel the grief clutching at her heart... again...the awful weight bearing down on anything that threatened to bring her a moment of respite...always there never letting her forget. She took a long deep breath and tried not let to let it overwhelm her...find some way to step past it so she could give her daughter something more than just tears.

"D'you remember when you were really small, Rosie? Before anything bad happened? I used t'tell you stories about Mister Pooh in Arizona...the time he went into somebody's kitchen and stole the ham they were gonna have for supper right off the table... or pooping in their gardens...or teasing the dogs across the street...?

"We'd all sit around at dinner and Grampa would promise to have a talk with Pooh...and Gramma would just throw her hands up in the air and resign herself to never having any friends in the neighbourhood *à cause du maudit chat*... "

"But you were all proud of him."

"Of course we were! We'd apologise whenever we had to, but then we'd go home and give him treats."

"I realised something, Mom."

"Like what, honey?"

"I realised I was angry at Grampa for leaving me. When I was little and we'd visit I loved it when he would pick me up and carry me and we'd go t'visit cows and the llamas down the road, just like he did with you in Ottawa when you were small. It was so warm and safe and I could feel how much he loved me...but I never realised how much he must have hurt when Gramma got killed."

"Rosie..."

"I'm so sorry for ever being pissy with you, Mom. It was the same for you, I know... worse even..."

"Rosie..."

She closed her eyes and could feel more tears but also something like relief because now her daughter knew...understood...and she'd never once even considered the possibility that she might ever be angry with her Daddy for anything, but listening to Rosalie she realised she too had been crushed...hurt so badly... enough so that she had not been able to forgive him for loving her mother so much he couldn't live without her.

Rosalie hugged harder and something slowly edged away from her heart. Finally.

"Where should we go for lunch, cute-face?"

"Wonton soup and egg rolls."

Christina sighed.

"Mister Pooh loved egg rolls..."

12.

When the supper dishes were washed and put away she left Sophie grading math tests and Rosie growling over the structure of Mendelssohn's *Italian* symphony #4 in A major.

"...I get that I need t'understand what he was doing, especially since it was one of the first big things to start in a major key and end in a tonic minor...but jeez it's a pain to tear it apart note by note..."

Sophie looked up and smiled.

"Better to just listen, right?"

Rosie nodded. "For sure...way better..."

Christina poured herself a glass of wine and headed for the back yard, stopping long enough to bestow kisses and offer encouragement. Grimsby raced past her as she went through the patio doors, arrowed off after a chipmunk as she climbed the hill in the wash of amber sunset behind her, then the limestone steps up into the tree-shaded quiet of Pooh's Garden.

Tucked into a corner was the double Adirondack chair her father had rescued from the local landfill. Repaired and refinished, it had been one of Pooh's favourite perches, a place where he had snoozed away his last summers whilst keeping an eye on the local rodent population. Christina folded herself into one side, set her glass down on the table between…closed her eyes and drank in the thick sweet scent of lilacs that lined the old roadbed above her, the cranesbill that rose up in pale pink-and-white flowers between the limestone slabs, spilled out over the hillside and surrounded the small enclosed space where Pooh had been buried.

She could hear the hum of fat bumblebees (Rosie had called them *bummerees* when she was small) buzzing from flower to flower…cicadas…the singsong of loons miles away on Camden Lake…sparrows and chickadees chirping their way to safe sleeping quarters for the night. A handful undaunted by her presence came to the birdbath set just beyond the edge of the flagstones, splashed for a moment or two and were gone. Killdeers squeaked out on the limestone where it rose up through thin layers of earth and lichen. She heard the chitter and squeal of outraged chipmunks and then felt a thump beside her, opened her eyes and found herself nose to nose with the cat before he did his requisite two or three turnarounds and settled down beside her wineglass.

"You like it here too, just like Pooh," she murmured, reached to scratch between his ears and then down over his shoulders where his fur was soft and dense, like a plush stuffy in pearl grey and white—Grimsby by Gund. He started rumbling and the big green eyes slowly went dozy and then closed sleepily.

"Daddy knew good spots when he found them."

She picked up her glass and reveled in a small swallow of the rich dry Cabernet, looked out past the house to where the sun was turning the sky to a palette of reds, golds and purples, the air losing its daytime heat, slowly growing cool and silent as the night drew closer. She looked down to where the stone covering Pooh was almost lost in the cranesbill, and the odd "guardian" set there by her father to watch over him...a teddy bear cast in dark indigo-blue bottle glass...

More and more in the time since his passing Christina had felt a suspicion become certainty; that on the day her father had buried Mister Pooh he had sent him on his way in company with her Mom's ashes.

For four years, from the time he'd come back from Arizona, they had been carefully tucked on a corner of his bedside table, in an antique white ceramic ginger jar glazed in a swirl of intricate blue and silver arabesques. She'd never said a word about it, only noticed that it was gone their first spring visit after Pooh had died, and after that her father had seemed to fade away, day after day, as if this last and final parting had brought home the reality of his loss.

So now it was almost ten years since that visit, and hundreds of slow walks up the hill with a glass of wine in hand, the times when neither Rosalie nor Sophie were around to hear her whispered accounts of the day gone by...or the endless unspoken wish that even now...somehow...someone might find her father somewhere and let her bring him back to rest, to be with everyone who had loved him. She began as always...

"Hi Mom. Hi Pooh..."

...But this time it didn't hurt quite so much, and the sense of sorrow was not so sharp.

"We're all goin' t'Arizona soon...me and Sophie and Rosie...for my high-school reunion I can't believe it's been twenty years...and everybody's gonna be there I'm gonna see Rosa and Dolly and Jorge...the whole crew, it's gonna be so good t'see them all again...

"Rosie's doing great in school. I told you all about her standing up for herself with that stupid boy...and you know what? A couple of days ago she was helping me do some laundry and cleaning and stuff and she just stopped and said *Thank you*...

"When I asked *What for?* she said it meant a lot to her that me and Sophie had let her spend so much time with her music instead of making her work at the Burger King or Walmart; and then she said she wished you and Daddy were here so she could thank you too, 'cause she knew it would've been impossible if the house hadn't been here for us.

UNTIL THE END OF THE WORLD

"You got a chance t'know her a little bit, Pooh...but Mom...she doesn't really remember you because she was just a baby...*merde*!...I know we never did the church or God thing but I hope you're both out there somewhere close by t'see her. She's such a good girl..."

She heard the rasp of the screen on the patio doors being drawn back, rousing Grimsby from Snoozeland, his eyes and ears radar-ed to where Sophie stepped off the back deck and traced Christina's path up the low rise of the back yard.

She'd changed into a light cotton sundress. As she came up the steps into the garden the last bit of gold from the sunset shone through it, turning her into a silhouette full of curves and shadowed places Christina had learned were her warmest and safest refuge from the world.

"I'm sorry I made you wait so long," she said softly.

Sophie only smiled and convinced Grimsby he needed to go hunting again...set herself on the table part of the chair beside Christina and reached down to strip off her t-shirt and bra... knelt to unzip her cut-offs and gently wriggle her out of her panties.... reaching again, this time to lift her up into her mouth. She sighed, making happy noises, teased her tongue through the tangle of Christina's pussy hair stroking up along her hips and her spine around to cup her breasts...a moment to breathe...fingers brushing across her nipples...

"*Il était un rien de temps, mon belle fille*...no time at all...I know you needed to be sure..."

Christina closed her eyes as Sophie's tongue moved up and down inside her.

"I just had to remember," she said. "I just had to remember how it was never better...with anyone but you..."

Sophie only moved her head from side to side, gently sucked at the soft folds of flesh hidden in the midnight curls, drinking in sweetness and salt as Christina tensed and wriggled and the muscles in her belly and thighs began to ripple against Sophie's face.

She sucked the wet out of her pussy and slipped out of her sun-dress, gathered Christina up in her arms and pressed first one and then the other nipple into her mouth... closed her eyes...rocked her beloved girl into the sunset...

They gathered up their clothing, now on the run from the twilight rise of mosquitoes and flying things that rejoiced in sucking hell out of unprotected naked flesh. Sophie said:

"Just in case you forget, baby, *je t'aime* forever."

Christina hugged harder; high-stepping past a nyger seed thistle gone to monster she said:

"I never forget, Sophie...never... me too you..."

They reached for the screen door together, felt the whisper and rush of grey-and-white fur past their ankles as Grimsby hot-footed indoors...did deer-in-the-headlights as Rosie came charging up the basement stairs and stopped dead.

"Oh," she said. "I thought I heard Noodlehead scratching t'get in. I guess you guys are gonna be busy tonight? D'you know where your toys are?"

Sophie reached out said *Come get a hug, wise-ass* and they made a threesome. Rosie purred it was three times better than hugging one at a time and...

"I got more music homework...how about I do it with headphones..."

...Scooping Grimsby up and heading back downstairs.

Christina kissed Sophie for a long long time.

13.

There was a beat up old Chevy station-wagon in the driveway when she got home. The garage door went up and went down as she hit the button by the door into the house, dropped her shoulder bag on the armchair and watched Grimsby hot-footing down the hallway into her bedroom. She heard a murmur of voices in the basement and thumps on the stairs and then a pair of shaggy heads rose up in front of her, one after the other, the first almost the colour of sunset and the other dirty blond like Sophie. The ginger turned at the top of the stairs...

"Oh...hi Mrs Haller..."

He took a couple of steps in her direction while the other one not near so tall came along in his wake both of them ragtag denim and t-shirts and sneakers with holes and suddenly a little bit nervous.

"I'm Sam," he said, offering a hand. "Hackett. I think I met you once last year...?"

The other followed suit.

"Charlie. Charles. Beauvais. Me too last year it was at that stupid PTA thing where I had t'come by myself."

Both of them were beautiful...enough so Christina had to stop and take a moment or two to say anything at all...big big soft eyes on the pair of them...green and brown...the rest of them lanky and slim and so incomparably young she wondered what they were doing coming up the stairs from her daughter's bedroom when all three of them should still have been in class in Napanee...

They looked embarrassed. Sam said:

"We ditched school today, Mrs Haller. Rosie met us in the parking lot this morning and said we needed to make music for something..."

Charlie nodded. Christina shook her head...a little bit stunned...a little bit stupid. They were so amazingly pretty and she realised in an instant they were in love with her daughter and would have killed anyone anywhere anytime all Rosie had to do was ask. Charlie said:

"I'm Rosie's drummer...and bass player..."

Sam said, "I'm her strings...violins and guitars and stuff..."

Christina double-taked again...had no idea Rosie owned guitarists or drummers...or anyone so obviously in thrall to her as these two. Sam said:

"She's really really good, Mrs Haller."

As if it explained everything. She said:

"I'm not really *Mrs* Haller. Christina...or Rosie's Mom would be okay. You guys wanna stay for supper?"

She made mental notes to corner Rosalie to find out what the hell was going on and Charlie said:

"We should get going good t'see you again Mrs Haller."

And they headed for the front door...closed it quietly behind them...light-footed it across the front porch. She heard the old Chevy sputter and then slide down the driveway into the turnaround...watched them go left up towards the highway. Grimsby made a cautious foray back down the hall. Christina looked at him and said:

"If anything bad comes from this it's all your fault, buddy..."

She didn't go downstairs. Sophie would be home in an hour. The luxury of her interns at the clinic let her come home early on slow days and she'd been jonesing for a lentil curry soup with shrimp for at least a couple of days so she just went to work and almost didn't hear the slow sounds wandering up the stairs from Rosie's room until she heard a piano intro and a voice she didn't recognise...singing softly...

There've been days & nights spent by myself
When the world just seemed to pass me by
I was all alone but I never felt lonely
I never stopped to wonder why
I would hear a song, walking down the street
About two people who had found their way
And it would make me think maybe we should meet
If I could find you somewhere someday

Bare bones Laura Nyro keyboard music...until it came to a chorus...drums and guitars and bass runs... doing that crescendo thing guaranteed to make you whimper and cry...

And every love song that's ever been written
Has been written for you and me
The names were changed

MICHAEL SUMMERLEIGH

The words were rearranged
The notes were written in a different key
But they've been telling the same old story
About something that stayed so true
Through a thousand years and a million tears
The song kept singing for me and you

And then soft again, the voice just aching with something that was so familiar and heart-breaking and so full of love she thought *Is that my Rosie...?*

We've been together since before the Beginning
We've known each other for twice that long
And from the very start whenever we were apart
The lives we lived always seemed so wrong
So now that we're finally together
I know I'm never gonna let you go
It wasn't hell trying to live without you
But you're the only Heaven I'll ever know
And it's always been the same old story
About something that stayed so true
Strange as it seems, in all of my dreams
There was never anyone loving me like you
Sometimes it feels like we've loved forever
That I've known you for as long as I've lived
But now every morning feels brand new again
With no end to what I've got to give
We're gonna have this forever I know it
I'll find the sun moon & stars in your touch
In all the deserts before I found you
I never dreamt I would have so much
And every love song that's ever been written

UNTIL THE END OF THE WORLD

Was written for you and me
The names were changed
The words were rearranged
The notes were written in a different key...
And they've been telling that same old story
About something that stayed so true
Through a thousand years and a million tears
That song kept singing for me and you
Every love song...every love song...every love song....

After a while she got lost in the sounds that began to thunder up from the basement...the beautiful crystal-clear voice soaring up over closing arpeggios...strings answering guitar fills...brass answering keyboard runs...the thunder of drums...a soft slide into the silence of fading strings...like the end of a Mozart symphony she realised she was on her knees in the middle of their kitchen with a paring knife in one hand and half an onion in the other and Grimsby looking at her like she'd lost her fucking mind...sobbing on the floor... listening to a last echo of all the heartbreak and hope she'd ever imagined...

Rosie found her a few minutes later.

"Mom...?"

She couldn't speak for so long...finally...

"Rosie that song...what is it...?"

"It's something I been working on, Mom...I'm sorry...I finished the words this morning on the bus and then I made Sam and Charlie come back here so we could make the music to go with."

"Rosie you wrote that?!?!?"

Her daughter nodded. "It's for all of us, Mom....but mostly it's for Gramma and Grampa…"

14.

She went into the lunch room at the back of the clinic, stripped off latex gloves and a surgical mask, the blood-spattered apron she'd slipped over her cut-offs and t-shirt. Realised she couldn't sit down yet. Nick and Wenda Burton were still in the waiting room, with four-year old Mandy and seven-year old big brother Jonathan.

She opened the fridge and uncapped a plastic bottle of no-name-brand water, frowned… realised she'd not made any kind of preparations to stop buying bottled water but it was something she needed and wanted to do as of yesterday. The two west-facing windows were blank and shimmering with late-afternoon-emergency sunlight. She was dog-tired…no pun intended …three-plus hours of working on Rusty's right hind leg. The Irish setter who owned the Burtons in the waiting room. Dumb as a fucking shovel. And utterly joyous in his complete and total obliviousness to sense of any sort. Like not to chase rabbits into traffic on a major country backroad. She emptied half the flimsy plastic bottle and grimaced at the oily aftertaste…thought:

They don't filter this any more than I do at home… just suck it out of the ground for pennies for every million gallons—thank you so much for letting them do it, government of Ontario—and then sell it back to us as pure spring bullshit holy fuck I wish I had their advertising people…maybe critters wouldn't get treated so poorly…

UNTIL THE END OF THE WORLD

She sighed, drank the rest of the bottle, tossed it into the recycling bin and started to the front of the clinic, making sure there were no spatters on her legs or arms to scare the children when she got there.

Nick Burton was a big farm-raised kid from just outside the reserve in Deseronto, with enough Amerind in his blood to get equal time from Wenda's blonde city-bred from Hamilton when it came to their children. They were still young enough that Mother Nature really hadn't had time to decide who they were going to take after, but all of them looked stricken and Christina was grateful she had good news.

"Rusty's gonna be okay," she said, mustered a smile and reached to take Mandy up on her lap. Jonathan followed protectively. She thought *Nick may be a country bumpkin, but some of Wenda is rubbing off in a good way...*

The real evidence was the credit card he'd handed over to Josee when they'd brought Rusty in off the bed of the truck. Wenda and the kids were in tears; Nick had been all business.

"You gotta fix him," he said. "Don't care how much. He's an idiot but we love him."

So three hours later she told them Rusty would be okay.

"That big bone in his leg got snapped in half..."

Mandy started snuffling and Jonathan tried not to.

"...But it was a really clean break and Rusty was lucky he got tossed onto something soft in the ditch...so he's gonna look really funny for a while, Mandy...I had to shave all the fur off the back part of him...but that's okay it'll grow back and he's gonna be as good as new."

The rest was for Nick and Wenda.

"I put a steel pin into the break to keep it all together and it really looks like hell. And he's gonna have t'wear one of those silly plastic cone things around his neck to keep him from chewing or licking at the stitches. Four six weeks we'll take the pin out if the x-rays look good."

Everybody started looking relieved, but Christina could hear the next question coming from Wenda, who looked after the family finances.

She said: "Five hundred"...shook her head when both she and Nick protested...x-rays and surgery and whatnot else...

"That's all I need, guys," she whispered away from the children. "Any number of other people around here would've come in telling me t'just put him to sleep...or not brought him in at all, left him in the ditch with a hole between his eyes. I'm good. He's gonna be good again too."

Mandy asked: "Can we go see him now? Can we take him home?"

"I'm gonna keep him overnight, honey, but he'll be safe here, okay...and you can bring him home tomorrow."

Rusty was dopey with sedatives, but just enough awake to be his normally dopey self with the kids. She stood back and watched them, smiled at the warmth of Wenda's hand on her arm...felt the gratitude in her touch. Somewhere in her heart was a memory of leave-taking...echoes in an Arizona airport...a nagging guilt for having left her family behind to do what she was doing now. She still could see the conflict in her father's eyes as she waved goodbye from the other side of the security checkpoint. Heartbreak of another kind of loss in his life would magnify it and become unbearable not long after, but on that day she'd also seen his pride in her, for having the courage to become what she wanted to be, even if it meant leaving him. She told the children:

"I'll make sure he gets looked after and we'll see you guys tomorrow, okay?"

Mandy and Jonathan nodded solemnly, thanked her with a little prod from behind by mom.

She waved at them from the doorway as they drove off, turned back into the waiting room where Matt and Josee were shaking their heads at her.

"You guys were great today thank you so much for...what?!?!?!"

They both looked sheepish, almost embarrassed.

"How're you gonna pay us if you keep giving this stuff away?" asked Matthew. "That was two thousand dollars easy."

Christina knew they weren't worried for themselves, said "My business not yours, Romeo," and went back into the lunch room for another crappy plastic bottle of water.

15.

"...Grimsby, *sortez de la table s'il vous plaît*..."

The cat twitched his ears in Sophie's directon, glanced at her quickly to see if she was actually addressing him and with what sounded like a feline sigh of resignation, or perhaps vast disappointment, gave up the fantasy of cadging some breaded haddock and chips from Rosie's plate. He unwrapped the tail from around his front paws, cast one last look of longing that stopped Rosie with a forkful halfway to her lips, and thumped himself down onto the floor.

"Now he'll be huffy all night," Sophie said.

Rosie's fork continued it's journey; she nodded with her mouth full. Christina poured white wine.

"He gets plenty all the time," she said pleasantly. "Sometimes he's kinda spooky though... just like Pooh..."

Rosie finished chewing and swallowed, speared a pair of French fries and dipped them in a puddle of ketchup. Sophie shuddered. In true *Quebecois* fashion she leaned towards salt and vinegar on her chips. Ketchup was so...American...

"He understands everything, Mom," Rosie said matter-of-factly. "Mostly he just decides when he feels like doing what we tell him..."

She got up from table to slide the patio door screen open; Grimsby went past it like a rocket, took off up the back lawn to a chorus of outraged squeaks as a handful of chipmunks scattered and then disappeared underground. Sophie laughed.

"He'll pay me back tonight...something small and dead on my pillow..."

Rosie looked wounded.

"No he won't, Sophie. He's not mean like that he's—"

Her defense of the cat was interrupted by a cell phone going off where three of them sat on the kitchen counter.

"Is that one mine, honey?" asked Christina.

Rosie shook her head.

UNTIL THE END OF THE WORLD

"It's mine, Mom. You really gotta let me change the ringtone for you so don't have t'go running every time somebody calls us."

She picked up her phone, checked the incoming LED.

"It's Sam can I answer real quick?"

Sophie and Christina nodded, went back to supper while Rosalie took her call to the other end of the living room they heard *Hi Sam!* and then an ominous silence... then *Oh no!* and *dammit!...and maybe Mom or Sophie can drive me...yeah...as soon as I can for sure...bye...*

She came back to the table looking frantic, almost in tears.

"Charlie got hurt he's in the ER in Napanee..."

Sophie was on her feet instantly.

"Somebody's gotta stay to get Grimsby indoors..."

Frantic had given way to something worse, Rosie just standing in the middle of the living room visibly shaking, not knowing which way to go. Sophie angled round the sofa and gathered her up in her arms.

"I'll stay here then, honey, your Mom can take you. And don't worry about Grimsby I'll make sure he's in before dark...I promise..."

Rosie nodded, swiped at her nose and eyes with the front of her t-shirt but still didn't move just watched as Christina swept her hair back into a pony-tail, picked up her phone, wallet, the keys to the Jeep.

"Call me when you get there," said Sophie, shuffling Rosie toward the door into the garage.

Christina stepped into sandals, hit the automatic opener on her way down the stairs and had the Jeep running as her daughter slipped into the passenger seat, waited for her to latch her seatbelt and backed them down the driveway into the turnaround.

"It's gonna be okay, baby, we'll be there in fifteen minutes..."

Rosie didn't say anything, stared straight ahead as they did an Arizona drift past the stop sign at the highway, clutched at the dash as her mother stamped through the gears doing fifteen klicks over the speed limit ten seconds later.

"Did Sam say what happened? Is it serious?"

Rosie didn't answer for a while, drew back into her seat with her bare knees up under her chin, bare toes curled down into the leather seat. As they came to the cutoff down into Newburgh she said:

"He fell. Sam said he fell..."

And that was all. Past the antique shop and the bakery in Newburgh village...on up the hill turning right towards Napanee...ten minutes later turning down Centre Street and then out Bridge to the hospital. Rosie was out of the car before Christina hit the parking brake... followed her past the ER triage room and found her sobbing in Sam's arms in front of the admissions desk he looked up:

"Hi Rosie's Mom," he said...smiling...trying for some levity to help her overlook the terror in his eyes. Christina felt her heart lurch at the ferocious shelter of his arms around her daughter.

"Is he okay, Sam?"

He nodded sort of. Looked down at Rosie kissed her hair gently before he picked her up to move them out of the path of someone else coming through the automatic sliding doors.

"They're takin' x-rays and stuff, t'make sure there's no internal bleeding."

Christina nodded sort of.

"Can we see him? Will they let us in t'see him? What happened?"

Rosie turned a tear-stained face twisted by fear.

"I told you, Mom. He fell...down some stairs..."

Sam said:

"They're tryin' t'call his parents...not sure if they wanna let us in..."

Christina said *Okay* and demanded an unspoken promise he'd look after Rosie before she turned around and started talking to the nurse at the admissions desk... opened her wallet to show her ID and continued to talk slowly and carefully until the woman put her lips together and seemed to come to a decision.

"I'll just clear it with the doctor?"

Christina softly said "That'll be fine...*merci*...thank you... "

"...We're going in t'see him right now," she said into her phone....listened to Sophie in her little pocket of cyberspace twenty miles away and smiled. "I'll tell her...yeah...big surprise he came charging down the hill, once he realised he was gonna get some of Rosie's supper after all..." Listened again. "As soon as we know...*oui*...me too, baby..."

Christina followed a dozen paces behind Sam and Rosie...stood a few minutes on the other side of the curtained ER cubicle...listened to her daughter crying and then her voice...a whisper af anger...Sam's soft but just barely-controlled, struggling to stay calm.

When she stepped through they were on either side of Charlie, hands fluttering over him, brushing helplessly at the saline drip plugged into his arm, over his face where one cheekbone and his lips had blossomed with purple bruising, a thin ribbon of blood just starting from one corner of his mouth. His eyes were open, bright with pain and pain-killers...

She went carefully around her daughter, gently put one hand on his forehead, could feel the heat of fever...trauma...radiating out from his skin she said:

"You're gonna be all right, Charlie...okay? I know some of the people here and they're gonna take good care of you, and we're gonna stay until we know you're bein' looked after properly."

He nodded...just a little up and down motion to let her know he was there. She smiled, nodded back and leaned over to kiss him gently where her hand had been. Behind them they could hear the scuff of rubber soles on the linoleum floor, the squeak of a gurney being wheeled past them, the murmur of voices and someone on the other side of the ER making unhappy sounds, could smell faint whispers of hospital disinfectant. Charlie sighed, drew a breath and winced, shivered, dancing on the edge of shock. Christina took another light blanket from the crash cart beside the bed and laid it down over him, signed to Rosie and Sam over her shoulder she would wait for them on the other side of the curtain, where she promptly walked right into the on-duty MD on his way in to see Charlie….

"Hi Daniel," she said, "Busy, eh…"

"Always, Christina," he said. "We don't get the funding for more than one sometimes two of us each shift. Gets crazy in a hurry. How've you been? This guy isn't yours, is he?"

"He's a friend of my daughter," she said. "I guess that makes him mine. How bad is he?"

Doctor Dan shrugged, checked his chart and shook his head. "Don't know for sure yet. We managed some preliminary x-rays fairly quickly…should have the film back soon. I promise I'll let you know as soon as I do… meanwhile…"

"Send the kids back out here on principle. Sam is the red-haired one and he's holding up okay. Rosie not so much."

He nodded, stepped past the curtain; Christina found a corner with some chairs, waved at Sam and Rosie as they got hustled back into the centre of the ER, waited until they had settled in beside her.

"One of you needs t'tell me what's really going on here?" she said softly, looking at her daughter, then at Sam.

"I told you, Mom, he—"

"Didn't fall down any stairs, honey. I love you but you know you can't bullshit me when it comes to damaged living things. Right, Sam?"

Sam ducked his head down, looked over at Rosie who got her t-shirt collar up where she could wipe snot and tears from under her nose, pushed her chin out at Sam he whispered:

"Charlie's parents are fuckin' drunks. His father went batshit on his mother for some stupid reason and she went off on him and when Charlie tried to stop it his father went t'town on both of them..."

Rosie sobbed out loud and Sam reached for her in the same instant Christina reached for both of them.

"How long has it been going on?" she asked.

"Fuckin' forever, Mom," cried Rosie. "Any time Charlie ever came home happy about anything that bastard had t'ruin it for him."

Christina took them both. Hung on. Kissed the tops of their heads. Babbled mindlessly just so they could hear the sound of her voice so they'd know the world wasn't anywhere near like that everywhere. She wished Sophie had come with, so her own heart wouldn't hurt so much with the heartbreak she heard in the voice of her child and her friend. She just hung on until they stopped shaking, until she stopped shaking with them.

"We'll fix it," she said softly. "Rosie...Sam...I promise...Charlie's gonna be all right and it will never happen again."

Rosie said: "What're we supposed t'do, Mom? Someday his father's gonna kill him..."

Christina said, "No! Not ever..." and rocked both of them in her arms until they were quiet.

She whispered, "You've both got t'tell the truth about what happened...the truth...and then we'll get a lawyer...somebody...and Charlie can stay with us until he's old enough to be free from them."

Charlie came to live with them a week or so later. His cheekbone had a hairline fracture. There was a small handful of cracked ribs and a ton of bruised bones from hip to ankle. There'd been a hockey stick involved somewhere, and he'd swallowed the molar been knocked out of his jaw, flushed it away the day before he got out of hospital. They left him at home with Grimsby...went back to his house the weekend after that, Rosie and Sam collecting his clothes and music and books, leaving the smashed remains of his drums and bass in the living room and glaring at his parents while Christina and Sophie dared them to do anything besides read the court order legally allowing them to look after Charlie from that minute on. They left with a veiled promise to have them both charged with physically assaulting their own child. Charlie took up residence in the upstairs guestroom until he could manage the stairs into the basement without pain. Christina decided to let Josee and Matt look after the clinic while she spent the days keeping him comfortable

"Are you sure, Mom?" asked Rosie. "Stayin' home from work...?"

Christina nodded. "He's gonna mend fast, honey, so it won't be for very long, and most of the spring calving is done so things are pretty quiet now anyway. Besides, I'm a whole fifteen minutes away if they need me for anything out of the ordinary, and I'll add a little bit of tax-free to their loan paybacks so they know they're bein' appreciated."

Sam took to picking Rosie up for school and bringing her back again in the afternoon. Once they got home he and Rosie spelled her mom by making a lot of Charlie's meals—mostly just eggs and soup and things he could chew or swallow without too much effort. Grimsby even started sleeping on his bed at night.

Meanwhile Christina settled into an easy routine not much different from what had passed for "everyday" before Charlie had been hurt—fixing breakfasts and lunches for everyone and waving goodbye when Sophie headed off to her third grade, when Sam came to get Rosie. Once the house was quiet again she'd clean up a bit, mow some grass, water the gardens, then spend the late morning and early afternoon keeping Charlie company. He got over being shy about her being Rosie's mother fairly quickly.

"I don't know what t'call you though."

He had to say it twice, because his mouth was pretty banged up and it hurt to talk.

Christina laughed. "Call me Mom if you want to," she said. "Christina is good too."

Charlie blushed a little bit, which was quite the accomplishment considering most of his face looked like a gay pride banner.

"Thank you for doing this, Mrs Haller," he whispered slowly. "It's been goin' on for so long I'd just stopped thinkin' about what I could do to get out of it."

"No relatives?"

"Not really. Who wants t'be related to raging alcoholics? My father was at it before I was even born, and my mom started after, because it was the only way she could deal with my father. I guess I cried when I was a baby and it pissed him off a lot."

Christina shuddered at the thought, took an uninjured hand in both her own.

"You love my Rosie so you've already thanked me," she said. "And you're important to her—"

"Mrs Haller I just want you t'know—"

She reached out to touch his bruised lips…gently…to stop him…shaking her head.

"You don't have go there, Charlie. Your friend my daughter is a grown-up. I'm usually a hundred percent with the decisions she makes for herself so you don't need t'be responsible for them. And if there's anything she wants t'share with me she'll do it in her own way in her own time."

He fell quiet, sipped some beef broth and puree through a fat straw.

"There's not a lot of people like you around, Mrs Haller."

"You mean like…lesbians?"

Charlie blushed harder and shook his head emphatically, even though she could see it cost him.

"No no," he said quickly. "I didn't mean that…"

"I was just teasing, Charlie," she said. "Besides, me and Sophie aren't lesbians. We're really just best friends in love with each other. I think there's a difference, even though I guess it still looks pretty much the same to anybody watching."

He looked thoughtful. "Maybe you could explain that t'me some other time," he said. "I just meant that you're not like most of the mothers I know; you're pretty cool about everything. You don't get all bent out of shape when Rosie gets into shit, like when she beat the snot out of Brandon Lockwood and you stepped right up—"

He stopped, realised what he'd said and waited to see if he'd crossed a line. Christina grinned.

"Lots of practise, Charlie, lots of practise. Rosie May has a fairly strong sense of what's wrong and what's right. I trust her judgment."

"She says she gets it from you."

"Well I got it from *my* parents," she said, wistful enough that he picked up on it.

"Rosie told us about them."

"Did she."

"Yeah...she was tryin' t'understand for a long time. It worried her...a lot..."

"What was she so worried about, Charlie?"

"She couldn't get why you couldn't let them go. How she felt helpless about it bcause there wasn't anything she could do..."

Christina could hear herself taking a long deep breath, felt herself instinctively backing away from the conversation...forced herself not to...looked at Charlie's ruined face—they'd had to put stitches across his cheekbone—and into brown eyes so soft and devoid of violence that she knew in a flash of insight that Rosie was every bit as much in love with him as he was with her; that somehow abused and battered Charlie had managed to preserve in his heart something that was overwhelmingly sweet and generous, in spite of his parents; and that Charlie had been the one who had given her daughter back to her...

"Can I get you anything else?" she asked urgently. "Are you feelin' okay?"

Suddenly she realised he was someone infinitely more than special in Rosie's life, found herself with an inkling of the frantic fear she had seen in her daughter on their way to the ER. She felt overwhelmed, compelled to make absolutely certain that the gentle thing in her care—who seemed in one startling moment so much like her father—was provided with every comfort and defense from further harm that was in her ability to offer. She watched him recognise the change in her, register the subtle difference in the way she had just spoken. She watched his eyes widen with a mutual comprehension of something neither one of them would ever be able to put into words.

He nodded, tried to shake off the welling of tears in the beautiful mirrors of his eyes. She brushed her fingers across his swollen jaw, leaned forward to brush the stitches in his face with a kiss. She took the mug of soup from him and said:

"You sleep for a little bit, Charlie. And you call me if you need anything okay I'll be close by I promise..."

***

As his days became less cloudy with pain-killers they talked a lot. When the sun got blistery hot she moved them out onto the front porch where they had comfy chairs and massive trees—an oak an elm and a cedar—to keep the upper portion of the front yard cool. Other days when there was a breeze they camped beside the glass-top table under the big green canvas umbrella on the back deck. Roundabout age ten Rosie had become pretty self-sufficient for a little girl; Christina found that looking after Charlie made her weepy inside, with a warmth that reminded her of the days before... uncomplicated...when someone else was depending on her for basic stuff...a return to some adult kind of innocence...like when she and Sophie made love to each other and would "wake up" after, feeling brand new, somehow having shed baggage they were not even aware they'd been carrying. She could feel Charlie radiating something that might have been gratitude, if not for the fact that for him she could sense it went much deeper.

"...It sounds stupid," he said one morning, after she'd delivered scrambled eggs and coffee breakfast to the back deck.

"What sounds stupid?" she said, buttering a slice of toast for him.

"Sometimes I feel like I'm a little kid...and I know you're Rosie's mom but you don't feel old at all except for when I get that feeling and then I keep hoping I'm not too old for you t'take care of me..."

His face was still swollen in some places, with weird shades of awful colour that were reflections of the awful beating that had brought him to her house, but couldn't hide the flush of healthy colour...his embarrassment...

UNTIL THE END OF THE WORLD

"That's not stupid, Charlie...that's what it's like when you're hungry for something you don't have...the physical contact of somebody else holding on to you so you know you're loved. Didn't your mom hug you when you were a baby?"

Behind the mask of damage to his face Charlie looked desolate.

"I don't remember anything like that, Christina," he said quietly, and he looked up the hill through shards of morning sunlight to Pooh's Garden, seeing nothing, trying his best not to cry even as she moved closer to him, aching to erase even the smallest portion of that emptiness from his soul. "Y'know after a while you just get used to things being the way they are..."

She remembered something her father had said to her...a quote from a Canadian writer... W.O. Mitchell... *Humans must comfort each other, defend each other against the terror of being human*...and in her heart wept for poor little Charlie...compared the emptiness of his childhood to the richness of her own... and again found herself thinking of him in terms of her father...the odd bits and pieces of their life together that had come from her Mom...of the nights when she had held him and just let him cry...whispered to him over and over again that he was loved and he wasn't alone anymore and that she would be with him forever. Christina said:

"That's over with, Charlie. My father used t'tell me that relationships between two people were only good for as long as they were good, and after that if they stopped being good then that was when you knew it was time t'move on...so I don't know how you and my Rosie are gonna turn out, but I know for damned sure how we will..."

He blinked...looked down to where she had taken his hand and started tracing soft patterns across his palm.

"You're mine now, Charlie. No matter what happens if you ever need that hug... anything... all you ever have t'do is find your way back here t'me and Sophie and we'll take care of you...fill you up again...make sure you know you don't ever have t'be alone again..."

"...It's so weird t'watch him hunting like that. He's this big lump at night...not like all over you, but y'can tell he's like two kinds of cat..."

Christina poured a pair of Waterloo Darks into a pair of blue-rimmed Mexican glasses—the ones with the little bubbles like someone had frozen carbonated water into the glass itself—and eased herself down into the deep-cushioned deck chair beside him, squeezed a wedge of lime into each one. They watched Grimsby, halfway down the front lawn, stalking something that squeaked in outrage and kept darting into the crevices between a half-circle stack wall her father had built to enclose a picnic table under the pine tree.

"We never did find out how he ended up here," she said, "but he sure hates being in the Jeep, or any kind of moving vehicle. Rosie thinks somebody just drove by out on the highway and pitched him out a window onto the downs...figures he was out on his own for at least a month, until he bonked his head against our back door. He was lean but not ever really mean at all...maybe nine pounds...and right off we knew he must've been hunting to stay alive..."

Charlie's grin wasn't quite so frightening anymore, though the thin white line across his right cheekbone seemed like heresy against a face growing back to beautiful.

"He's got a good spot now."

Christina clunked her glass against his. "Both of you."

"Rosie is really lucky."

She shook her head. "No Charlie I'm the one with all the luck. I've been so busy crying over all the love I lost I forgot to appreciate all the love I've been given t'make up for it. My folks were different from anybody else I've ever known, but they showed me...gave me... most of the things I needed to get by, even if they didn't have all of it themselves."

She watched him, his tongue playing with the big empty space where a tooth had been, leaned over and kissed his face, the place where the stitches had left the thin white line.

Charlie blushed.

"That chipmunk is screwed," he said

Christina nodded. "Yeah pretty much. Don't tell Rosie..."

16.

A week later he moved downstairs, into the extra room between Rosie's bedroom and the television room, newly repainted, click-floored with rugs on top, a futon bed/couch and a mini-component stereo system Rosie had salvaged from the dump. A small computer table that had been collecting dust in the garage came downstairs as well—a place for his laptop—and a bookcase for his favourite CDs and books.

After dinner the next day she could hear a faint murmur of voices downstairs, Rosie and Charlie in close quarters. She slipped a bookmark into her place midway through a giant trade paperback edition of Garrow's *Bearing the Cross* and listened...felt peaceful and someplace where, perhaps for the first time in a very long time, she could actually look down at herself from a comfortable height and say she was happy. Sophie said:

"Oh look! My girl is smiling!"

Standing in the door of their *ensuite* in danger of losing her towel, another one in both hands raised up above her head to dry her hair. Christina shook herself like she was waking up from a dream and said:

"You are so beautiful..."

While Sophie kept towelling her hair...

"So incredibly hot..."

...Wriggled just short of losing the one held up by surface tension...

"Come on over here and let me lick you from armpit to wherever."

...Wriggled one more time and lost the towel as she climbed up onto the bed beside Christina, bending forward to kiss her, one hand feathering down across her belly. They came up for air five minutes later... laughing... Sophie said:

"I need another shower."

"Me too," said Christina. "Thank you...always thanking you, Sophie."

"For ravishing you?!?!"

"No-o-o-o...well yes that too," she said, laughing again then turned serious. "But for Charlie first...for not even blinking...this young guy suddenly living in the middle of you and me and a teenage daughter."

Sophie didn't bother to respond, combed a tangle out of her hair with her fingers and then put them back where Christina couldn't ignore them...

"I love you, Anglais poophead lover girl," she said quietly. "I love you forever... just you...and Rosie and the cat..."

Drew her up where she knew Christina was always most comfortable...eyes closed. They drowsed for a while...

"Rosie wanted t'talk t'me today," Sophie whispered. "Said she had a problem because she needed t'talk t'you but she didn't know what to say."

Christina opened her eyes, a question drowsed in afterglow...

"Charlie."

Christina nodded a little bit.

"I told her I didn't think it was gonna be an issue."

Christina smiled, thought how fine it was that the only other person she loved as much as her daughter knew her so well.

"I said it was between the two of them...that I thought you would never even think about making something like that difficult for them...but I wondered how Sam was gonna deal with it."

"What'd she say?"

"She did a Rosie thing."

"Where she pretends like she didn't really hear what you said and answers *No problem* anyway?"

"How on earth did you know?" said Sophie.

Christina closed her eyes again and rolled herself deeper into her warm places...

"I guess we're all okay for tonight then," she said sleepily, "...except maybe for Grimsby. He might have t'look for someplace t'sleep..."

17.

Charlie got back to school a couple of weeks before holidays kicked in for the summer... just in time to become the recipient of what had become a grass-roots sort of GoFundMe campaign engineered by Sam and Rosie that had started in their high school, became county-wide, spread into Kingston proper, and then beyond when somebody in their music classes made it known he had a relative worked at the Godin guitar factory in La Patrie on the Quebec side. When it was over, Charlie's new bass was a top-of-the-line fretless, donated by the company, and his drum kit was vintage Ludwig from the late 60s with a brand new set of bronze bangers by Zildjian—a smokin' deal from Renaissance Music in Kingston that left the fund with more than a thousand dollars that ended up at the Sandy Pines Wildlife Rescue place just west of Napanee. Rosie mapped a layout for the drums that filled the entire centre of the television room without making it impossible to see the television.

was funny as hell anyway? She'd do it on purpose, y'know...t'make your dad laugh. She was like a *quebecoise* version of Charlie Chaplin or Groucho Marx...and she taught my mom how t'do the same thing because she knew just how much Therese loved to make my father crazy with craziness. As far as your mom was concerned, the only thing she was missing was one of those bendy-twirly canes...or maybe a cigar and glasses with the moustache attached..."

Christina was stunned into silence. Not a bad stunned. Stunned by the flood of warmth Sophie had just conjured up with the memory of life with her parents... how her mother really had revelled in dead-panning absurdities...almost like she was entertaining herself by being silly for her father. It had happened hundreds of times, starting when she was barely old enough to even understand the concept of "funny" when it came from a frame of reference other than her own.

"You're smiling again, baby," said Sophie.

Christina said, "Am I really?"

Sophie nodded, tilted her head ever so slightly...unspoken joy in the radiance of her lover's smile.

"Sam traded that Chevy beater in for a van in even worse shape," she said at last "I told him they could use the truck to get all their stuff to the gig in Napanee, but he said he might as well look ahead some...get something they could use for a while..."

Christina looked puzzled. "What gig? Tonight? I thought they were going to the graduation dance thing tonight...at the Strathcona Centre..."

Sophie said, "It's called a junior prom and they *are* going...to provide music for the occasion. We're supposed t'go over a little bit later t'watch...the debut of Rosie May the band, with our Rosie May in it..."

"No movie tonight."

"No movie," grinned Sophie. "It's their first real gig."

Christina said, "Is the world ready?"

Sophie said, "Probably not...but it's for all their friends so I don't think we have t'worry much...not tonight anyway..."

19.

She woke slowly, kept her eyes closed soaking in the sounds and smells of the morning... first Sophie... breathing softly...her heartbeat where Christina rested her head...the warm place between her breasts where new sunlight and heat had sheened them with old sandalwood oil and perspiration....the rich curves beneath her waking fingers...the deep mysterious well of her navel and the swell of her hips...the long smooth elegance of her thighs and ...always...the delicious place between them...

The breeze through the door onto the back deck was dry...empty of moisture almost like Arizona...toasty flavours of leaves and grass gone too many weeks without rainfall, redolent with different from the day she had found this place for her parents...the thousand and one lush greens of four acres and a spring season full of rain. She snuggled closer to Sophie only half-roused murmuring *It's okay Tina I'm not awake yet but I'm here*...and sighed herself back into sleep. Christina listened to the chipmunks squeaking... the every morning omnipresent idiot coo of a renegade whippoorwill...over and over...the buzz of insects...a mosquito dive-bombing bare skin...she eased herself out of bed trying not to disturb Sophie, listening for any sounds in the house...

Saturday morning and only days left now before their flight to Phoenix...still plenty of things in need of doing. She met Grimsby in the hallway, bowling-ball head bumping her ankles as she sat down to pee in the main bathroom, following her into the kitchen Christina nuked a cup of day-old coffee and said:

"It's still too early for breakfast, buddy...oh....all right...let me put a load of laundry in and when I come back upstairs we'll get you some food..."

She headed for the stairs, halfway down feeling the coolth rise up around her knees she realised she'd not bothered to look for knickers or a t-shirt...shrugged *Oh well it's early* because she remembered Sam, Charlie and Rosie up late, watching a counterculture double bill—*Easy Rider* and the extremely silly *Psych-Out*, complete with popcorn, beer and probably a toke or two just because Jack Nicholson as a going-bald "Smoky" was a bit much...

She ducked through the door under the stairs into the laundry room noticing along the way that the poster of six-pack tattoo boy had disappeared from Rosie's door. She reached for the light switch, toes hitting cold painted concrete floor, and started hopping from one scrap of carpet to another, bumped a stack of boxes, knocked a handful of plastic hangars from the overhead rod they used to dry clothes indoors rather than pay extortionate rates to Hydro One...

She threw a load of girl stuff together...brassieres and panties and whatnot... punched in the code for a short cold-water delicate cycle...didn't hear the click of Rosie's door behind her. When she turned around, Sam was framed in the doorway back out into the basement.

"Oh...hi Rosie's Mom," he said quickly.

His gingery hair was all stood up and spiky around his face, his eyes had been half closed but they were wide open now. He did an up-and-down once, really quickly, and then made certain his eyes never left hers.

"We were pretty late...and a little bit...you know...so I just crashed here. I hope it's okay."

She had to give him credit. He stood there doing his best to not to look at Rosie's Mom naked and did a pretty good job of it. Then too, all he was wearing was a pair of raggedy-ass jeans riding down around the neighbourhood where six-pack tattoo poster boy had begun, so she tried not to stare at him.

"I was just gonna go to t'the bathroom," he said.

Christina put on her best serious face.

"Well don't let me hold you up on that, Sam. When you gotta go you gotta go..."

He nodded. Carefully.

"Okay then. Nice t'see you, Mrs Haller."

She hoped she hadn't blushed. Anywhere. He turned around quickly and ran away, which was good because Christina stifled a huge laugh and then just collapsed against the side of the washing machine. She heard him levitating up the stairs two and three at a time...Grimsby trying to talk him into providing breakfast...a quick dash of bare feet down the hallway. She grabbed a bath sheet scheduled for washing later that morning and wrapped it around herself, grabbed a can of Friskies on the way out of the laundry room, and followed him on up the stairs...

"...*Bonjour* my love," she whispered, slipped back into bed, bumped her face up against Sophie's boobs and felt herself go a bit cross-eyed with happy when arms came round to hug her tightly where she was.

"G'morning t'you, Tina, I love you."

"I love you too Sophie...Sam stayed here last night. I think him and Charlie and Rosie all slept in her bed."

Sophie wriggled and nuzzled and said something along the lines of *Oh...isn't that lovely...*

Christina said, "I'm not sure if I should be upset or not."

Sophie said sleepily, "I don't think you should be, Tina..."

"No?"

Sophie said *No* with another wriggle, and "They love each other...all of them..."

"I know."

"So no worries then?"

"I guess not...but I forgot t'put any clothes on when I went downstairs t'do some laundry and Sam caught me on his way upstairs..."

Sophie woke all the way up and started laughing.

20.

They started early, about the time Sam chugged up the driveway in the van at O-dark- hundred because he'd forgotten when it was they were leaving to catch their Southwest flight out of Hancock International in Syracuse.

It had taken some doing, but both Sophie and Christina had managed to convince Rosie that being a *fashionista* of anything but swimwear in Phoenix in the middle of the summer would be a complete waste of time. Heat and Perspiration trumped Stylish every time. She'd ended up packing mostly shorts and t-shirts and sunscreen but insisted on making her debut in the desert in bronze-and-black camo—a skirt, jacket and black tank top to go with her top-hat and goggles....

They piled into the Jeep, but not before she spent a good quarter of an hour with Grimsby, explaining how Sam and Charlie were gonna look after him and he'd better behave because as much as she loved him, Sam and Charlie had a few things on the table that he was never gonna match. Grimsby got huffy, but didn't struggle much either when Charlie picked him up and made him wave from the front porch. They all waved back. Sophie got them out on the highway with the sun smack in their eyes...

"They looked kinda sad," she said, checking Rosie out in the rear view mirror.

"Are you okay, baby?" asked Christina.

Rosie nodded unconvincingly. Sniffles could be heard, a paisley handkerchief lay in her lap, clutched in one hand as she kept looking back over her shoulder.

UNTIL THE END OF THE WORLD

"We're only gonna be gone a couple of weeks, honey. And they'll take good care of Grimsby. They're gonna be fine..."

Rosie nodded. "I know. It's just that I...well...I mean...I just don't like not bein' able t'see them whenever I want to. Stuff could happen and I wouldn't be here."

"Stuff could happen and they'll deal with it," said Christina. "Matt and Josee said they'd be stopping by too. When we get back there'll probably be hundreds of kids who've been here for at least a week, all dancing naked all over the place."

Rosie asked Sophie if her mom had smoked anything that morning, and after that the spirit of adventure kicked in. In the years since her father had gifted her with the four-wheel drive Jeep, there'd been a big stereo retro-fit for CDs and thumb drives. The original Allman Brothers *Live at the Fillmore East* got them to the border at Thousand Islands...

Christina leaned across Sophie to hand the customs guy three passports...two US and one Canadian... explained they were all going back to her twentieth high school reunion because when she was eleven her parents had moved them all to Arizona and Sophie had visited once but her daughter had never been and oh...Sophie was her best friend...and now they were all going back and yes she was a Canadian citizen too...so was her daughter...in the back seat...

Rosie said: "They promised we could go t'Disneyland..."

And after a while the customs guy's eyes started to roll back into his head with an overload of information and Sophie swore she was coming back with them as opposed to selling herself into white slavery...ponied up three sets of return plane tickets as evidence...took all three passports from him, batted her eyelashes and waved *Bonjour merci bien so much have a nice day* as they drove off...

With at least two hours to kill they stopped in Watertown for breakfast before running the last seventy miles down to Syracuse on Interstate 81. Rosie volunteered to drive, said she wouldn't mind some highway-time practise if that was okay. With Sophie riding shotgun, Christina moved into the back seat and daydreamed twenty-five years into the past, the day she had left Canada...with her parents...and Mister Pooh howling beside her...looking back over her shoulder just like Rosie had done, and wondering if she would ever see Sophie or any of her friends again.

The sun started climbing past mid-morning and she got a little bit drowsy, not really paying attention to anything even after Rosie turned the Jeep's A/C on she felt wrapped up in cotton wool...her daughter's voice and Sophie offering advice sounding so far away she suddenly remembered something from that first day...an incident...sort of spooky but funny too...

Somewhere along I-81 everyone had gotten a little bit hungry, the car needed gas, and she had needed a bathroom badly, her stomach in knots and not at all happy with Mister Pooh being unhappy. Her father had taken the first exit off the highway, but the usual easy on-off for services didn't seem to apply. They had driven on for what seemed like forever, under a canopy of trees growing close up to the two-lane blacktop on either side, leaves that should have been bright with autumn colour gone drab and dull because the day had gone cloudy. She could feel her father's concern for her, wanted to tell him he didn't have to drive faster she was okay; instead she had just closed her eyes and stuck her fingers through the door of Pooh"s carrier to scratch an offered ear, whispering *Don't be upset Pooh we're all here*...and finally she could feel the car slowing, a quiet breath of relief from her dad, her mom announcing their arrival...somewhere...

She had opened her eyes, heard the tires crunching them across the gravel parking lot of what looked like a truck stop, or maybe just a local quick-stop grocery store. She promised Pooh she would be really fast, undid her seatbelt and scrambled out of the car, keeping close to parents because the clapboard building looked really old and rickety and as they approached one of the screened outer doors, a couple of people came out first, and she could see them staring. Once inside, her mother had looked around quickly and then said ... *Vas-y, Christiane, les toilettes sont à l'arrière*...pointed her down the wide aisle that went past the check-out counter and on to the back of the store. She didn't want to go by herself, but she also didn't want to show she was afraid or nervous.

It was musty inside, full of smells she didn't recognise at all, stuff on the shelves packaged with plastic sleeves that looked dry and brittle, the labels on the canned goods ragged and sun-faded so much she couldn't tell which ones had corn or which ones had peas. As she neared the end of the aisle she heard voices, moved slowly past the last bank of shelves and found a half dozen people seated on low round stools at a lunch counter, drinking coffee and having breakfast. They all stopped talking...stopped eating...stared at her. As she inched past them, one man in overalls smiled, his face seamed and bristly in need of a shave, with a lot of teeth missing from the smile. She said *Bonjour* quickly and for a moment the stylised female figure tacked beside the door she wanted just didn't register. Then she pushed through and could feel her insides getting really uncomfortable as she raced to the rear of the rest room and bolted the wooden door of the stall behind her, unzipped her jeans and pulled her panties down, her nose wrinkling at a new bunch of smells she preferred not to think about.

She closed her eyes again, her stomach beginning to settle as she did her business. She tried not to breathe too much and just sat there until she was sure she was finished... sat there and heard the door to the washroom open and the sound of feet scuffing along the cracked linoleum...saw a pair of old shoes stop in front of her stall. The door rattled and banged violently. She said:

"*Je suis ici*. I am in here....please..."

Rattled and banged again.

"I am using this one please...*celui-ci est occupé*..."

Then she didn't speak anymore, realised she was scared and wishing whoever was out there would listen...go away... She held her breath until finally the shoes disappeared... scuffed some more...seemed to go back the way they had come without even using one of the other two stalls. Hurrying now, she wiped herself and flushed the toilet, trying not to look at the rust stains on the stainless steel and the porcelain, the black seams on the linoleum floor. She rushed back out into the narrow corridor grateful no one stopped to look at her again, desperate to find her father or her mother...grateful when someone at the lunch counter said:

"Didja see them fuckin' longhair hippies up in the front...?"

And she realised Sophie had called her name softly, had reached into the back to touch her cheek she shivered, opened her eyes...

"I dozed off."

Sophie nodded. "You did, honey....and you were makin' funny sounds...like you were scared..."

"I guess I was dreaming...but it was something I remembered, Sophie, something that happened...the first time I came this way...with my mom and Dad..."

She retold the story, found the funny part of it in the re-telling. Rosie said it sounded like a scene out of that weird movie *Deliverance*...

"Was there anybody playin' a banjo, Mom...OW! cut that out I'm the driver..."

"Don't make fun, Rosie, it was scary when it happened."

"*Ma pauvre fille*," said Sophie sympathetically, "but today we're going to places that you know...to see all your friends."

"Maybe I'm just nervous about seeing them all again."

"Well....me and Rosie are looking forward to it...it's another grand adventure..."

Rosie promised she wouldn't stop anywhere they couldn't see the highway, and thirty minutes later braked them cautiously into the exit and around the big curve that emptied onto the airport causeway.

PART TWO - BACK TO THE DESERT

21.

They stepped through the hatch of the Southwest jet and she tasted desert...glorious heat and the dry salty whisper of wind out of the Sonora. All along the accordion passage leading into the terminal it all came rushing back from when she was sleek and brown and her world was half as old as it was now...

Rosie said, "Wow is it ever hot!"

Sophie offered, "Not as bad as it could be?"

A question. Christina shrugged. "Not quite. Dolly said it was a good spring but then things went from comfy to Dante in a hurry..."

She stopped, dragged them out of the small tide of humanity crowding down the enclosed walkway, let other people pass them by, making thumps and shudders with their footsteps. Christina closed her eyes... scared...waited until the warm of Sophie on one side and Rosie on the other slowed her terror. They followed the last of the passengers out past the security doors and stepped back in time as a dozen familiar faces lit up with smiles and roared:

"Bienvenido de nuevo al Valle del Sol!"

...Scared the crap out of all the other passengers in front of them...stopped Christina in her tracks for an instant before she rushed forward, dragging Sophie and Rosie along behind her as the welcoming committee closed around them. She heard voices naming themselves to her daughter and to Sophie, a rapid-fire dance around the family tree of their relationship to each other, twenty years older but suddenly all over again her *crew*...her *familia de su corazon* from their last year in high school.

"*Dolores mi amor! Jorge! Alisa, donde esta tu nuevo bebe...y tu hermoso niñito... llamado Gervasio? Madre de Dios* you are all so beautiful..."

Sophie and Rosalie stood by while all the hugs and kisses were exchanged, Rosie looking a bit stunned and definitely amazed to hear her mother chattering away in Spanish. She asked Sophie if she knew any of them...

"Not one, Rosie. When I came to visit with my mom and dad, your mom didn't really know anybody yet..."

"How does she know Spanish so well?"

"She took Spanish all through high school," Sophie explained. "I think that's how she ended up with everybody here. She was always the girl with the Canadian parents even though Joshua was American he sort of *acted* Canadian...and she was always just that little bit different from the white kids...enough to make her feel like she belonged with the Mexican kids instead..."

They milled and danced around each other long after the party moved to the baggage carousel. Their luggage went around three times before anyone thought to claim it...finally Dolores said:

"*Vamonos, chica*. It's time to go and everyone else is waiting for you. *And* you have to meet my three boys. *Me hacen loco*! but I love them—Alejandro will be eight next month, Rodrigo is six, and Leandro just turned three..."

They allowed themselves to be herded out of the terminal through flashes of afternoon sunlight and then the shelter and relative cool of the covered parking where they split up into four separate vehicles and caravanned their way out of Sky Harbour airport...I-10 South onto the Superstition Freeway. It had changed a little bit but Christina closed her eyes and the trip became one she knew very well as she sat beside Dolores in the passenger seat with the ever-smooth Jorge in the back, wedged between her daughter and Sophie. As the lead cars in their cavalcade sped past the Val Vista exit, Christina turned to Dolores.

"Dolly don't you live down along here?"

Dolores smiled.

"You're not staying at my house, *hermana*...not tonight, anyway..."

In the back seat Rosie said:

"Holy shit! Mom is that *it*?"

Sophie whispered, "Watch your mouth, sweetheart," but didn't really mean it.

Superstition Mountain rose up like a wall on the horizon to the northeast of them, Rosie leaning forward with the brim of her top hat tilted back so there was nothing between her and the magic she had known only through photographs.

"That's it, honey," Christina said proudly, like it belonged to her...an heirloom finally bestowed upon the youngest member of the family.

Rosie said *Wow!* again and slumped backwards right into Jorge's lap, scrambling red-faced to move a bit off to her side of the back seat.

Christina asked: "Where are we goin', Dolly?"

"*Ya verás...ser paciente...*you will see, just be patient..."

They drove on past all the exits she still could name one by one as the mid-afternoon traffic thinned the farther out they went into the east valley.

"Yay! We're gonna go to Dirtwater for supper!"

Dolly looked away from the road for a moment and grinned. "We got the place for the night, your *jimmy jangles* pre-ordered, and Dick can't wait t'see you again."

Rosie asked: "Who's Dick? What's jimmy jangles?"

"*Chimichangas*, *chica*...your mama's favourite *comida Mexicana* served up by one more guy who fell in love with her the minute she arrived in Apache Junction. How old were you then, *Racha*...?"

"Twelve."

"Who's *Racha*?"

"*Su mama, niñita...en Espanol* we called her Streak because she could outrun all of us *and* all the white kids too..."

"Mom you never said."

"I didn't want you t'know I could catch your ass any time I felt like it," laughed Christina, and then she went silent as the exit ramps got closer and closer to where she had become a grown-up and she remembered not being there on the day her mother had left Life...and her father...behind...

Sophie reached forward. Christina turned with tears in her eyes. Dolores took the Ironwood Road exit into Apache Junction and played tour guide for Rosie as they came up past AJ High School...turned right on Southern Avenue. Christina sobbed:

"Dolly...?"

Who only put one hand to her friend's face and whispered:

"I'm taking you home, my love."

They stopped in front of a butter-yellow house on the corner of Del Rio and 22nd Avenue, where a forty-foot *ficus nitida* she remembered being only six feet tall the day she helped her father plant it cast its shadow over a Y-shaped pathway of pink sandstone that narrowed down to a front door under a canopy of blood-red bougainvillea...an arcade filled with everyone from the airport...at least two dozen more...children half-grown and small...and one face that had not been there to greet her at the airport.

"He bought it back for you, sweetheart," said Dolores. "Last year, as soon as he knew we would be seeing you again..."

"You said the other people had painted it blue."

"He repainted it the same colour it was when you lived here."

"Look at the *cholla* it was still so small when I left."

UNTIL THE END OF THE WORLD

"You're not going to believe the back yard, Christina...it's what your Dad wanted it t'look like when it was done. We'll come back after supper..."

She got out of the car slowly, her eyes drawn to another pair as dark as her own...the slender. handsome but gone-almost-totally-grey-haired man who had been the boy who loved her...who came slowly down the flagstone walk her father had made and stood waiting for her...

"Welcome back to us," he said softly. Rosie watched his eyes get shiny.

~~~

En masse they headed uptown to the Apache Trail, a much larger caravan now, that took up most of the parking at Dirtwater Springs. Sophie had been there before and provided a running commentary for Rosalie, including advance warning of all the stuffed dead wildlife that accounted for a large portion of its Wild West interior decor. She watched her mother get big-hugged by yet another (but older) guy and then stood open-mouthed as he turned and offered one to Sophie as well...stammered a polite *Nice t'meet you too* to Rosie, and introduced himself as Dick, the owner of the establishment who had known her family quite well...who remembered Sophie from her visit twenty-plus years before.

Everyone scattered to tables and booths all over the front and back rooms while the wait staff was loudly instructed to provide everyone with whatever they wanted for as long as they wanted it. Dick winked at Rosie, then leaned over and said something to her mother, turned away quickly. She watched her mother sitting beside the man who had hugged her in front of the yellow house...eyes closing again as she laid her head against his chest.

"He's some kinda hottie but...who *is* he?"

Sophie said, "I think he's the one took your mom t'the senior prom, honey... Alvaro...Dolores' brother..."

"My mom went t'the senior prom? That is so lame..."

"He was head-over-heels in love with her."

"Looks like that hasn't changed so much."

"Not so much at all," Sophie said thoughtfully.

Alvaro's head went down to where he could whisper to her...started her crying again... holding on to him...

"Sophie what's goin' on...?"

"Leave it be for now, honey...besides, it looks like you've already got a couple of admirers at the next table so you should pay attention and make sure not to step on their tongues..."

Somewhere in the middle of the festivities all the lights went out, and Dick reappeared with a massive cake lit by a ton of candles and everyone started singing *Feliz cumpleaños Christina y Rosie,* and Sophie just looked deliriously happy and proud and almost a hundred people took advantage to do more hugging and kissing.

Christina and her daughter looked at each other.

"I forgot," Rosie said.

"Happy Sweet Sweet Sixteen, baby," said Christina.

"It's Gramma and Grampa's anniversary too."

Christina nodded. "As old as me..."

UNTIL THE END OF THE WORLD

Well after dark, in twos and threes and fives a goodly number of Apache Junction High School's class of '97 along with their families waved and headed off into the night, promising another reunion in two days when the official one began...and then a weekend of crazy in the back yard just like the old days. Dolores and Jorge and their kids joined them beside a truck that everyone had seen before. Alvaro smiled.

"*Si...es el mismo camion*...the same one." He shrugged. "I couldn't bring myself to sell it so I kept on repairing it over and over and then I had it repainted and...here it is..."

Christina turned to Rosalie and Sophie, said:

"I went to the prom in this truck. This is the one in the pictures..."

Her daughter said: "Sophie told me I can't believe *you* went t'the prom."

Sophie said, "Y'know...Tina...I think me and Rosie are going to head into Mesa and hang out with Dolores and all these handsome boys." She nodded and smiled at Alex and Roddy, who were miniature versions of their father and already knew they were hot stuff enough to also know how to take compliments. She scrubbed three-year old Leandro's nose and made him giggle. "How about we see you...Friday...for lunch maybe...?"

Rosie started to say something that a gentle nudge in the ribs convinced her was totally unimportant. Dolores and Jorge grinned conspiratorially. Alvaro cocked his head to one side...puzzled...then slightly wide-eyed with comprehension. Christina only stood in a kind of stunned silence. When they had driven off, Alvaro turned to her.

"After you left I kept telling myself that you would come back to me...that no one could ever love you as much as I did. I think I was wrong..."

He took her back to the butter-yellow house, now bathed in starlight with the massive shadow of Superstition Mountain rising up into the eastern sky. He handed her down out of the truck in the carport where a long-haired grey-and-white cat named Mister Pooh all the way from Canada had often waited for her to get home from school...through a screened security door that creaked and then rattled the same way it had when she first had opened it twenty-five years before. Some of the furniture was different and the television was bigger, but somehow inside it still held the scent of patchouli and Coppertone and the smell of two people making love that had never failed to make her feel safe and loved.

In the tiled space between the kitchen and the sunroom he kissed her face and said: "Your Sophie is beautiful...and Rosie is exquisite...like your mother...like you..."

The silence was exquisite too. He led her slowly down the hallway into the room where she had managed to always walk in on her parents "doing it"...the place where she had learned never to be ashamed or embarrassed of who she was or what she might look like...and into the room across the hallway where she had become a grown-up in her very non-traditional prom dress and the man who had chosen to be her father had cried... speechless with love and pride...and then the room that had belonged to her she said:

"*Amado*...it's too hot for us to sleep indoors."

So together they moved a mattress out into the back yard. He went inside again for candles and wine. In the sunken garden they undressed each other in new moonlight... wept for lives not large enough to allow for all the love...

"Alvaro I'm so sorry—"

"No Christina...no..."

"You're alone."

"Not tonight. And you've always been in my heart. Too much so, I suppose...but also never enough..."

She sensed his ironic smile but heard no sadness, marveled at the spareness of his body, so different from the rich warm curves and softness of being close to Sophie.

"Her name is Elizabeth?"

"*Si*. She lives in Tucson...with our little boy..."

"How old is he?"

"He'll be seven in November. His name is Daniel Joseph Morales... *para tu madre y padre*..."

He had grown hard again, but their intimacy had become something all-encompassing and she put him in her mouth as if to swallow him like the words from his heart and their acts of love as life and breath. She moved slowly in time to the rise and fall of his hips and when he came she stretched out alongside him again and kissed him...spread him across his lips and his face and then licked him clean as newborn...

"Your Sophie has given me a gift I can never repay."

"I don't think she would ever dream of asking, Alvaro."

"Elizabeth realised she was never going to be what you had been to me..."

Another silence grew between them. On the other side of the block wall that enclosed the yard was a world that turned in its own fashion to time and tide, but for a moment Christina thought Time had bent itself to her heart's desire and she felt the feathered touch of a cat's tail across the back of her thighs...heard soft passionate cries through the open window of the back bedroom...

"After I left everything began to go wrong," she said, and began to cry again. "You...my mom...my poor sweet cat...my poor sweet father...my uncle Parry...and I was never there... they all died alone I don't even know what happened..."

"Christina stop...please...it had nothing to do with you...*es Vida...y estamos en el mundo*...it is only Life and we are in the world...at its mercy...

"There are days when the sun shines and the air is so still and so pure that we go about our lives believing that nothing can come between us and what we wish for in the deepest places of our heart...and then comes the wind, and we learn how fragile the balance can be...that our dreams are always vulnerable to Life...that the promise is no promise at all...only a Hope and a possibility..."

Here was the barbed hook behind the bait she had, perhaps knowingly, swallowed...the good times that had drawn her back to Alvaro and Dolores and Jorge, and Rosa flying in tomorrow from Chicago with her husband and children...everyone... memories of when her world ...finally...had been perfect...devoid of fear...but perhaps like a China doll on a shelf in Paradise in the instant before an earthquake sent it crashing down onto a concrete floor. She said:

"When we were small in Ottawa, Sophie and I would have sleepovers all the time, but she loved sleeping at my house because my bed was right up against the wall to my parents' bedroom and we would listen to them...sometimes almost all night...and my mom would talk dirty when they made love to each other...to tease my father...to show him that the words had nothing to do with what she felt for him...and she loved to do it... sometimes she would say the filthiest things and then burst out laughing...

"But one night I think she was scared or sad...for him...for us...I don't know...she said:

Fais-moi l'amour, Joshua ... baise-moi aussi fort que tu peux ... pour qu'ils sachent que nous sommes vivants et je t'aime toujours et je m'en fiche s'ils s'en foutent ...

"I don't know French, Christina."

"She said *Make love to me Joshua... fuck me as hard as you can...so they know we are alive and that I love you forever and I don't care if they don't care...*

"I was six or seven years old and I didn't know what she was saying. I didn't really know then what fucking was...had no idea who *they* could be. And I still don't know...but now I understand exactly what she meant...exactly what you said...

"It's just Life…and we're in the world…and all we've got is each other. Please tell me what happened," she begged him. "He never ever talked about it. Sometimes he just stopped believing she was gone…"

"…They were so good to me, Christina. They were so good to all of us. Whenever there was something we couldn't take home with us we went to *your* house…*your* mother and *your* father…and we were *never* turned away…not once…it was like we had become just as much their children as you…that it was for them to share our joys and ease our hurts… to explain what we didn't understand, make it something that was bearable as long as we believed in each other…

"Once they sold this house Joshua was terrified to leave your mom and Mister Pooh here alone. He pretended that everything would be all right…he was going to re-connect with some old friends in New York and then go back to Canada to make the new house perfect…

"I drove him to the airport and he asked me if I would look after them…stop in every couple of days. I said I would. I swore it. Your mom and I…after your uncle died, we knew what loss was all about, but it was nothing compared to what stalked your father day and night.

"I was supposed to pick your mom up in Scottsdale and we were going t'meet his return flight at Sky Harbour…except on the way up I heard a newscast on the radio about a gang shoot-out at Fiesta Mall…and when I saw Pooh sitting in front of the casita in

UNTIL THE END OF THE WORLD

Scottsdale...waiting for her...someone...that's when I knew something horrible had happened...

"I was scared to death. I knew I couldn't leave him there and I knew how pissy he could be...but not that day...I walked up to him and he knew...just let me pick him up and put him in the truck he never made a sound and the next few days were a nightmare...the three of us...trying to find out what had happened to your mother...making all the arrangements...

"In the end all he had left was a small cardboard box with your mom's ashes in it...not knowing what he should do or where she might find the most peace. He couldn't leave her behind, even though there was a part of him that felt she should stay here, that the mountain had been her fascination, and the sunshine...the heat...had worked some strange magic... each feeding the other...the furnace that fueled her passion. One night he told me how they had hiked together in the Superstitions...made love at high noon in caves and on outcroppings of rock, on blankets in the sand with nothing between them and the sky... hawks overhead singing them into each other. I didn't know what to say...or what t'do for him...but your mother had saved my life and I would have done anything to make the pain in him stop...

"Nothing worked. A couple of days later we had breakfast together. Pooh stayed in the car and when we went out into the parking lot he just said *Thank you* and kissed me goodbye... got in the car with Pooh and drove away...and I never saw him again....can't even begin to imagine how he managed to drive all the way back to

Canada just him and the cat and your mother in that cardboard box beside him..."

"...What shall we do today, *bonita*?

For a moment she had no idea where she was, or that it was Alvaro not Sophie with his arms around her as she opened her eyes to cool night air slowly soaking in morning heat and Arizona sky gone from indigo to translucent blue on its way to blistering summer white...utterly still at the bottom of the bowl in the back yard where she had demanded her father tell her what Love was all about so she would know what it was when it found her. She burrowed deeper into his arms could feel him growing hard against her belly, gently taking him in one hand...moving up and down slowly...feeling him grow slick with anticipation wishing they were three...wanting him to be inside Sophie too...so she would know...

She looked up and smiled to see him gone stupid with her hand around him...leaned into his chest and licked upwards to his throat closing her teeth around the place where she could feel his pulse jumping...

"*Nada, mi amor*," she breathed. "Nothing today...just hold me...all day...and all night tonight until our dream is something else tomorrow..."

A phone message brought them to breakfast in Mesa the next day...a tiny Mexican restaurant filled with seemingly hundreds of her friends and their families, but now there was Rosa and her family and "the crew" was complete...her beautiful twin boys only a year or two younger than Rosie...her breath-taking eleven-year old daughter...and her smooth sweet-talking husband Max who knew exactly what to say and when, all the while looking over his shoulder to make sure everyone was paying attention. They had to leave after three hours because the locals came crowding in for lunch, and as most of the wait staff conveniently had forgotten just when it was alcohol was allowed to be served in the morning, afternoon began in a genial haze with promises that the official reunion beginning that evening would be more than the Anglos could manage.

Sophie walked up to them and put her arms around Alvaro said:

"*Bonjour mon beau garçon j'espère que vous avez bien pris soin de ma fille.*"

Alvaro looked stunned. Rosie said:

"She wants t'know if you took good care of my mom. I wanna know too..."

Christina couldn't remember the last time she had felt so happy. For a moment, Alvaro looked stunned with Rosie up in his face, until he realised she wasn't at all serious. Still a bit uneasy, he managed to put on some bravado and said:

"You're gonna have to ask her that yourself, *chiquita*."

Rosie stood back and because she'd been teasing all along just grinned...touched Sophie's hand and then tippy-toed up to kiss his face.

"Don't have to," she said, and took off because she had business with Rosa's boys. Sophie said:

"We're all doin' the water park this afternoon…"

She moved slowly up between them, gathered them up one on each arm…

Somehow it felt as if no time had passed at all, drenched in the smell of chlorine and suntan oil, surrounded by glistening bodies; the younger children shrieked and laughed in the wading pools with big white swatches of sunblock all over their faces; the teens slunk around with casual glances for just about anything in their age group that moved, struttin' their stuff and lookin' for adventure.

The grown-ups…the AJHS Class of '97…took over vast tracts of poolside concrete, moving constantly, finding old friends with slightly older faces, cranking up smartphones and sharing jpeg files, continuing conversations begun days and weeks and months ago online and by telephone.

Christina was nervous in spite of every assurance from Sophie. Beneath an oversized plain white dress shirt she had decided to go with some swimwear that twenty years before had passed into the stuff of which legends were made, gold and white nylon in what was only a just-barely-legal excuse for a string bikini…the one she had borrowed from her mom on graduation day. Sophie was already stripped down to a one-piece that showed off all her best features, and, after a couple of days, now was thoroughly at ease with Christina's *posse* from the good old days…exchanging stories for possible future blackmail and generally carrying on as if they had known each other for their entire lives.

"*Nous sommes les trois mousquetaires et je suis d'Artagnan ... seulement en espagnol...*" she said, translated for Dolly and Rosa, then blew a saucy kiss at Max who was lounged on the perimeter of their little enclave with a blissful grin on his face, checking out his wife's friends and pretending he and Jorge weren't comparing notes.

She contemplated some outrageousness in return, but got distracted when a tide of laughter and splashing came from one of the deeper pools, and everyone turned to see what the commotion was all about. On the far side she could see Rosie and Mariela surrounded by a large contingent of admirers, all of them young and very enthusiastically male.

"What's up with them?"

"I think our girls are getting swimming lessons from the boys," said Rosa.

Christina tilted her head to one side, looking a question at Sophie, who only seemed to smile even more.

Sophie said, "I'm pretty sure Rosie didn't bother t"tell them she already knows how t'swim. How about Mariela?"

Rosa said, "She's like a little fish. And she's got her brothers to look out for her."

And Rosie to look out for all of them thought Christina.

She watched her daughter holding court... Mariela looking slightly embarrassed but taking her cues from Rosie. She realised that her daughter, though only a few years older than the oldest, was totally comfortable... relaxed...soaking in the adulation and bestowing innocent favour on them all, paying special *girl* attention to Mariela to put her at ease.

For a few brief seconds she saw herself in Rosie...certainly no great leap of imagination, for already there had been a dozen comments to the effect that they seemed more like sisters, in the same fashion as she and her own mother had often been indistinguishable as parent and child...except Christina marvelled at Rosalie, how she had almost always moved with an unshakeable confidence in herself, something Christina had only partially learned from her parents. Alike in so many ways in spite of the recent cataclysmic shift of generational attitudes, she recognised in Rosie that major difference; that somehow her daughter had come to her with some options that were, in her, standard features...factory installed...

She shook her head slightly, moved out of wherever it was she had gone...heard Rosa speaking as if she had been reading her mind:

"...I hope our girls will become friends. I mean, Chicago isn't so far from where you are, right? And Rosie is so good for her...my poor Mariela she is only eleven and already she is getting these things..." Rosa shook her front "...and doesn't know what t'do with them...or what to do with the boys who notice everything...so fast... *gracias a Dios* I am not like Dolores that way..."

Christina nodded. "I hope so too, *querida amiga*, she's so sweet and adorable... but you know something, *chica*...I think she will be fine as long as she knows she never has to hide anything from you and Max."

"*Como tu madre y tu padre*. Like with your mom and dad..."

"*Si...*"

"Come on, *Racha*," said Dolly, reaching over to tug at Christina's sleeve, "Sophie told us what you got on under that thing."

"What about you? Aren't you gettin' wet today?"

Dolores made a small *moue* with her mouth, shook her head and looked down her front before rolling here eyes heavenward.

"Not in public, Christina. Not anymore," she laughed. "But now it's time for you t'shake it out again, honey. The world is *never* gonna be ready for you so get on with it."

She glared daggers, took a quick glance around and said *Fuck it!* Mustering some of her own courage from her daughter's example, the dress shirt came off with a flourish...heads turned...and she had the great satisfaction of watching Max and Jorge become instantly more attentive.

"Thank goodness *that's* over with," she breathed to Sophie, and reached for her Coppertone.

───※───

They had come upon a lull in the excitement, now lay side by side stretched out in the sun, drowsy with heat and not a few clandestine visits to a select bunch of insulated Colemans fueled by Jose Cuervo.

Sophie traced a finger along the tie of Christina's bikini bottom, opened her eyes just long enough to make sure that an instant of *too far* wouldn't be cause for any unwanted attention.

"I remember the day in Las Vegas when your mom wore this."

Christina sighed. "It was pretty memorable."

"I gather the times you borrowed it for your graduation pool parties were pretty memorable too."

"Don't tease, Sophie. We were really young and we all loved each other. Nobody even noticed...well...not much anyway..."

"I find that hard t'believe, Tina. You're the most beautiful girl in the world."

"As long as you don't ever stop thinking that," Christina said quietly...and then: "Thank you Sophie... thank you so much."

Their hands met. Christina felt like she was in kindergarten...five years old on the edge of adventure. Sophie asked:

"Was it good?"

"It was wonderful, baby. Back then me and Alvaro were both mostly brand new and he was kinda terrified."

"Not this time."

"No...not this time at all...and he was so gentle, Sophie. Nobody can make me melt like you, but it was so good to be with him and have no doubts or fears about anything...

"I kept wishing you were with us. Sometimes it even felt like you were. It was so different from when we were kids...and you've managed sainthood as far as he's concerned."

Their hands came apart, feather-touched each other's hips.

"We're we gonna see him before tonight?"

"He said he had some stuff to look after but he'd be here this afternoon for sure..."

Christina elbowed herself up to where she could look down at her, then slowly dropped into a long slow kiss...felt Sophie's arms come up around her up through her hair, their skin gone to sun-warmed oil and silk against each other.

22.

Friday night's official opening festivities had been a small stand-up buffet, lots of announcements, and although no one cared to admit it, a trifle uncomfortable wherever local and national politics bumped into cocktails and conversation. Someone had forgotten to inform Christina that as the class valedictorian she was supposed to give a welcoming speech, so she did the best she could under the circumstances, in many ways simply repeating some of the thoughts she'd voiced at their graduating ceremony, wishing everyone well and thanking them for showing up and sharing. As had often been the case twenty years before, socialising instinctively seemed to run along lines of ethnicity, something that Rosie remarked on with no small amount of disgust once things had broken up and they were all on their way back to Apache Junction.

"...It's Arizona, honey," said Christina, trying to explain. "Historically it's not really ever been a hotbed of progressive thought, but with so many people from up north and back east moving into the state, there's always been a bit of tension when their attitudes and beliefs clashed with those of the people who grew up here."

Rosie just shook her head and curled her lips disdainfully. "It's just stupid," was all she would say, and no one could disagree with her.

※

"...This is better than the hotel," said Rosa, pouring more wine. "Next time I don't think we should wait for an excuse for all of us to get together. I keep expecting t'see your mom and dad though, bringing more food or tequila...or Señor Pooh the Shit waiting for a chance to steal something off our plates..."

Christina reached for a *taquito* and salsa, closed her eyes and munched...Tito Puente and Santana on the stereo... almost the entire *latino* contingent of her graduating class and their families... crammed into the back yard of the house...

She opened them again saw Alvaro playing the perfect host looking perfect in loose linen trousers and a blouse-like shirt blindingly white against his dark skin...slow-dancing with Sophie...Rosie dancing with Mariela in and around a circle of boys...her brothers Jose and Rafael having a hard time deciding who was needing more of their attention. Sophie caught her eye and winked, spun herself into Alvaro's arms and rocked him through *Esperando*, *Black Magic Woman* and *Oye Como Va,* while Dolly boogied with Jorge and the night started to come down around them from a sky streaked in purple, rose, orange, crimson and gold. Christina took a deep breath of the first cool air coming in from the desert, closed her eyes again.

"This is that Mexico City concert, from 1993," she said. "The one my dad got on a bootleg in Tucson."

Rosa nodded. "He made copies for everyone."

"I can't believe we're all here..."

"You haven't changed at all, *mi amor*," said Rosa.

"Rosita we've all changed, but we don't notice because we remember who were were when we found each other. It's wonderful to finally meet your Max...and your babies... *Dios mio! Los chicos son tan guapos...y Mariela ...ella es exquisita...*"

Rosa beamed. "Sometimes I don't believe how lucky I am," she said quietly. "When we graduated and you went back to Canada it was so strange...I mean, all the rest of us we knew each other all through school but it was almost like we were waiting for you...and your mother and father...

"Before you came along we kept to ourselves... *nosotros éramos latinos y luego estaba el resto del mundo*...you know what I mean. Us and them..."

Christina nodded. "I was an outsider too."

"But you were one of *us*."

"It went both ways, Rosa. You shouldn't have welcomed me the way you did, but when I realised all of us were feeling like we had been marginalised here...your families *way* longer than me...I didn't want to be anywhere else."

"I'm so sorry about Joshua and Danielle, Christina. I was already in Chicago. I didn't find out about *su madre* until months after."

Christina fought the almost instinctual urge to give in to grief...again...shrugged instead.

"It is what it is, *chica*. I've been crying over them for so long. First my mom and then my father. Alvaro just said *Es Vida*...and he's right. What can we do? They were so special not just for me...for all of us...even though they had no real place in the world except with each other, somehow they convinced us all that each one of us already owned our place here, all we had to do was claim it."

They watched each other's eyes go bright... leaned into each other's arms and stayed there.

Rosa whispered, "*Te amo, Racha.*"

Christina whispered back, "*Y te amo también, Rosita*...but tell me...where did you find your guy? Jorge was always showing off, and we know he'll never change. He's so smooth and charming and he knows it and all Dolly had to do was shake her front at him and it was all over. But sometimes I see Max get really quiet...not cold or nose-in-the air stuffy...but you get the feeling he's always keeping an eye on the serious side of things..."

Rosa grinned. "Well, he's a lawyer just like Jorge so what else is new? But you're right, *hermana*, he's got a side to him that's always business. He's always watching out for his people...and next year he's probably gonna to try for mayor back home, or the legislature.

"I met him when I went north the summer after you left, to visit with cousins, and we ended up in the same protest march on City Hall...better housing...better services for minorities... more watchdogs for the police department...you know what I mean, all the shit that we have to put up with because we're not white…and he's just as smooth as Jorge, but he figured out how to be slick, too.

"He knows things, *chica*…about everyone who is anyone in Illinois. They all looked at a poor *latino* from west Texas and never considered he might be keeping tabs on them…so they've been careless, and he's never put it in their faces, but they know he knows their secrets, and he figures if he runs as an independent he can make changes just from them *thinking* he's willing to play the same dirty games."

"He's gonna make a difference then."

Rosa nodded. "I think so. I hope so. The boys brag about him all the time, and once we knew we were coming back for this reunion he made sure he got in touch with Jorge *and* Alvaro. This is business as much as pleasure for him, especially since that *hijo de puta* was elected *el presidente*."

"He's in the news every day back home," said Christina, shaking her head. "Is it bad where you are…or here…?"

Rosa's face became cold. "So far all of our families have been lucky. ICE hasn't found an excuse to bother us yet, but the everyday is worse than what it used to be," she said bitterly. "Now it's acceptable to be a racist…to cheat or to lie, even when there's no reason for it. It's the Internet, Christina, and that bastard in Washington. Before the Internet all these stupid people were never sure what kind of response they would get if they opened their mouths in public to spit hatred; they would hide under their hoods and white sheets and pretend God was on their side…but now because even stupid people can be online and they are everywhere, and because that bastard gets away with saying anything day after day, these people think their sickness and hate are just fine."

Christina nodded. "It's the same in Canada, she said sadly." We have such a diverse population...immigration from all over the world. As long as they're willing to contribute they're mostly welcomed in Canada. I guess a lot of it is looking ahead economically... but you almost never hear about hate crimes from minorities, it's always the white people, who feel entitled to sit on their butts because they're white, and they resent anybody who works harder than they do...or succeed where they've failed..."

"That's why Max is trying to network across the country," said Rosa. "Jorge is altering his law practise here in the Phoenix area to accommodate every facet of *la experiencia latina* in Arizona *and* New Mexico...to provide free legal advice and service wherever it's needed. I don't know if Dolly told you, but next year she's getting her own law degree so that when Leandro is old enough to go to school she and Jorge will be able to work together.

"Alvaro was already in construction when the housing market here fell apart, so he started buying and borrowing for every house he could lay his hands on, to renovate and repair them, bring them up to code, make them available to our people at prices and on terms that were affordable.

"These days Money is the only voice that gets heard in America, and sometimes the hate is so loud that even money can't talk...but this will be our *fuck you* to Trump...to fight back and beat him in terms he will understand, even if he will never acknowledge it, or even know who we are and that we will never lie down without biting back at his ignorance and stupidity. And also because he is a fat-ass motherfucker with ugly beady-eyed children."

Rosa grinned, high-fived her and said: "Enough of this, *Racha,* now we party. Let's show them who can shake it down an' what happens when we do..."

23.

For Christina, Saturday's program of events mostly went the way of Friday night—a brief appearance at the hotel, dropping in on some of the group discussions to reminisce, table- hopping in the bar and restaurant, chatting a few minutes at a time in the lobby, or stopping to introduce Sophie and Rosie to some of her Anglo classmates before slipping quietly back out into the parking lot and pointing themselves in the direction of Superstition Mountain...

Happily stretched out on long deck chairs in the sunken patio, attired less controversially than in the previous day's swimwear, she and Sophie got shiny with tanning oil and gratefully accepted slushy mango margaritas from Alvaro as the back yard began to fill up all over again. Rosie wandered down the flagstone steps looking for a taste, but encountered two parents gone open-mouthed with astonishment

"What happened to all your gear?" Sophie asked incredulously

Rosie was wearing a pair of her mother's old silk running shorts, a lightweight linen blouse with spagehtti straps, and some new pink flip-flops with purple geckos on top.

She shrugged. "I couldn't wear the camo anymore," she said, frowning.

"Too hot, eh?" grinned Christina, offering her a sip of mango slushy. "I told you it was gonna be toasty..."

Rosie shook her head. "It's not that, Mom," she said . "It's those sneaky little Casanovas masquerading as Dolores and Jorge's kids."

"Casanova was Italian."

"Yeah...well he must've given these kids lessons. The middle one kept looking under my kilt. Every time I turned around there he was with a smug little grin on his pretty little face, and the hem of my skirt in his pudgy little fingers. The little shit..." she finished bitterly.

"Oh Rosie what's the big deal he's just a kid..."

She took another swig of Christina's slushy, demanded equal time from Sophie.

"The big deal is I was so hot in the kilt that I wasn't wearing knickers...and with Rodrigo standing there grinning and me bare-ass swearing at him, who should be standing right behind us admiring the view but Mari's brothers..."

Sophie got her margarita back and said, "Well...just don't forget to put your sunscreen on everywhere, honey."

Not long after Rosie's visit the music kicked in...post-psychedelic Santana mixed with Mongo Santamaria and Malo, redolent with the flavours of jazz, funk, and salsa from all over the Hispanic world...and then the barbecues got fired up with *chorizo* and strip beef and chicken for *fajitas*. They wondered just how well Rosie would hold up with that kind of temptation, but only as long as it took for a tall dark-haired *latino* from west Texas to sit himself down between them

"*Buenas tardes, señoritas. Cómo estás hoy?* Can I freshen things up for you?"

Christina giggled. "Shut up, Max. There's no use you putting the moves on us we're best friends with your wife and also impervious to your charms."

Sophie leaned over to hand him her glass as she kissed his cheek, a wicked smile on her face. "Oh Tina does that mean we've stopped not being lesbians?"

Christina handed hers over too. "Shame on you, Sophie," she said happily. "Now look at what you've done! Max is blushing!"

Max was smooth enough to know when he'd lost a round to the ladies.

"Ah well...Rosa has told me but I could not believe it was true."

Christina shook her head. "*Estás lleno de mierda, Max...*"

Sophie asked, "What did she say?"

Max put on an air of wounded pride.

"Your lover has told me I'm full of shit."

Sophie took their glasses from his hand.

"But also you're charming and *très beau* so don't feel too badly. Shall I bring one for you too?"

Max asked for single malt neat and Sophie wandered off with a backward glance full of meaningful nonsense.

"*Es bueno conocerte por fin*," he said, following Sophie's shimmy up the sandstone flags. "She is very beautiful. And also the daughter you have named after my wife."

Christina followed his gaze, felt an extra flush of warmth in the afternoon sun.

"She's my girl," she whispered, and "It's very good to finally meet you, Max. It's been so long and so much has happened. And today...yesterday...except for a few things... people who should be here...it's almost like no time has gone by at all...*es maravilloso*..."

"I hope you will come to visit us in Chicago."

"You guys have t'come to Ontario."

"Rosa told me about your mother and father," he said seriously. All of the playfulness and pretense in his voice was gone now. "It is very strange that so many of us here today have been here before...knew them so well...and feel that having known them was a gift... something precious in their lives, when they were young trying to find their way out into the world. Alvaro said all the good things we would ever need to know of your parents we could find in you."

"You're trying to do the same thing now, Max," she said. "I don't know what's happening in the world anymore. Once upon a time I suppose it made sense, but not anymore, not to me, anyway. My mother and father were outside of the world, certainly the one we have now...but they found each other and together found a way to teach me to survive, along with everyone else who came here for some peace and refuge from the craziness.

"On our drive to the airport I had this dream that was really a memory of the day when I first left Canada to live here. I was ten or eleven years old and I was scared to be wherever it was that we were, but I remember someone calling them *fucking hippies*, like it was an insult. Today I think it was the most intelligent thing that stupid man ever said..."

Christina watched his face become transformed with a smile that made his already handsome features transcendent with a reflection of his heart. He took her hands in one of his own and made an elaborate ritual of touching them gently to his lips.

"I wish I had known them, Christina, and I see why it is Rosa loves you the way that she does. Please promise to visit us. We must go back on Monday, but please promise me..."

She nodded wordlessly, leaned into his embrace lost in the heat and the scent of his cologne, looking up as Sophie came back with more liquid refreshment...smiling eyes...singing along in a language she didn't know, old songs become new, reminding her of what it was like to be in a place where everything was right and proper, and all of the people she loved all were safe in the knowledge of being loved.

24.

Monday morning at Sky Harbour watching them go...Max and Rosa...Jose and Raf with a much much deeper appreciation for Rosie, who didn't want to let go of

Mariela. It was all too familiar to Christina, suddenly thrust back into re-enactments of things that had gone before...farewells...in hindsight, unseen-tragedies-in-waiting...except this time there was a tomorrow to look forward to that somehow, for her, had managed to extricate itself from the horrible sense of impending doom...the fear of bad things happening...

When Max and Rosa and their kids were in the air, they all piled into a rental car and from the airport began a smaller version of the Great Western Safari, visiting some of the places that Sophie and Christina had been to with her parents twenty-five years before...

The headed north to Sedona for lunch and the afternoon before continuing on to Flagstaff and the Canyon, because Rosie couldn't visit Arizona without seeing the Grand Canyon. They spent the night at the El Tovar Lodge...Christina and Sophie haunted...in mid-morning the next day south again to Flagstaff, to catch 89 and then 160 to Kayenta... Lake Powell... Monument Valley...

There was a Navajo man who took them out onto the floor of the Valley...who looked at them and was looked at it turn...

Christina said, "*Mon Dieu* you're Ahiga,"...softly... stunned at how the universe sometimes could maintain its own continuity...redefine the definition of what might be termed a miracle.

Ahiga now more than fifty years old nodded.

"I know you."

UNTIL THE END OF THE WORLD

"Yes," said Christina, pulling Sophie closer. "You brought us here a long time ago...with my parents..."

"I know you," he said again, this time meaning something entirely different he smiled and looked at Rosie. "And this one can only be your daughter."

They stayed long enough to watch the sun make black cut-out castles of the Mittens as it began to sink into the western sky. They spent hours in the whisper of wind that was like the breath of the gods, and he told Rosie all the stories he had told her mother and Sophie more than twenty years before...kissed them all on their way at sunset...

In the motel room in Kayenta that night Christina told her daughter "I once told Grampa this would always be the best adventure of my life."

"Except now maybe for this one?" suggested Sophie.

"Except now maybe for this one," agreed Christina. "Did either of you guys get the feeling we had company, especially when we stopped somewhere?"

Two wide-eyed faces nodding provided all the response she needed.

"I started getting a little bit freaked out in the helicopter over Lake Powell," said Rosie, "especially when we did that big dive and started skimming so close to the water...right into the sunrise as we came up to Rainbow Bridge. I thought I heard one of you whispering to me not to be afraid and I felt somebody's hand on my shoulder...and bein' afraid just went away..."

Sophie said, "Last night in our room...and now...right here right now..."

They waited for Christina...as Christina waited for what had for so long been the almost instinctual reaction to anyone's recollections of time spent with her parents. She found herself puzzling over something that once might have been nothing but a crippling sense of loss, yet now seemed like something else entirely new.

"For me it was yesterday at the Canyon," she mused. "The place where we had turned around and suddenly realised that Daddy had climbed over the guardrails. D'you remember that, Sophie? All three of us begging him to come back...and then hanging on to him? Afterwards he felt so badly about scaring us like that...tried to explain to me what had happened. He really didn't have any words to describe it, but I got the feeling that for a little while he'd stepped out of our world into a place that existed in that same moment, but somewhere between his past and the future...that only just barely connected to where we were...

"It was one of the most frightening days of my life...the thought of losing him like that, but going back yesterday...being there...it was peaceful...like maybe wherever he is now, he's not scared anymore..."

"You didn't really wanna go to Disney World, did you, honey?" asked Sophie.

Rosie wagged her head. "No not really," she said brightly. "I just said we were going so the customs guy at the border wouldn't give us a hard time. It's more for little kids anyway, and besides, this is way better...goin' t'some of the places you guys went to...listening to your stories. It must've been so awesome doin' that with Gramma and Grampa."

UNTIL THE END OF THE WORLD

"They were pretty wacky together," said Sophie. "It was like they were taking care of us... making sure we had a great time...but bein' kids just like us at the same time. I missed *my* mom and dad a lot...really wished they were with us...but your mom and dad, Tina, like Rosie said, they were awesome...always let me call home anytime I wanted..."

"Speaking of..." said Christina to Rosie. "You talked t'Sam and Charlie last night, didn't you? How're they doin'? How many critters has Grimsby killed since we left?"

Rosie began to glow.

"They're good...really good. Sam's been stayin' over almost every night and they've been playin' music and listening t'all of Grandpa's music and watching all the videos...and oh oh oh Matt and Josee dumped their *others* and are hangin' out with each other now...and Grimsby's hardly even been outdoors because it's too hot so there's been almost no dead anythings at all. Can we get something t'eat now? I'm starving..."

Somewhere in some last bit of sleepy conversation later that night, both Sophie and Christina keeked over the pillows to where Rosie was curled up on the other twin bed in their motel room.

Sophie said, "We can't stop, Tina...we can't stop living just because shit can happen..."

A little bit of outside neon crept past the curtains of their room, falling on Rosie's face, a mirror of Christina's.

She nodded without any words, kissing Sophie between her shoulder blades...wrapping her arms around her waist she made spoons as they drifted into sleep.

Early the next morning they headed back to Phoenix, days to be spent in Mesa with Dolly and Jorge and the boys over their last weekend, and at the house in Apache Junction. Alvaro was bringing his son Daniel up from Tucson to meet them.

25.

Rosie was in the back seat hop-scotching wi-fi hot-spots on her tablet as they travelled south to Phoenix on I-17. As they passed through the Coconino Forest and doglegged west toward Camp Verde she began to get breathless with *ohmygods* and when Sophie who wasn't driving turned around to see what was going on found her open-mouthed and almost jumping out of her skin.

With no rest areas in sight and in that moment no regard at all for the signs they'd seen warning *Emergency Stopping Only*, Christina declared an emergency and stopped, braked them slowly onto the shoulder right up next to the guardrails so they all had to pile out on the highway side and hope like hell no one was riding the rumble-strips. Rosie was hopping up and down, and doing a little bump-and-bounce with her bum on the front fender of the car.

"Charlie just emailed me! We're goin' t'Toronto," she said in a whisper. "Holy shit Mom...Sophie...we're goin' t'Toronto...and before that we gotta start practisin' our brains out because *somebody* we know wants us to open for him at the Grand in October and maybe go on the road with him for his tour next summer!"

An eighteen-wheeler thundered past them, the driver looking at three women dancing on the shoulder like he knew they were out of their minds but laying on his air-horn anyway because in his mind in that instant there was nothing in the world to match three beautiful crazy women dancing on the edge of the interstate halfway between Flagstaff and Phoenix. Christina said:

"D'you guys have enough stuff you can record?"

And Rosie nodded, half in tears...

"You've got a whole record-full of songs...?" asked Sophie.

Rosie nodded again.

"We do we do...after the first one...remember, Mom? After that one it was like a freakin' cloudburst for all of us we'd be wakin' up every day with new ideas and words and music..."

"And you're gonna be the band," laughed Sophie

"Yeah we're gonna be me, we're gonna be Rosie May. Sam and Charlie said so."

Traffic got crazy alongside of them...

"You guys really wrote a whole album full of songs?"

"We did, Mom...we even got a name for the record..."

They all decided any more conversation where they were was less than ideal, took the Camp Verde exit and the excuse to sit somewhere quiet with coffee and tea. Rosie usually traveled with a godawful-green Army-issue canvas bag as a purse, something large enough for the laptop and anything else she cared to carry with. When they were settled in the corner of a small diner just off the highway she carefully extracted another canvas sleeve out of her bag, and something she put on the table in front of her mother and Sophie....

"Before we left I was lookin' through some of those boxes of old cards an' pictures an' stuff. I found this..."

An old handmade card already going yellow with age, with a wash of water-colour sunrise on the front...and words inside written in small sweeping curves, dated 13 July 1985 it read:

Mon cher Joshua
avec tout mon coeur
Je t'aime
pour toujours
jusqu'a la fin du monde

"My mom wrote this...it's from my fifth birthday," said Christina. "The day they got married. She must've given him this card. I've never even seen this, kitten."

Rosie nodded.

"Charlie and Sam said we should speak for them. If the record company signs us we want t'call the record *Love Songs for Souls Remembered*..."

26.

Not long after, as they cruised through Black Canyon City, Christina's cell went off and Sophie answered it for her...read the caller ID...

"*Bonjour*, cutie," she said, and turned on her most evil grin.

"It's Alvaro," she whispered.

UNTIL THE END OF THE WORLD

"...*Si*...we're just north of Phoenix now...and you and Daniel are in Florence...an hour or so...?"

She listened intently for a minute for so and then nodded.

"Okay see ya soon. *Adiós* Hot Stuff."

She studied a map conjured up on her own phone and asked Christina if she remembered the 101 or 202 loops running down and through the East Valley.

"I think maybe they'd just started planning them about the time I went home," she said. "What do they do?"

"Alvaro wants us to meet him at the house in AJ...said if we turn off on the 101...that's the Pima Freeway the exit's only a few miles in front of us...it'll take us east and then south through Scottsdale so we don't have to go through all the spaghetti downtown...and then we can pick up the 202...the Red Mountain Freeway—that loops farther out and dumps us east of that big mall—or just keep going until we hit the Superstition at Price..."

They opted for both the 101 and the 202, crossed the dry-as-bone Salt River bed just east of Rio Salado Park...arc-ed over the East Valley with the peaks of the Mazatzals stark and sun-blasted away to the northeast, then dropped south along Power Road until the Apache Trail took them the last eight miles into the Junction. Alvaro's truck was in the carport when they turned into the driveway. A little boy with inky black hair and huge brown eyes came running out the carport door to see who had come to visit. From between them Rosie looked out the windscreen and said:

"Ohmygod he's adorable!"

MICHAEL SUMMERLEIGH

She tumbled out of the back seat before Christina had a chance to put the car in *park* and stopped a couple of feet from where Daniel stood beside the bed of his father's truck, barefoot and nut-brown against the white of a short-sleeved dress shirt and a pair of khaki shorts he said *Hola* quietly...and Rosie said *Hola* back...and Alvaro came out the carport door as Christina and Sophie came up behind Rosie...

"You made it," he said.

Christina nodded. "We did..."

Alvaro grilled hot dogs for everyone because Daniel loved hot dogs better than any other food in all the world, and he grilled some salmon for Rosie—on a cedar plank with sliced zucchini and tomatoes and fresh-cut rosemary from the now-massive bush beside the house that Christina had planted herself. They drank ice-chilled Coronas from a cooler and watched the sunset turn Superstition Mountain into a brick-red-and-gold splendour, and Beethoven came out of the big living room speakers, floated softly overhead where they sat on the sunken patio. Daniel stopped after every bite, to look first at Rosie and then at Christina and then at his father in an unspoken attempt to figure out how they could look almost exactly alike. Introductions had been made in the carport, explanations came with supper.

Rosie said, "She's my mom, Daniel. I look just like her and she looks just like *her* mom looked. We're all the same."

"And Sophie is your mom too?"

"Yeah. I can explain that if it's okay with your dad."

Alvaro only smiled....

※

"...He's usually so shy with people he's never met before. *Son mágicos* ...all of you..."

Rosie and Daniel had their heads together a couple of levels up on the flagstone patios, in porchlights bent over a book he was sure she needed to see...or simply needed to be shared with someone new and suddenly welcome in his life. Alvaro still had no idea how to deal comfortably with his old love and her lover, sat in front of them across a small circle of stone, unwilling to presume upon his prior status.

"He looks like a little boy with his older sister," said Sophie. "Rosie is...well... she's Rosie... a pain in the ass sometimes, and then there's times when my heart just doesn't know what to do with her because she's so..."

"Rosie," said Christina, and twisted the caps on another trio of Coronas, passed them around, lay back in her chair and breathed up into the night.

"Pooh is here somewhere," she whispered. "I just know he is...I can feel him..."

※

"...I hate it that he's down the hall, all by himself."

Christina caught her breath, ran her hands through Sophie's hair and drew her up from between her legs to kiss her, the familiar taste of herself in Sophie's mouth...the surprise that she would think of Alvaro there and then...

"We could change that," she said slowly, cautiously.

Out of the darkness Sophie said, "I know...but not tonight. I'm selfish, Tina, tonight I want all of you just for me...your fingers and your tongue inside me all at once...just yummy up...and the toys would be nice too..."

"*Quelques jours de plus, mon amour*...a few more days...for the toys, anyway..." Christina whispered, reaching for her hips. "My turn now..."

In late morning they caravanned into Mesa, returned the rental car, crammed themselves into Alvaro's truck and headed south to the house in Val Vista Lakes that Rosie and Sophie had visited the week before—a long side-split ranch with a short fence panel on either side promising all sorts of space in the back yard.

Jorge welcomed them through a marble foyer and into a kitchen tiled in *saltillo*, that faced the back yard through a large number of floor-to-ceiling windows and sliding glass doors. He began ferrying coolers and trays of food out to the barbecue. Dolly was already out beside the pool, keeping an eye on Alex and Rodrigo annoying the crap out of each other while Leandro gurgled happily in her arms, having a late breakfast.

"See what I mean?" she said to Christina. "They haven't gotten any smaller, *chica*, not after three children, and Jorge who won't stop acting like them. *Jesu Cristo*! Roddy still gets jealous that this one still gets some of his meals here."

"No surprise there," said Rosie, making sure her bikini bottom was where it was supposed to be under her shorts.

"And they all think it's funny when I fall out of my clothes," continued Dolores with mock bitterness. "Next time you see me, Streak, I'm going to be fifteen twenty pounds lighter."

"They'll be heartbroken," observed Christina, "...*especially* Jorge."

Dolores shrugged and covered Leandro's ears.

"Fuck him. He's had twenty years to be friends with them," she said with a smile. "Besides, when I get my papers how am I going t'walk into a freakin' courtroom with these things in front of me? I'll have to say everything at least three times before anyone with *cojones* will listen, and the women won't listen at all. And what happens if I drop a pencil? *Dios mio!* it will take three bailiffs to get me off the floor if I tip over!"

Her logic was irrefutable. The sunny yellow one-piece she was wearing looked more than a little bit challenged by the expansiveness of her front.

Christina said, "*Mi pobre dulce amor*," trying to appear sympathetic, but it was too funny and she began to laugh...joined immediately by Dolores who had expected nothing less, and finally by Sophie and Rosie, until Jorge noticed as he walked by with a plate of sausages in hand and started casting nervous glances over his shoulder.

"You better be nervous, *perrito*," she called after him; then, "Come on, girls, let me get this one where his brothers can look after him and we can have the big children look after us all afternoon."

"...Jorge tried to make this just like it was at your place in AJ, when we were all together that last year in high school," she said. "The people who bought it from your mom and dad started changing things right away; we would drive by whenever we went up to Dirtwater and just shake our heads."

Christina was slightly dozy with tequila, overwhelmed by the blazing heat and sunlight flashing off the surface of the pool. She felt sleepily peaceful, her hair fanned out over the top of her deck chair, Sophie glowing beside her getting more and more brown with sun by the minute, and Dolly her usual outspoken outrageous self, testing and teasing them every time she bent over on purpose...

Jorge and Alvaro kept watch on the boys. Daniel knew them all fairly well, having visited in the past, but every now and again, after a bout of horsing around in the water or driving Ritchie Valens the resident golden retriever crazy, Christina would notice him gravitating to where Rosie had set up camp a bit removed from everyone else...plugged into her phone... reading...every now and again charming Alvaro into more than her allotted share of recreational beverages. Dolly said:

"Sometimes he's so sad it breaks my heart. I met his mother a few times, and she's a very remarkable woman, but I think that when she found out about you, *Racha*, and realised she had married someone who was still in love with someone else, she stood back a little bit. Daniel is the one who pays. He's lonely...so hungry for warmth... someone to wrap him up in their arms and rock him to sleep the nights when he cannot be with his father."

"He's fascinated by Rosie," said Sophie. "You can see him light up every time she pays him any attention. Mariela was the same, but for different reasons, I think."

Dolores nodded. "*Cómo puede ser diferente?* How can it be otherwise? She has the same *generosidad* as her mother and her grandmother…someone who cannot turn away from anyone who is needing a kindness in their life."

Christina watched them—her daughter just now fully grown into the almost supernatural adulthood of all the Lariviere/Desjardins/Haller women…the seemingly endless cycle of reincarnation of one another from each generation to the next, regardless of who provided the seed to create them.

She heard the murmur of Daniel's soft voice, saw Rosie look up from her book and reach for his hand, draw him up alongside her. He put his arms around her waist and his head down on her chest and Christina didn't need to hear Rosie reading to him to feel the physical intensity of her attraction to him.

Rosie. Her sweet almost-grown-up daughter. Ready for love. Already there. And then the child-woman who somehow seemed to be a beacon for the little boy who belonged to the man who still loved her mother. Daniel. Now her baby brother by some strange cosmic proxy…

Christina said, "Please don't ever let me take anywhere near so long to come back to see you again."

Dolores looked at Sophie. "You and me we'll make sure…?"

27.

MICHAEL SUMMERLEIGH

After dark, when all the dishes had been washed and the paper plates and cups had been recycled, and everything else left over consecrated to the god residing in the *chimineo* in a corner of the yard...when Ritchie Valens finally had found himself a spot where the sun-stunned children wouldn't bother him, they headed back to Apache Junction.

Rosie was half-asleep on her feet, but seemed to be half-asleep with one arm protectively around Daniel. She said goodnight. Daniel said *Buenos noches*. They disappeared into the guestroom Christina's father had made out of half the detached garage...and when they themselves had settled again on the patios, flickering candlelight danced through the bay windows, and they could hear the murmur of Rosie's voice singing soft lullabies that sounded suspiciously like old Beatles songs slowed down to put seven-year olds to sleep.

"I worry for him," said Alvaro. "He is not capable of violence of any kind...except sometimes to himself... when he gets angry or frustrated. I know I am to blame..."

A bottle of old brandy sat on a small table before them, out in the first coolth of the night...large round-bellied glasses holding dark amber dreams to come. He looked at Sophie and apologised.

"I'm so sorry. You are more precious than I have words to express, and you are integral to something here that happened without you ever being part of it."

Christina was very tired. Not really paying attention. Buzzed with tequila and brandy and errant bits of light making tiny shimmers in Sophie's hair, she only half-listened, drowsing in the sound of her voice.

"It's not too late, Alvaro," she heard her say, cryptically. "And you don't have to apologise to me. I've been caught up in this for a very long time...almost from the very beginning... and no matter how grateful we are for the things that make us feel safe and loved, *il y a toujours un prix à payer, par quelqu'un...* There's always a price to be paid.. by someone...for our searching...

"This time was meant to be. Coming together again after so much time...learning our family was so much larger than we have ever imagined. And it was also meant for your little boy to become free. For the five of us right here and now in this moment Rosie is the magic. She's the one who's risen above all the tragedies...all the grief...finally..."

She tossed back the last of her brandy, reached to caress Christina's cheek.

"*Ma pauvre fille endormie,*" she whispered, reached further to gather her up in an embrace she turned back to Alvaro.

"*Rosie s'occupera de Daniel ce soir.* Maybe we three should look after each other."

Christina saw her Sophie mirrored in Alvaro's eyes...first narrowed...again not fully comprehending what it was he had heard...and then widening...stunned once again with complete understanding.

She let herself be drawn upward onto her feet, felt like she might be floating... stars falling away behind her...the familiar coolth of a house she knew very well...and finally the night coming to breathe on her bare skin...and two souls learning to love each other both of them loving her.

There was one more afternoon, once again scheduled for the shimmering back yard of Dolores and Jorge. They awoke together in mid-morning making love without benefit of coffee or true consciousness, in a pleasant exhaustion...Alvaro then suddenly concerned for Daniel...stayed by Sophie's hand and her promise there wasn't anything to be concerned about anymore... reminding him that something new had come into the world of his son.

Freshly showered and finally presentable, they found him and Rosie in the sunroom at the back of the house, bent over a ring-bound sketchbook of pencil drawings that Daniel had brought from his room. He looked up and when he saw all three of them smiled... suddenly without any warning a smile of brilliance and untrammelled joy...as if recognising that somehow miracles had been visited upon them all and they had come to take away some of the shadows that had fallen upon his life and that of his father.

He said *Good morning!* and in turn came to each one of them. Rosie ducked her head down so they wouldn't see her smile she said:

"He's amazing. Look at what he's done!"

She offered up the sketchbook...one page especially...a small finch...like the ones that came to the feeder out by the garage—the drab little females of no real colour at all, the males all *machismo* over the tiny splotch of purple on their chests. The one Daniel had chosen to draw was still only half-grown, hunched up and anxious...

"It was a baby," he explained. "I looked with binoculars."

The drawing was remarkably detailed, so much so that it left no doubt about the age of its subject, or the "expression" Daniel somehow had managed to capture perfectly.

"He was scared...waiting for his mama."

They all nodded...solemnly...because it was a solemn drawing...a reflection...

Rosie said "You're gonna be a famous artist, Daniel, I know it. This drawing is r*eally* good"

He shrugged, embarrassed, but also thrilled...looked to his father for confirmation, as if too much praise might be suspect. Alvaro dipped his head again, reassuring him... and so unmistakably proud...and then cast what might have been a puzzled look in Rosie's direction, perhaps remembering something Sophie had said the night before. Daniel said:

"Rosie is the one gonna be famous. She makes music."

"Not as good as you draw, Daniel, nobody is better than you."

He smiled again with naked adoration, and Christina saw her daughter crying as the little boy leaned against her and she put her head down to kiss him.

It was a late-night flight back east...due to be much much later by the time their plane set down in Syracuse in the dawn of the next day's sunrise. Sophie was curled up in the window seat, fast asleep, catching up so she could drive them home. Christina sat beside her with Rosie on the aisle, the cabin of the 747 mostly dark...humming...lit intermittently where someone not sleeping was watching an in-flight movie, or reading in a tiny umbrella of light.

"Did you have a good time, kitten? Did I drag you off so I could get some of my past back and make you miserable in the bargain?"

Rosie shook her head. The slow glowing smile on her face made something inside Christina go breathless.

"I had a *great* time, Mom...really...Mariela and Daniel...it was like finding brothers and sisters where I didn't have any before...and it was so cool to hear all those stories about you and everybody I met there...and Sophie was so amazing Mom I don't know what I woulda done but me and her we talked so much the couple of nights you were with Alvaro...

"She's always been so good to me and sometimes I kinda thought it was just because you and her... well... y'know...but it wasn't anything like that at all...and I started t'see why you loved Grandpa and *you*r mom so much...to really understand what it meant for the two of them...and for you...and how Sophie loves you so much that she can't be jealous...and that's what Love is really all about...just giving..."

Rosie kicked off her boots and slipped out of her coat, undid her safety belt and crawled into her mother's seat, straddled her hips and took her face in both hands before she kissed her.

UNTIL THE END OF THE WORLD

"I still have no idea how really lucky I am…to have so many people to teach me how not to be petty or stupid or afraid to give away parts of me to people I care about…and how even if it turns out to be crappy it's still way better than if I'd been afraid to do it in the first place…to always have *t'think* before doing stuff that never should have t'be thought about at all…

"I don't wanna be like that, Mom. Not ever. I'd rather get hurt than always be afraid of getting hurt. You and Sophie and everybody I met in Arizona…I feel like I was supposed t'know all of you so I'd be sure t'learn it was the only way I wanted t'live my life."

Christina didn't say anything right away. Couldn't. There was a brief instant when she consciously acknowledged that people really could get lumps in their throats and it didn't let them say anything for a while, so she just wrapped her arms around her daughter and was grateful inside until she could talk again…softly…a whisper from her heart for the most precious thing in her life:

"Grampa was broken, Rosie…he was broken so badly…and I think maybe Gramma was too, in a different way…but our world was all they needed, the three of us and Pooh…

"And I think somewhere in there I got busted a little bit too…maybe because Daddy tried so hard to keep me from getting any kind of hurt at all…"

She realised in that instant she was exactly like her parents, that after her mother's accident she had started to fashion her world small enough that she could make it all safe...and by going back to someone...Sophie...where there had never been any doubt...

"...But whatever is broken in me is perfect in you, Rosie May. You're not afraid of anything in the world. Somehow me and Sophie managed t'do all the right things, and now you and Sam and Charlie have plans and you can't wait t'get started..."

"Mom I need t'tell you something about me and Sam and Charlie."

Christina shook her head. "No you don't, honey...not at all."

"You're not freaked?"

Christina laughed.

"Baby, why would I be freaked? Look at us holy shit sweetheart...you've been walked into being a grown-up by two girls who've been best friends almost all their lives...both of them raised by parents who were anything but conventional...who realised that what they felt for each other was better than anything they could find anywhere else no matter what it looked like to the rest of the world.

"If what you've got with Sam and Charlie makes you feel safe...like you're floating in warm salty soup when you make love to each other...then you've already found the most precious thing you're ever gonna find in your life..."

"I don't wanna choose Mom, I love them both so much...and they love me."

Christina smiled.

"Then don't choose at all, Rosie May. Take both of them. Your Grampa was so lonely before he met Gramma, but she loved him so much...gave him the luxury of loving without fear...of living in the music he wanted to share with her... *I don't really see why you can't go on as three..*"

"That's David Crosby."

Christina felt stoned. "Yeah...and Jefferson Airplane too."

"I wish I'd known them better. I wish I'd known Gramma better..."

"They're both alive and well in you, honey. They'd be so proud of you....both of them..."

EPILOGUE - THE BEGINNING

They sat side by side in front of the vanity, a direct descendant of sorts to the one Rosie had in her room, that had belonged to her grandmother. Reflected in the round mirror were two faces; one deeply tanned and framed by long dark hair that fell like ravens' wings down over her shoulders to pool around her behind on the *banquette*; the other face was rounder, only just seriously browned by a southern sun a couple of months before, but glowing in shagged waves of dirty blonde hair bleached almost white by that very same sun.

A large grey-and-white cat sat on the bed behind them, having a bath that was punctuated by snorts and other assorted horrible sounds that only cats are capable of making once they are totally absorbed in chewing hell out of a paw, or some other body part suddenly perceived as in need of a wash. Christina leaned into Sophie's arms, bent her head...a moment...to kiss the nipple on her left breast.

"I'm so sleepy," she said, could feel herself smiling.

It had been a long day, made longer still by anticipation of what was to follow.

"You could do that again," said Sophie.

Christina did that again, knew they were dozy in the unseasonable heat, and with the bottle of red wine they had shared over a hastily-contrived meagre-at-best supper of olives-and-greens salad and day-old *fettucini*...

"I love you, Tina," said the blonde girl.

"Oh good," said the other. "Otherwise I'd be embarrassed kissing your beautiful boobs..."

They laughed and melted into each other, the heat moving them right along, making them giddy...

"We should get our shit together," said Christina. "Rosie's depending on us to raise hell when we get there."

Sophie started shaking with quiet laughter, the kind that made all the parts of her that were round and soft so comfortable to be next to...

"We should," she agreed.

"What should we?" asked Christina. "I forget..."

"Get our shit together."

"D'you really think so?"

"*Incuestionablemente*...!"

"Use that word in a sentence," demanded Christina.

"I just did!" said Sophie.

"No that was just...that was...well....it was...whatever it was..."

"So you say, almost *Anglais* poophead lover girl!"

"I love you, Sophie."

"I love you more," said the blonde girl.

Rosie came rushing down the hallway...a hanger-full of clothing over one shoulder...

UNTIL THE END OF THE WORLD

"...I gotta go now, guys. Sam and Charlie are gonna be here any minute will you *please* make sure t'give Grimsby his supper before you leave? I gotta do sound-checks and stuff..."

"Like he's gonna let us get out the door if we don't?" asked Sophie.

"So we'll see you after the show? We'll tell them to let you in back-stage. Sam and Charlie said they wanna party with you guys after."

"We'll be sure to get our game on, baby," said Christina...very...slowly...

Rosie shook her head like *Stoned again*...gave both of them high-fives...put her head down for a moment, said:

"*Je t'aime tellement les gars*...forever..."

Sophie said, "Us too, kitten. Blow the roof off the place."

Rosie grinned and was gone.

Sophie said, "Those were your mom's boots. I remember them...that Christmas... all my uncles with major hard-ons in their pants..."

Christina hugged harder. "Yeah...they were my mom's...not right for me... Rosie found 'em in the closet, said she just wanted to wear them a couple of songs in because she'd rather be barefoot when she's playing anyway, and takin' 'em off onstage would make the boys go crazy...

"I figured that was the best way my mom could ever think of anybody else ever wearing them."

"Well now we need to get it together, Hot Pants," said Sophie, looking meaningfully at make-up and the clothes that Grimsby had decided to sit on.

"Not yet, baby," said Christina. "I don't mind another shower, but there's no point in doing this stuff twice..."

The sun was only just going down when they went to claim their comps at the box office.

Dressed to kill...a little bit higher by one or two tokes in the parking lot...and tonight feeling like being out together was like being in bed at home. They got to their seats front row centre in the balcony and started dancing to music they made between themselves.

Fifteen minutes later the house lights went down.

They recognised Sam and Charlie being ragged and sexy, and then there was this perfect young woman with midnight eyes and midnight hair shagged down over her shoulders...in denim and leather, buckles and belts, a stunning pair of thigh-high black suede-and-silk-ribboned boots, and a vintage black top hat with brass goggles perched on the brim...who revved up her bank of keyboards with a series of drone chords, played low under an introduction... almost *a capella* they made a spoken-word harmony...

Heart beating time to the universe drum
Out where the stars paint the sky...and hum...
We are timeless...

And then...utterly fearless...with voices like those of angels making love...they sang rock'n'roll and played Mozart until the end of the world.

DANCING WITH SHADOWS

PROLOGUE

Silver hair danced on the wind, coiled itself up into sunlight, caught glistening drops of salt spray and dropped restlessly onto brown shoulders...slicked across bare breasts and down her back as the ocean surged up onto the beach and foamed around her ankles. Above her were towering cliffs and Big Sur, a hollow on the other side of the PCH where she had stashed the VW bug out of sight for a day or a night or however long she had intended to stay was irrelevant now. The decision once made was a done deal...reality finally bumping into what had seemed to be a good idea at the time...

She took one last plunge into the surf, turned onto her back and drifted...face upward...watched scruffy gulls sarabanding their way across the sky, a lone pelican back-dropped by a big fat cloud gliding right over her looking for lunch. She let the sun warm her belly and the waves lift her up and drop her down again...rocking her back into a semblance of calm... leaching some of the frustration out of her soul until she imagined the sunsets she was going to leave behind this time around and spun over in the water, began to stroke her way back to the shore...angry again...with herself...the world in general...

When the wind had dried her skin she twisted her hair into a pair of loose knots down her back and slipped into cut-offs...a threadbare t-shirt that read *Downchild Blues Band* across the front...slogged up to the base of the cliffs to the overhang of rock that sheltered her sleeping bag and back-pack, where she had slept the last three nights with a small driftwood fire for company, a few tins of food, some bread and cheese and a gallon of Almaden Mountain Burgundy...

She kicked and buried every sign of her brief residence down into the sand and when she had everything else ready to go for the climb up the cliff-face, she hoisted one last item and walked back towards the ocean...looked out over the Pacific...considered what passed as her options...punched holes into the vacuum seals and pitched everything into the water. She shook her head once and walked away...decided to move while she still had a choice...

CHAPTER ONE – RUNNIN' JUST T'BE ON THE RUN...?

1.

"...Honey you think maybe you could sweeten this coffee up a bit?"

She sighed, looked out the window of the diner where Interstate 80 somewhere east of Cheyenne and west of Pine Bluffs ran by beneath them...wondered when her car would be road-worthy again...went back behind the counter to pick up a steel-bottomed glass coffee pot cringing at the millionth play of *She Thinks I Still Care* on the Seeburg... and wandered back to the asshole trucker who couldn't seem to focus on anything but her tits. She topped him up and stood back from the table, ignoring the other two guys in the booth. They were letting the asshole run point for them.

"That about right for you then...*honey*?" she asked softly.

She cocked one hip, rested the pot there and looked soulfully down into his eyes... bloodshot from way too many whites. It was barely seven in the morning...less than two hours into her shift and she was already walking a thin line.

All unknowing the asshole said, "Not quite what I had in mind," with a big wide smile.

Incredulously she thought *Does this toothless dumbfuck really think that smile is gonna make my panties wet?*

She reached across the table slowly, so he got a good solid look down her blouse, and commandeered the sugar shaker. The trucker reached up her skirt and she clocked him with the shaker...full on between his nose and the three days' on his upper lip that went red on contact. He howled and she hit him again...this time beside his left ear bringing the heavy ribbed glass round with her right hand in one whistling arc half a mile long. Asshole got glassy-eyed and went to sleep. She looked at the other two and said:

"Take your brain-dead Neanderthal friend someplace where I won't kill him," and walked away.

They left most of their breakfasts on the table and didn't leave a tip.

"I can't have you beatin' the piss outta my customers."

Sam was so pathetically stereotypical she could almost forgive him.

"He stuck his hand up my skirt."

Sam looked at her like she was out of her mind for feeling put out.

"Gloria didn't knock my customers fuckin' unconscious."

"Yeah...but you ever wonder why Gloria's not here anymore...?"

He got red in his stereotypically unshaven fat face.

"Do you have kids?" she asked.

"I got kids," he said, confused. "I got Dennis is twelve and Patti is fifteen."

She smiled.

"So if Patti was workin' here with me...or your wife...it would be okay if that sonofabitch put his hand up their skirts, too?"

"Fuck no!"

She leaned forward across his desk so he could look down her front just like every other guy who came through the doors.

"So am I movin' on...or shall I plan on another lovely fuckin' shift here tomorrow morning?"

Winter in Wyoming turned out to be more desolate than pretty much anything she'd ever encountered back home in Ontario...or at least it seemed that way. A couple of days before the snow started falling she drove two hours into Colorado to find something that approximated a real bookstore...bought what she hoped was a winter's-worth of used paperbacks...read them all holed up in the motel room she rented by the month...

Hermann Hesse and Tom Wolfe. Neitzsche, Nabokov and Camus. Mario Puzo and Schopenhauer. Izzy Stone. Dickens. Dostoyevski, Robert E. Howard and John Fowles and just about anyone she could buy for less than a buck a book. She ran out in the middle of January...had to wait for a good-weather window to go back to Denver...

There was no warm in her bed but she read words...thought thoughts...decided Philosophy was for people who had forgotten how live their lives properly. She didn't want to be one of them even though she knew she would stay where she was until she got desperate enough to move again, but she was grateful for the block heater her father had installed in the Volkswagen's engine, that gave her the small luxury of knowing she could move if she had to. For the time being it was enough.

Sam behaved himself, but there was no end to the bastards who thought she worked at the Halfway to Heaven Diner so they could fantasise about fucking her. One morning in the spring, as she was walking down the side road to the diner with the sun still not certain about making an appearance that day, she saw a white '64 ragtop T-bird in the parking lot that seemed too familiar for comfort...just enough light from the neons to let her see the California plates, the dark red leather interior. She turned and went back to the motel, packed her books and gear into the VW and cursed all the way to an eastbound

I-80 on-ramp. At the next exit she doubled back toward Cheyenne, took the interstate south to Denver again. She hated leaving a week's-worth of wages with Sam the Greaseball Man, but figured it was time to put some more miles between her and the Left Coast...

Philosophically. How to accept the realisation you were being imperceptibly fucked by a life you thought you had under control...

In Denver by lunchtime, she went back to the used bookstore on Colfax. The older guy who'd worked so hard to look her in the eyes both times she'd come in for books asked if she was okay. Softly. Like he might really give a shit if she wasn't...like as old as he was there was a spark of something in his soul that understood what it was like to be adrift in the world. He asked if she was looking for a job and offered her twenty hours a week with a couple of bucks over minimum under the table. She asked *Why?* and he said:

"Because my two daughters aren't quite as old as you are...but all three of you are too pretty to get much more than trouble from guys who mostly just want one thing from you."

She took the job...kept it through the summer and on into fall...listened to Denver radio... read more books. She felt safe with him...slept with him twice before he began to feel guilty about his wife and the daughters he planned to get through college. He kissed her forehead and apologised...for wanting into her pants just like everybody else...and for deciding not to sleep with her again...

"As long as you need or want t'be here is okay...just leave me a note when you decide to go...and promise you'll be careful..."

A week later, with a bloody sun setting down behind the mountains and the first intimation of winter in the air...before he went home and after they'd locked the door to his little hole-in-the-wall beacon of light and learning on Colfax...she hugged him in the dark for a long time...said thank you and goodbye.

At first light she headed south again, following the interstate along the eastern edge of the Rockies. She turned the VW's heater on full against the chill wind that whistled in past the doors, threatened to toss her off the gravel shoulders. She kept a steady fifty-to-sixty mph, trying not to do an encore on the piston rod that had stranded her racing headlong past Cheyenne.

Somewhere past Larkspur she saw something small standing at attention beside the highway, thought it moved directly in front of her as she drove by and braced for a bump or a crunch beneath her wheels. In half-light she searched the microcosm of her rearview mirror for the flattened corpse of the roadrunner and then let out a long sigh of relief to see it once more at parade rest on the other side of the roadbed.

"Meep meep y'little bastard," she shivered. "You scared the crap out of me. Who cut you loose from your cartoon, anyway?"

She watched him dwindle away in her wake, grow smaller and smaller she realised she was crying and laughing at the same time to see it do the exact same animated flippity-floppity hop off into the high desert. Ten miles later she passed the exit for the Air Force Academy and then she was running through Colorado Springs, with Pike's Peak away to the west, already snow-crowned and rising up in the cold new morning sunlight.

She wasn't paying a lot of attention...listening to Denver radio fade away and her stomach rumbling...thinking about how good one of her made-it-myself omelettes at the Halfway to Heaven would have tasted in spite of the company. She was past him before it even registered he was there...long brown hair spilling over hunched shoulders in buckskin and fringes and denim...moustaches curling round down past his chin...one thumb in the wind and a big army duffel to keep his toes warm. She pulled cautiously over onto the gravel, rearview-watched him hoist the duffel bag onto one shoulder and start to jog towards her...slowly at first...then faster as if he could sense her impatience. He pitched his bag into the back seat. She winced as he fell into the passenger seat and slammed the door hard.

"Hi thanks it's starting t'get cold out there where ya goin'?"

It occurred to her she had no destination...said:

"Away from here...south...wherever..."

UNTIL THE END OF THE WORLD

"I'm goin' west once we get a-ways past Pueblo...a place called *Huerfano*..."

"What's that?"

"A little valley sittin' down under the Sangre de Cristos. I got a friend there... *huerfano* is Spanish for orphan."

They both stopped talking and took turns staring at each other in the heat coming off the dashboard. Some mutual admiration stoked it higher. She had no illusions about her own appearance, or the present state of her affairs. *Huerfano* sounded about right... and he was almost as pretty as she was so she said:

"Just tell me where to turn."

2.

He said his name was Tango and she laughed, asked him if that was his first name or his last name, ragged him enough to make him admit it was really Bernard Rosenbaum but there was no way he was ever going to answer to it. She reassured him:

"Your secret is safe with me, Bernie."

"Now you owe me one of yours," he said... smiling...half in fun whole in earnest.

"Sorry pal I don't have any secrets," she lied. "Besides, we didn't make any disclosure deals so as far as you're concerned I'm gonna mostly stay Mystery Girl on principle."

"Well then what's your name?"

"Francine," she lied again, and remembered the title of book she'd read back in Wyoming. "My friends call me

Cat Dancing, on account of my slinky disposition. Cat for short..."

She could tell he seemed to like that, dreaming a little bit about how maybe *slinky* Cat Dancing might feel like doing a Tango after dark. A few minutes more and she took them off the interstate in Pueblo, went looking for a place near the highway to stop her stomach from growling. He thanked her a second time and rolled a big fat joint from a small pouch inside his jacket. They got high and kept stealing glances at one another. She stopped looking long enough to pull into the parking lot of what could just as easily have been a twin to the Halfway to Heaven. Inside there was more warmth...and the comfortable fuzzy cocoon of stoned with the sound of his voice smooth and easy. They sat across from each other in a booth by the window; he played some word-games with their waitress, finally ordered them both big breakfasts as the munchies sat down beside them...

Through a mouthful of scrambled eggs and sausage he said, "You're a long way from home, Miss Cat."

A small spark of dope-induced terror ran through her as she suddenly realised she was running expired Ontario plates on the car...wondered if it was going to be a problem... how she was going to fix it if-and-when. As the thought slipped away she sipped black coffee from a big ceramic mug.

"Home is wherever I happen t'be, Mister Tango," she said casually, shrugged her hair over one shoulder. His eyes were big and bright with marijuana...attentive...so very appreciative. His smile was radiant with lust and empathy.

"I can dig that. I been workin' on the road myself... started back in Ohio... two weeks after that motherfucker Rhodes sicced the National Guard on us."

"You were at Kent State?"

He stopped eating and his smile became death-like...the reflection of some kind of bad joke played on a corpse.

"Yeah. My second year," he said bitterly. "I went fuck it I don't wanna be a part of this goddamn system anymore so I just took off."

"I bet your parents were thrilled."

"I'm not even sure they noticed I was gone." He laughed with no hint of humour. "After the shitstorm I let 'em know I was okay but I was probably gonna get some work in Kent and stay there for the summer. That was the last time I talked to 'em. What about you?"

She sipped more coffee, weighed the wisdom of telling some Truth against the work of making up more fairy tales and decided she'd have less pretense to keep up if she went with some fact instead of fiction.

"After I managed to graduate from high school I wanted t'go to this fine arts college in Toronto but it was more than me or my folks could afford. My dad bought me the bug secondhand as an apology and I went to Woodstock, spent some time in upstate New York...and then I just didn't feel like going back..."

He nodded, understanding nothing and everything.

"So here we are."

She nodded back. "So here we are...the two of us...does that make us *huerfanos*?"

"I guess," he said. "Riders on the storm..."

"On our way to this Valley of Orphans. What's there?"

Tango shrugged, the rustle of leather fringes, a glisten of sausage grease in his moustache gone with an inviting flick of his tongue.

"Can't say for sure 'cause I've never been. A friend from school came down this way, said there was some sorta commune started up there and it looked like t'be a good place to be gone from the world. I don't think it's more than a couple of hours from here."

She said, "So far I think I'm still good with that."

They finished breakfast and he offered to put some gas in the Volkswagen before they took off. As she climbed back into the bug she realised she was dozy with smoke and really tired even though it wasn't even noon. Relieved to know she was at least going somewhere now, she just wanted to strip down someplace warm and curl up in a ball...go to sleep...or maybe take Bernie Rosenbaum for a ride if his boyish charm held up long enough to get them to where he was going. Back on the interstate she shifted them up to fifty-five and put her right hand down on his thigh just to let him know she might be interested.

"How'd you get t'be Tango...?"

He took his time answering. When he did she could hear it was costing him in the way of something he'd never intended to tell. She moved her hand an inch or two for some encouragement but he didn't seem to notice.

"I'm from this little town in Indiana with like five other Jewish families. My mother got me Arthur Murray dancing lessons when I was ten or eleven ...so maybe I could fit in at all the parties I never got invited to by all the KKK assholes we had for neighbours..."

His hand covered her hand, raised it up to where his moustache tickled a prelude to a soft kiss on her palm and suddenly she felt a surge of contempt...for letting them fuck with his head... and for being so damned obvious trying to fuck with hers.

He asked her, "How come you didn't go back?"

She figured she was already in for the ante she might as well play the hand...

"I was tired of living with stupid rules...and my mother, who didn't fucking care if the rules were good or not so long as they were *her* rules. She liked t'play me off against my younger sister...

"For some reason my dad never said anything... worshipped the ground she walked on, even though she was a manipulative bitch...and I understand it was because of the way she grew up...the only thing she'd ever known...but she could've decided t'be different with her own daughters. Instead she just passed that shit on..."

They drove south in silence, both getting lost in past lives that in no way resembled what they presumed lay in front of them. Tango rolled another joint and she played with the radio dial, getting static and DJ chatter from Santa Fe and Albuquerque...Amarillo... country and western on a signal that somehow had managed to bounce itself through the mountains from Grand Junction. After an hour or so

Tango shook himself out of his stoned, said they were getting close.

"...We're lookin' for a cut-off...Red Rocks Road heading west. My friend said it was State Road 610 runs down into 69..."

She eased off the gas, cursed as three sixteen-wheelers laid on their air-horns and passed them like they were standing still, slipstreams tossing the VW all over the highway. They saw the sign too late for her to do anything but curse some more. Tango said:

"It's okay we can pick up 69 further on..."

In Walsenburg they did, turned northwest on two-lane blacktop that looked like to run them smack into the side of mountains climbing up into the sky in front of them, at the last minute always dipping right or left, up or down, threading its way through the foothills like bread crumbs on the road to Shangri-La until there was no mistaking the weight of all the earth, rock and Time that surrounded them. After another half hour she said:

"This looks like it."

Tango nodded.

"We can stop somewhere soon, ask our way..."

Huerfanos. Orphans. She heard a small voice in her head telling her maybe she should let him do his own dancing in this place...

3.

They stopped at the merest shadow of a general store in a place called Farisita, where a pretty little thing behind the counter checked her out bigtime before even noticing Tango stomping along one step behind her. She smiled warmly, in such a way that Hippie-Chick knew there was at least one girl in the room who wouldn't be caught dead in love-beads and a gauzy fuckin' tie-dye skirt. Something nearby hissed. It could have been the coffee pot sitting on the woodstove; more likely it was both of them deciding not to be friends. Sensing trouble, Tango hustled himself front and centre, turned on his smile, introduced himself and exchanged pleasantries. Hippie-Chick said her name was Sandi with an "i". Watching them she sensed herself becoming a non-entity in the proceedings, did a mental back-step as Tango turned the charm up a notch like he couldn't help himself.

"So listen...I'm lookin' for a friend o' mine told me this was cool place to hang out. Maybe you know him...his name's Steve...Steve Bergson...?

Sandi felt the sudden vacuum around the new guy and did her best with what she had... made a big show out of wracking her brains for a memory of Steve before batting some baby-blues and saying:

"Ohhhh....yeah...that guy...from Ohio..."

"D'you know where I can find him?"

Sandi shook her head. "He split around Christmas last year, Tango. He was stayin' up near Libre in one of Danny Moyer's outbuildings but..."

"But what?"

"Danny caught him fucking Melissa an' he was gone the next day. Danny beat him up pretty good."

"Melissa is—?"

"Danny's wife."

"And how'd she do?"

Sandi shrugged. "She's okay I guess. I just hope the kid looks a little bit like Danny 'cause I think she'd been ballin' your friend for a while..."

Tango wagged his head like he was stunned his buddy had been caught in somebody else's henhouse; Sandi did her level best to show Tango how much she understood whatever deep emotion he was feeling. Together, like the ritual stepping away of Japanese corporate samurai, they managed to distance themselves from disgraced Asshole Steve. Hippie-Chick opened her blue eyes real wide and threw some major invitation at Buckskin Boy.

"D'ya think he's still got some space, Sandi?" asked Tango. "I'm thinkin" maybe this would be a good place to spend the winter."

She just stood by and watched the drama unfold.

He got directions to Danny Moyer's place out past Libre, along with a whisper that he really shouldn't even mention Steve Bergson at all if he had something he could offer in return for accommodations. Tango nodded, thanked her and they flashed peace signs at each other. Sandi didn't even bother to look her way when she said:

"Tom's gone t'Taos yesterday for winter shelf-stock, if Danny's got no room. He should be gone for at least another couple of days. We got an extra room upstairs, but it's really only big enough for one person..."

The irrelevancies of both statements were totally lost on Tango, now engaged in a parody of thought with some of the more primitive aspects of his sensory input. She allowed herself an instant of regret...a lightning review of the afternoon...implications... intimations of what might have been if the world wasn't such a shit-hole. Prescient, she saw Bernie Rosenbaum ten years in the future, neatly dressed in a three-piece suit selling mutual funds in a place where he didn't have to deal with being a Jewish kid with baggage and could hit on the upscale wives of his clients.

They got back in the bug and met Danny Moyer half an hour later. She watched Tango doing his thing...Danny suddenly getting interested...Melissa waddling herself out into the yard looking scared with less than a month to go before Judgment Day. Tango pulled something small and squarish out of his duffel bag. A quarter mile down the road there was a was small ten-by-ten foot whatever built round the trunk of a Ponderosa pine with a dirt floor and a bed-frame beside the fire-pit in one corner in imminent danger of becoming kindling.

"Here we are again," said Tango, smiling like it was Hawaii and virgin strands of volcanic black sand beckoned from the other side of the plank door. She knew a lot about small spaces...hated them...made up her mind in that moment and spared him a withering glance.

"I like you, Bernie. I think you're an okay guy even if you can"t quite keep your eyes from wanderin' over anything that smells like pussy. But there's no fuckin' way I'm playin' pioneer woman here with you, so thanks for buyin' us a crash-pad for the night and I'm gonna take off in the morning. You go on and see if you can get lucky with what's-her-face from the store."

"Fran—-"

"You stupid shit! Francine's not my real name! Go fuck the moon-bunny for god's sakes I'll even drive you back there. Just leave me some o' your smoke so I can get some sleep..."

He looked stunned again, different from finding out about Steve. And even no small amount of disappointed. Sandi might have been willing and ready to jump out of her sweet little tie-dye in a heartbeat, but they both knew without it she looked like an abandoned Girl Guide with no cookies.

"Are you sure?"

She shook her head...happy for him...that he didn't give a fuck where he put his cock so long as it was female.

"Yeah Bernie I'm sure. Put your bag back in the bug and I'll get you on down t'Sandi's before sundown where we can see how long it takes for you t'get into her knickers. Just make sure you get your ignorant ass out of there before Tom gets back from Taos with the rest o' the fuckin' wagon train..."

She had her sleeping bag and a ground-sheet. The bed-frame did indeed become kindling. She got high... opened a can of chili, ate it cold with some of the red wine from the ass-end of another big old bottle of Almaden burgundy...read Kafka by the light of a candle she found in a cupboard on the wall. She missed dumbfuck Bernard Rosenbaum for about a minute and a half before he became a minor footnote in her past...still knew best what made her feel good...

4.

...Had stumbled into the learning of it...Saturday evening...weaving her way down the hillside to within a couple dozen yards of the stage when Canned Heat was mid-way through their set...just breakin' into a half-hour boogie when the monster took hold of her and she started dancing...stoned on the clouds of smoke inhaled along the way...daylight leaping away on winged rock and roll feet...

At some point she opened her eyes and there he was...denims crusted to the knees in mud and whatnot-else...a leather belt cinched and knotted with endless tangles of leather laces...a tie-dye t-shirt shucked and tucked into the waistband...sun-browned abs...lovely wide shoulders with just enough muscle showing through, and a Greek god face under long black curls down past his shoulders he whispered *Bonjour belle fille* without any intention of her hearing the words...kept his eyes where he knew hers could read them off his lips she said:

"*Canadien...?*"

And he nodded...smiled like the sun...

<hr />

It was her first time. Not in terms of actual events. *That* first had been stolen from her, over and over again. But as Woodstock Day Two wandered on into the night and became Sunday morning of Day Three they found a spot where they were in no danger of being trod or sat upon and when Paris-Paul Lariviere eased himself inside her, stroked her hair down the length of her back and sit-upped his lips to her nipples and breasts, whispered *en francais* things she'd never bothered to learn in her French classes...

The night dissolved...became something endless... soundtracked by the Dead, Creedence, Janis, Sly and the Who...and morning maniac music with the Airplane...

drowsy and hungry for more until he somehow...with his mouth and his cock and his fingers so gently he managed to make sparks start jumping up and down her spine and behind her eyes and she could feel herself starting to melt...getting lost in wave after wave after wave of gut-wrenching glorious fucking and it was only his eyes in rapt attention to her sudden terror that kept her from losing it all...

Sunday at sunset she said "...Yeah...in the morning... Nine ten o'clock? I'll meet you at the gates to the raceway in Monticello..."

On Monday morning with Jimi star-spangling the sunrise she hiked out to the pale blue Volkswagen, took NY 55 back to the Quickway and fled east into the Catskills...a few months of respite, until someone else found the open places in the wall she had never intended to build around herself. Then she was gone again, a single breath taking her down to I-84...into Pennsylvania, high-tailing it through Scranton and Wilkes-Barre until I-80 left her nowhere to go but west...

5.

She slept in until she realised she could see her breath; that where she was it wasn't going to begin to get much warmer indoors or outdoors for another six months. She dressed inside her sleeping bag with extra socks and a sweater on over her t-shirt before she dashed out to the VW and dragged her winter coat out of the trunk...stopped long enough to put her nose in the air and smell the weather...an early winter on its way.

The extra split second it took for the bug's engine to turn over thumped her heart rate up to thirty seconds of terror that she might get stranded there. On her way past the store in Farisita she downshifted to a slow crawl, knowing Tango was near an upstairs window... watching and waiting to see if she really was going to split. She flipped him a bored *fuck you!* and a peace sign. Then she was gone, on her way back to the interstate... took the southbound exit, turned right heading for New Mexico.

6.

She had an aversion to the cold. Liked the idea of as little clothing as possible. Where she had been born in Maritime Canada—the eldest of two daughters by two years—her earliest memories were of snow and bone-chilling winter light sneaking through cracks in the walls of a single-room shack perched high above the banks of the St John River in Woodstock, New Brunswick. The uppermost drawer in a tallboy had been her crib and cradle for the first eighteen months of her life. She had been a preemie...so small that she had come home from hospital on an Indian motorcycle, tucked into the front of her father's leather jacket with mom riding behind him.

When she was two she loved being outdoors in the summer sun, playing with butterflies and making pictures in the dirt down beside the river. It was the winters she grew to hate, when their shack was so cold she spent months never allowed out of her parents' bed because her feet might freeze to the wooden floorboards. When she was old enough to go to the one-room schoolhouse two miles down the road it wasn't much better because it too was less than a model of modern construction, and it was there she found out she was badly dyslexic, even though dyslexia hadn't been invented yet. She was, in the words of her teacher, a "less than promising student". She couldn't make words with letters, had to *see* the word all by itself...when it was finished...when it was already whatever it was supposed to be...before she could understand how she could use it within the context of her education.

By the time the family moved to Ontario both she and her younger sister were old enough for middle school, where it became evident her sibling was destined for a more successful career in the hallowed hell of high school. That was when mom chose sides, and dad chose in self-defense...

She was his firstborn and he loved her with the same measure of devotion he had felt duty-bound to serve the pretensions of his upwardly-mobile bride. That all he had was a third grade education—it took him more than a day to get through the four-page local daily—pre-disposed him in favour of his underdog daughter, the one who had to struggle to get by in her world same as he'd done from the age of eight in his own. He worked two and three jobs at a time, but never failed to spend a few minutes with her when he got home, usually well-past her bedtime, before much-needed sleep drove him into her mother's service for the night.

Mom preferred the other one, who expected the world on a string and was bright and quick and never much for being fussed over, the one who even as a grade-schooler always had plans for the next day being *better* than the one before. Theirs was the unholy alliance of ambition, the daughter as living proof Mom was right—that diligence and a total disdain for the less-than-brilliant herd around them could and would pay off in the end. If the spilling of blood had been involved, they would have invented *collateral damage* well before the imperialists of the world decided that the lives of innocent Third World bystanders didn't count.

So Siana...her given name from a moment when Daddy forgot his place and put his foot down...the heroine from the very first book he had ever managed to read end to end... became the rebel...and the very first member of her family ever to use a bad word over the breakfast table, following an incident when her younger sister complained about being knocked on her ass in the middle of the night.

Siana had said, "I was sleeping and she came home from her big date with fuckhead Richard and turned on all the lights and the record player like I wasn't even there."

She emphasised the extent of her outrage by walking into the bedroom they shared and laying waste to half of her Beatles records on the living room floor, along with the warning:

"You go near my stuff and I'll knock you on your fat ass again."

That was her one-up on the distaff side of the family. Siana's ass was not fat. It, like the rest of her, had turned out more than just pleasantly attractive, as if to make up for not being able to read very fast or see very well, or fit in anywhere as effortlessly as her younger sister. Soon enough she'd begin to realise that one-up at home didn't necessarily translate well elsewhere. It made for a mane of dark hair that went white and silver before she was eighteen.

7.

Albuquerque late that afternoon lay sprawled out in old sunlight under a haze of shit that soon would mutate into something unacceptably toxic in despite of the cautionary existence of Los Angeles eight hundred miles to the west. She parked the bug on a shoulder overlooking the valley and consulted her road atlas compliments of Rand McNally...chewing on beef jerky from a roadside stand just off I-25 near Santa Fe... looking left and right east and west where Route 66 lay early on in the Age of Aquarius, before being reborn as US Interstate 40. Road signs for places named Cimarron and Pecos and Domingo Pueblo made her stupid with romantical daydreams of the Wild Wild West, but she knew the air would get warmer if she could only drop another few hundred feet closer to sea level...that she'd be okay then for the winter. She went looking for an exit and a side road before she hit metro Albuquerque, smoked some of the camel-shit-passing-for-hashish Tango hadn't missed in his haste to get into the hippie-chick's panties...finished her Almaden wine and watched a billion stars light the night overhead. A long way from home she made love to herself...stared up into the dark...shed not a tear because that sort of thing wasn't allowed...

8.

Before Siana Lynn and her sister let Mom turn them into arch-enemies under the same roof it was a given that there were some things you never fuckin' ever talked about in the Darrow house. Finances was one of them. Daddy had given that over to Mom a long time ago. He just put his head down and did whatever it took. Mom did the math, doled him out a few dollars each week and otherwise made it her business to keep them afloat, but always with enough on the side to make sure little sister never lacked for a trendy new blouse or a shiny new #2 pencil. Siana's dreams always seemed to be a little bit beyond the family's means. A baby sister's surprise arrival on the eve of some modest prosperity only served to make their mother more determined than ever to see her chosen one become "successful". The rest of them mostly went begging.

Another taboo was emotion...personal stuff...raised voices or tears...any kind of wilderness cry for warmth or consideration or shelter from a world viewed by Mom as a permanently hostile place where no one could be trusted and everything female was out to steal her man. Siana watched her father struggle for self-esteem... working his ass off to provide, to make sure all of his girls had food and clothing and a roof over their heads...making no distinctions once he realised he wasn't allowed to have a favourite daughter. He stopped tucking her in at night...spent what free time he could find in some inarticulate emotional swamp beyond her reach where he wouldn't... couldn't...risk allowing her to save him from being swallowed up in the muck. Someone might notice. Siana prayed for the stony silences that bore fruit as cold suppers and petty, vengeful "oversights". Her father let himself get buried beneath them.

9.

The next day she went west, stopping in Gallup to do laundry where she stood a proud five-foot-five amongst a milling herd of Navajo, Apache and Hopi braves who from the lofty heights of six-foot-twenty in sunlight seemed to shimmer with silver and turquoise and ink-black hair down to their asses. They all looked...some incuriously...most others with a studied indifference...a few hungrily, for whatever they imagined she was offering. She gave them back stare for stare and read her book, walked across the street from the laundromat and bought herself a bottle of Jose Cuervo, plunked it down on the orange plastic chair beside her and invited them all to keep up with her if they dared. She wouldn't admit she was scared, but laundry day in Wyoming had been overdue and what little she owned in the way of clothing was starting to smell like she'd slept in all of it for a month. So she stayed where she was...staggered back to the bug around sundown...

She heard footsteps and realised she'd been asleep standing up against the side of her car. She turned in sickening sodium vapour light and the stench of diesel...deafened by the roar of pickup trucks with no mufflers...tried to focus on the concerned face of a thirteen-fourteen-year old girl with a paper sack full of stuff from the 7-11.

"You can't stay out here," she said. Thin with quick dark eyes that held no questions, that darted right and left always watching. A scrawny refugee from the reserve in a threadbare plaid shirt, jeans and sneakers, with long black hair like everyone else.

Siana staggered upright, struggling to be all there for as long as it took for her to try to make words in response to the Indian girl...failing miserably.

"You can't stay out here," she said again. "Not after dark. Are you okay t'drive?"

Siana shook her head. Fell backwards against the bug.

"Gimme your keys then okay I got a place where you can stay."

She watched stupidly as the brown face with the broad cheekbones filled with shadows. The girl shoved her laundry into the back seat along with the 7-11 bag, then dragged her around to the passenger side and kept her head down while she collapsed into the shotgun seat...closed her eyes and heard the bug's engine go boom. She put her head back and gave herself up to all the gods she didn't believe in...

"Ontario. Canada, right?"

Siana made yes noises.

"That's really far away. How come you're here?"

Siana made noises to the effect that this was where she was.

"Well you're okay now. You're really pretty I like your hair."

"Somebody put some Cherokee in my blood and then I had t'pay for it."

She was so tired...said:

"You're not gonna fuck with me?"

"No. Just promise don't be sick 'cause if you throw up then I will."

She nodded cautiously. "Who are you? I'm nobody t'you. Nobody having her ass saved by whoever you are."

She could hear the gears going from reverse to drive and felt the car moving underneath them, fought to keep her promise about throwing up.

"Everyone calls me Mosi. It means *cat*. If I told what my real name was you couldn't say it."

Siana nodded a little bit more and regretted it instantly.

"'Kay," she said quietly. "Thank you, Mosi. Go slow please, and if you know where the bumps are don't go near them."

She heard a giggle.

"I won't. You'll be okay."

⁂

"...Wake up don't go t'sleep! If you do you'll be *really* sorry in the morning..."

They weren't moving anymore. Mosi was trying to help her out of the Volkswagen but having no luck. It occurred to her she was about as thoroughly shit-faced as she'd ever been in her life, but at least she was no longer hovering on the brink of a cookie-toss.

"Gimm e a second," she slurred. "I can do this I just have t'pay attention."

She managed to get herself upright on what felt like some broken pavement, with only a hint of light from somewhere nearby crawling under her eyelids. Mosi provided encouragement, a surprisingly strong shoulder, and navigational skills that included a warning when three short steps down brought them up against a dark rectangle set into the rear foundation wall of a small building. Somewhere inside was quiet whispering.

"I'm gonna get you settled and then I'll come back for our stuff."

Mosi quietly tapped some sort of code onto what sounded like a hollow steel door and the whispering stopped. She heard footsteps and the door opened...a sliver of light...a face at first anxious and then relieved with recognition.

"Open the door...*haneetehee*!"

It swung wide and Siana felt herself guided into a small room close with warmth from an ancient space heater...walls and the one window shrouded with blankets... flickering candlelight that made the shadows dance. The face from the doorway belonged to a young man of Mosi's age; two other girls not much older than six or seven and a small black puppy were the only other inhabitants, as they all converged on her to make sure she got comfortable in a tatty stuffed armchair in the far corner. Mosi issued orders quietly, seemed to be bringing them all up to speed before turning to her.

"This is William," she said, indicating the young man. "Then there's Maggie and Flower and the puppy is Smudge. I'll be right back. I told them you're feeling sick so no noise or jumping on top of you."

William had a sharp pointy face, ragged black hair and frightening blank eyes that seemed to burn through something darker in his soul. He followed up on Mosi's directives, sent one of the little girls off into another room to bring her a big glass of cold water and two white pills.

"It's aspirin," he said. "Drink all the water. Mosi says maybe you won't get a hangover."

Smudge the puppy camped on her feet.

10.

Mosi returned with her laundry and the garbage food from the corner store, kept up a slow conversation to keep her awake while the others camped on the floor, drank Dr Pepper and tried to eat ripple chips quietly. Maggie and Flower looked like big-eyed scarecrow twins lifted from a painting on black velvet; William looked like a young wolf who couldn't decide if he was protecting them or fattening them up for his supper.

"...the Indian Affairs people took all of us off the reserves," explained Mosi a bit later on. "They said we weren't getting' looked after properly so the government was gonna do it instead. Turned out it was just a different place not to be looked after properly so we ran away...a month ago. Right now we're just lookin' for a way t'get up past Shiprock where my uncle lives..."

Groggy questions, more water and a couple of hours focusing on her steady voice started Siana's brain working again, cleared away some of the tequila haze. The twins' mother had tried to sell them to a female undercover cop in Farmington so she could buy heroin for her new boyfriend. William's father was angry at the world in general and had beat him regularly just on principle. Mosi's parents just disappeared one day back in February and she'd not seen them since. The BIA case-workers moved in, sent them off to Gallup, and then moved on.

"...We don't have no money but what we can beg on the street," she said at last. "That's why we don't have any real food to eat. My uncle's a good hunter he'll take care of us if we'll pitch in on chores and stuff, but you can't trust hardly anybody here so I been careful..."

"Except with me."

Mosi shook her head. "No I saw you get that bottle and I could tell you were freaked out so I kept checkin' on you."

"But I could be anybody meaning you no good."

Mosi shook her head again. Just shook her head, said nothing. Waited for Siana to tell her what she wanted to hear.

"Shiprock's not that far from here, is it?"

"Only a hundred miles. I didn't wanna get us stuck between here and there and I didn't wanna ask the wrong person for a ride."

Siana nodded. It wasn't as risky a proposition as it had been earlier in the evening. Smudge was trying to chew one boot off her foot and the twins were looking like bedtime. William hadn't said a word, but the feral light in his eyes hadn't dimmed at all. She said:

"I'll take you back. Tomorrow. If I'm not dead."

She grinned ruefully and Mosi's answering grin was the first bit of positive light to shine on her day.

"Yesterday I told somebody to call me Cat Dancing," she told her. "He turned out t'be an asshole but after I decided I wasn't gonna sleep with him I sorta felt like one."

"A cat dancing?"

"Sideways."

"Then we must be related," said Mosi.

Siana said, "I imagine so."

11.

William was out on the street early, came back with McDonalds food for everybody. Siana was grateful her stomach was still too wonky to do anything but issue warnings when the stuff came too close for comfort, but everybody else tucked in and then it was time to start loading up the VW for the run north. She had a few leftover French fries and called it breakfast.

She'd heard of Shiprock...seventeen hundred feet of volcanic razours rising straight up off the desert floor. Mosi said it was the great bird that had brought her people south from the frozen lands. Siana sensed a sea-change in her wanderings, an intimation of radical transformation that gave her pause for some thought and the possibility there might be consequences, but only so long as it took to decide that she had been going nowhere and Mosi, perhaps, had saved her sorry ass for a reason; that there were consequences for everything, and she needed some good karma to make up for some of the shit she'd dumped on the world. They were heading north by noon, up through more and more desert the farther they ran from Gallup.

The twins were sweet and quiet, solemnly did their best to help pack up the Bug, never making a sound. Siana bled for them, knew that any time they'd ever made any noise at all had only brought them terror. They sat in the back beside William, who was so single-minded in his survival mode that he scared the shit out of her even though he was only twelve years old. Mosi was the balance. Somehow she had become self-reliant enough to spread Serenity over all of them...dissolve their fear or anger in the totally unwarranted belief that Life was going to be good to all of them some time soon.

The trappings and bullshit of civilisation disappeared quickly as they moved up NM 491. Soon there was nothing on either side of them but open desert that disappeared into haze and highlands to the east and west, blazing sunshine with very little warmth, the season too far gone into the demesne of winter-approaching. Every now and again Siana would take her eyes off the road and Mosi's eyes would always be there fastened on her with something in them Siana remembered from being small, when her father would stand over a tallboy drawer in the dead of winter and look at her.

"Are you sure your uncle's gonna be good with this?"

She nodded, said, "And we'll be back with our own people," as if it explained everything.

It made Siana wonder who *her* people were...if maybe she'd left the only one of them that mattered behind back east...in fit of pique...just not getting her way quick enough there'd never been a night as warm since then...

"Thank you Cat Mom," said Mosi who was *Cat* looking after her own litter.

Unkindly Siana said, "Just shut up and tell me where we're goin' when we need to."

12.

Shiprock took her breath away. She had to stop and catch some of it back never having seen it's like before except in photographs. The reality made her shiver with the sense of her own infinite smallness in the great grand universe. It was there, in a sweep of crimsoning desert swirling upwards into the sky, a dirt track leading away from the highway, off into something that in no way belonged to a world where humans walked and fucked each other's lives up for fun and profit. One of those places that you could believe only *seemed* to reside on Earth, an illusion of something that stood somewhere else...a universe unto itself...because the immensity of its indifference to the affairs of Man was far greater than immeasurable. Mosi whispered:

"My people call it *Tse Bit'a'i*...Rock with Wings...that brought us here from the northern waste..."

"And then you met white people."

"Siana...?"

"I'm okay, Cat."

"Thank you for bringing us back home."

"Somebody else would've come along."

"Not you."

"Somebody not me."

"It wouldn't be the same."

"You'd be here though..."

"No. You'll see I'm right."

"You're a child, Mosi."

"We're here t'save each other."

Mosi kissed her face. William's eyes grew cold. Maggie and Flower said Smudge had shit on the back seat.

13.

She delivered them. Thirty miles further west to a place somewhere east of Red Mesa that had no place on any map, in the middle of sacred ground where the wind whispered to gods no longer listening. Mosi's uncle spent the better part of five minutes simply staring at her...eyes never leaving her eyes as he herded the children into something built into the side of a bump in the desert landscape. His face was brown and creased with far too much knowledge...the legacy of a hundred year's-worth of Great White Father ass-fucks. She might have been bringing his niece and her friends back where they belonged but she knew she would never be entirely comfortable there...never entirely at home...that this was where she was to pay a small installment on an ancient debt she had never incurred. He echoed Mosi:

"Thank you for bringing her back."

Siana dipped her head.

"She kept me out of a bad scene I was stupid enough to make for myself."

He held out his hand, going through the motions. If she had not been there she sensed Mosi would have been buried in his arms...that he reverenced her...thought he'd lost her forever...

She took his hand, looked him square in the eyes, and then offered a name she barely remembered from when she was very small and her grandfather had taken her to a place with people who had looked at her...granted her a small token of sustenance for the trace of Cherokee in her blood...spoken words she didn't understand, that somehow had conveyed an assurance that if she remembered the name there might yet be a place of refuge for her somewhere. Mosi's uncle said:

"My name is John."

Siana blinked, gave it a moment of consideration and smiled.

She said "Okay," and he started to laugh a little bit, slow and deep.

"Will you stay?"

She said, "If I'm welcome...if you'll have me..."

He looked to where Mosi, the twins and Smudge had discovered a small pen with goats and a handful of sheep.

"I love her. I thought I would never see her again and I had nothing to offer them in exchange for letting her come back. She doesn't know her mother is dead, or that her father got drunk and beat her to death for dancing with another man."

"Your sister?"

"Yes."

"So where's her father now?"

"With his gods."

"You know that?"

"Oh yes," he said softly.

He turned away. Siana followed him, put a hand on his shoulder, faced him round again but couldn't explain how his sense of loss diminished her.

"Now you have part of her back," she said. "I don't let anyone see me cry either."

He told her his real name, and she went back to the bug to get her pack...

UNTIL THE END OF THE WORLD

14.

...Settled into a simple daily routine with no real responsibilities, just doing whatever needed to be done on any given day—driving into Farmington each weekday to deliver the children to a new school that had nothing to do with the snake-pit the emissaries of the Great White Father had thrown them into...buying groceries or doing laundry...looking after the twins who seemed most happy simply playing in the dirt with the goats and Smudge and the sunny-dispositioned mutt who lived with John...spending hours with Mosi who throve in the absence of paranoia, who took her wandering to places half-remembered where the whispers of high-desert breezes were unnerving, but tempered with the caress of fine mists of sand that reassuringly spoke to them with an unspoken promise of the future.

John scavenged some paneling and two-by-fours and partitioned off a portion of his one-room cabin, a place where all the new ladies in his life could have a little bit of privacy. The twins hauled the studs one by one from the truck, dragging them through the dust, making cautious laughter as the dogs chased along beside, barking and snapping. William had decided to sleep on the floor in front of the stove, refused to have anything to do with them, refused to go back to the school, ended up spending his days in silence and solitude looking after the goats and sheep. John and Siana grew blisters and banged the walls together. Mosi watched Siana carefully....all the time...

One day in December with school out for the white man's Christmas they took a day trip together just the two of them...huddled together for warmth as they sat on the edge of an outcropping of rock overlooking Monument Valley, with the Mittens gone soft and hazy in a distant swirl of snow...

"You could stay forever," said the girl. "You could belong. We could get you books and you could stay. Uncle says you aren't like the rest...you're really one of us..."

Siana shook her head, wept tears in her heart.

"No I'm not, Cat-girl. That's the problem with being on the outside looking in. Even when you find people who are outside with you, you still don't belong. It's why you're outside in the first place..."

Mosi just hung on tighter.

"You don't have t'go on like that, Siana," she said. "All you gotta do is just stay here..."

"It's not that simple, honey. You don't get a choice..."

"You *always* get a choice!"

"When it comes to everyone else, Mosi. Not when it's for yourself."

"Oh that's bull Siana don't make stupid excuses if you don't wanna stay..."

"I do, honey, I wanna stay so much...but we both know I won't..."

"But why...?"

Siana watched the snow dance. Heard the faint whispering of the wind across the valley floor...saying nothing that meant anything to her. She put her arms around the girl, put her head down closing her eyes so she wouldn't have to look at herself mirrored anywhere in somebody else's life.

"I don't know why," she said. "I just don't fuckin' know…"

There was lots of daylight left. Back in the bug Mosi took them on a magical mystery tour along the fringes of the Valley…trying to remember a place she'd been… pointing out wrong turns…backtracking…trying again… They found the right track and wound slowly up and down on the edges of the valley…came to a box canyon with cliffs soaring up into the sky…shadows tucked into the stone towers…

"My mom brought me here a couple of times."

It was like being back at Big Sur. The same sense of things in the wings she didn't necessarily want to know or see or hear. They climbed anyway…Mosi like a monkey in blue jeans and sneakers and a second-hand down parka too heavy for early winter but it was all she had. Siana followed her…always ready…always making sure there was somewhere for her to anchor herself…catch the girl if she fell it seemed like they had climbed forever, but when Mosi stopped…panting on a ledge looking down on the Volkswagen…it was only a half a dozen yards over the cul-de-sac…

"My mom brought me here," she said again.

They took a few minutes to catch their breath and then Mosi took her hand and led her through a crevice in the rock-face.

CHAPTER TWO – DOWN INTO THE DARK
1.

Not long after the bad-word incident, things at home became less than acceptable. Just as one never raised one's voice in the Darrow house, raising one's hand was equally *verboten*. She'd never seen her father get drunk but eventually learned that once upon a time early on in her parents' relationship it had happened a few times... when the going had gotten a bit too rough for him to withstand without something to take the edge off, and he still hadn't learned who was really in charge in his own house. He'd gotten angry... frustrated...balled his fists and then was given to understand in no uncertain terms that even that small measure of un-restraint wouldn't be tolerated...

So younger sister's selfish discourtesies became totally lost in the greater magnitude of Siana's minor transgressions...the sunshine of motherly love shone upon her even less brightly than before...and there were some weeks when most nights brought another phone call from the principal of her school or a neighbour "sassed" in response to innocent remarks. One afternoon when she was fifteen she simply didn't go home... ended up downtown after dark...stepped off the street and found out she looked old enough that the bartender was more than happy to pour her drafts without any questions; that if she danced with one guy there were three more waiting for the next one; that it was liberating to let go...to face no disapproval...to not give a damn who was there and just be herself and have so many admirers in the bargain.

The down side came when she woke up in a place she'd never been before...in the dark...with no clothing...

2.

UNTIL THE END OF THE WORLD

A voice startled her when she finally came fully awake. Told her she was not going to be hurt as long as she behaved; that she could scream if she wanted to, but no one would hear her. She asked questions, received no answers…realised she'd been *collected*…sort of like in the movie she'd snuck into the year before. Someone had dumped something into her beer while she was dancing and now that sonofabitch someone had plans for her.

"…It's a matter of re-educating you, teaching you it's not okay to take advantage of men just because you know how to wiggle your ass and shake your tits in front of us…"

She recognised the voice. The dark-haired one…the first one she had danced with…good-looking but in a soft way she knew he was a "soft" person even if she herself had no clear idea of what she meant by it.

"I wasn't trying t'take advantage of anybody," she said cautiously. "I was just out dancing trying to have a good time. You don't have t'do this…whatever it is…you don't…"

He was quiet for a while, long enough she thought he might have just dissolved in the darkness around her, even the sound of his breathing lost in the background sounds of wherever he had taken her.

"Are you still there?"

"I am."

"Why didn't you answer?"

"I was thinking over what you said."

"Are you gonna let me go?"

"No."

She sensed him coming closer, a change in the temperature of the air around her body. There was only a moment between the sound of a sudden sweeping movement and the instant when his fist smashed into her face. Half-conscious she heard him say:

"You shouldn't make excuses like that. You're just going to make us angry..."

Us turned out to be three of them. Only the first face stayed bright and clear in her memory. It was more than enough.

3.

She wasn't cold. The other end of the chain wrapped twice around her right ankle was looped around a radiator that worked so she wasn't cold. There was a thin blanket neatly folded on the end of the cot wedged into one corner of the unseen eight-by-eight room that was their very own playtime-with-Siana place, but it disappeared once they realised it was her only defense between her body and them.

They would let her go two or three days without food...a small cup of water once or twice whenever...so for the first little while when they brought her the doped food and water she never gave a thought to why she got so tired in such a hurry until she woke up and sensitive body parts that had never received anyone's attention but her own felt bruised and painful when she touched them. It was frightening.

"Why're you doing this to me?"

"You know why."

"I didn't do anything wrong."

The second time he hit her it was hard enough to put her out instantly.

UNTIL THE END OF THE WORLD

4.

In the dark there was no Time. Just the dark. The sound of water hissing in the radiator. The hum of something rumbling somewhere close by. Air moving across her bare skin there was no way she could curl up so it wouldn't touch her in the places where *they* had touched her...and worse. She knew they were washing her after every time they raped her. It was part of their idea of education, but she could still taste them in her mouth no matter how much Listerine they swished around there before holding her head over the bucket they left for her shit and piss.

It was frightening. And then it became more than she was willing to tolerate.

5.

She found a loose portion of the flooring and most of the water went under the boards. She ate just enough so when she shit and pissed in the bucket it was just enough to make it unlikely they would discover how much of their food she hadn't eaten. The drawback was that for a while she was almost conscious when they fucked her; that in the half-light they brought with them she found out why her pussy and her asshole and her mouth hurt so much; that their idea of education involved toys that were obscene.

She stopped being frightened. Suddenly she realised that Siana the Fuck-Doll had a power greater than her own terror; that Siana the Fuck-Doll was something they wanted and needed.

She stopped being frightened....got angry. And then she decided it was time for them to pay.

6.

The first one must have been the owner of the place they had taken her; must have been able to do her whenever he felt like it. She waited for one of those times when he wanted her all to himself. Knowing they took the chain off her ankle when all three of them fucked her at the same time she prayed it was also standard operating procedure for just him, that maybe the key to the padlock would be in his pocket.

She heard him coming. Heard the door open. Heard it gently close. Heard him breathing. Faster harder as he got undressed he thought she was sleeping...drugged into coma...his fuck-doll waiting...

When he tried to put his penis in her mouth, her hand in two coils of carbon-steel chain-link lashed up into his testicles.

7.

She was stunned to find out that beyond the door of her own prison were three others on a short hallway at the bottom of a steep flight of stairs...each one opening onto a room just like her own...all sound-proofed so there was no way she could have known there were three other girls being "educated".

Her first instinct was simply to run...find clothing and run...

Instead she went back with the key that had freed her...looked into eyes that mostly were only just waiting for their own next lesson...

One of them said *I don't know where to go* and Siana spat:

UNTIL THE END OF THE WORLD

"Just go wherever the fuck you want to. I'm not your goddamn mother."

She found clothing for all of them. Rifled the pockets of the unconscious motherfucker now chained to his own radiator and divvied the proceeds in thirds once she realised that the house...a little bit isolated from any neighbours where it stood at the end of a cul-de-sac... was less than a mile from where she had once upon a time lived the normal life of a pissed-off teenager..

She watched them stagger off into a chill winter sunset. Found a calendar and near shit herself when she realised it had been almost five weeks. She found a mostly comfortable out-of- the-way spot on the ground floor and sat down to wait.

8.

The other two showed up early the next day. Siana was grateful they came separately, so she got to use the same shovel on both of them. Used some nylon boat cord to tie them to their friend wearing the chain. Silently thanked her daddy for showing her how to siphon gasoline from their truck into his motorcycle tank.

She wound their heads in duct tape...did something with her face that was meant to be a reassuring smile...told them: "You can scream if you want to, but nobody's gonna hear you."

In the place where she had learned all the lessons they felt she needed to learn she emptied their pockets of cash, bathed them in high-octane and backed her way up the stairs before she conjured up a fifteen-minute delay with one of their cigarettes and a book of matches and left them, secure in the knowledge all three of them would do a lot of screaming before they died.

Then she walked away...

CHAPTER THREE - CAT, CAT DANCING & MISTER D

1.

"Siana are you all right?"

They were just past the first bend in a downward-spiraling passage already gone black. She could hear Mosi scrabbling around in the dark and knew she was pressed hard up against an unseen rock wall with a scream in her throat and that her eyes were wide open and her teeth clenched together so desperately that she remembered what it was like to have let them open her mouth...to have pretended not to be aware of what they were doing....waiting for her chance...

"Siana...?"

She could have wept at the flare of the match...the smell of rags soaked in hi-test... the cloud of light that washed over one friendly face instead of three with eyes like slimy fingers...

"Siana..."

"I"m here, Mosi," she said. "It's history. I'm gonna live..."

"What happened?"

Cat became the first one Cat Dancing ever told.

"I paid them back," she said.

"I don't know how bad that is. I'm only thirteen."

"I was a couple of years older."

"Siana don't hurt..."

"I'm tryin' honey just don't let go right away...just don't let go..."

On her knees she felt the Navajo girl's arms around her. In the flickering dark it all came back—-five weeks she had never consciously tried to forget...five weeks she had left alone in a corner of her brain she had simply avoided...

"We'll go back," Mosi said. "It's not important."

Siana shook her head...violently...

"No...no...you brought me here for a reason."

"My mom used t'say it was a magic place."

Siana shivered...said: "I could use some magic..."

Mosi brought them both back up onto their feet, the torchlight painting the walls with their shadows as they took each other hand in hand and began a steep descent into the well of darkness below them. Mosi seemed fearless, perhaps having twice been to wherever they were going and come back out into the light it no longer frightened her; Siana suddenly found it otherwise in her own thoughts, and in the hammer-strokes of her heart that pounded against her ribcage.

At first she tried to hang back, lag behind to slow their progress, but Mosi's hand would not let her go and any attempt she made to protest met first with the Navajo girl's looks of reassurance and then with a burgeoning echo of even her smallest whisper until they were surrounded in thunder and even the sound of their footfalls was lost in it... buried beneath as much weight as the mountain of stone above them.

She remembered an old Penguin paperback she had read the previous winter...a pivotal chapter...about India and another woman finding herself lost in the same situation...deafened and feeling blind in the dark... overwhelmed by something unseen... perhaps even unreal...nevertheless terrifying in its impersonality...the coldness of something primitive and unyielding...careless of any human concern...

"We're getting closer, Siana."

Mosi's voice was steady...warm...unafraid...clearly heard, as if spoken directly into her ear. Siana's terror was instantly transformed...thoughts become answering strokes to the thudding in her chest...reaching out into the dark and soundlessly tiding against it...

Breaking through it...cracks in the walls of a prison below a house less than mile from the one in which she had been prisoned by resentment, bitterness and loss. She remembered how totally divorced she had become from all sense of Time...or of self. In self-defense she had willed herself to be numb for as long as it took the anger to come

back...to serve her instead of enslave her. Realised it had been her constant companion ever since.

"My mom said Changing Woman lived here...White Shell Woman...where the world could be reborn...where girls who got hurt could always come to be healed..."

Siana could feel the crazy...simmering... bubbling...the place where she had been hurt and stripped bare from bone rattling like Death in nowhere trying to find light...

"Mosi."

They turned a corner and torchlight burst into a million fragments of light as they stepped into something that could have been a million years in the making...an hollow space beneath the earth filled with the crystalline breath of water drops uncounted through limestone, and dreams waiting to be born in a wish and a prayer.

"Mosi."

She stepped into the middle of the cavern where each curving wall shimmered and shone…where each crystal upon crystal was a promise of Life as it should have been lived…where it could be lived…

"Don't be afraid, Siana."

"Mosi."

"My mom said we would always be safe here…"

There was a small pool of water at the end of their odyssey…a place where life-blood in clear liquid made magic—coruscations of light dancing in the dark. The Navajo child dipped her hands into the water, brought them an essence of Life to be shared on lips grown cracked and dry with an absence of Love. She hung on to Siana because they were Nowhere if not together.

"Please stay with us."

Siana was lost. The roar of the Marabar was too loud in her heart. The condemnation too sharp. She stroked Mosi's hair and hugged her until the poor thing couldn't breathe, and there under the earth something spoke and was heard though no ears could have listened. In the way of all Revelation there was suddenly Understanding… comprehension beyond all language.

"I can't, Mosi," she said. "I'm gonna miss you forever…someday…but not just now."

2.

They climbed back into the world. Bumped and bounced and rumbled back to John's sanctuary on the edge of the universe. Something radical had happened. Siana wondered how she could feel so much the exact same *me* as the thirteen-year old who loved her.

Mosi only smiled. Radiant. When Maggie and Flower yipped and yammered to see them coming home and Smudge crapped in the cabbage patch, Mosi leaned over the stick in the VW and planted a kiss on the topside of where Siana's right breast would be without the cloth between she said:

"Not just now..."

And the goats and the sheep and John came round to greet them.

"William's gone," he said. "He took some money and my shotgun. He's out there... somewhere..."

They stood on the edge of Monument Valley...waiting for the gods to get their shit together...

Maggie lifted her nose into the breeze and frowned.

"He's not here anymore."

Mosi said: "He's going back....after the ones who hurt him."

3.

They left her with the chickens and the dogs and the twins, piled into John's pickup and headed back to Gallup with some sketchy details about William's life before being dumped into the system. Mosi wasn't even sure of his last name, only that when she went looking for him after busting loose from the child services house she'd found him scrounging in the dumpster behind a bar on South

UNTIL THE END OF THE WORLD

Third Street and had snarled at her to fuck off. The second time she watched him from a distance, an hour without moving as he paid special attention to a small falling-down old clapboard house near the Catholic school. The third time he had found her, simply attached himself to their little band of refugees with no kind of explanations, adding only some frightening survival skills and the sense that someone had already lit a match to a long fuse that ended in his back pocket.

"I have a bad feeling," John said.

Shiprock rose up in silence behind them, drowned in their dust, and the dying sun bloody with no warmth, waiting on winter, cold air stealing into the cab of the truck to fuel the shared sense of impending tragedy.

Siana nodded. "I don't think this is gonna end well, John. After that first night I don't remember him saying more than a dozen words to me…ever…"

"He's had all day in front of us."

They traveled in silence after that, both of them trying not to imagine anything at all rather than the possibility of something beyond their imagination. The desert on either side of the highway had become frozen in a moment of time…motionless but for the rush of their headlong motion…a landscape in muted twilight colours waiting for a slow fade into black and white…an Ansel Adams photograph from Hell.

Gallup seemed deserted. Scraps of newspaper thrashing their way down the asphalt on Route 66. Amerind bucks stomping their way across neon package store parking lots, splendid and dying in silver concho belts and cockroach-killer boots, long black hair whipped in the wind...

Siana had barely found the time to even recognise the strange heightened sense of consciousness she had found down in the dark with Mosi. Now she shivered in the shrill whistle of wind creeping past the doors of the truck...suddenly terrified...knowing this␣was␣a␣different kind of cold reaching out into her life...John's...Mosi's...

This cold was smooth...insidious...a caress of icy fingers in places not even three pairs of charred hands had ever been before in her life.

It was the end of Innocence...all over again...

4.

Somehow they knew it all would end in the clapboard house. A local radio station started interrupting its normal programming with news reports about a shooting at the BIA offices in downtown Gallup...and then an update from the Catholic school...and then there was a cautious crawl as they searched for the house all the while trying to navigate around and through police cruisers and ambulances and the dozens of emergency response people who clogged intersections and crosswalks everywhere they turned, hoping no one would notice them paying too close attention to the carnage.

Siana felt like she was going to throw up, afraid to look at John as they slow-rumbled up and down side streets in search of the house...wondered how they possibly could know it when they saw it and knowing for damned sure they would when they did.

John said: "We should go, Cat Dancing. It's too late..."

And there was nothing Siana would have preferred to simply turning around and leaving it behind them, but she knew it had never been an option; that William's horrendous silence had driven a spike into her heart and she had not yet even begun to bleed.

"He's not finished, John," she whispered.

"I know."

"We can stop him."

"No..."

"Then why the fuck are we here!"

He shook his head, checked rearview and side mirrors. Pulled the truck to the side of a residential street that somehow had managed to remain untouched by the ongoing horror in this one early winter night.

"We're too late. I thought we could be here before he began. Now we can do nothing."

Nevertheless they found the house fifteen minutes later. Unmistakably the house, set apart from its neighbours. Siana had been in a house like that before. If they had been in Greece in the last light of an ancient Athens night the glow through a pair of duct-tape-mended windows would have been like Charon's eyes on the far shore of the Styx. They parked a block away and walked in...waiting for the sound of chaos, realising with every step that whatever had happened had done so without benefit of their presence....

5.

Somehow, William was still alive...slumped in a corner of the living room with half his face shredded over the ragged scrap of carpet on the bare wood floor. A small table lamp on a small end table in the opposite corner of the room shed barely enough light to lend colour to the blood seeping from the splinters of bone where his left eye had been. He had worn a secondhand UCal-Berkeley sweatshirt to celebrate the valedictory of his life; once upon a time it had been a sunny yellow; now it was turned orange and black in a past-due Halloween mummery. He couldn't speak because most of his mouth was gone with the rest of his face.

"Siana we can't stay."

John picked up his shotgun, prying it loose from William's bloody hand. They followed the sight line of the barrel and finally got round to noticing the something that lay sprawled on the sprung couch beside the end table with the small table lamp on top of it.

One severed arm still held an old .45 revolver. Everything else was unrecognisably William's father, from the waist up no more than a shapeless mass of blasted flesh and bone and blood. Seven or eight shotgun shells lay on the floor at his feet.

Siana turned away, knelt beside the boy, felt a dim fading consciousness regarding her from his remaining eye.

"I'm sorry, William" she said. "You scared me. I didn't know how much you were hurting."

He blinked once or twice with one wide staring eye she saw he was still alive enough to be crying.

"I'm so sorry," she said.

John put his hand on her shoulder.

"We have t'go."

She leaned over and kissed William's forehead.... watched the light and the life go out from him.

6.

Ducking down side streets to avoid the aftermath of William's last will and testament to the world, eventually they drove north again in silence with the radio updating the body count minute by minute. Five dead at the government office. At least another six at the school. Mosi had told her about her time in the care of the federal government; she could almost hear the voices that had haunted William's fragile existence.

"He was quiet...not a word even when we beat him for speaking his native language...or burning those smelly bushes in his room..."

"We put him where he needed to be in order to fit in and all he ever did was cause trouble."

"He never fuckin' listened, the little bastard...his mother was the same way..."

Siana turned the radio off as they barreled through the dark.

John exhaled slowly and said: "He took a whole box of shells...who knows how many he used...I still don't know how he managed what he did to his father..."

Once they were headed west from Shiprock he pulled the truck off into the desert and disappeared for half an hour...took the shotgun with him...came back without it...

"It's finished," he said quietly.

His face once had held a majesty of self...an inner peace and a calm born of simply being an outcast faced with simple survival...outside the petty concerns and bullshit triviality of life in America. She looked at him and the dark liquid sorrow in his eyes, never even tried to imagine...suddenly aware that she would never know that kind of desolation or loss... that if you were white you could get away with just about fucking anything unless it became an inconvenience to someone...or got in the way of them turning a profit...

Them....faceless...*the gang of those who rule us*...and everyone else just bit players in a second-rate threepenny opera...

It really was finished. For William. He wouldn't cause trouble for anyone ever again...

7.

She didn't want to see anyone she knew...went out of her way and stopped for breakfast before she went home... the early morning crowd gone from the diner. She ordered two of them...eggs and bacon and sausage, toast and home fries and coffee and pancakes it all tasted brand new as if she'd never eaten anything like it in the life she had been living before.The waitress wore a tag said her name was Brenda, never blinked, but Siana saw the puzzled expression on her face as she went for more of this or that, refilled her coffee mug. When she brought the bill back the puzzlement was gone.

"You look different from the photograph," she said quietly, slipped an old newspaper down onto the table... front page news from over a month ago...another local girl gone missing...

Siana didn't feel all that different. She recognised numbness growing over the sharp wounds of memory...

the scrapes and tears and abuses on her body and in her soul...but she didn't feel different in any way she thought might show until she went to the washroom to get rid of some of the coffee...walked past an image of someone who might have been her if not for the rampant tangles of bone-white and silver in her hair. The waitress was waiting for her, concerned.

"Should I call someone?"

Siana shook her head. "No...thanks I'm okay..."

"You were big news."

"I just needed to get away. Me and my mom... y'know..."

Brenda nodded like she knew.

"Yeah...me and mine got into it when I was your age. Are you gonna be all right? If you don't have money breakfast is on me."

Siana smiled, one more thing that felt like it was something she'd not done in a long time. A couple of miles away she thought she could hear sirens, foghorn blasts conjuring images of big red trucks with chrome fittings and hoses...a house hopefully being eaten by flames too big for anyone to do much more than just stand by and watch them chew...

"Thanks for the offer," she said. "I'm flush this morning..."

She reached into the pocket of someone else's corduroy trousers and pulled out a handful of bills...left two twenties on the table for ten dollars'-worth of breakfast she said:

"Would it be okay if I wasn't here this morning?"

Brenda said *Sure no problem*, and Siana walked back out into a bright bright sunshiny day. When she got home the house was empty so she showered for an hour and went to sleep in her own bed...

8.

She woke up mid-way between the highway and John's digs a mile off into the desert... bounced into consciousness and an apology from him she shook her head it wasn't necessary. A few more minutes and she could see Mosi out in the yard waiting for them, a small dark shadow in bright moonlight. Siana half-slid half-fell off the bench seat of the truck and did her best to look her in the eyes with a small wag of her head.

Mosi said: "He's not coming back, is he?"

Siana said: "It's done for him, honey. He didn't have your heart or anywhere near enough of your hope."

Mosi began to cry...soundlessly...just big fucking tears falling down her face as she grew smaller and smaller in the night wind out of the valley. Siana reached for her, nodded to John it was okay they'd be inside in a minute. She watched his back over top of Mosi's head, the slump of his shoulders as he went through the plank door. Mosi was hanging on to her so hard it was painful.

"He wouldn't say anything the first week he stayed with us. He always went out and found us something to eat, but he never said a word....and one night I could hear him in the corner under his blanket and it was so horrible, Siana...like his heart kept breaking over and over and over again and he couldn't do anything to stop it from hurting...

"He hated anyone coming near him but he was keeping the girls up and he sounded so alone. I went over and hugged him until he went to sleep. In the morning he kissed me really hard on the lips and watched t'see what I do...

"He wanted me t'be angry at him..."

Siana pushed her away some, pulled a tail of her shirt out and wiped gently at her face, staring up into the sky, shaking her head at the stars. In the space of a few seconds thoughts loomed, coalesced and became the stark reality of the wall she had constructed inside herself...high enough and deep enough to never let anyone in where they could do her any more damage. She cursed silently...drew the girl back into her arms...

"He's flyin' now, Mosi...back t'somewhere he can be happy again..."

"Siana..."

"It's okay, Cat...even if it's not..."

She turned her around put her arm over her shoulders. Mosi's went round her waist and she put her head down where Siana could put her nose in her hair...breathe in some innocence...

9.

She woke up drowsy...felt a rush of panic... disoriented until her nostrils picked up the sticky sweet stench of her sister's godawful mine-only don't-touch-it perfume...opened her eyes to a prim little tartan skirt and a fuzzy sweater and something typically shrill and stupid leaking out of a face open-mouthed and stunned with surprise.

"Nice t'see you too, Pollyanna," she said. "Just go away or shut the hell up I'm still sleeping..."

"Where have you been?"

"Someplace would've done you a world of good for sure..."

She turned over, buried her face in a pillow.

"Why did you do this? Why didn't you call? What's wrong with you we were worried to death...."

"Not near close enough so now just shut the fuck up."

"I'm calling Mom."

"Whatever..."

She dozed off...shivered awake...drifted off again until Pollyanna shrilling in the living room became too intrusive. She threw off her blankets and followed the noise to where she found a moment of extreme satisfaction by walking starkers into the kitchen past Mom and Sis...poured a glass of milk...lounged in the doorway.

"Well I'm back," she said brightly....

10.

Mosi slept with her from that night on. Climbed into her flannel pj's and then just cuddled up against her as winter closed in. The twins shared their accommodations with Smudge. As he grew into the dinner plates masquerading as his paws they tended to sleep on top of him. In the middle of the night they whispered secrets to each other. During the day you could beat them with tent poles and they'd never make a sound. Mosi expressed concern.

"They're not doing so good in school," she said. "I know they understand what's going on but their teacher's not happy with them. Siana. If they don't start talking to other people they're gonna take them away again..."

Again...they...the faceless *they*...

She'd never imagined she would ever be mother to three children; Mosi's innocent half-awake kisses in the middle of the night made tides of warmth go through her...half-guilty pleasure remembering some of them from two winters gone when she had forgotten about her walls and let someone in. In the darkness Siana promised to talk to the twins... make them understand they were safe now...that it was okay to make sounds and be little girls...

She wept for them on her own time.

11.

"Maggie...

"Maggie listen t'me..."

Maggie turned a sunny smile in a round face with fat cheeks and inky black bangs and said:

"I'm Flower. Maggie is not so nice as me."

Siana said: "You're both angels and I love you but you gotta start talkin', baby...if you guys don't show them you're okay when you're at school they're gonna take you away from us."

Flower frowned.

"If we make sounds they'll hurt us."

"No they won't, honey...I won't let them. You don't have t'be afraid anymore. Nobody's gonna hurt you."

Flower thought it over.

"Are you sure? Will you promise?"

Siana closed her eyes and hoped tears didn't squeeze out from under her eyelids.

"I promise I'll do everything I can t'keep you guys safe."
Flower thought it over some more.
"I'll see what Maggie says...okay...?"
Siana nodded.
"Okay...but you tell her it's important..."

12.

"...I should get some work in town," she said. "I'm driving the girls in every morning anyway. I might as well look for something...and I'm runnin' out o' cash I don't wanna be a drag on you."

John sipped his lunch coffee, turned away a bit to watch snow dancing past the window on the kitchen side of *Casa de los Perdidos*.

"I can manage," he said. "For all of us. And I'm still in your debt...forever..."

He shrugged. Smiled over the remains of their midday meal. Siana thought it was beatific when he smiled. It happened so infrequently if you didn't know to watch him when he looked at Mosi or the twins...or when he threw sticks for Smudge and No-Name Dog. She poured herself a small measure of bourbon from a dearly-bought bottle.

"You're not no way and I need to keep up my people skills."

John snorted coffee through his nose...convulsed himself away from the table and tried to laugh through choking to death. Siana leaned over and tried to keep his hair from getting snarled up in bodily expectorations. Her hand came to rest against his cheek and they both looked up...startled...

Siana said: "I would, y'know...girls has got needs..."

John started choking again. When it had passed he just shook his head.

"I don't know anyone like you, or where you come from."

It was her turn to shrug.

"I don't fit in, either. That's all it is. For me it's just dealing with bullshit. For you it's Life and Death."

"You don't guilt."

"I haven't really done anything t'feel guilty about, John...not yet anyway. Maybe once...but none o' my people have ever fucked your people...so here I am being people with you and the girls and the fucking dogs and right here an' now is one of the few times in my life I've felt maybe I was where I was supposed t'be...for a little while..."

John said: "I'm not gonna sleep with you. You're one hell of a good lookin' white girl, but I won't do it. I'm old enough to be your grandfather. It would be insulting you, him, and your daddy."

Siana drank more whiskey.

"Then just thanks for taking me in....for letting me stay. I didn't really have anywhere else t'go. I know where I *should* go, but it's a long drive and it's been a while... She's probably moved on...

"Meanwhile...I'm gonna look for something...just t'keep the wolves away."

John nodded okay...put one hand on her knee, and for just a moment it felt like one of the days when there had been nothing between her and the people she cared about...

13.

Her father just hung his head.

"I love her, Siana. I know what it looks like t'you but I've never even looked at anybody else from the day I first looked at her."

"Daddy she treats you like you're a servant...like you don't even live here!"

The stricken look on his face hurt more than anything she'd ever felt before. She'd only spoken the obvious, but there was a good chance it had never been painful for him until the moment when he knew that she had noticed.

"When I was younger than you out in Halifax I had no place t'live because my mother was dead and my father's second wife hated me. I hung out with this other kid and we found a wooden shack that didn't seem t'belong to anyone, and a small steel drum for makin' a fire an' we just got by that winter. In the spring there was nothing inside that shack because we had burned it all t'keep from freezing to death..."

Siana slipped a carton of milk, a sleeve of Wonder Bread and some Kraft slices into a paper sack...took a five-dollar bill from Mrs Hoity-Toity and made change...sent her on her fat-ass way...

"You need to be more friendly."

Her manager was ten feet away, behind the other cash register, shaking her head and looking daggers.

"And you need to get over the idea that you're anything more than a kiss-ass to the guy that pays us," she said. "That woman's a foul-tempered hag."

"I can always replace you."

"I'm sure you can, but we both know I'm here because I know how t'count past ten, I don't skim anything out of the cash drawers, and the boss plus most of the boys in this neck of the woods like buying their beer from someone who makes them go hard inside their panties."

She did a bump and wriggle with her hips that slammed her cash drawer shut, smiled with malicious sweetness...then turned away...suddenly...feeling uncomfortable...a feeling that might have been guilt.

"I've done this gig before, Kathy," she said quietly. "I'm just tryin' t'get by with what I've got...keep as much of it as I can. Can't we just try t'get along instead of you always bein' in my face over shit that doesn't really matter...?"

She didn't get a response. Finally turned back to where Kathy was wearing this stricken look on her face...twice her age and five times her dress size...just trying to get by...likely with a husband who bought his beer the days when Siana was doing the early afternoon shift on her own she said:

"I'm sorry. From now on I'll try t'be...nice... whatever..."

CHAPTER FOUR – NOW IS THE WINTER OF DIS & CONTENTMENT...

1.

A freak winter storm descended upon them; the wind came howling down the valley and laid siege to the small collection of planks and nails doing it's best to remain recognisable as their refuge, windows rattling, the soft snuffle and shuffle of goats and sheep...safely indoors in the enclosed pen next door, inside with the wood stove starting to take on a decidedly rusty colour as Maggie fed more wood into the flames.

"Be careful, honey," Siana said. "Don't touch anything it's really hot..."

Maggie was talking...not as much as Flower but beginning to feel like her voice had every bit as much right to be heard as anyone else's. She leveled a ferocious stare at the firebox, clamped her lower lip firmly between her teeth and chucked a chunk of wood into the fire.

"I have a stick, Cat-Mama," she said.

So saying, she used said stick to clang the door of the stove shut, came back to the blanket she was sharing with Mosi and Flower and waited for story-time to resume. John dried off the last of their supper dishes, poured himself a cup of tea and settled in with his own book, borrowed from Siana's traveling library...a paperback copy of *The Killings at Kent State*.

"I guess it was only a matter of time before they started murdering their own children," he said.

Siana looked up...startled to hear him make words out of a thought that had been floating around in her head for ages. She made *back in a minute* sounds to her listening audience, sipped her whiskey...said:

"That's been goin' on way longer than just Kent State," she said.

"What will they do when they're the only ones left to prey upon...?"

"Like the when the rest of us have been bled dry?" John nodded sadly, stared at Siana without really seeing her:

UNTIL THE END OF THE WORLD

"My people are bones in the desert. All of us. Even those who still walk and breathe the air, we are only ghosts...flesh and bone memory of a different world that will never come back."

He called her by her Cherokee name.

"Can you tell me why white people must obliterate everything they cannot understand or use to their advantage?"

Siana nodded brightly, with bitterness....

"Sure. It's simple. We're like a fucking virus. We soak up what we want, fuck everything else up for everyone left and then move on. It's not really a question of why, John...it's a question of something in our genetics that makes us batshit fuckin' crazy that way... and if you refuse to join the Great Rolling Thunder Caucasian Road Show...give up whatever kind of culture or values you had before they found you...then you're pretty much basically screwed."

"But you're different."

"No-o-o-o...I'm a girl. In the grand white male scheme of things that's not much better than a nigger or a spick or a fucking Indian..."

John shook his head and sighed.

"White Man make-um big fucking mistakes...have no clue..."

Siana laughed, said *That's for damn sure, and not in front of the children...* went back to reading to the girls about the adventures of Mr Toad, halfway through *The Wind in the Willows*.

Outside the storm piled snow up against their door and threatened to freeze the windows shut until spring;

inside it stayed warm, well away from the Road Show for at least one more night simply because on that blessed day they had nothing white people wanted.

2.

Nobody knew if the school in Farmington was open or not. Outside the snow was bigger than the dogs and the twins; inside next door, sheep and goats in anthropomorphic revel gave each other high-fives and said *We got a roof,* all the while shuddering about and bumping into shared walls.

Maggie and Flower looked at Mosi who looked at Siana who said:

"I'm not goin' anywhere t'day."

Maggie got brave and said:

"Can we have pizza?"

Mosi started laughing but Flower was very serious.

"Maggie we can have *two* pizzas if you know how we can get them."

Which put paid to pizza dreams. Siana sipped coffee and looked questions at John.

"I don't know," he said. "Not much of anything t'do today except dig ourselves out...?"

She nodded, wondering how and why she could be so peaceful snowed in out in the middle of fucking nowhere with a bunch of Indians, and a small army of stinky animals in a barn attached to the house. Mosi's head on her knee, the softness of her hair under her fingers, was one of the most wonderful feelings she'd ever had in her life. The twins whispered to each other and Smudge ducked under the blanket, made them giggle. No-Name Dog was older, stayed close to the stove where it was warm. She realised she had simply stopped noticing the smell of kerosene in the lamps that gave them light... didn't even care that doing her business meant ten minutes climbing into a ton of clothing just to get to the outhouse for the time it took between doing her business and her ass beginning to go numb with cold on the wooden seat. She laughed, and when John looked up to see why she shrugged helplessly.

"How 'bout snow angels after lunch?"

He grinned back.

"I'm game," he said. "Can't grow anything in the snow."

"We can grow snowmen...but they're all gonna be white..."

"We'll have to make them sign non-aggression pacts."

"We'll need some weaponry t'maintain a proper balance of power, otherwise y'know they'll come for us with pitchforks and torches."

It was a giant *non sequitur*. Nobody but Siana had ever seen a Frankenstein movie. Mosi said *We can hide all the carrots,* which struck them all as ridiculously funny...even the twins who didn't quite understand what was going on but were beginning to feel safe in the sound of other people laughing...

Later in the afternoon, with a small generator going to keep the truck and VW batteries warm, a big iron pot of soup over the fire started to bubble in the twilight hush creeping through their windows. Maggie and Flower put brightly-painted ceramic bowls on the plank table, added paper towels for napkins, mis-matched cutlery and re-cycled jam jars for whatever they would be drinking.

Mosi sliced a loaf of sourdough bread that Siana had picked up on their last trip to town. John bent his head before they tucked in, muttered something... looked up to see if Siana had understood.

"It was my prayer of thanks...for you," he said. "Just in case somebody was listening..."

She had so little in the way of defenses when it came to kindness...some old memories of when loving her had not cost her father in every other aspect of his wretched existence...a few months'-worth of warmth in the bed of a beautiful blonde girl who had shivered and wept beneath her fingers and her tongue, the two of them blindly seeking shelter from storm.

Flower said, "Don't be sad, Cat-Mama. We love you."

Mosi looked at her trying hard not to cry, knowing that for *her* Cat-Dancing it was not near enough and never would be...

But on that particular night the soup was thick with beans and rice, a small shredding of venison and old vegetables, and the wind when it decided to speak was only a low whistle out in the valley that never reached them where they ate quietly in the warmth of the stove.

3.

No one ever mentioned her disappearance after she woke up that afternoon, or questioned why she had started putting long streaks of white and silver in her hair. When her father came home that night she watched shock and an infinite sense of relief flutter quickly across his face; then their eyes met and she saw sorrow, because suddenly he knew she had been somewhere he had been unable to protect her...that she had traveled too far a distance on her own and neither of them would ever again cross the gulf that had come between them.

If the local news reports of a nearby house going up in flames in any way seemed to connect itself to her, no one pointed it out. After a large fireproof metal box of photographs was recovered from the ashes, it became common knowledge that the three crispy critters found in the basement had, in life, been imprisoning and sexually abusing young women. By that time her absence from the Darrow house had become something else that never got talked about. She went back to school, and as her hair grew longer and slowly leached itself of colour, she became *Morticia* to the boys who never stopped trying to get into her knickers, and much worse to their girlfriends who were pissed off they wanted into them at all.

One guy from her lit class started following her around, tall and thin and less objectionable than any of the others. She let him take a few steps into her world because he was one of a handful of "hippies" in her high school. Long lank hair. Ragged jeans and denim shirts. He didn't hang out with anyone, and he didn't play hockey or football...but he listened to strange psychedelic music from California and once he had turned Siana on for the first time, appeared willing to pay for her company with what seemed like an unlimited stash of marijuana.

One day near the end of her junior year they got high out behind the maintenance building, sat with their knees up and their backs to the concrete wall staring up through the treetops into blue sky and clouds, blowing long streams of dope smoke into the sweet lilac smell of early summer.

"Why'd you do that t'your hair?" he asked.

"I didn't do anything to my hair," she said drowsily, feeling peaceful. "I had a bad Halloween."

He choked on a toke and she reached over to relieve him of the joint and pound him on the back until he he could catch his breath.

"Really...?" he said, finally.

"Don't be an idiot," she said. "It just turned white on me. Maybe now I can go t'Hollywood and get a movie career playing witches."

"You wanna be an actress? That's so fucking plastic."

"Right now I don't wanna be anything, except maybe somebody sitting here quietly and doin' another one of your doobies."

He dutifully rolled another one, politely offered her the first hit, waited until he saw it curling out from her lips and nostrils.

"You know why witches never wear underwear?" he asked cautiously.

"No...why?"

"So they can get a better grip on their broomsticks."

"That's fucking gross."

"But it's funny, right?"

Siana shook her head in disgust and took the joint back.

"It's hilarious, Jeff, and if that's your idea of a suave-motherfucker-intro to get into my pants you can pack up and go the fuck home."

He looked hurt.

"What am I doin' here with you then? You don't have anything t'do with anybody else…"

"I'm thinkin' you're the only one can answer that question, Jeff. I'm here because I'm just as big a fuck-up as you are and since you were kind enough to share I've decided I like gettin' high…and talking to you…most of the time, like when you're not bein' gross…but that doesn't mean I wanna fuck you."

He got thoughtful for a while. Took the joint from her fingers and slowly dragged more smoke into his lungs.

"Oh well," he said behind the billow of exhale. "I was hopin'. You're a beauty, Siana."

He looked over at her hopefully…one last ditch pitch for some honey. She wouldn't look at him.

"Thanks, Jeff," she whispered. "You're a good guy too. It's just not a good time…"

They had a couple more short little hits and sat in silence, watching the clouds morph into early summer cotton sky sculpture.

"Whattaya gonna do after next year?" he said.

She shrugged. "I wanted t'go t'this art school in Toronto but it's not gonna happen. Maybe I'll just go away…just get the fuck out of here. This isn't a good place t'be different."

"That's for damn sure," he agreed,

They did some more silence, then Jeff said:

"You're the only one I talk to, y'know."

Siana laughed without any laughter.

"You poor bastard. Stuck with fuckin' Morticia."

"They're all assholes."

"Yeah they are...and most of what they have t'say is shit. Remember that when you look at yourself in the mirror..."

4.

Mosi was curled up under the blankets when she came to bed, reached for her...not even half-conscious still drawn into soft and warm. Siana stripped down to a t-shirt and panties and wondered how/why this was something she treasured over anything else in her days... someone who trusted her...found safety and total peace with her...

She remembered whispers in the dark...the blonde girl not so much crying as racked with guilt for finding her own best loving with Siana, instead of the high school sweetheart she was supposed to marry.

Nearby on their own cot each of the twins wriggled and squirmed for a one-third share of the mattress mostly now owned by Smudge getting bigger by the day. Mosi wriggled closer too as she always did; she could never seem to get close enough...and Siana didn't get wet anymore...became aware that in her own consciousness there was this place that demanded attention...a simple innocence of warmth...being close to someone who loved you just because...

No rules.

No demands.

Nothing at all but stay close I need to be near you.

She thought of the blonde girl all the time but rarely by name, because doing that, thinking too hard, was asking for trouble...an acknowledgment she had fucked up badly... that she missed her...that having left her behind had become painful…the source of something she had never experienced before…

Regret. Bone-wrenching fucking regret.

Siana cried for a girl named Karin and Mosi kissed her face…half asleep…until she could go to sleep too.

5.

Every month or so she got caught with weekend shifts…all day or mid-afternoon to closing. More often than not it was just a marathon to keep the beer coolers full and everyone civil with each other whilst in the process of getting shit-faced and mortally hung over for Saturday or Sunday morning.

Her truce with Kathy had weathered the better part of the winter; knowing nothing of her circumstances Siana was stunned…sorrowed…when even the least bit of kindness or consideration on her part was met with something that seemed to approach gratitude….

"I can do the weekend if you'll do my Wednesday Thursday," the woman said one Monday early in the morning. "That way you don't have t'drive in just t'do the shifts."

"I really don't care one way or the other, Kathy," she said. "You deserve some weekend time. You look after everything and I just show up. But I sell more beer than you do, so the numbers on Monday make Dickhead smile for the rest of the week. I figure we got something good goin' on…"

The older woman almost smiled. Siana figured maybe weekends weren't such shit-hot fun that staying home was a good thing.

"Why don't you just take off for the weekend then," she suggested. "Put a six-pack and a fuckin' meat loaf in the freezer for the mister, go see somebody somewhere you haven't seen in a while..."

"It's not that easy."

"Sure it is...you just have t'think of yourself every once in a while, is all..."

On Tuesday after the big rush that followed fresh bread deliveries Kathy said:

"I'm goin' t'Albuquerque. I called one o' my high school friends and we're gonna have lunch and I'm gonna stay over..."

Siana grinned. "Good for you. Don't forget t'raise some hell...*and*...bring me back somethin' nice..."

She winked, let Kathy blush and fill in the blanks any way she chose....

So it got dark on the Saturday and she was hoisting cases of Bud and Coors into the coolers, came out front again with a handful of pick-ups in the parking lot and just as many guys already one-and-a-half sheets in the wind...sold them their two-fours and pints...found the last one in the queue was somebody she'd looked at once or twice, when he and nobody else was looking.

Six foot. Early twenties maybe younger. Big black eyes in a face that reminded her of Neil Young but with a better tan, helped along by a homemade haircut ragged over his shoulders. She could say with a near-certainty it was done that way just for the benefit of any hottie felt the need for some honey and pretty-boy company. She knew she was being suckered, but there were some things she'd been missing of late...a girl had needs y'know...

She said, "Howdy Neil," just to let him know she wasn't oblivious.

"That's not my name," he said, sliding a case of Coors and a pint of Jack Daniels down the counter.

"It is now, handsome," she said, smiling so he wouldn't take offense.

He seemed secretly pleased, and suddenly the possibility of not having to do the long midnight drive home across the desert seemed pretty damned alluring to her, like his long legs and the braided leather belt slung down low over his hips like a promise.

"Maybe we can get together later?" he asked softly. The *aw shucks* shy smile was about as contrived as anything she'd ever seen but it still looked like sugar.

"I finish up here around eleven," she said. "If you're allowed t'be up that late maybe we can."

She rang him up and made a big show of rippling the silver down her back.

He drawled something unintelligible...long and slow, and when she handed him his change she reached over the counter and ran her fingers down along one side of his face.

"So I'm gonna see you," she said

"Ten-thirty," he grinned.

"Neil you are *so* smooth..."

She could hear his truck rumbling into the empty parking lot, watched the headlights flare in the dark and then fade against the plate-glass storefront...saw his breath billowing out the driver-side door into the cold winter night...winced when she saw the flash of a match and the pinpoint laser burn of a cigarette.

Gonna make that boy brush his damned teeth she thought out loud, slid the cash drawers shut and zipped the night deposit bag.

He was slouched against the cab of his truck smoking another cigarette when she keyed the alarm inside and slipped out through the front door, turned and sent a cloud of *Hi, you made it!* into the air. He pitched his cigarette and nodded, did a slow saunter on his ankles, his boot-heels hardly making a sound on the snow-tatters and asphalt.

"Gotta stop at the bank first," she said, holding up the day's worth of sales.

"We could take it with us and head for the sunrise."

"But then I'd have t'shoot you, and *that* would be a shame."

"Think so?"

"Oh yeah."

"What"s your name?"

"Alix," she said. "But it's got an *I* instead of an *E* and that's why I'm a girl."

She could see him smile, the flash of it in leftover bits of light with nothing else to do but light up his pretty face.

He asked, "Are you hungry, Alix?" and she nodded once...slowly...very slowly...making sure he could see that her eyes were locked on his, because the game was fun and she knew it was her game and they both were having a good time playing it.

UNTIL THE END OF THE WORLD

He reached into the back pocket of his jeans and brought out the pint of bourbon, offered it to her. She shook her head.

"Don't really want anything in the way," she said softly, and for a moment he looked like a little boy...intrigued...and then she could hear him thinking...casting his fate to the wind. She knew where most of the blood flow was going now...said:

"Have we got someplace t'go?

He nodded.

She said: "Then after the bank you lead and I'll follow..."

───※───

It was a small room in the basement of a split level house with a "private" entrance round the back. Next door beyond a thin line of scrawny shrubbery was neon and a biker bar.

She followed him down the steps and into some welcome warmth. As the door closed behind him she slipped out of her sweater and denim jacket, reached under her t-shirt to unhook the clasps on her bra, feeling dangerous with anticipation...some innocent fun and the who-are-you-kidding chance at some romance as he came up behind her and put his arms around her...

"You...are...so...sexy..."

She could've forgiven him that stupid line...overlooked any number of things with an interesting something bumping up into the crack of her ass through the seat of her jeans, but when she turned around he'd managed...somehow...to get out of his clothes and still keep his boots on. She backed up.

"You're pretty, Neil, but I'm not getting into bed with anyone still wearin' boots...and I sure as hell am not gonna stand on my tippy-toes for a first-time-around fuck. You need to screw with your boots on you go find a cow."

She could see the sudden frustration...feel the pounding of lust in his crotch. It made her sad.

"Maybe you're not a bad guy," she said. "But I'm not here just to feed your fantasies. I was hopin' for a little bit of warmth, y'know..."

He seemed dazed...confused...like he'd been part of something he knew real well but then somebody had changed the rules without telling him. His big soft black eyes got cold and hard like splinters of volcano glass she said:

"Don't, Neil...just don't okay...?"

She remembered the slip knife she kept in her hip pocket, for slicing open cartons and boxes of frozen food. The point came up into the hollow between his collarbones. She could hear herself speaking words she would never have dreamt of speaking ten seconds before.

"Just don't...please...think about what would happen if I tore my t-shirt up and ran into the parking lot next door screaming my brains out about how a fucking Indian was trying to rape me."

She started crying, could feel tears leaking down her cheeks. She cursed herself and cursed him and felt relief when he finally backed up and the lovely promise between his legs got lost and far away, him standing there looking stupid and angry, and her gathering up a sweater and a jacket and edging toward the door.

It was hours...a fucking lifetime...before she crawled into the bed Mosi had kept warm for her.

6.

It took some doing, but the weather was warm and the sergeant on duty at the desk in the city jail had a good imagination when it came to perspiration and young girls who chose to make undergarments optional. She followed some guy in a uniform until they stopped in front of a barred cell and geeky Jeff looked up... surprised...didn't actually say her name out loud but she could see his lips move in a way that if she'd been listening would have heard the note of terror singing alongside it she asked him:

"Are you okay?"

And he shook his head. He wasn't supposed to shake his head. He was supposed to nod like *Yeah everything is cool* ...but he didn't and it wasn't. Jeff look scared. Jeff looked lost and alone and there was nothing she could do to change it.

"I bought some *sensemilla* seeds in the mail, Siana. I planted 'em on my grandparents farm outside of Sunbury. They followed me. They said I'm old enough to get charged as an adult...for growin' with intent to sell..."

"Jeff it's just us...you and me..."

"Siana, I know. They're tryin t'say I'm the one sellin' t'the whole school."

"But that's bullshit!"

"You shouldn't have come, Siana. They're gonna start keepin' an eye on you now."

"I don't care...!"

Jeff said, "But I care, Siana...and since they need somebody t'fuck for all of it, just let me be one..."

7.

Mornings were always entertaining. Nobody wanted to be the first one out of bed, the one who got to shiver and shake and feed the wood stove back up to fighting weight against the cold. No-Name Dog and Smudge could be depended upon to unfailingly provide moral support, especially as the daily ration of food for them usually followed stove-stuffing, even if it was just a careless toss of a plastic beach pail full of crunchy things into their bowls. It was John's muttered curses that woke them to clouds of their own breath in the air...or one of the twins still dopey with sleep passing on encouragement and advice to the other...or Mosi dashing out from under the blankets just long enough to do what needed to be done before diving back into the warm place she had found in Siana's arms the night before.

Everyone laughed at Siana doing stove-duty. She couldn't hurry...refused to move fast...or ever remember to put socks on her feet before they hit the floor. The twins whispered. Mosi giggled. John usually thanked her but you could never be certain it was a thank you because he never bothered to come out from under his own blankets if someone else had been foolish enough to volunteer for first-thing-in-the-morning warm-it-up patrol. The daily round got off to a sluggish start at the best of times...

Siana took the truck into Farmington one morning in late February...dropped off the kids and went grocery shopping while the laundry dried...did her six-hour shift at the grocery store but in between she kept bumping into places where there was a television or a radio and that was where she heard about Pine Ridge...brought the children and the news home to John who already knew about it.

"It's going t'be bad," was all he would say.

A week or so later Siana ducked through the blanketed doorway separating the girls from John and the rest of the house, found him sitting at what passed for their kitchen table with a fresh pot of coffee on the woodstove, and some in his cup as he bent over yesterday's newspaper.

"Have you seen the keys for the Bug? I'm gonna be late for work."

John looked up from his newspaper.

"Take the truck, Siana. I'm not goin' anywhere today."

He nodded toward the hooks by the door, where the Bug's keys were noticeable by their absence. Siana frowned.

"I'd rather take the Bug," she said. "It doesn't use near as much gas..."

John got up slowly and poured another mug of coffee.

"You've got the weekend off and you got paid yesterday," he said, smiling as he handed her the mug. "And I found the money you left under the plates in the cupboard."

"John what're you talkin' about?"

"I'm talkin' about Flower watching when you thought nobody was watching... throwin' stuff into the trunk of the car...some quiet rearranging of things so it would be easier for us when you were gone."

"Gone where...John, are you stoned or somethin'...?"

"Wounded Knee," he said, sitting down again. "I know that's where you were going. And then Maggie said the same thing."

"Those kids are fuckin' scary, John. I mean they're sweet and good-tempered and all that but I keep expectin' stuff t'start movin' around just by them lookin' at it....and I'd swear Maggie never uses matches anymore when she lights up our candles or lanterns."

John started laughing. "Don't change the subject... and please don't go.

"Sit down and talk with me, Siana, this is not your fight. This is that fucker Williams...Oglala Sioux...siding with the government against his own people so his family can become wealthy and powerful."

She sat, sipped at her mug of coffee in stubborn silence, glaring at him across the room... turning away only half-listening...hearing echoes distilled into out-of focus images bright with winter sunlight, seen through ancient scavenged glass panes gone watery with age, looking out over a never-ending parade of Tragedy to celebrate mankind's inability to just get along with one another.

"Mosi told me some things, Siana," he said softly. "She was very careful not to say what was only for your voice to say, but she said you had come from a difficult life of your own... and also about this young man in town not long ago."

She shook her head, refused to acknowledge him, engage in a discussion that would batter too heavily on the walls that enclosed her deepest secrets.

"I know him," John continued. "He's young and good-looking and in many ways he is like Williams at Pine Ridge...or a song by Janis Joplin..."

Siana faced him again, questioning. His face lit with a huge grin.

"*Get it while you can*," John sang softly. "Take the same advantage a white man would take in your position. Your Indian brave would not have been unkind, but he has a temper, and mostly he's looking only for his own pleasure. Whatever you said to him, to get away from him without damage, is only what he deserved."

"People are gonna get hurt," she said angrily. "*Your* people are gonna get hurt."

"Indians always get hurt when they try to take back some of the things that have been stolen from them. It's only worse today because one of us has become one of them, which is how they will finally win their wars to make the whole world a safe playground for white people. All they have to do is hold out the carrots they have never given away, make us beg for them, dole them out one by one until we all are strangers to what we were meant to be. Then we will fit neatly into their world and make no more trouble."

"I still should go."

"And do what, Siana? Freeze your ass off? Let Starvation become the one thing you can share with your Amerind brothers and sisters? Maybe get shot by some nineteen-year old farmboy from a place no one has ever heard of, who is defending whatever bullshit *American* value looks best on the television? Please...please stay here...stay here where you can make a difference for Mosi and the twins."

"I'm useless here, John!"

"You are anything *but* useless, Siana! You show them how to be little warriors... who can grow into women who don't have to be afraid to be who they want to be. You're teaching them self-respect and self-reliance...*you* are their bridge to freedom..."

She turned back again to the ancient windows, drifted into the off-kilter fluffy white clouds drifting by in an off-kilter winter blue sky listening to her heart stop pounding... grateful that he wouldn't let her go...

"Maybe once *they* go I'll get to follow them..."

8.

She could see his lips moving as he read down the front page of the newspaper, the struggle to connect the letters into words that meant something in context and concert with all the other letters and words on the page in front of him.

"I'm sorry I wasn't there," he said, taking off his reading glasses. Each one of his tears made a soft *snap* as it hit the newsprint in his lap.

She shook her head. "*It's down t'me*, Daddy," she said, for some strange reason channeling words from a song by the Rolling Stones. "My stupid not yours. I'll be okay."

He started to say something else but she put her fingers against his lips and leaned over to kiss the shiny spot on his forehead where a long unruly lock of hair once had fallen across his eyes.

"I know," she said.

UNTIL THE END OF THE WORLD

9.

Mid-March and the Valley became something approaching magical. It was cold, but the sky was a clear icy blue and the sun turned the swoops and sheets of stubborn snow on the hillsides and the ground into shimmering carpets before the wind started to skim it up into the air in swirls of crystal that caught the sunlight and exploded into curtains of daytime firefly diamonds. By early afternoon most of the landscape had been scoured of it, exposing the hard flat desert floor to the first whispers of Spring. When Siana brought the girls home the transformation was startling; it was near sunset head-count, herding the sheep and goats in for the night after their first day of foraging, that Mosi noticed three of the sheep were missing.

She could see John was angry, mostly at himself for letting it happen, but also with a hint of the kind of unreasoning anger that showed up when Fate decided to monkey-wrench a balance already skirting the edge of precarious. They couldn't afford to lose the sheep. They were wool to be traded to the blanket-weavers in return for any number of necessities. John stood in the doorway of their hobbit-hole and shrugged.

"They're done," he said. "The dogs and coyotes all are hungry after the winter. We'll find nothing but their bones."

Siana felt someone tugging on the sleeve of her coat, looked down into Maggie's round face, her eyes just the smallest bit glazed...unseeing...or looking elsewhere...the little girl said:

"Not yet."

Two words in a sing-song voice that ended on an upbeat note, the way children sound when they knew something you didn't know. Siana knelt down to where she could look her in the eyes. John turned in the doorway.

"Maggie...?"

Flower was beside them in an instant.

"She can find them, Cat-Mama."

"Flower she wasn't even here today. You guys were in school."

Flower said, "She can find them," in a tone that was considerably more uncompromising than most anything else she said on a daily basis. "We can all go... you'll see..."

Siana looked at John and John looked at Siana. The light was fading from the sky, shadows getting long and longer and then becoming part of the onrushing night.

"We could try," he said. "I've got one good flashlight, and we'll have the moon three-quarters full...but it will be cold..."

※

It was. They ate a quick hot meal of beans and rice and then bundled themselves into the twilight, filled up a pair of army-isue canteens with water. John brought the new shotgun thathad replaced the one that had "disappeared" in the aftermath of William's leave-taking. For Siana and Mosi he dug two staffs of heavy almost-striated wood from a corner, viciously pointed on one end and knobbed but not much less so on the other.

"Saguaro bones," he said. "They're older than the twins...foraged them off the ground in the superstitions east of Phoenix."

At the plank door of the long lean-to where the sheep and goats spent their nights they turned to Maggie, not knowing what to expect. She stood beside the door and then started walking out through the wide gated pen onto the valley floor...out to the perimeters of where they had spent most of the day grazing on the first bits of green to sneak their way into the light. She put her nose up into the night, seemed to look around without seeing anything at all, and started walking again, following a path only she could see as it would between two low hills and then began to climb into the heights that surrounded the valley.

At first No-Name Dog shuffled along at John's heels as they went sideby side up into the hills. The path narrowed and he charged ahead, then from side to side, nose to the ground, picking up old scents of jackrabbit and mice, until John called him back to the rear of their single file. Without any discussion Maggie simply took the lead, appearing to be almost asleep, her eyes nearly closed but every so often catching a glint of early starlight as her head lolled first to one side and then the other. Flower walked a few paces behind, every now and again leaning forward to whisper into her ear. Siana and Mosi went three of four steps behind them. The only sounds were No-Name's aimless nosing along the ground, the rasp of boots and makeshift walking sticks across pebbles and stones, the rhythm of their breathing carried upward as the air rapidly cooled back down below freezing and new frost began to grow and glisten on the moonlit heights above them.

Their shadows grew longer as the moon rose over the hills to the east. Maggie never faltered, never slowed even when the way became steep and required attention to loose stones, and shadows that could have been shelter to any number of unwanted mischiefs. Eventually their path leveled again, then started winding downhill. Siana had no idea how much ground they'd covered, how far they had come from home. She felt like they'd been walking for hours, fingers growing slightly numb against the strange iron-like sensation of cactus-bone against her fingers. Flower leaned forward to confer with her sister, a few breathless whispers before she dropped back to Mosi and Siana:

"She says soon."

Thirty seconds later the silence erupted into yips and howls and Maggie broke into a headlong rush down a scree-covered slope to their right, dodging boulders and ducking down into a wash that began to rise again up beween two large outcroppings of stone outlined in stark moonlight showing only darkness beyond.

Siana heard John cursing softly behind her, telling the twins to slow down. No-Name began to bell, charging ahead of them, seeming to follow Maggie's outstretched hand...pointing...and then they could hear the frenzy of the pack just around another upthrust spur of rock, and the unmistakable shrill of three ewes well beyond fear.

UNTIL THE END OF THE WORLD

John shouted and the twins began to slow their pace. He followed his dog to the fore with Siana and Mosi directly behind him on either side, now forming a semi-circular shield in front of Maggie and Flower as they turned into a small cul-de-sac of black and silver shards of light...seven coyotes inching the sheep backward into their killing ground.

No-Name Dog tore into the hindquarters of one, rearing up and then down to bury his teeth into its neck just above the shoulders. One of the ewes bared her teeth and stamped forward, protecting the others, just enough time for John to come alongside No-Name Dog, firing three shots in rapid succession into the rear of the pack, taking down two, Siana in silence swinging her cactus-bone like a Louisville Slugger, knocking one sideways to lie still with its jaws flecked with foam its eyes staring sightlessly back along its broken spine. Mosi screamed at the top of the lungs, stabbing at another with the sharpened end of her club, running it down and pinning it to the earth with one thrust down through its ribs.

Two coyotes broke and ran. John's fourth shot took the head off the last of them that insisted on staying behind. In less than fifteen seconds it was over...no more snarls... no more bleats of terror... only heavy breathing and each of them waiting for the pounding of their hearts to slow down and let them listen to the silence.

Flower and Maggie walked up to the sheep, began crooning to them...just wordless sounds to quiet them...running hands through their oily coats... whispering to each other, smiling as if nothing at out of the ordinary had occurred.

They formed a small caravan for the journey back to the valley floor. John and a strutting No-Name Dog licking at his muzzle took the lead this time, followed by the largest ewe who had held off the coyotes that one crucial second. The twins chattered to each other as they rode the other two sheep homeward. Siana and Mosi brought up the rear.

"How did she do that?"

Mosi shrugged. Flower swiveled around on her wooly charger.

"She just knows," was all the explanation she would offer, "but she wants bells so next time it won't be so hard to find them."

10.

Spring came soon after, the winter chill in the air suddenly gone as quickly as it had come the previous fall. The sun came up hot and bright, boiling over the eastern heights to spill warmth and life-giving light to the desert floor and the hillsides, now dotted with tall yuccas blooming purple and white, fragrant brittlebush sporting little yellow flowers,

desert sage and pepperplant. The goats and the sheep grew restless, tired of winter feed, anxious to be out and chowing down on the brand new growth. Over breakfast the twins seemed excited, doing their usual whisperings behind cupped hands, giggling, darting quick glances at the rest of them to see if they were being noticed.

UNTIL THE END OF THE WORLD

John noticed...said: "Looking forward to school today? Something special going on?"

They looked at each other, did a little pantomime between themselves, raised eyebrows and small frowns, another giggle or two...and then Flower said *Nope* and went back to spooning cornflakes and making mysterious faces at her sister. Siana and John shook their heads, knowing something was in the wind...curious...but also long-resigned to the way the twins behaved with their little secrets.

Eventually Siana got them into the truck and they headed east for the day, the usual for all concerned. The twins and Mosi helped with getting three loads of laundry into the washers before they were delivered to school. Just as Siana was about drive off, Flower hoisted herself through the open passenger window, leaned into the cab and said *Ooljee is coming* with a big grin on her face.

She went back to the laundromat to put everything in the dryers, went about her other business in the hour she still had before her shift at the grocery store. Non-perishable stuff at the hardware store and the tack shop, where she was well enough known to be on speaking terms with the people who worked there. She asked about *Ooljee* ... explained and asked what Flower had meant by saying it. The woman whose name was Takala laughed at the question.

"She is playing with you, sister. *Ooljee* means moon...and tonight is the first night of the waxing quarter."

Siana collected her gear, collected the laundry and did her six hours at the grocery, rumbled up to the front of the school just as the twins waved goodbye in unison to a small group of children in the yard. Mosi was next, crowding onto the bench seat and making a big deal out of wriggling Flower up onto her lap...oblivious to meaningful looks she exchanged with Maggie. Siana said *Ooljee is coming* and they both smiled, nodded enthusiastically. Mosi looked puzzled. Siana shrugged as if to say *I have no idea*...

Until they got home...long before moonrise...and noticed a small pinto filly, mostly a ghosty white but with a black crescent on one flank, quietly snuffling through the feed trough in the goat pen. Flower was off Mosi's lap and out of the truck like a shot. Maggie pointed with her nose...

"*Ooljee*." she said, climbed over Mosi and pelted after her sister.

John came out to help unload the truck.

"She showed up here just after lunchtime. I saw her a few miles off, thought she might be running from something, but she came along in her own time, and then made herself at home."

Mosi said, "I guess her name is *Ooljee*."

John said, "That seems right."

Siana shrugged as if to say *I have no idea*...

11.

...And learned to bake flatbread...plant squash and beans in the small garden...gather nuts and seeds...mend jeans and braid leather...watching as the twins fearlessly rode Ooljee bareback all over their corner of the world...found Mosi's old constant scrutiny now softened to a small quiet smile of pleasure every time Siana would catch her at it.

Apart from taking the kids to school, her shifts at the grocery store and doing necessary errands, she found herself feeling less and less need to go into town at all…became comfortable with the people who came to visit John and, quite often, meet the rest of them for the first time. Mosi became cautiously ecstatic.

"You see, you *do* belong here!" she said once, as lightning forked far away north in the night sky, the sound of its thunder never even reaching them, they sat on the wooden bench beside the front door and ate supper.

Siana forked some steaming chili onto a piece of fry bread and considered the possibility that Mosi might be right; that the measure of acceptance she had found in the desert, by being rescued and rescuing in turn, was something entirely new in her experience. It occurred to her she no longer had issues to intrude upon the simplicity of her existence; though aware of the rest of world and all that it embraced, whether it was joy or sorrow, celebration or catastrophe, it was not for her to truly change any of it, for better or for worse….only to do the best she could with what had been given to her, and to live with herself and the people who came into her life.

When everyone else was asleep John said, "You are growing peaceful here… learning stillness…"

This too seemed to be an accurate assessment. She told him she felt as though a hundred different weights had been lifted from her body…

"And your soul…" he added quickly.

"And my soul," she agreed, fished a pair of Budweisers out of the cooler tucked into a small cupboard set into the hillside behind them. She knocked the caps off on the edge of the table, handed him one, and they drank to each other in silence.

It had seemed so far removed from what she had come to view as her normal day-to-day that she had almost forgotten it entirely. As the summer sun grew strong in the sky and the air went dry and still in the afternoons, she sensed something, in the same way the twins had sensed the coming of Moon, but nowhere near as plain...just an uneasiness... something that the long evenings somehow contrived to heighten, until she took to climbing the outcropping of rock up above the house, sometimes spending hours staring up at the stars, or the shadows that crept into her valley with every sunset, until someone would climb up after her, remind her that sleep was something she really ought to consider in between her days.

"What are you doing, Cat-Mama?" the twins would ask, and she would say things like *just sitting*....or *listening*...answering them in the same cryptic fashion they themselves used, leaving them to interpret as best they could.

To John she would say, "Trying to be peaceful," and once he sat down beside her she would be peaceful again.

Mosi—who had become joyous by simply being near her, by living the days *with* her as they became weeks and then stretched into months—never asked at all...most often was the one who came to sit with her quietly for a while, before reminding her about the sleep thing.

One afternoon had been religious, the two of them, watching eagles soar on thermals until they got lost in the sun. As dinnertime approached she followed her Cat down the hillside and suddenly felt like all the breath had gone out of her body...realised that all the while she had been sitting and listening and being peaceful, she also had been waiting...

THE LAST DANCE
1.

They were three-four miles from home when one of the twins leaned over from the back seat of the car and whispered something into Mosi's ear...repeated the whisper this time more urgently and Siana suddenly felt an uneasiness of her own...looked over to Mosi who said:

"Maggie says to stop, Siana."

They had stayed in town for a while after she got off shift and picked up the kids at school. They said they wanted hamburgers and French fries with extra junk food for the dogs...

"...Smudge likes his hamburgers with lots of those pickle slices..."

There was still plenty of light left in the day but the desert was just starting to turn gold in late afternoon. Siana looked at Mosi who nodded soberly and she downshifted... slowed the Beetle down to a crawl finally stopping in the middle of the dirt track, engine idling. Maggie whispered to Flower and she pointed and said:

"Somebody's visiting," and leaned forward between them.

"How d'you know, honey?"

"The dust is still jumping, Cat-Mama," whispered Maggie from the back seat

Siana turned, gave her the facial equivalent of *Huh?* and then followed the line of Flower's forefinger out past the windscreen where she saw...absolutely nothing but what was always out there—scree-littered desert...outcroppings of razour-edged rock...rock worn smooth by the wind and sand...sunlight building shadows with a big orange ball dropping lower on the horizon.

Maggie wriggled past Mosi in her passenger seat reaching for the door handle and half-falling into the dirt as she struggled out of the car, walking in front cautiously until she knelt down in the roadbed about fifty feet away. Everyone followed her.

"You can see," whispered Maggie.

Siana didn't see anything but everyday...the same things they saw every afternoon

coming back from town.

"What're you lookin' at, honey?"

Maybe it came out too sharp-edged. Maggie jumped a little bit and looked for Flower's hand. Mosi tried to soothe her.

"Whattaya see, Maggie?"

The little girl pointed again and now Siana could see another set of tire tracks slowly being shifted into non-existence by errant breaths of wind...tracks that didn't belong to Siana's Volkswagen or John's truck out here in their small corner of the desert it was suddenly obvious that someone *was* visiting, though how Maggie had known was one more mystery the twins shared between them. The problem was that Siana knew the "somebody visiting" was not good somebody, could feel her sense of uneasiness churning into the certainty of a shitstorm to come; that after today she could stop waiting.

"Mosi I want you t'take the Bug off the road... someplace where you can't see it from here...and stay there...and if I'm not back by sundown or you don't see a car coming back this way you're gonna have to camp out here for the night...or go back t'town for help..."

Mosi's eyes started to grow dark with terror, an unspoken question.

"I don't know exactly, Cat," Siana said, "but I know it's not good. You guys gotta hide out for a while. Will you do that?"

Mosi nodded. Maggie and Flower clutched at each other, got wide-eyed...

"I'm gonna walk in from here. Take care of each other...okay?"

This time all three of them nodded. Mosi started crying...soundlessly. The twins wrapped themselves around Siana's waist.

Siana said, "I love you... all of you...so much... Thank you for saving me."

Mosi would not speak, only stepped up close to her...looked up at her for a moment before she took her face in both hands and kissed her on the mouth.

Siana swallowed hard and turned away...started walking...

⚜

Three quarters of an hour later, jogging up onto the rim of the small bowl that enclosed the house and pens, all now cast in deepening shadow. She could see the goats and sheep milling behind the fencing...edging their way nervously into the lean-tos and sheds...the little pinto that had just magicked into existence one afternnoon now dancing on the outermost edges of his paddock...and a white "64 Thunderbird ragtop with California plates parked sideways across the path between John's truck and the door.

She blinked into the westering sun...closed her eyes...

The gunshot was short and loud in the silence... echoes swallowed up by the dark coming down she tried not to howl into the dusk...drew a couple of deep breaths...and then started to zigzag her way down the slope to the house. When she got close she made enough noise so they would know she was coming...took one more breath before she opened the door and stepped inside.

⚜

There were two of them, identical for all the small differences between them made in the cold-eyed stares that narrowed on her... both of them were about six feet tall...surf-boys...blond and blue-eyed, no doubt great fucks as long as they got their way. One of them stripped her with one look.

"I can see how he got stupid over you."

She said: "He was dumbfuck stupid t'start with," and gratefully found John behind them, tied to a chair...but No-Name Dog was bleeding out at his feet.

"If you do any more damage here you're never gonna see your shit. If you wanna most of your thinking with your dicks I don't really give a damn...but nobody else here is gonna pay, otherwise kiss it goodbye for good..."

The second one looked over his shoulder at John and said, "How 'bout I start with his knees...maybe a hand or an eye...?"

"How about you both can go fuck yourselves twice I can't stop you...but in the end you're still not gonna see your snow and you're not gonna find it unless I show you where it is..."

She watched them mulling that over, an undercurrent of rage in blank shark stares. She looked past them...to John...

"Are you okay?" she asked, used his real name. He nodded. Siana begged forgiveness with her eyes and he shrugged. She could hear him absolving her of all responsibility...

This is what was meant to be...I will miss you...I love you...

She remembered the day they learned to love each other in a way that was best for their souls...when she offered something else and he said no but thank you...

I don't let anyone see me cry either...

Surf boys were getting restless.

"How the fuck do we know you're not full o' shit?"

Siana smiled.

"Can't help you with that, blondie. I know what I did wasn't very bright but we can fix it if you're smarter than you look.

"And how is *Trevor*? He could go all night when he wasn't too fucked up with all the coke and whatever else he was stealin' from you. I could always see myself in his eyes because there was so little else behind them."

She smiled again, because now she knew she had stepped into a place where there was nothing left to lose and the surf boys were only thinking in dollar signs. She could see them processing pros and cons and actually trying not to give in to the urge to beat the crap out of her and worse.

The first one said, "Trevor's fuckin' dead. Where are we goin'?"

Siana said:

"Back home. Big Sur. That's where I stashed your stuff..."

She nodded once to John before she let them frog-march her back to the ragtop... tie her hands before they dumped her into the back seat.

2.

Two days driving. She led them back to the hollow where she had parked the Volkswagen in another lifetime, climbed out of the bucket seat the colour of dried blood with a nine millimeter handgun pressed into the base of her spine. She turned slowly and said:

UNTIL THE END OF THE WORLD

"Here we are..."

"Don't fuck with us, cunt...where is it?"

She shrugged over her shoulder, carefully looked both ways like her Daddy had taught her to do whenever she crossed a street. She realised she should never have just run off without saying goodbye to him...that she had become just one more heartbreak in his life and now he would never know how much being his special girl had meant to her.

She led them across the highway and down through scrub and twisted cypress gone like willow in the wind off the Pacific. When they came to the top of the cliffs she stopped...on the edge of nowhere...breathless and breathing in the delirious salt smell of the ocean going on endlessly into the deep blue sky and the clouds starting to turn gold with a young sunrise just behind them, filling the early morning with soft loving light.

"Down there," she said quietly, nodding down to the beach where the sand had clung to her and then whispered away as the afternoon heat had dried her wet skin. "Y'see the spur of rock at the base of that cliff? I buried it there."

"You're full of shit, bitch.

"Fine," she said. "Your call..."

"Keep it up and you can say goodbye to whoever else was livin' with that old red nigger back on the reserve."

"Good luck with that. Whoever else you're talking about will run your stupid white-bread asses into the desert where the coyotes'll strip your bones and the crows will mix fuckin' martinis with your tiny little surfer-boy balls for onions..."

She'd been hit in the face like that twice before in her life, and even though her legs went out from under her and she ended up on her knees between them she could begin to see where it was all going....could hear a clock ticking in her brain. The backhand hadn't been meant to put her out, just to let her know they meant business...to prove they were in charge.

They thought they'd hurt her...that the tears on her face were there because now she was scared...ready to cooperate. To herself she said *Go fuck yourselves, you dumb-ass jock motherfucker dickheads*...got back on her feet... taking her time so the cobwebs would go away and the blood pounding through her head would slow down...just enough...again she said:

"I buried it down there," with a catch in her voice... head down so they'd think now they had her terrified and willing to do anything they wanted. "I'll climb down... I'll get it..."

The wind rippled across the headland, danced her hair in a silver cloud around her head. Up above on the highway she heard a transport go rushing by, then the whisper of swallows darting through the trees. She blinked away more tears...the ones for John, No-Name Dog...Smudge...for Mosi and the twins...the little brown-and-white lamb bouncing around for the very first time on newly-discovered legs. Her father. She scuffed her way out of her boots...unsnapped her jeans and stripped them off...

"What the fuck are you doin'...?"

The clock in her head wound down to sixty seconds...then thirty...

UNTIL THE END OF THE WORLD

"I can't climb in these...they get snagged on the rocks..."

Reached down and pulled her t-shirt up over her head...slowly...fifteen seconds...so they'd both have a good long look at her breasts...ten seconds...

"And y'know...I really think we should do this together."

...So they weren't looking at her hands when they went into their waistbands and she dragged them all backwards into the light of the new-rising sun.

MIRANDA MOON

for Dolly

1.

"...I guess it's just the two of us now, baby brother," she said softly.

She kept her eyes on the road but looked away just long enough to see tears glistening on his cheeks he was crying...soundlessly...

"Manda, how come people die?"

She swallowed hard and clenched her teeth together, slowed down a little bit as the tires on the right side of the Toyota plowed through some snow that had drifted off the shoulder on Route 9. Then the pines and spruce closed in on them again and the road was clear, dry white salt patterns cold-etched over the blacktop. The sky was all overcast and grey around them, the sun just a faint promise behind the clouds.

"We just do, honey," she whispered. "We get old or we get sick or we have accidents and that's what happens."

He asked every time, even for animals, and she was never ready with anything more than what she knew was, at best, no explanation at all, because he wasn't asking about the mechanics of Death, the physical end-product-everybody's-doing-it destination of Life. He wanted to know the all-encompassing cosmic fucking *why*... and she might just as well have been honest and told him that she didn't have a clue, because that part of it was as much a mystery to her as it had ever been to him.

"I miss Mom and Dad a lot. Paul...and Smoky so much...I miss everybody."

"Me too, Oliver," she said. "Me too."

It felt like yesterday...had started with their older brother...a drunk driver in Tucson running a red light and their older brother thrown a hundred feet from the wreckage of his Harley. Then it was the stroke that killed their mother...and two years after that, grief that got fatal for their father when it made him careless with a chainsaw, taking trees down behind their cottage on the lake. She thought after that maybe they could be safe for just a little while...but three days ago their older sister... Lisa...five weeks after the doctor had found the cancer in her pancreas and it was over. Suddenly...it felt that way... suddenly all the Woodroffes were gone and it was just her and Oliver.

"Don't die, Manda."

"I'm gonna try like hell not to, sweetheart," she said.

"And you're still gonna be my sister?"

"Of course I am, honey," she said, and was grateful the stretch of Route 9 west of Hillsboro in front of them had no curves because she closed her eyes and had to suck the snot back up her nose and pretend her heart wasn't maybe finally breaking beyond repair.

"And you're always gonna be my brother...and Uncle Oliver for Lisa's kids..."

Oliver's sweet little brain had stopped growing somewhere around eight or nine years old. He still wept for the baby raccoon had died in front of their cottage years ago... and Smoky, their yappy happy Keeshond.

"Manda...?"

"Yeah, honey."

"I'm sorry. I didn't mean to make you cry I'll be quiet okay?"

She nodded. Rubbed her nose with the sleeve of her parka. He got hungry so they stopped in Keene for hamburgers at McDonalds and fifteen miles later picked up I-91 in Brattleboro and headed south. An hour after that they arced round a dogleg in the Connecticut River, took exit 19 onto Bridge Street in Northampton, crawled past the park and playground, and came to rest in the driveway of their small house on Walnut Street.

Miranda said, "Home again home again."

Oliver had already pretty much forgotten the cemetery in Concord, or why they had gone there in the first place.

2.

The next day they went back to the small school she had opened just for him...fighting for accreditation so she could, at the very least, map the potentials of children like her brother...find ways for them to survive once they were grown beyond the safety nets of their childhood.

Oliver was the best thing about her school. Never having surrendered his innocence to cynicism, adulthood, or the harsh realities of Western capitalism, he was the one who most often made the connect with the kids who came to them. He served as the gentle reassuring soul between them and the small staff, managed communication miracles where PhDs and all the clinical studies in the world could find no way to breach the walls of fear, chemical imbalance or physical short-circuiting that came with each new face.

Oliver had been her *raison d'etre,* the driving force behind her BA at UMass Amherst, the Masters from Clark and the doctorate at NYU, all in search of answers and solutions to the whats and whys of lost children…the cruel twists of Fate and physiology that often brought them into the world already damaged, in places where nothing and no one could ever reach them. Oliver was the soul of her crusade, had become the love of her life, because he needed everything she had to give, and she remembered the awful moment she realised he would never stop being the sweet little boy who had filled up most of her life through high school; that more than anything else in her life, it had become important to her for him to be able to stay that way.

"Miranda…?"

She shook her head, focused on the face leaning past the door of her office—a Saudi refugee she'd met during her post-grad work in New York City. Small and fierce in the freedoms she'd won by leaving Arabia, Rajiya Barakat was a different kind of crusader, with degrees in sociology, Middle Eastern studies and business administration, most grateful for American citizenship because it allowed her fiery activism to flourish unchallenged by the societal constraints of her homeland. She wore her short-cropped head of dark hair and her blue jeans proudly, regarded trendy trappings with a sneering disdain, and was utterly fearless when it came to standing up to red tape, racism or intolerance of any kind. She managed the clinic's day-to-day, kept it running smoothly for Miranda and the children.

"I knocked a couple of times are you okay?"

She had a heart-shaped face and almost-black eyes lit with a watchful, protective wariness that never seemed to waver where her friends and responsibilities were concerned. Miranda shuffled some papers in self-defense, mustered a smile.

"Yeah mostly," she said. "Come on in, Jiya."

"You guys could've taken the rest of the week off, y'know…we can run the place a few days without you."

She flung herself down into one of the comfy chairs in front of Miranda's desk, and her eyes went a bit softer than their usual ready-for-action brightness. "How's Ollie doing?"

Miranda shrugged, laughed uncomfortably. "Oliver's doing Oliver," she said quietly. "Sometimes it seems like his brain just goes into this savant-like overdrive and he remembers everything. Then he starts to grieve all over again, like the memories are too grown-up for the rest of him. This morning he was fine again."

"So then how're *you* doing, Miranda?"

She mulled that question over a couple of times, taking too long to come up with an answer, to where Rajiya leaned forward and started to look worried.

"I don't know how I'm doing, Jiya," she said. "No idea, really. Numbed out, maybe? It doesn't matter. I'm dealing with it, and I can't let losing Lisa get in the way of me being all here for Oliver and everybody else."

Rajiya leaned closer. "You can and you should if you need to. Everyone here knows the drill, and we're all more than capable of making sure it gets done."

"I know that, Jiya, it's not even an issue."

"So...?"

"It's just that this is my life. I loved my parents and my brother and my sister, but I got to take care of Ollie because I was the youngest, and then I made the decision to keep on taking care of him. And after that...I didn't stop loving them when they were alive or after they were gone, but the nature of what I chose to do by necessity put some kind of distance between us. I'm gonna cry for Lisa and my mom and dad and my brother some other time. Right now is right now, and right now I guess I'm all right."

"You're gonna tell me if that changes though..."

They got up from their chairs together and met beside the desk, arms encircling each other.

"I promise, Jiya. I swear it. Thank you."

Rajiya spoke in Arabic. " *'Ahlan bitawajudik dayiman 'ukhti* . You are welcome always, my sister..."

3.

There was always paperwork, the clinical kind that Rajiya would have done happily if she had decided to get qualified for it with another couple of post-graduate degrees. Miranda always bitched about having to do it, would have preferred to have had more time working with the kids, but as her office manager had said, the staff she had hand-picked knew the drill, could do the work, and never failed to come to her to discuss every aspect of what they were trying to do.

Mark came through her door with his classroom/session reports for the previous week, forever eleventh-hour on the mid-week deadline they all had agreed upon, but every bit as ferocious about their children as Rajiya was about all of them. Six months before, after she'd told him that sleeping together wasn't the best idea if they were going to work together too, he'd moved on, but his charming smile and genuine warmth had never left their relationship so there had been some extra time spent with her...some Lisa stories...a red-and-white bandanna offered when she finally did let some tears out. When he was gone she was thinking about someone else she'd known who was so much just like him, bandanna and all. After Mark came her Oliver...serious...a frown on his face...

"Hi Manda I can't remember. What's for lunch today?"

"It's Wednesday, right?"

"I think so." He leaned over her desk to look at the big desk-blotter calendar with all of her scrawls and notes on it. "Yeah it's Wednesday...I think..."

"Then it's tuna sandwiches with soup."

"Do we have the potato chips and pickles to go with, like always?"

Miranda started to smile and then she started to laugh.

"C'mere and gimme a hug, Ollie," she said, standing to get wrapped up in one of his enthusiastic embraces. "As far as I know we got everything, honey. What's with all the questions?"

UNTIL THE END OF THE WORLD

He stood away from her, looked out the window. Got real interested in a pair of chickadees wrangling over seeds in the feeder she'd perched on the outdoor sill.

"I just wanted t'make sure," he said, still looking at the birds on the windowsill, but showing signs of relief that making sure had turned out the way it did.

"So are you gonna be the one to pick some music for us today, or should I get Mark or Abby t'do that?"

He gave her one last squeeze and headed for the door.

"Abby picks good stuff," he said. "See ya later..."

Most of the rest of the morning went by quietly. Phone calls....referrals...parents checking in...after one last call Miranda put the desk phone receiver back in its cradle and eased back from her desk...thinking again... bandannas...a day long gone...

She reached down past her feet for her purse on the floor, suddenly frantic that what she suddenly was looking for wouldn't be there even though the last time it had been there when she hadn't been looking for it at all...

Two sheets of lined paper carefully torn from a pocket notebook, carefully folded and hidden between her Social Security card and a photograph of Mom and Dad and Paul and Lisa all crowded round her and Oliver at their cottage on Newfound Lake. Pencilled poetry from a visitor when she was still an undergraduate at Amherst...

Childhood eyes transparent with innocence
Step lightly sweet child the garden crawls
Each moment in Life another for Death

MICHAEL SUMMERLEIGH

A sunset for my Life with every breath
Kiss me gently sweet child before sinking
Your teeth in passion it"s all guaranteed
I dream to be all the wings you need
Together to fly...together to get high...
No better way in any world to die

The words brought back images...a tall beautiful boy with long black hair and grey eyes flecked with gold...an afternoon spent together...listening to music on the stereo. She had been knitting gloves or a scarf or something for Oliver; he had sat on the floor almost at her feet...told her how pretty she was...seemed sad...the way she had started to feel as they sat in their constrained silences...waiting...

There are no more heroes in this desperate land
When they come to lay waste to our garden
There will be no one between us & them
The flowers will sigh one last time
And then there will be only exile
And sinful night-roaming under the moon
Elysium is there...waiting for us somewhere.
Streams swell into rivers to fuck with the sea
Sunlight is honey...the taste of you in me

She remembered how it had all seemed so familiar, how easy it had been to sit there and confide...say things she'd not had time or courage to say to anyone else...and how the look in his eyes had made her feel that she was something precious to him even though they'd only just met...

What knowledge have I of saints & patriots?
What need for a standard to bear

When Elysium awaits us so wondrously fair...
Sweet child with transparent eyes
Shall we go now across the Bridge of Sighs
To be running free on golden sand
To love and make love hand in hand
Elysium is there...
Waiting...

She folded the papers back into its place in her wallet, and put her wallet back in her purse...

4.

Just before lunchtime Abigail came roaring into her office, all sorts of hippie-*chic* with bells sewn into the hems of her vintage-store denim trousers and the distinct aura of Aquarius in her waist-length hair.

"You gotta come see this, Miranda," she said... grinning...dodging round the desk to grab her hand.

"Oliver just did it again," she said...now laughing... shaking her head like it was something that happened every day where her brother was concerned. She dragged them out into the hall and down towards the common room where they served meals, had all the group sessions and the big screen television on one wall for after supper...

"I was sitting down with the new kid...Jimmy Rossiter...the one come in last Saturday...right before you...you know... Lisa...?"

She stopped in mid-stride halfway down the hall... turned...Miranda said:

"It's okay Abby what the hell...?"

Abby just said: "Tiffany Brewer."

Who had been with them since the end of the summer...speechless...cowering in the corner of her room never leaving it without hours of reassurance no one was ever sure she had heard. Abby brought them up short of the common room and pointed...at Oliver... sitting with a thirteen-year old girl...round-faced with big haunted eyes and ragged blonde hair...wrapped up in one of her brother's bear-hugs....

"I was talking with Jimmy...talking *to* Jimmy...you know, our usual trying to find out where the boundaries are...an idea of where to go...

"And suddenly I'm hearing this voice I've never heard before and I look over and holy shit it's Tiffany... she's crying, 'Randa...she's sobbing and *talking* to Ollie...!"

"No way!"

"Yes fucking yes, Miranda! She's leaning up against him with his arms around her and she's weeping...crying...wailing...I heard her she said *Why do they all go away I hate it when they go away they don't care they just go...*

"She's been here for months, Abby. Not a sound. What happened?"

Abigail shook her head. "Oliver. I don't know..."

5.

"Shit," said Miranda. "What have we done to ourselves that loss can turn some things into life-shattering catastrophes?"

Abigail just shook her head. "How long have we been doing this, Randa? D'you think I've figured it out? Good luck."

UNTIL THE END OF THE WORLD

They sat in Miranda's office, considered the ramifications of challenged... retarded...Oliver doing something they themselves couldn't do, not with years and years of...education...and just sat in Miranda's office, each of them measuring the length and breadth of their own catastrophes. Years and years of them. They'd been best friends for a long long time.

"Abby, when we were at Amherst. D'you remember? It was like right about now, the middle of winter. I knocked on your door first thing in the morning and you let me sleep in your dorm room for two days..."

Abby said, "Never gonna forget. That sonofabitch Dorn dosed you. A big fucking dose of acid..."

Miranda nodded. "It was like somebody was trying to tear me out of my skin and chew me up there was this huge empty place in front of me and I was getting sucked down into it to die in all that horrible emptiness...and there was this guy...his name was Joshua... Dorn had brought him back from some dope sell in upstate New York. He saved me Abby...this beautiful boy who didn't know me from a hole in the wall he saved me... stayed with me out in the snow all night and he held me and talked to me and made me tell him stories about Oliver and in the morning he called me Miranda Moon and made sure that there was nothing to hurt me and nobody to carry me away he handed my life back to me, Abby... in the morning...he did...he gave it back to me so I could go on taking care of my baby brother and do this with you and Mark and Jiya..."

"I remember..."

"Where would Tiffany have gone...who would she have found...where could she have left the hurt if Ollie hadn't been there t'help her leave it behind...?"

"You know I can't tell you that, Randa. I don't have those kind of answers. My parents would have said God was working in mysterious ways."

"We don't need that kind of mystery in our lives."

"Preaching t'the choir, girlfriend."

"I know. It just makes me crazy sometimes...the way it almost always comes down to this hit-or-miss equation..."

"It happened, Miranda. When it did. It's gotta be good for Tiffany."

"I hope so. Oliver doesn't even realise..."

"Maybe he does, Miranda. Maybe it doesn't have t'be something consciously recognised by anybody. What matters is he found a bridge...a way through all the desolation in that girl's heart..."

Abigail went back out into the world a couple of minutes later. Miranda was sitting at her desk staring at the chickadees still being pissy with each other...kicking up fluffs of snow on the windowsill, their squeaks stealing through the double-paned glass she looked up and Oliver was standing in the doorway.

"I'm sorry Manda I was listening," he said apologetically.

"It's okay, honey," she said. "No secrets...never any secrets for us, right? You're my magic, honey. You're so good. I don't know what me or anybody here would do without you."

Oliver looked embarrassed.

"I remember that guy Dorn. He had blonde curly hair. He made you cry a lot."

Miranda nodded back. "He did, Oliver, he most certainly did..."

"I didn't know he did that bad thing to you, though."

She smiled at him, as hard as she could because he looked worried...because his sense of Time was as off-kilter as everything else in his brain and it seemed like maybe he was thinking the *bad thing* had been yesterday...or so recent that *he* needed to be doing something to make up for it.

"It was a long time ago, sweetheart," she said. "Not something you have to worry about. I'm okay. And that guy Joshua took good care of me."

"I woulda took care of you too."

"I know that, baby," she said. "You would've liked Joshua. He would've liked you."

"D'you know where he is now?"

"No, Ollie, I don't...he had to go home the next day and I never saw him again."

"Could you find him maybe...I wanna say thank you."

"Why d'you wanna do that, honey?"

"Because he saved you when you were gonna die, when you were afraid the dark was gonna swallow you up and take you away..."

He stopped...looked up at her with his beautiful innocent face...the eyes of a child...struggling with the words for one last thought.

"Because if you were ever gone, I don't think I would know enough stuff by myself to be here now." He leaned over and kissed her cheek. "I should go see if Tiffany is okay. I told her today we were having tuna fish with soup and potato chips and pickles and if she would come out of her room for lunch I'd sit with her so she wouldn't be scared."

Miranda watched her fifty-five year old baby brother toddle off to save another soul from the darkness.

THE CHEWING GUM GOD

"....Really...sometimes she's like Jimi's Dolly."

It had been so long since they'd spent any real time together it took almost half an instant to process...to make the previously-instantaneous leap to Hendrix... *Dolly Dagger*...

"Her love makes you stagger."

It was a statement of nebulous even dubious fact, waiting for the current definition of *heavy* from her twin brother. She was surprised to find herself suddenly... *annoyed*...rather than mock-maternally amused as usual. She was, after all, almost ten minutes older...

"Jamie," she said slowly, "you...are being...a fucking asshole..."

Each word was measured and careful...she had always tried to be honest with him...but never cruel...

"She puts up with *so* much shit from you."

It was his turn for surprise, that she would take side against him...not offer immediate consolation she was, after all, his big sister...

"You're not serious?" he asked incredulously. "Ran you're kidding, right?"

She shook her head, said only:

"No."

He wagged his head twice. Beneath the still handsome face worn by years—and too much of everything come with them—to a less than pristine nobility, she could sense confusion in the spun-gold-gone-to-grey brows knit together... and then an almost frantic dismay.

"Ranna...?"

She turned away from him. Refused to let him see that for what she just now had inflicted upon him, she had in one sense damaged herself as deeply...and consciously became aware of something she had known in her heart for a long time.

"Jamie how many times has she waited up all night for you? Have you ever stopped to count them? Have you ever stopped to think how she would feel, knowing you were out fucking someone else?"

He was stunned into silence. She could see him turning it over in his mind as if there were a real possibility it never had occurred to him before. It made her sad that he could be that way...to have spent sixty-plus years on the earth bound to him by their birth without ever having taken notice...

"She's half your age and there's nothing wrong with that but she trusted you, Jamie...to be whoever it was she was looking for...and almost from Day One you treated her so badly...carelessly...just like everyone else before her, except out of all of them she's the one who really doesn't deserve it at all."

As she had done so many times before when he was hurt she wanted to put her arms around him and tell him *Things are okay little brother okay we've still got each other*...but today she couldn't do it...today something had changed...

They sat drinking whiskey before dinner, watching the sunset splash crimson and gold down across the lake, listening to steaks sizzling on the barbecue and Canada geese coming home in great honking arrows overhead. All around and below them down to the shoreline the pines were deepening into dark green, the ash and the maple and the birches beginning to leaf, growing joyous with the fresh flood of life coming up from the ground.

He shifted in his deck chair, leaned over and refilled his glass from the bottle of Mortlach on the railing of the porch. The dog snuffled in his sleep, wriggled higher up on his instep to discourage any further movement. Jamie drank two fingers'-worth in one swallow, took another sip and stared out at the shadows where the sun could no longer go...brooding now...trying to find something to say in response to what she knew he felt was a betrayal.

The day before, he'd phoned her from Halifax, told her he was coming for a visit; that he'd be flying into Toronto that night and would see her in the morning in time for brunch. Just after eleven she heard the engine of his rental revving out of the village and started walking out towards the road to meet him, the big Pyrie dog padding along beside her, checking the wind for intruders. Minutes later she waved him down as he raced by her in a red metal-flake Ferrari, did a perfect hand-brake 180 less than a hundred yards down the road and rumbled back to where she stood at the unpaved drive to the lakeside cottage. The Great

Pyrenees stood to her hips, growling ominously. Her brother rolled his window down.

"You told me you'd gotten a dog, not a small horse," he said. "Who's this?"

"I call him Jon Snowball, the bastard son of another big white dog. Put your hand out the window."

"I still need it."

"You use your right hand. Shut up and let him smell you."

She turned to the dog. "Snow, this is my baby brother Jamie Roderick Craigen. Don't bite him unless I say so."

The small horse masquerading as a dog sniffed outstretched fingers suspiciously, settled back against her leg. She nodded back over her shoulder.

"It's about an eighth of a mile in, but go slow or you'll take the bottom out of your fancy car. I'll walk back with Snow..."

He'd brought three bottles of champagne and orange juice and a swanky bag full of expensive finger foods from an airport clip-joint. They drank two of the bottles and got a little bit stupid together it had been over a year since she'd seen him...and if she had not happened to glance into her own mirror earlier that morning she would have been more than a little bit unsettled to see that he had grown older, no longer her stunningly beautiful seemingly ageless twin brother.

After the champagne had worn off some he asked for a tour, never having visited her new digs before, and she took him along the pathways and overlooks that had seduced her from the moment she had laid eyes on the property...then drawn him into the separate outbuilding a stone's throw from the cottage that could have been another house but was instead one large studio space, with north-facing skylights and windows and a wood stove she swore kept itself banked for whenever she felt the urge to bang hell out of a piece of stone or slap paint on a canvas.

She had always been able to impress him by the mere fact that while they shared so many of the same sensibilities...likes and dislikes...only she had been the one to translate talent into vision and creativity. She could tell by the way he ran his hands over the sculptures, reached to within a hair's-breadth of her paintings, that he was both proud and a little bit envious.

"I've got a show in town in August," she told him. "Anything and everything I care to have shipped down. You and Tess should come..."

He was cuddling up to a half-size nude in pink marble that was at the far end of the room so she didn't quite catch his response, but his tone spoke volumes and presaged a topic of conversation to come. They went back to the house for the last bottle of champagne and headed down to the lakeside...uncorked the bubbly and plonked into a pair of Adirondack chairs at the water's edge.

"Snow helped me drag them out here yesterday morning. I think he knew you were coming."

"This is a ways out from civilisation, big sister," he said without too much concern. "I haven't seen any neighbours. Don't you get a bit strung out with the quiet?"

She smiled quietly and sipped her champagne. Overhead the sky was impossibly blue streaked with thin tatters of clouds that seemed frozen between winter and the threat of warmth. They watched the first loons come paddling across the still surface of the water, making ripples that lapped soundlessly at their feet...listened to the first whippoorwills mindlessly cooing through the still air.

"I've got my small horse," she said contentedly, "and I'm only five miles from the village where I know everyone and they know me. There's some truly good people in around here, Jamie...another painter on the other side of the lake. I've got people dropping by all the time, and since we've been lucky to have been born with silver horseshoes up our arses I have all the comfort and luxury of living in town without all the fuss and the stink and the noise."

Again she caught that faint whiff of envy coming off him. He didn't begrudge her anything, she knew that for a fact...but he was jealous of her being at peace with the world. He got up suddenly, startled Snow into a warning growl at her feet, but showed him his hands and turned away to the lake, knelt and starting skipping slivers of shale across the water.

"What's goin' on, little brother?" she asked. "You didn't come out here to throw stones in my lake..."

And he had made a face at her...rueful...suggested they finish the champagne and then go back up to the house...put potatoes in the oven to bake...dragged themselves out onto the porch with the single malt in tow and thrown a pair of monster steaks on the barbecue. Ranna had waited...wounded him...waited some more...went inside and put an old McKendree Spring album into the CD player...came back outside and waited some more. Jamie wouldn't look at her now...

"I just don't know what t'do," he said plaintively. "You know Tess...she's sweet and smart and lovely and we fuck like bunnies..."

"But."

"But it's too much, Ran! I feel this weight of her love on me, and I don't mean to hurt her but it's too goddamn much....her expectations...me trying to live up to whatever the hell it is I'm supposed t'be for her. With us it was always so easy..."

She could have wept for him...understanding... knowing exactly what he meant...how he must feel. Inside on the stereo Fran McKendree tried to break her heart by singing to her brother...

"If I gave you everything you wanted...would I be the one who'd have t'cry..."

...And then it was her turn to look away because she didn't want him to see her crying for him...didn't want to chance falling back into something that had not been wrong but had not been right either and giving him some reason to believe she was still the one who would make his life sunshine-and-roses for him.

"Ranna. I need to ask you something okay?"

And she knew what was coming...had been waiting for it all day for almost fifty years...

"D'you remember in '70 when we did that music festival?"

"We went to a lot of them that summer, Jamie."

"You know which one I mean...the last one..."

"I know. The Isle of Wight."

"It was never the same after that," he said.

"You mean we never shared the same bed again."

"Yeah."

For a moment she remembered what it had been like when they were sixteen... running away all over Europe...cash-proud...clinging to each other totally fucked up and happy... and one weekend in amongst another six hundred thousand people crammed onto a tiny island off the south coast of England. Like it was almost yesterday she could taste the freedom of being out in the world totally free with her beautiful baby brother and the way he tasted when he kissed her or they leaned against each other swaying in slow stupid dances together in the sun and the rain it had all seemed exactly the way it should be....

"How's Mom?" she asked. Somehow it seemed like a relevant question.

"Remembering less and less. It took her a while to figure out who I was the last time I saw her. She doesn't remember Dad anymore...but the time before that out of the blue she said you had told her..."

Ranna whispered back.

"She asked and there wasn't any point in lying to her because she knew. Jamie I'm pretty sure she knew right from the start. Never mind beds that didn't get slept in, all you had t'do was look at us in our rags and tatters...finishing each other's sentences... trading secrets without even talking...fucking off all over the place for weeks at a time. There was no way she didn't know..."

He nodded, and she forced herself to meet his gaze because after a lifetime it was time for a Truth between them, far too important to allow herself the cowardice of looking away when she told him.

"I don't know how it happened, Jamie. We were so stoned and stunned with the music and I hadn't planned anything at all but I sort of woke up behind the stage and walked right into him...touched his face... He never said a word. I put my fingers in the waistband of his trousers because I was all tottery after bumping into him and he looked down at me for a second before he put an arm around my shoulders and leaned on me a little bit, like he was really tired..."

Now she had to look away...could see the worst damage was already done...that the rest would be just as hurtful but nothing she wanted to see.

"They had played for almost two hours and I remember watching his hands and his fingers...how they were so ferocious...tearing the music out of his guitar strings...but you could see...you just knew...when he was done...when the music was over...then they would be so light and gentle with each touch that I wanted to scream for more than just being teased.

"The skin on his belly was so smooth and silky...his skin was sweet like chocolate cream...with veins running down into his crotch. I never saw them in the dark but I could feel them under my tongue...

"He was the best night of my life Jamie...I'm sorry...better than we could ever have been because we were just following up on the outside what we'd been on the inside, before we were born...but *he had no idea who I was I was a total stranger to him*...and he knew for a fact he'd never lay eyes on me again...but nobody since has ever been that brand new sweet and generous as he was to me that night. He was so tired but it was never about him...and in the morning when he kissed me goodbye he *thanked* me. He smiled that shy little smile and *he thanked me...*"

She heard his breath catch in his throat, could feel him straining not to cry out loud.

"Little brother we're so fucking old now please let's stop playing at this. I know it's not a game to you I know you're not heartless, but we're all bearing the weight of something on our souls. You're not the only one. At least admit it to her face...apologise if you're really sorry...don't pretend if you're not..."

She got up...staggered a bit with all the alcohol... turned the steaks over on the barbecue and then knelt down in front of him forcing him to look at her she held his face in her hands.

"I know we're both missing pieces...somehow we both lost the one where we find real true love forever and a day...but after that night I realised even one day with someone could be enough, and that searching for something that might not even exist might ruin my life. Maybe we could have been what we were forever, but the reality is that the world was running out of time for the life we were living...our little bubble of peace love and happiness...and one of us...maybe both...would have started to wonder what it was like outside the bubble.

"I'm so sorry it wasn't that way for you. I never meant to cut you loose like that I thought you could work it out same as me..."

They ate supper slowly, quietly, in candlelight. Chopin just barely heard on the stereo.

The dog seemed to understand that something long unspoken had finally come into the light and found a small if grudging measure of acceptance; stretched out in front of the fireplace he twitched and snuffled in counterpoint to a piano prelude. Jamie kept his eyes down she could see him trying to process through all the years...put all of his feelings into the context of what he too had known all along. She wanted so much to touch him, hold onto him the way she used to, because even with the one transcendent night that had sustained her understanding of self and the world around her, and all the lovers and friends who had followed...there always came a night spent sleepless with longing for the innocence and the senseless joy of what they had shared.

"However it ends, Jamie, try to be kind. That's what I learned from him. All it's really about is the kindness..."

Later that night she heard him on the telephone in her guestroom...talking to Tess... crying...trying to explain... asking her if it was all right to come home. In the morning she made coffee and fresh-baked bread...saying nothing...both of them starting all over again in a different way.

In the moring he said, "I'm gonna go, Ranna."

She nodded, picked up his overnighter and walked him out to the car...walked alongside with Snow until they reached the road.

"Drive careful, Jamie. Travel safely. Hug your lovely girl for me."

"It drove me crazy that he chewed gum all the time."

She leaned down through the window to kiss him softly on the lips.

"Not with me," she said, and smiled. "Promise me you'll be okay from now on."

He said he'd try. Snow chased a rabbit back toward the house. She waved once, watched the Ferrari kicking dust clouds off the pavement, stood listening until she heard the car downshift through the village.

IN TRANSIT

Aaron looked around at the empty apartment...sunrise through naked windows setting newly-emancipated dust motes to dancing...a table and a chair...the laboured hum of the old refrigerator now reprieved from cooling anything at all...

In the freezer was a small glass vial that he put in his pocket...picked up the small carry-bag with a toothbrush ...a cell phone...a change of clothing and two things he needed to put in the mail...he took one last look...from the doorway...closed the door and locked it before walking slowly down the stairs...one step at a time...slipped the key into the super's mail slot...

Outside it was already shaping up to be a scorcher... humid...heat from the day before that had been trapped in the city streets...now escaping into the brief cool of morning. In front of his apartment building he called a cab and then stood perfectly still...waiting... watched pigeons on the sidewalk across the street wrangling over a scrap of something...some finches arrowing around a bird-feeder on a window sill three floors up...

Some local kids poured out of a doorway...waved good morning he waved back...briefly wondered where they were off to at barely-past-five in the morning...then noticed the baseball gloves and the broom handles it was never too early for stickball when school was waiting in September...

Up over the rooftops the sky was blue, smudged white with wisps of cloud being lazy. He breathed in air still sleepy enough not to be spiced with diesel fumes or exhaust.

The city would wake up around him soon enough, but he intended to be well on his way way by lunchtime. He brushed some damp strands of hair from his face and slowly walked the half block to the mailbox on the corner...retraced his steps to wait for the cab.

When it arrived he handed the driver a twenty and gave him the address, nodded to the East Indian accent of *Good morning*...suddenly cautious with the twinge in his chest he tried to be polite...smiled when the bearded face beneath the turban made the connection and offered small-talk requiring no response from him...

In front of the hospital he said *Good luck sir* and Aaron thanked him...waved off the offered change back from his twenty and stood for moment to catch his breath...let the sudden pounding in his chest slow down a little before moving again...

When he turned he realised there was a man not far from the entrance to the hospital dressed in tattered camo...scarecrow thin...bearded...not as filthy as he could have been...still needing a place with some extra kindness and clean water. Aaron saw a small cardboard sign...hand-lettered with black marker...looked into the man's eyes and again reached for his wallet... emptied it...another twenty...a ten a five and three ones...

"Breakfast," he said softly. "There's enough for breakfast...and then the whisky afterwards. Have the first shot for both of us..."

He couldn't really say which war had been young enough to wound him, but the ageless ancient ravaged face for a moment softened and became human again... lips moved and whispered some gratitude. Aaron nodded and half-lifted his hand...flashed a peace sign...

"I was in the battle of Chicago," he said. "Nineteen sixty-eight. I wish we'd tried harder..."

Inside then, the candy-striper at the information desk was named Brianna...fresh-faced and cheerful he could smell soap and just a hint of something she might have dabbed on a day or two before...bright blue eyes...shiny blonde...he gave her his health card...

"Mister Standish?"

"That's me," said Aaron, another little twinge of heartache for the way she had called him Mister...not recognising the possibility there might still be a prospective suitor alive somewhere inside of him. "I'm lead-off today..."

"Six o'clock..."

"Triple bypass," he nodded.

Brianna reached for a folder and handed it back to him with his card, pointed him in the right direction for his last-minute prep and pep talks. He thanked her by name, so she would know he had noticed, and she wished him good luck...fresh-faced and cheerful...

He found a seat three or four removed from one of those occupied in the cardiac unit waiting room, put his bag on the chair beside him...still a bit winded. Even though they'd offered a wheelchair he had insisted on walking...

The air was hospital clean and sterile but there was the smell of perspiration anyway...and fear. Aaron looked at the guy three chairs away reading the newspaper... older... heavier...ferocious grey eyebrows over eyes chewing up the words on the page with some last-gasp bit of sustenance...a frenzy of intent to keep the terror at bay...

"I'm sure you're gonna be all right," he said, as kindly as possible...and realised he was calm and totally unafraid himself...somehow...and he should try to share some of it...

The older man looked up...angry as well as scared...

Aaron said, "Really...they're all very good here. Who've you got?"

"Andrews."

"He's doing me in a half hour," Aaron laughed. "He should be in the groove by the time he gets t'you."

"He's a prick."

"Well he *does* have a pretty good opinion of himself, but I hear he's the best of the bunch... except for his grasp of musical history..."

"Huh?"

Aaron tried to explain. "You got the whole prep talk, right? This is what we're gonna do...this is how long it's gonna take...blah blah blah...?"

"Yeah...I told him I been smokin' since I was twelve and he says t'me I better quit or I can find me another fuckin' doctor..."

"I sort of got that too...but when he was done he wanted t'know if *I* had any questions, so I said I had one and it was really important..."

"Yeah...so what happened?"

"I told him I needed to know if he knew who the lead singer for Jefferson Airplane was. He thought about it for few secnds and said Stevie Nicks. I said *Wrong!*...he was gonna have t'find me somebody else t'do my surgery."

"What'd that have t'do with it...?"

"Absolutely nothing. He looked at me like I'd lost my mind."

The old guy laughed...finally...coughed a smoker's cough into his fist.

"Well he's still a prick...not as bad as these fuckin' terrorists...or the bastards runnin' this country...but almost..."

He offered the other hand...introduced himself as Joe Pantiglione...plumber's union this number and that...

"My daughter was supposed t'meet me here but she's late as usual..."

"Not married?"

"She died two years ago. The cancer chewed her up. How 'bout you?"

Aaron shook his head ruefully. "Nope. Don't know how I managed it..."

"So you got anybody t'look after you when you get out...?"

Aaron shook his head again. "I'm on my own..."

Pantiglione looked at him as if he'd lost his mind. Aaron shrugged.

"I guess I'll just have t'go slow for a while..."

The nurse at the desk called his name and he stood up. He and Joe shook hands again. Joe said *Good luck maybe I'll see ya around* and Aaron leaned over, patted him on his knee and told him to count on it.

Sharon was all business as she led him down a corridor, indicated a curtained cubbie where he could change into the gown and told him she could get him something for hisr feet if he hadn't brought anything...the floors... germs...Aaron said thanks he was good.

"Nothing to eat?"

"Not since yesterday afternoon."

"So I just have to check all this before we get you ready to go...your wife is Sandra... daughter is Haley..."

Stocky and all business in her floral scrubs, Sharon rattled off telephone numbers and addresses and Aaron smiled and nodded it was all the same information he'd given them at the start...no changes.... When she was gone he slipped out of his clothing and into one gown facing front and another one facing back...

No hurry now...in the pipeline...he stuffed all of his clothing into his carry bag...kept the glass vial from his pants pocket...back out into the corridor for a moment he found a water fountain and quickly swallowed the three tabs of lysergic acid...took the empty vial and his wallet and his bag and walked barefoot back to the trash chute he had passed on his way down the hall...sat in another small waiting room...

UNTIL THE END OF THE WORLD

Waiting...hoping the acid wouldn't kick in too soon...so tired...thinking...

Of the girl he didn't marry. The daughter he never had. The Battle of Chicago... and how they had somehow managed to let things go so badly that after all this time gone it was worse then ever...the greed...the corruption...the hatred...the lies now as good a currency as the Truth had ever been...and the myth of America...land of the free and home of the brave...where anyone...regardless of race creed or colour...could grow up to be somebody... just one more lie told over and over and over until it might just as well have been the Truth...

❦

Kenzie came for him. Something tall and willowy with long brown hair and beautiful dark brown eyes that were warmer and more lovely than anything Aaron had ever seen in all the days that had come and gone since Sandra had walked away...

Her voice was soft and reassuring; not realising he wasn't afraid, she went on about silly things trying to make him feel more at ease...promising he'd be just fine...he said:

"Are you going to be there the whole time, Kenzie?

She nodded. "Andrews like to have newbies around so he can show off. He's good though...you don't have to worry..."

"Can I ask a favour...a big one...?"

"Sure of course you can, Mister Standish."

"Would it be all right if I pretended it was you who was holding my heart?"

They stopped right in the doorway of the operating theatre. He could hear them all inside checking this and checking that. Andrews was on his way they only had a few more minutes...

Kenzie tilted her head to one side and Aaron watched sterile fluorescent light coming alive in the curls and the waves of her hair...the sweet curve of her lips and the cinnamon spice on her breath...

"And no matter what happens...*no matter what*... don't freak out it will be okay."

She nodded...not understanding...and he went inside. A few minutes later she was back, helped him up onto the table, gently tied his left arm down...the one where they would harvest the artery for the bypasses...stood close by as the anesthetist prepped his other arm they stretched him out like Christ on a fucking cross and she stood close by not understanding...her hair trapped in a surgical cap...her lips and the touch of her breath behind a mask...he heard the arrival of his surgeon...felt the sting of a needle in his right arm and dutifully began to count backwards from one hundred...felt the chill and the darkness traveling up his arm into his brain...

And somewhere between the worlds he knew there had been a passage of Time...that pale ghostlike figures stood over him with scalpels and clamps and sponges and no one of them knew he was still there...watching and waiting...

He opened his eyes.

She stood over him...he watched shock and horror pass through her...shook his head ever so slightly...

It's okay Kenzie...it's okay...

Watched amazement and then calm in her wondrous sweet brown eyes...he could feel the acid in his blood expanding...every cell in his body Disconnecting... slowly... singing songs in the key of every colour that had ever been created by whatever it was Man had intended God to be...

He tried to smile at her around the tube in his mouth...thought:

Thank you...thank you so much...

And the deep deep brown of her eyes seemed to melt into the halo around her silhouette, cold white light that had turned to gold and rainbows...he closed his eyes again...felt something soft and gentle lift him up and carry him away.

UNDER THE GUNS

"...Doctor Torelli will see you now," said the receptionist. "Just through this door..."

Regretfully he hoisted himself out of the velvet cocoon masquerading as a chair in the waiting room, nodded and followed her snug curves to a panelled oak door, ducked his head and said *thank you* as he inched sideways past her. He found himself bathed in light from a wall of windows...floor to ceiling...the Potomac a glistening ribbon below him in the afternoon sun... Georgetown and DC blossoming northeastward from the Arlington Memorial Bridge...Theodore Roosevelt Island...

He stopped dead a couple of paces onto carpeting that felt more comfortable under his feet than the mattress he slept on...wagged his head for just a moment...enough to appear as though the postcard picture was something new.

"Thank you, Barbara...and hello, Mister Hogan. I'm Patricia Torelli."

The heavy door snicked shut behind him and the voice materialised in front of him, shoulder-length blonde hair framing wide-spaced brown eyes in a faintly oval face... lightly tanned for April...pale rose-glossed lips a bit thin but welcoming. His hand totally engulfed the one she offered him. Not so much she was small only that he was so big...

"Doug is okay," he said, making sure he kept the volume down. "Douglas if you have to, but please not Hulk."

It took her a moment to process, gave him time to check out the rest of the package she presented—understated upscale casual...an open-neck blouse in pale cream silk under a sculpted jacket and skirt in light chocolate. Expensive and tasteful. From the knees down he figured she played golf or tennis regularly. Suddenly he felt like a character in a Raymond Chandler novel.

He lied, "I've never been in the Towers before. This is quite the view," and she seemed pleased. From where he stood he could spot every landmark he once had visited for the first time when he was in the sixth grade.

She smiled warmly, but not with her teeth showing... a bit of professional reserve...

"I expected a uniform."

Listening more closely now her voice was not so much cold as it was cautious... waiting for more information...chess on a psychological chessboard. She was calculating the amount of distance she would need in order to do her job properly. He appreciated that...not wanting too much closeness. He didn't intend to see her again.

"I left it in the car," he explained. "I'm not back on until tonight. Special session."

"Did you have any problems parking?"

"None at all, thank you. Lots of space. And I've got a ton of clearance high enough I can park just about anywhere I want if I have to."

He liked that she was barefoot on her carpet. And that she turned her back to him as she invited him to sit...

"You asked for the afternoon, Doug, so please just call me Pat and if you'd prefer something stronger than tea or coffee or water I try to stay well-stocked. Sometimes it helps to get the words flowing..."

The rest of her office space was almost spartan. A small low desk that looked superfluous to her work...a matching credenza that seemed to be the wellspring of her offer of refreshment. A few things on the walls... photographs mostly...one large oil that looked like it might be a real Impressionist and expensive. Haphazardly between him and the wall of glass were three mismatched but expensive-looking armchairs and a fainting couch in the ubiquitous velvet...all very comfortable. He chose an armchair with a view and examined the effect of sunlight bouncing off the Reflecting Pool between the Washington Monument and the Lincoln Memorial. The dome of the Capitol reared up behind them.

"I've never been accused of being stingy with words," he said. "Scotch would be great. Johnny Walker...?"

Pat asked "What flavor?" and he turned round to see if she were serious...decided he liked her immensely... wished there was more time...

"Whatever you think is appropriate," he said. "I've never done anything like this before but so far you're definitely not fitting any of the stereotypes."

UNTIL THE END OF THE WORLD

She laughed. A nice sound. Nothing personal in it she was still casting about for the role she would play in their relationship but it was an intimation of what she might be outside her office and for an instant he wondered how it would sound if they were to be together...a few weeks into something that had nothing to do with why he was there. She handed him a glass...three fingers...he ran it under his nose and then took a drop on his tongue...

She said "I usually record my sessions so I don't get distracted by having to take too many notes."

To himself he said *I know*...

Aloud he said "I have no problem with that." Sipping his scotch. "I've never had this before."

"It's the Blue label."

"That would explain it then. I'd have to retire and rob a bank before I could justify a bottle of this."

"You're probably selling yourself short, Doug, but you're more than welcome. Honestly...our session is going to buy me my next bottle so please ask for seconds..."

She poured herself an equal measure and they shared the ring of crystal as they bumped rims. She padded across a few feet of carpet and sat on a corner of her desk, crossed one knee over the other.

"You're a luxury for me. I don't drink with everyone...*and* you appear to be very normal."

She seemed quite at ease, but he knew she was still probing for boundaries, that they were fencing he said:

"I seem to have issues."

"Don't we all?"

"Yeah, but mine seem to worry my immediate superiors."

"How is that?"

He put his head down, wondering where to begin it was so much more difficult knowing only how it would end.

"I was driving home...well...it was the end of my shift and I was going back to where I sleep...and some asshole in a Lincoln SUV pitched a McDonalds bag full of garbage out his window right in the middle of an intersection. I stopped...I'm allowed to do that...picked it up and followed him back to Georgetown..."

Pat Torelli sipped her Scotch and nodded.

"I guess I was a little bit hasty when I smashed the bag down onto the snappy leather seat that was still warm from his lazy ass sitting on it. There was still a lot of oozy stuff in the bag."

"Anger management."

Doug nodded. "I'd gotten served by my wife's lawyer a couple of hours before so I wasn't at my best."

"So you're in the middle of a divorce."

"Not for much longer. I don't want t'fight about it. I'm gonna miss her, but somewhere along the way it just stopped being good...for either of us."

"Is that why you're here?"

"Maybe a little...actually no, not really...but it was the beginning of this *thing*... three weeks ago...he lodged a complaint and I got called onto the carpet and I had to promise them I'd get a bit of *counselling* while I was going through my personal shit..."

"So far that all seems reasonable."

"Yeah mostly...but I've always been outspoken and the problem is that lately I seem to have lost some of my filters...the patience to put up with the double-speak in favour of the status quo...to simply keep my mouth shut when I should *keep* my mouth shut..."

Pat Torelli nodded...commiserative...sipped JW Blue...noticed he had finished his and offered more. Doug poured a few more fingers and set the bottle down beside his chair. The wall of glass in front of him caught a stray ray of light and went blank with bright...

"Maybe paranoia is my problem, but I'm fairly certain they want to put me out to pasture...any excuse to get me there...shut me up...PTSD..."

"I could bankrupt you, Doug. Why don't you let the US Army pay for your rehab?"

"I think they've already made up their mind, Pat. I wanted an independent observer."

"How did I get to be that?"

"You spoke before a Senate sub-committee...the application of civilian psych protocols in the treatment of military PTSD. I run a security detail at the Capitol...was on duty that day. I stopped in, paid attention and I was impressed."

She mulled over the compliment for a few moments

"Do *you* think you're suffering from PTSD, Doug?"

He emptied his glass again and shrugged.

"I don't know, Pat. I really can't say."

She opened a file folder lying beside her on the desk, briefly looked at what was inside. He got the distinct impression she already knew everything there was to know about it.

"I was curious when Barbara told me about your appointment. Usually my new clients want a short session to start with...to see if we're going to get along. You asked for an entire afternoon right out of the gate and, according to Barb, made it clear you were career military. I looked you up."

"And...?"

"Highly decorated....valorous to the point of near-legendary and, considering where you've been and what you've probably seen, I would imagine you might be a stellar candidate for PTSD..."

"But I don't seem to be."

She shook her head. "No, you don't...but you have concerns so I guess that's why we're here. I'm going press some buttons on this digital thing and we can get started."

Hogan nodded, poured more whiskey but only to warm it up in his hand. Torelli left the recorder on her desk, walked over to sit facing him in one of the two remaining armchairs.

"I grew up on a farm in Nebraska...and I enlisted straight out of high school because my old man had been Army and I'd grown up being taught that serving my country was an honour and a privilege.

"I'd been in less than a year. On March 8 in 1985 I was in Lebanon just a few days short of my nineteenth birthday and I rode shotgun on a detail that delivered a vehicle outside an apartment building in west Beirut. Extremists took credit for the explosion, but for all intent and purpose it was the US of A that engineered the whole thing. We killed eighty people...seriously injured two hundred more, almost all of them women and children, the rationale being that the Moslem cleric we were trying to assassinate was himself responsible for violent acts of terrorism...."

Torelli remained silent, met his gaze and for an instant she let something personal show through on her face. Hogan looked away first, back out through the plate glass. If he tilted his head the tiniest little bit he could almost line up the dome of the Capitol right off the top of the Washington Monument.

"I was still a kid. I told myself I didn't know all there was to know about something like that. We didn't have access to all the Vietnam papers we have now, or what came after."

"So how did you feel after the fact?"

He turned back to her.

"I was a few days shy of my nineteenth birthday... serving my country... At that point I didn't know what to make of it. At that point I didn't even know that I *needed* to make something of it..."

※

Torelli shifted around in her chair, faced him more squarely.

"What's going on with you and your soon-to-be ex...?"

Hogan looked down into his glass, swirling the whiskey around watching it coat the glass in pale transparent amber and gradually drift back into something richer and deeper at the bottom of the glass.

MICHAEL SUMMERLEIGH

"We got married right after I got back from Lebanon. Eleventh-hour high school sweethearts. Refugees straight out of the Fifties me and Lacey...but I'd mooned at her for three years and gotten the shit kicked out of me playing front line offense/defense for our football team trying to impress her and one day she actually noticed me...

"She said I looked stupid in a buzz-cut. After that I became a with-it dude, even if I couldn't dance worth shit."

He smiled...remembering Life a little bit simpler.

"I was in Central America when Chase was born in '87...wandering around Guatemala and Honduras and Nicaragua...but I was actually home when Charlotte was born in '89...got t'see Lace get chubby all on account of me. It was great...

"And then it started to stop being great. I was too good at whatever it was they wanted me to do. I never got home for more than a few weeks at a time...my children grew up hardly even aware that they had a father...

"When I'd manage some leave Lacey used t'keep me up nights telling about everything I'd missed. We'd fuck like there was no tomorrow and then she'd tell me some more. And then I'd go away again...this time back to the Middle East...the first Bush war... *serving my country*... tearing down a guy we'd set up because he'd stopped being cooperative..."

"And your wife?"

"My wife got lonely."

"She started seeing other men?"

"Yep."

"How were you with that?"

UNTIL THE END OF THE WORLD

"I was angry as hell...but I was busy at the time, trying to keep myself and a bunch of other people alive and somehow being angry slipped away...and then I just got sad...back then I just got sad...I thought I was doing what was right...not blind and stupid like these blowhard assholes wandering around America thinking automatic weapons make them soldiers of freedom. I got to where it felt I was just paying for the privilege of being an American for me and for my family. I knew some of it wasn't right, but I knew I didn't know all of it and I trusted them to be making choices for me. Behind all of that I also knew better than anyone I was letting Lace and my kids down..."

Pat Torelli got up, walked across to her desk to make sure the recorder was doing its job. While she was about that he topped up her glass. Held his up to hers and clunked them again. He could feel sympathy coming off her in waves, and perhaps an instinct for kindness that was being held in check simply because she took pride in doing her job professionally at all times. Again, he wondered what it might be like if she put her arms around him...kissed him...anything else...realised none of that was going to happen...that she was warmly empathetic and very attractive and he needed her for something else that had nothing at all to do with either. She sipped her whiskey...held the highball glass in both hands it reminded him of a photograph of his son's youngest daughter...four years old with a sippy-cup of milk he wondered if a trickle of JW was going to run down Patricia Torelli's chin...

"I've never seen my grandchildren," he said, appalled that for the first time in recent memory the thought made him want to cry. "Photographs. Chase and Charlotte started out by wondering why their father always missed birthdays...communions... graduations... weddings...and along the way they found out why and stopped caring whether I showed up or not...stopped talking to me, right about the time they were old enough to instinctively know what it's taken me an entire lifetime to figure out..."

He emptied his glass and reached for the bottle. Left it on the floor. The afternoon was running along and he didn't want to be driving with too much alcohol in his system.

"Douglas, you're not suffering from post-trauma stress," she said.

He looked up at her, shook his head.

"No, Pat, I'm not..."

After that they talked about all sorts of other stuff. She asked questions and wherever he could he replied with things that closely approximated real answers, and then outright fabrications where they best served him. He knew she was mapping him, finding the boundaries of his feelings about as many things as she felt might be helpful to her in a preliminary diagnosis. Just about the time he thought the receptionist should be making a reappearance there was a knock on the door to the office...an apology...a question...

Torelli looked away for moment, said "We're going to be a bit longer, Barbara, thank you. Go on home and I'll lock up when we're done."

UNTIL THE END OF THE WORLD

Barbara purred *Good night Mister Hogan* and closed the door. Some bustling ensued in the outer office, then quiet. Pat turned back to him, apologising for the interruption. He just waved it off.

"Were you ever scared, Doug? In all the places you've served...I'm assuming you've been under enemy fire dozens if not hundreds of times. Are you trying to deal with the fact you were scared?"

He shook his head again, but smiled.

"I near shit myself for far longer than I will admit to anyone but you...and of course I was scared. Terrified. But my father told me some things about his time in southeast Asia... before it crept up on him...

"He was the one with PTSD, Pat. It took almost forty years for it to bleed through, but in the interim he told me it was okay to be scared...okay to want t'run away and hide it was only crazy people who were never afraid...

"So I looked at it and I looked at all the other guys around me who maybe hadn't been lucky enough to have that tiny precious thought explained to them and I held it together for me and for them and I was afraid all the time, but whenever they gave me more people to look after it got less and less scary...

"Now I'm a fucking hero...with a big mouth..."

"Where's your Dad?" she asked softly.

Hogan considered refilling his glass after all.

"In the ground. When my mother died he started reliving Vietnam...waking up in the middle of the night thinking he was back there...like she had been the buffer between him and all things he'd never told me. I was back in the Middle East when he killed himself."

She was quiet for a while he could watch her processing information...mentally weighing the things he'd said against statistics and her instincts. He sensed it was coming close to the time for him to go...

"Doug, what is this?" she asked, frowning a little, speaking very slowly. "I'm starting to feel badly about my new bottle of Johnny Walker Blue. You could have chewed the ear off a bartender in any DC tavern for a lot less. You're desperately lonely and horribly disillusioned...but you're not crazy or anything that anyone could misconstrue as being crazy."

He smiled, nodded.

"You're right. I'm really just angry...now more than ever after this last little circus called an election..."

And that was the final act in his performance...the real distillation of why he was there. In between all their talk had been long long silences and the afternoon was going away... the time *was* coming closer...a few more minutes and there would be nothing else to say.

"I'm like that guy in the movie. I've had enough and I'm not gonna take it anymore."

Her frown grew deeper, drew her eyebrows down towards the bridge of her nose as she slipped in her chair, looked up at him...startled...almost afraid...

"Are you still with me, Pat?" he asked softly.

She looked up at him blearily...dazed...

UNTIL THE END OF THE WORLD

"Douglas...I'm so sorry...I think...I think I'm going to...have to...cut this short..." she said slowly. "I am...suddenly...so tired..."

He stood up...walked to her chair and scooped her up into his arms...no weight at all he felt as if he had grown wings and had only the sky before him...placed her gently on the couch.

"It's just the little something I slipped into your last glass of whiskey," he explained. "I'm not here to hurt you I promise, but you're going to sleep through the night."

He read the puzzlement in her eyes.

"The real reason I'm here is I need a witness, Pat. I checked you out...read up on the things you've done...the things you've said...the causes you've stood up for...and I came to you because I needed someone to know the Truth. I'm *depending* on you to tell the Truth...to take that digital recording and put it out in the world so when you wake up tomorrow and they try to paint me as some radicalised Muslim convert...or right-wing racist nut-job...or some left-wing commie sympathiser out to turn the US of A into a Russian satellite nation...there'll be a record of what it was really all about...

"That it was just me. Major General Douglas MacArthur Hogan. Someone who has done murder for them for over forty years and just wants it to stop...wants his son's daughters to be able to walk to work in their executive suites bare-ass naked if they feel like it and never have to worry about getting groped or being assaulted because *they were asking for it*. Somebody who wants his daughter's sons to respect women, never know the weight of an automatic weapon, or blow the crap out of innocent human beings in wars that are being manufactured for profit. I want my family to be able live without fear...without a gun under their pillows at night...in a country where they haven't been taught it's okay to hate people for any reason that feels right on any given day."

He found a light coverlet in a lower drawer of the credenza and draped it over her.

"Just tell them I was tired of the bullshit, Pat. Tired of being lied to, scammed on the American Dream, thrown crumbs and bullied into believing America was this great principled nation full of kind generous loving people. Tired of football-and-beer sideshows and flag-waving as an easy out for the responsibility of what we've let our leaders do to us and the rest of the world."

She was entirely out now. Snoring softly. He hit the STOP button on her recorder. Hit SAVE. He looked back at her from the doorway, washed in the light bouncing off the Potomac...shadows crawling into the inner corners of her office...

"Tonight they're all going t'be there, Pat," he said quietly. "That gibbering idiot from the White House right on down. Heaven knows how much more damage they're intending to do to this country.

"But tonight I'm going to put them all under the guns. If I can kill enough of them, perhaps We the People can start over and get it right the second time around."

AU 'VOIR

The first time she laid eyes on him she was certain he could not be human, rather something elemental, a behemoth, some wild crazed thing of storm-cloud and thunder raging across the stage, stamping the boards to splinters, fists like hammers raised up against the sky railing against Fortune. If there yet lived any gods upon Olympus, she knew they could hear him, and were bowing their heads in deference to his greater majesty.

It was just after the war, visiting with an aunt and uncle in London, and she was fourteen years old, wide-eyed at so much of the damage from the Blitz still visible...all forgotten in the instant he had appeared. She might yet have her ticket stub to tell her the name of the play or even the theatre...after so many years all driven from memory... everything but the almost physical recollection of a tempest clothed in Elizabethan finery.

"Can I get you anything, William? Are you comfortable?"

He stirred in the chair, a rustle of blanket in half-light from the arched leaded windows ranked along the wall like the nave in a cathedral.

The knave in a cathedral...

MICHAEL SUMMERLEIGH

That had been the second time. A touring company come to Oxfordshire ten years later there had been a rustle of humanity behind her where she sat through the dog-end of a service...the mock solemnity of his entrance...the transparency of his poor attempts at respectful silence. Grandstanding. She remembered how her heart had jumped to recognise him, and the smile she had kept hidden when her fiancé expressed his disapproval. Thereafter his performances were sell-outs as no doubt he had intended them to be, but she had managed tickets for one of them, a girlfriend providing the necessary subterfuge and companionship for her to get away.

He stirred in his chair...dislodged a tuft of fur from somewhere. The dogs lay scattered on the floor about him...big snuffling throw-rugs waiting for rebirth and the energy to chase something...anything...anywhere...

"A cup of tea would be nice," he said. "Maybe with some of that wonderful honey we brought back from Havana...?"

She turned away hoping he'd not heard the quick intake of her breath...her heart jumping...

"I'll put a pot on for both of us then," she said, knowing any honey would do...or perhaps even some brown sugar, because the honey from Havana had been from their first real holiday together. Long gone...now almost fifteen years ago...

She filled an electric kettle and watched him while it hissed and spit and lurched towards a boil like a leper on the road to Jerusalem. It was almost too much for him to stand on his feet. A trip to the fucking bathroom was akin to the preparation of an African safari. She warmed the china teapot with tap water, spooned the very last of their Russian Georgian into it. There would never again be Russian Georgian tea for the world. The cataclysmic ebb and flow of Eurasian politics had destroyed the last of the tea-fields; now the cataclymisc ebb and flow of Life was destroying the last of her heroes.

Beyond the windows and thirty feet below them the river ran rushing by on its way to a lake and then a river and then an ocean...the cold-cold-even-in-summer north Atlantic. She wondered if the tiny currents that made for the whole of it knew of the journey before them...that when it came to their time in the sun and a rising up into the sky if they would be aware of it...the endless cycle... Ourobouros snaring its own tail...that someday they would begin again right back where they had begun...and likely rush by the very same house and never even know the last souls to have witnessed their earlier passage through that place were now gone.

"Dear do you remember...?"

There was a deceptive rumbling of strength in his voice as he called to her she filled the teapot...watched the agony of the tea-leaves writhing in the hellish stream of boiling hot water. For a moment his voice was as it had always been...the deep and elegant *basso profundo* to shake the windows and rattle your bones for the times they were indeed a-changin'....

And she did indeed remember that time. Carnaby Street. Kickin' down the cobblestones lookin' for fun feelin' groovy and her two beautiful daughters just now learning to walk the walk in the very best of times and the very worst of them she remembered...looking through a boutique window and seeing him surrounded by shopgirls...each one with a velvet coat in hand or a brocade waistcoat...waiting on his every word...vying for his attention...

She also remembered the hurt...of being too free with her thoughts and her desires...speaking them aloud to her husband who preferred to keep that sort of thing to himself, where indulgence would not threaten his standing amongst his peers she asked:

"Do I remember what...?"

But he had already forgotten whatever it was he had remembered. She poured a thin bone china cup for herself and a sturdy ceramic mug for him, with a fat dollop of local honey...delivered it to a hand gone frail and bone white. She sat on the sofa beside his chair to keep him company. On the big screen television a soccer match unfolded without benefit of sound.

"Are you hungry, my love?"

"This is good," he said. Sipped at his tea. Tried to set it down somewhere and gave up. The dogs wriggled and snuffed.

"Caroline...?"

"Yes, William."

"Did you remember to tell the Queens people that we won't be attending that dinner...?"

She closed her eyes, struggled not to let the scream out where he could hear it. The *dinner* had been years before.

"I did."

"Oh good then..."

"They were disappointed, but I told them you had a prior engagement..."

She covered her face with both hands, turned away where he couldn't see her. The quiet got deep and long. She dared to look back at him. He seemed lost in an obscurity of grey and white monochrome, the once vivid raven-black bristling spikes of hair as he raged about the stage all gone to a Procol Harum whiter shade of pale... no longer the valiant conquistador...just a tired old jouster in the lists...her Ivanhoe laid low and murdered by the chemicals meant to save him...

William...sweet William...

He turned his head as if she had spoken aloud and in his cloudy eyes she saw for the first time a spark of something that might have been alarm...a look of sudden startled awareness—that if *she* recognised the imminence of his end then it must surely be upon him.

He had never been afraid...not even on the Saturday in 1983 when the Irish Republican Army bombed Harrods...Christmas shopping...the girls would be coming home for the holidays...

She had been on the fourth floor, well away from the actual explosion below...not far enough to avoid being flung against a wall by the blast...feeling the displaced air rush past her carrying shards of plate glass and then the stench of her husband's terror. In the smoke and the chaos she heard that voice...*his* voice...cutting through the cries of pain and fear calling out to survivors...now cast in real life...heroic and unflinching...

She had followed him to a stairwell...waved him on with someone more seriously injured in his arms...later watched him go back for others...tirelessly...until the immediacy of search and rescue was gone and his reputation was loosed forever from the bonds of mere stage stardom. She had wanted to thank him...but more than a decade went by before it became possible...

"...I *thought* I heard someone calling my name," he said in mock perplexity.

He turned away from the knot of people with whom he'd been engaged in conversation...elegant and assured with a flute of champagne in one hand. She had never been that close to him...introduced herself he was instantly attentive...and beneath the self-assurance sincerely flattered that she would remember in such detail the three times their paths had crossed... and then he became severely embarrassed by her thanks.

"I was there and it was horrible," he said. "What else could I do?"

The rest of the party had become dreamlike. She could not say why she had gone at all, except for friends who had told her to mourn a marriage gone bad for too long was not healthy; that it had been well over two years ago even Ariel and Regan had begun to worry about her...

"Your daughters, then?" he had said. "What happened to Titania?"

And they had laughed when she told him she had loved her new children far too much to saddle one of them with a name like Titania, no matter how grand its pedigree. And then they began a ritual of courtship, and she found him old-worldly and thoroughly charming as she knew he would be. And Ariel and Regan were very impressed...found his easy solicitude for their mother and themselves irresistible...

"We've had so many adventures together," he said.

She nodded, came to arrange a blanket around him, bent to kiss his forehead.

"We have," she said simply.

Almost twenty years of them she cried to herself. *We waited such a long time...*

"I imagine we had good lives before....mostly..."

"I thought you might have turned vain and pompous."

"Well I had," he said, smiling a little. "But then I turned around at this dreadful party where I was expected to be vain and pompous, and there you were..."

He had never failed to compliment her. Never once had he *not* been there to support anything she ever did or wanted to do...or failed to treat her children as though they were his own. She wondered that for all the good things that had come to her because of him there was one thing that always had seemed to be missing.

He grew drowsy again, she could see the haze slowly covering the brightness of his eyes. She caught his mug of tea as it left his fingers and pottered around the kitchen... close by...for when he woke again...

He murmured something. It was scarcely more than a breath she was not even sure he had spoken yet she heard him clearly enough. She wound her way through the maze of dogs...moved towards him in his chair that was become like a moth-eaten damned coffin...drew back his blanket eased herself down beside him...put her head down on his chest...too tired to fight anymore...

He whispered: "You mean quite a lot to me."

Suddenly she was so *weary*. A word from another time...a word from so long ago...a word that spoke so much more deeply than just being tired she said:

"You might have mentioned that before now, William."

Beneath her the great bellows of his lungs exhaled with something that might have been mistaken for a sob, eloquent with regret.

"I'm sorry. You're right. I should have spoken. I should have told you."

"You're so damned British."

"But so are you..."

"Not like you, William," she said kindly, "not so damned British as you, who never learned that his love might be something someone else might hold to be precious."

He was quiet. This then was perhaps as close to a cruelty as she could inflict upon him...now...finally...to hold up before his eyes the mirror of his life...to make him see the wonderful reflection that had been there through his lifetime, only just waiting for his acceptance.

"I love you Caroline," he whispered, and put his hand gently on her head.

She said *Oh sweetheart I know* and laid her head down again...listened to his breathing begin to stagger and crawl...watched as the afternoon drew deeper grey shrouds down around them and the greatest measure of light she had ever known went out from her life.

LOST & FOUND

No coverage, not even one bar, the battery was dead anyway. It was still daytime, but there was an overcast and the sky had a perfectly even dullness, so there was no way to tell what time of day it was, much less which direction was north or south or anything else for that matter. A two-lane blacktop road snaked up into the distance and disappeared into some trees, or a forest if you wanted to get technical about it. It also snaked down toward some lumpy hills and disappeared there as well. What sounded like a two-stroke chainsaw could be heard in the distance, but it was impossible to tell whether it was up in the forest or down in the lumpy hills. This had been happening more often lately. Two different ways to go, with a dead battery and no signal, and nobody left to blame.

Both of them were running, though neither could say exactly what it was they were running from, only that the lives they were leading had stopped being important, and there had been a night when all caution and pretense had been swept aside, and thereafter no explanations had seemed appropriate. Both of them had simply walked away; now they were stopped in the middle of nowhere, lost along the way to wherever it was they were going. A road atlas would have been helpful, certainly better than a smartphone with no smarts... but looking at each other they each realised it didn't really matter where they were...*lost* was the way it was going to be for a while.

Shawna brushed strands of hair from her face, the cloud cover making the air thick and humid she could feel her blouse and jeans growing damp with sweat, felt crushed beneath a sudden deeply oppressive sense of weight as the chainsaw sputtered and died in the distance. Silence rose up to swallow them standing beside the car...

Rick hadn't made a sound since they had turned onto something that in spite of tar and chip really didn't even qualify as a tertiary backroad. No signs. Nothing to tell them where they were going. Shawna had not spoken, but watched him hunch over the steering wheel a bit more with every passing mile, watching for another ribbon of dirt or asphalt to return them to civilisation... refusing to back-track...wild-eyed... like some poor soul in a Stephen King novel driving deeper into something dark and dangerous but refusing to give an inch to dismay or common sense.

Fair to Shawna's dark and exotic he had pale blue eyes that had been sharp and stubborn in the Caddy's air conditioning, but now he seemed to be drowning in the heat, his white dress shirt starting to darken with perspiration, the lines of his face losing some of their strong angularity...softening into something Shawna realised was terror; that the passion, the sheer desperation and need of their flight, that had fuelled *him* over half a continent, had somehow been sucked out of his soul and had left him adrift in something utterly beyond his comprehension, without a map or a compass...a reference point of any sort...in exile from all the comfortable things in the world he had given up in order to be at this crossroad on this day out in the middle of nowhere with her.

She felt a sudden sadness for him, and then a surprising sense of almost bitter disappointment; that all the strength that had attracted her to him in the beginning seemed to have gone in the first wave of a minor crisis. Instinctively she wanted to walk around the front of the car and put her arms around him...offer him some sort of refuge from what was making him so crazy-scared...then she realised it was that very same thing in her other life that had driven her away; that she had given all she had to give to it and now was looking for something in return. She stayed on her side of the car, ready for the wave of guilt she knew was coming...

The silence around them started to shred with the hum of cicadas in the tall grass lining the roadside, growing louder and louder until it was almost deafening she could see Rick's lips moving but still couldn't hear what he was saying. He didn't even seem to be talking to her and the look in his eyes kept getting more and more distant, as if he was retreating into himself, away from whatever was upsetting him, not made any better when the humming just stopped dead and both of them were startled by the raucous jeers of two crows arrowing overhead, black shadows against the gun-metal sky. Now she could hear him cursing, the deep rumble of his take-charge voice drowning in anger growing sharper, edging towards hysteria. The pair of crows disappeared into the trees, a last chorus of derision echoing in the stillness.

She called his name once...then again...louder this time and he seemed to wake up from the nightmare, recognition replacing the glassy stare into nothingness. He shook himself loose from where the collar of his shirt clung to his neck, ran both hands through his hair and when he found her looking at him closely flushed even darker in the suffocating heat.

He was embarrassed, dimly aware that for a while he'd totally lost it...something new and alien in his life he'd always been the one to pay the bills and make sure everything was where it was supposed to be when it was supposed to be there. His kids were in college and it was all paid for and he was so fucking tired of always being the one in charge and then *she* had come along... given him these strangely wonderful moments of reprieve...a deep brainless world of fucking where there weren't any consequences and he could sleep again...without the worry... buried in the sweat and perfume between her breasts when the night had driven them to the edge of exhaustion...

He had never seen it coming. Just a morning when he woke up and consciously recognised he didn't want to get out of bed or go to the office or ever touch his dearly-beloved-until-death-do-us-part ever again. Not that she had done anything except perhaps fall into the same traps that had snared him, set him racing after the common definition of the American Dream. Just that it suddenly all seemed like utter bullshit and he was tired of it.

He had forced himself out of bed, stumbled into the bathroom. In the middle of shaving he realised he had no idea who was staring back at him from the bevelled glass mirror over his side of the twin sinks. Two nights later staying in town for a drink with a client—staying for one more before heading back to La-La Land—he'd met Shawna. Her voice had been so low and so comfortable in the half-light...her casual office-acceptable clothing nowhere near enough casual to hide the honey hiding inside.

And he had started working late every night that week. Two of them staying in town with phone calls back to the 'burbs that were full of lies, and everything after that full of Shawna...no words... just a blessed relief in not having to talk or think...

He watched her watching him over the roof of the El Dorado and he was embarrassed...ashamed for having given in to fear...for having gotten lost in it. It had never happened to him before and her eyes were like mirrors... dark, but without the judgment he had made that morning when he was shaving, yet he could see that somehow he had slipped in her regard...the tweo of them less than a few weeks old and already he somehow had managed to fall short of her expectations.

For the space of a dozen heartbeats she saw that same hangdog expression she had left behind...the look that had become so frustrating...so goddamn infuriating she dealt with the same everyday shit he did why was she the one who always had to be the safe harbour? Who was gonna hold her and say *There there it's okay I'm lookin' after you baby you don't have t'sweat a thing I got you safe and warm now...*

She watched him come back to where they were... answer the unspoken clarion call in her voice she didn't want to have to tell him...to admit that even now every minute was a test he needed to pass. She didn't care about the sex. He wasn't the best lover she'd ever had, but he was gentle...maybe too cautious because they were new...but he was considerate and it wasn't just about him getting off and then rolling over to go to sleep...

She mustered a commiserative smile, something that would let him know she didn't give a damn if they had no idea where they were because that part of it was true. In the martini-charged moment when she had made the decision to walk away she also had sloughed off all need for any kind of certainty except for the one where she took up with someone who would be willing to dare the Unknown with her. Step over the edge. Take a chance take a chance ollie-oxin-free.

He told her stuff she already knew. Maybe another thirty miles in the tank and the phone didn't work but they'd turned off the interstate to find a gas station that had been out of business for at least a year... and then just followed another road off into where they were now.

She nodded *I know* and he wished they were somewhere for the night he just wanted to see her naked again...be inside her. If she fucked back hard enough he could stop being terrified. He put his head down and waited until his breathing slowed enough for him to speak again, through the awful sense of failure...

Finally he looked up, afraid of what he would see... but whatever was in her eyes wasn't condemnation or disdain. He spoke slowly, said they might as well pick one way or the other and eventually they'd have to end up somewhere. She grinned at him, sharing the joke... already comfortable with the complete silliness of what he had only just discovered...and if by chance she could figure out where she'd stashed the charger cable for the phone...

They climbed back into the Caddy and he started the engine, turned left, up into the trees thinking *What the hell maybe the crows know where the fuck they're going* and that they couldn't get more lost than what they were.

At the top of the hill the roadbed became an underwater ocean of dull greens and shadows, but as they started coasting down the other side somehow the world managed to transform itself, as if the hilltop had been a border between the worlds of darkness and light. From nowhere the sun struck tentative fingers through the cloud cover and then exploded...joyous...roiling like a furnace...flooding the next valley with gold and promise...and a filling station. Shawna whispered *Holy shit!*

and they laughed... together...sharing a vast unspoken sense of relief. Salvation had been just around the corner after all.

They got the Caddy tanked up and the teenager in his bib-overalls shared some laughter when they told him they thought they were never going to find their way back to the interstate. He pointed down the road...four-five miles make a left...then past the fairgrounds another couple-three more...

That simple. They bought Nestea in ice-cold cans, and a suspicious something-or-other that looked like it might be a ham sandwich but could have been bad cheesecake... just to dull the rumble in their stomachs. One was plenty in case it turned out to be fatal there had to be someone to warn the next unwary lunch-hungry victims...and then on down the line in blazing afternoon sunshine. Left-turning and the fairgrounds, where the kid in the overalls had neglected to mention there was a county fair in full swing. Rick asked if she wanted to stop and she smiled.

He swung the car into a vast dirt parking lot, found a spot in the shade of a huge elm tree at the far end, where the fairgrounds met the primeval forest. Shawna reached down for her purse and stepped out of the Caddy...turned to him with a triumphant grin and the snaky black charge cord for the phone that had been hiding under her seat.

She plugged it into the cigarette lighter and the phone made wake-up noises. She shrugged as if to say *Not so bad after all* and saw another weight come away from his shoulders, and then they could smell hot dogs and hamburgers sizzling on open fires...see the broad arc of the ferris wheel against the afternoon sky, hear the shrill delight of children being whirled around on the Cyclone ...the ching-ching-ching of a pinball arcade and animal sounds from the petting zoo. She ran on ahead, came back to grab his arm and drag him along faster... suddenly excited with old childhood memories.

This was new for him. Or at least the memory of some similar experience was so old as to be forgotten. With the imminence of net contact re-established he felt better in the same breath he took to feel stupid at how much his peace of mind was dependent on the technology.

Her face was laughing and her eyes sparkling with an almost childish excitement. He couldn't figure out why or how he could be at all reluctant to simply join in...let some of the *sameness* from his old life just slip away. She grabbed one hand and drew him along in her wake, a glimmer of mischief in her eyes...and now a sense of relief crowding into his thoughts that it would be okay this was why they were where they were...cutting loose...trying to break free. She urged him into a dog-trot and she paid their admission tickets to the midway, with a triple handful of the ones they would need to get on some of the rides.

She could see him struggling with his old sense of *malaise*, the tiredness that had made him an observer on the sidelines of his own life. She knew that feeling very well, after years of not wanting to start a day because there was nothing to look forward to at the end of it. When she felt him hanging back she turned to him... kissed him hard and fast... challenged him...breathed an inner sigh of relief when he rose to the challenge and let himself be drawn back into the land of the living. They sauntered back into the world, hand in hand.

The noise was immense after the great silences that had shrouded their thoughts, and the uncomfortable ones between bursts of conversation that were really just there to ward off the silence.

The carousel blared calliope music; the ferris wheel on the edge of the fair moved to its own soundtrack, moving in slow arcs against the blue almost-white-with-heat sky and the pale cotton candy clouds. The air filled with the shrieks of children and young girls on the roller coaster; the boys put up a brave front and tried not to grip the safety bars too hard.

The dry summer earth of the fairgrounds rose up to cover boots and denim overalls with a thin skin of dust...crept between painted toes in leather sandals...the feet and calves and thighs that belonged to them. Shawna kept turning to him, urging him on, coaxing him with her eyes and the sense of freedom she felt growing in her heart.

The air filled with the sweet thick stench of manure and farm animal...the sound of cows lowing in their stalls, the goats baa-ing in the petting zoo. A clown walked by juggling five apples without missing a beat, winked at her, and she could feel Rick smiling beside her...slowly growing into the adventure his hand around hers easing away from tense...edging towards softness.

They tried a couple of the less extreme rides...a monorail that wound around and through the grounds twenty feet over the heads of the locals. Tried getting close to each other...perspiration and the meeting of flesh outside of lust or passion, simply gone dazed and dozy in the heat...together...he would lean forward every now and again his attention caught by something below. She closed her eyes and let the slow movement lull her almost into sleep...contentment...

It went on long enough that getting back on the old *terra firma* was funny...a bit of a stagger...another reason to be close, knees and elbows bumping trying to match strides in two directions at once she started laughing again and couldn't explain why... laughing so hard until he started laughing with her and she caught a glimpse of him she'd not seen before...the silly part that had been buried by *being in charge* for so long...the Responsibility she herself felt no reluctance in sloughing off...

They bought hot dogs and French fries, the suspicious supposedly-ham sandwich long gone and gratefully forgotten...and jumbo Cokes with crushed ice. Felt their lives becoming something that approached the realm of Normal. Rick saw a pair of crows perched on the roof-tree of the hot-dog stand, doing that herky-jerky-hop dance-step thing crows did before they descended on a discarded bun...democratically each taking one half before taking off again they watched them lazily soar away over top of the funhouse...which was enough of an invitation for both of them...

They walked gratefully into the half-dark and the coolth...let the outdoor clamour fade away behind them replaced by spooky Halloween-type music and the entertaining funhouse groans of souls in torment. She could feel his ultra-pragmatism kick in...recognising the sheer foolishness of funhouse-as-entertainment...yet it was only for an instant and as long as it took them to almost bump into the mirrors... heartbeats of *ohmygosh!* before they recognised themselves in the distorted images.

They'd not gone more than a few dozen steps further, still laughing at their cartoon reflections, when they heard voices raised behind them and someone shouting *No no no that's not me I didn't do it please I'm so sorry I didn't mean to do it* and then a crash...splintering glass...a woman screaming they stopped... turning to each other... one glance and then Shawna just went instinctively, broke into a run back the way they had come. Rick reached for her, thought to tell her *Don't get involved!* but she was already gone.

He caught up to her seconds later, hugging the walls as a family raced past him terrified he stopped dead in his tracks behind her. Over her shoulder there was a broad shadow shambling towards them in a kaleidoscope nightmare...sobbing...making sounds that seemed to be filtered through running water as it came closer...moved into the blood-red glow of the passage and collapsed at Shawna's feet.

His face and arms and upper torso glinted and shone with splinters of light reflecting off the splinters and shards of the shattered funhouse mirrors embedded in his flesh...rising and falling to the laboured breath...the words choking to find their way through the bubbling pools of blood pouring out of severed arteries and shredded veins.

Shawna dropped to her knees beside him desperately trying to find and stanch them. She knew better than try to pull the broken glass from his wounds...already knew he was beyond her help but calling for someone to call 911 anyway....wishing this once that she was back in the city with her ER people.

Rick stood over her for a moment, stunned, before he stripped off his shirt and started tearing it into something she might use to stop the blood growing into a thick black river across the floor between them. He watched her...amazed...realised she knew exactly what she was doing and he'd had no idea...known almost nothing about her at all there was chaos exploding all around them yet he could swear he heard her voice talking softly to the dying man in front of her...cool and calm and comforting making promises no one could keep...until the pretense became too much for her.

She leaned back on her heels and let her hands fall away from him... helplessly... there was nothing more she could do he'd be gone long before anyone would arrive who could save him. She could feel her fingertips teased by the slow tide of life pooling on the floor beneath them. The knees of her jeans grew black with it and in the sudden stillness she couldn't hear him breathing anymore, only the slow pounding of her own heart coming down off the frantic adrenaline high, now counting time to the last sluggish beats of a heart gone empty...

The sound of an ambulance siren filtered its way into the labyrinth, and after a while there were footsteps... voices calling out to someone...anyone...they shouted together...until they were found and paramedics asked questions and did whatever they needed to do...protocol and procedure and then just stating the obvious.

Rick helped Shawna to her feet, followed along behind as they staggered back out into the light and the carousel...Joni Mitchell's painted ponies going round and round and up and down as if nothing at all had happened. State troopers were already all over the place interviewing witnesses; they each got one of their own...told their stories...learned what had drawn them into it.

He was twenty-two years old. His name was Todd McCreary and after being away for the better part of a year he'd come home three weeks earlier...clean and sober... the only wedding gift his *fiancee* had wanted... the only girl he'd ever dated...all the way through high school and his long-weekend visits when she was away at state college she had graduated that spring and the wedding was supposed to have been tomorrow...

Except Todd had fucked up. Disappeared for three days and the word gone round that he'd gone back to the alcohol and the drugs and there had been a woman he'd met at the rehab facility...and *that* perhaps, more than anything else, had done for the wedding bells...and for

Todd, when he got his ring back in a special delivery parcel that everyone in town knew about.

Shawna was exhausted, realised her clothing was soaked in his blood...going black and stiff in the dying of light creeping into the shadows between the midway tents and stalls. Rick looked down at her and she looked up at him and somewhere in all the strangeness of a day gone so very horribly strange they both seemed to come to the same sort of revelation...

He went back to the car to get clean clothing for them, let themselves be led off to somewhere they could change and she could wash away the last of Todd McCreary. She couldn't speak, couldn't begin a process of rationalisation or interpretation to give meaning to what had happened. Tragedy was tragedy. Shit happened. She wanted to cry.

He reached for her hand, brushed a few flakes of dried blood from her wrist with a tenderness that was thoroughly new to her experience with him...rose to her feet and felt a deep sense of gratitude he was there, not because she was incapable of going on alone, or unwilling to do it out of necessity. It was as if they had found something between them that was more than the desperation of two strangers running away together; that the sexual attraction, the attractiveness of *personality* now had less to do with what they had been, and more to do with what they had become...in one moment...having shared something that had belonged to neither of them before, now free to share everything else if they chose to do so.

He put an arm around her shoulders. She put hers around his waist. Together they moved slowly back out

UNTIL THE END OF THE WORLD

into the glare and the glitter of the midway, past the cotton candy vendours and the arcades, the barkers and the jugglers, parents trailing in the wake of excited children, young lovers kissing and old lovers holding hands.

They passed a clothing concession and he saw a cotton dress in pale tangerine patterned with slate-blue lotus-flowers, that tied with a bow in the back he said it belonged to her, wanted to buy it for her if that was okay it would go so well with her hair and her skin and the lotus-flowers were the same colour as her eyes in the first hours of evening drawing down around them.

They made their way through the crowd, and back to the car. As they approached it, a crow flew directly over their heads and landed on the hood and then looked at them. They stood some distance away and watched the crow watching them. Another crow flew directly over them and landed beside it. The first crow squawked and then both flew away. They watched them disappear, looked at each other, and then got in the El Dorado. Only one way to go this time, with five bars and a full battery.

A DREAM OF NATALIE

She had never been late coming home from work. Bonker and Zoom got supper at 5.30 without fail, so when she turned the corner he sensed...knew...something was wrong. The sunset shone through the three high-rise towers to the west like solstice through the sarsens at Stonehenge, ran rivers of gold down through the streets, struck red-bronze sparks from the mane of her chestnut hair; the linen of her lily-patterned dress blazed white against her skin and even at a distance she was startlingly beautiful...but she was more than hours late, and the normally confident swing of her stride was slow and painful to watch. When she finally reached the concrete walk to her townhouse door she stumbled, turned an ankle in one of her cork-soled rope sandals and staggered back against a parked car. He was already halfway across the street, moving towards her. As she tried to stand up he was there with an arm around her waist, catching her before she fell. She struggled instinctively, swung around in his arms with a clenched fist that connected just below his ribs and actually knocked the wind out of his lungs.

"Leave me alone," she sobbed, still fighting against him. "Get your fucking hands off me I'll—"

"Natalie stop it's okay it's me...Jackson...it's okay..."

She turned, stared up at him blearily through the tangle of her hair.

"Jackson...?"

Her eyes matched the deep rich brown of her hair, but they were dazed, muddy, filled with pain. She seemed to look right through him, seeing nothing, and repeated his name, this time with a tiny crease of concentration coming between her eyebrows as she tried to process two syllables into something with meaning.

"Yeah," he said softly. "I got you now you're gonna be fine..."

She sagged against him, reacting to the calm in his voice, or maybe just exhaustion.

"I think I caught something," she mumbled. "I wasn't sick this morning."

She wasn't really talking to him, feverish enough that he could feel the unnatural heat through the thin layer of her clothing. He half-carried her up the few steps to her door, reached into the bleached canvas bag dangling from one shoulder to find her keys, fumbled one into the deadbolt...cursed to need a second one for the handset lock...finally swung the door open with one hip and then picked her up bodily...down a short hallway that opened into a kitchen on the left...the open expanse of the sky-lit living room.

"I gotta get supper for the guys," she whispered, almost in tears. "Please..."

He laid her down on the wood-frame futon/sofa, tucked a pillow under head.

"I'll feed them, Natalie," he said...then repeated himself a bit louder to make sure she had heard him. "In the kitchen, right...?

She nodded slowly, her eyes clenched shut, the rasp in her breathing sounding like it was bubbling up from deep in her lungs. He got her sandals off, looked around for something to cover her, found a rough woollen Mexican blanket folded up inside the low cabinet beneath the widescreen television Two cats stood in the archway off to the back bedrooms.

Zoom was green-eyed, a short-haired marmalade tabby...sleek, unobtrusive, silent and slinky as running water from a distance. Bonker was a massive black-and-white longhair, one green eye and the other one spooky gold...intimidation on four paws.

They both looked at him as if to say *Who the fuck are you?*

He said: "Relax boys, I'll be with you in a minute..."

He turned and went back into the kitchen, located their food bowls, vaguely aware of at least one set of paws having thumped along in his wake. He turned to the counter with the bowls in hand...found them both staring at him again.

"I'm on it guys really...your mom's not feelin' good so just chill okay?"

He found an open can of mixed seafood whatever in the refrigerator and an unopened one in the cupboard. He shovelled half a can each into the two bowls, emptied and refilled a larger one with fresh water from the sink. Once he had them on the floor, the cats eyed him warily as their noses got a whiff of dinner. Zoom got hungry first and edged past him. Bonker decided he wanted whatever it was in Zoom's bowl and they exchanged a few pleasantries. The short-hair seemed to debate making an issue of it, decided that scrapping wasn't worth the effort once he realised the stuff in Bonker's bowl was same as the stuff in his .

He left them in the kitchen, making horrible noises as they inhaled their food. When he walked back into the living room, Natalie was unconscious on the floor.

He didn't do much thinking over the next hour or so. Someone had stoked the fire on her fever and he could almost see the heat coming off her. On his way down the back hallway with her in his arms he managed to kick off his boots and undo the zipper on her dress. In the bathroom, he got them both down to their underwear and into the shower, trying to find a spray that was cold without being too cold, all the while with one arm around the waist of a someone gone limp and delirious. She didn't have the strength to actually fight him, but they stood under the hiss and sting of the water sheeting down over them and danced to two totally different tunes.

It seemed like lifetimes later but she stopped struggling, draped her arms over his shoulders. The pain seemed to rush out of her in a long sigh that brought her close into his embrace where he could see it disappear in the places it had etched itself on her face. She was light in his arms, slender and small-boned, but her breasts were large and heavy and swelled upwards where they pressed against his chest. He wrapped her in a bath-sheet and carried her into one of the bedrooms. The cats stood in the doorway watching him, leapt up onto the bed beside her the moment he tucked a blanket around her and stepped away.

He was surprised to find it was still an hour short of midnight. He got out of his shower-damp shorts and slipped back into the rest of his clothing...left his boots in the front hall and revisited the kitchen...found an old bottle of Scotch under the counter maybe a third of it left...poured all of it into a big tumbler. Sat down on the woodframe sofa/futon thing in the living room and started breathing again.

In silver moonlight the walls seemed to have been done in an impersonal rental off-white, but covered with posterised prints of her photographs, framed original drawings, a pair of photos in the archway that were studio-posed nudes. There was a bookcase as well... eclectic titles on history, philosophy, some old textbooks and a biography of Michael Jackson. He drank her whiskey, too wired to sleep, unwilling to let himself drift off so he could keep checking on her, make sure the fever stayed away.

Once upon a time he had been so grateful for the warmth and the company of the woman he'd married. A blessed sense of relief that had felt like asking questions was unnecessary...like what it was they wanted for the rest of their lives...where they wanted to be ten twenty however many years down the road...the nuts and the bolts of what it would take to hold them together as those days and weeks and months and years went by...

And now he was sitting in the living room of somebody he'd only just met after three days of what anyone would have called "stalking" her, never mind that maybe he'd saved her life he suddenly felt like somewhere along the way perhaps he'd lost some sort of perspective, his sense of reality, inched himself all unknowing into the land of sickos and perverts.

When he woke up it was only a few hours later and the glass was empty in his hand. She was sitting in the chair across from him, rubbing sleep from her eyes, still looking a little bit dazed but most definitely levelling a wordless WTF at him.

"Jackson," she said.

He nodded.

"Facebook Jackson."

He nodded again.

"You live four hundred miles away from here."

"I wanted to see you. I didn't think...I just...well...I did..."

She took some time with that thought, found another one she felt was more in need of clarification.

"I don't remember coming home."

He said, "You were running a really bad fever... almost collapsed out in front...on the sidewalk..."

"And now I'm safe and sound and in my nightgown with a bunch of wet towels and my underwear on the floor next to my bed."

"I didn't know what else t'do. You were totally out I thought you were gonna burn up on me if I didn't do something."

"9-1-1 maybe?"

"I was afraid it would take too long for somebody t'get here."

She crossed her arms beneath her breasts, reached for a throw pillow and hugged that too, folded her legs carefully underneath her all the while keeping her eyes on him, weighing the words.

"So?" she asked.

He looked at her, not understanding.

"What d'you think?"

"What do I think about what, Natalie?"

He couldn't tell if the note of contempt was meant for him, or perhaps just intrinsic to the nature of her next question.

"Am I fuckable?"

He realised he had gone speechless, turned away when he felt a flush of heat rising up into his face he said:

"Fuckable?"

He turned the word over in his head because it was something he'd not really ever heard before. He was pretty certain Webster had never considered the term for inclusion in his dictionary…knew for a fact it was a concept he had never once even thought in the way she meant it.

"You're everything a beautiful forty-one year old woman should be," he said, still not looking at her.

"You could try answering the question," she said derisively, taunting him for being embarrassed. "Well…?"

UNTIL THE END OF THE WORLD

"You know that's not how I look at you," he said defensively...but a few hours ago, after he'd managed to wrestle them out of the shower, he'd stripped off her panties and bra, towelled her dry while she was only half-awake...combed her wet hair out over her pillow... put four loose bows in the lace ties down the front of the night-dress he'd slipped around her.

"You're a guy."

"We're not all the same."

"Sure you are," she said, now not even hiding the contempt in her voice. "Some of you just pretend better."

Desperate, he said: "Natalie what d'you want from me with all this?"

"What d'you want from *me*, Jackson? Why the fuck are you here at all? Does your wife know where you are?"

"I wanted to meet you. I was gonna call, ask if you would have supper with me."

That had been three days ago, after driving almost eight hours, standing outside her door a block away, nights in a rented room borrowed from a novel written by Franz Kafka.

"What *about* the missus, Jackson?"

"We don't answer to each other anymore. You know that."

"How about being nice to her for a change, instead of sneaking off to ask me out on a date?"

He looked at her helplessly...dishevelled with sleep and still so stunning he had nothing to say that could possibly be the answer she was looking for...wondered how on earth he had thought she could be anything else than what she was, what she had claimed to be during their online conversations.

"Jackson, don't you know that eventually every relationship turns to shit?"

"I don't believe that. I don't believe you do either. Not after some of the things you've said."

She shook her head at him, like he was a five-year old incapable of any kind of

understanding... loosened a sleep-tangle of hair that fell down over one shoulder and made him ache inside, desperate again, for something... anything...to keep her there... talking to him...he said:

"So where's what's-his-face?"

"He went off to some gaming convention for the weekend. Says he gets ideas for his commercial work from looking at all that shit, and probably from fucking the brainless twenty-something he's in bed with right now."

She didn't even seem angry...just exhausted she stood up and said:

"Jackson I'm going back t'bed. I have to go to work in the morning."

He looked down at her bare feet on the rug...a few steps away from each other... separated by something endless, infinite and incomprehensible.

"Can I crash here, on the couch? I'll just get a couple of hours of sleep before I take off."

"Do whatever you wanna do, Jackson," she sighed. "Move yourself into fuckin' Tony's bedroom if that's what you want..."

UNTIL THE END OF THE WORLD

In the archway, she stopped for a moment, looked over her shoulder at him and said:

"Thanks for getting me in off the street."

When the sun came up he was still awake...sleepless now...haunted...slowly coming to terms with something he wasn't ready to acknowledge with any kind of coherent thought.

He walked down the hallway and looked at her asleep....curled up under the blankets... faceless beneath the spill of her hair...

Bonker and Zoom left off washing...glared at him from where they'd spooned up against her back and thighs. He whispered *Be safe and happy* and hoped that someday somebody would come along who would convince her that love and trust weren't just words in a cheap romance novel.

He picked up his damp underwear, slipped soundlessly back into his boots and let himself out her front door, stood in the watery new sunlight breathing in damp and diesel as the city came awake around him. He walked back to where he'd parked his car the day before and ripped up the parking ticket on the windscreen. Then he drove aimlessly for a little while, in rush-hour traffic, until he found some public parking and spent the day wandering around the sprawl of a park that was less than a mile from her house...studied stone statues raised up in honour of city fathers and historical heroes ...sat beside a fountain as the ebb and flow of people still living their lives ran by him...considered going back to her house a dozen times...waiting for her...again...and found it no longer seemed as important to him as it had the day before.

He could have been sleepwalking all day and simply not known. Another sunset shone through the three high-rise towers to the west like solstice through the sarsens at Stonehenge, ran rivers of gold down through the streets. He got up slowly, found his car in the parking lot and joined the evening commuters on his way back to the interstate.

The highway unwound in front of his headlights...dotted lines strobe-like with the passing of time and other vehicles...solid yellow ribbons a prison bending him to the dawdle of drivers closer to home than he would ever be. At some point in the middle of the night when he was alone on the highway and the quarter-round slice of his world bordered by thousands of lives being lived beyond the reach of his high beams, he looked back across all the years of traveling he had done...most of them on his own...always moving...or running...even the years and years with his wife.

He shifted uncomfortably...too many hours...no respite...no sleep...miles to go before he could lie sleepless staring into a different kind of dark than the one on the other side of his windscreen. He reached for a bottle of water...found it empty...thin plastic drying in the absence of moisture and a wash of dashboard heat. When the rain started to splatter down and his wipers slashed away ineffectually as it grew into a downpour he let out a deep breath and thought perhaps he could simply stop at the end of this journey… live out the rest of his days quietly in surroundings that were at least familiar… make an end of the endless highways.

The thought should have brought comfort. Given him a sense of relief that it was over. But he knew what it really meant…that in the last twenty-four hours something dreadful and intolerable had happened and he simply had run out of places to hide.

He realised he was having a hard time breathing; that his throat had gone raw; that all the muscles in his body suddenly felt like they were being stretched and twisted and that someone had lit a chemical fire inside his head. He realised he had waited too long to get back on the road and now whatever killer virus had tried to take Natalie was mindlessly intent on taking him instead.

"You're not going home," he whispered, more tired than he had ever been before in all the sixty-odd-almost-seventy years of his life. "You don't even know what it means."

He closed his eyes…felt the tires on the passenger side of the car sliding off onto the shoulder…found himself back in the wash of soft golden lamplight in her bedroom, looking down at her in the few brief moments before he reached to do up the first lace tie on her nightgown.

Her hair was a glistening arc across the pillow, already losing dampness, beginning to wave and curl back down across her shoulders. Her head was turned to one side...eyes closed...eyelids trembling slightly, moving the long dark lashes in small shadows across her cheeks she was breathing easier now, into a cupped hand flung up into her hair on the pillow...child-like... helpless...so much more than just fuckable he...

...Touched her once...so gently...where he could see her heart beating softly up into her throat... closed his own eyes for an instant when he felt her pulse under his fingertips...opened them again...saw the slow rise and fall of her breasts....the sweet curve of her hips and belly down to the elegant mound of her pussy, and the neat tiny triangle of dark hair that disappeared into the shelter of her thighs...

He imagined for a moment what it might have been like for them to kiss... together...to feel her body in response to his...satin skin...warmth...to see her dark eyes open for him...focus for a moment...and then become soft and dreamy...to close slowly to the worship in his touch...

In the bleak howling lightning-blasted wasteland of his heart there was... suddenly...an absolute silence...and peace...one last exquisite moment when she adored him, and what little he had left to give was more than she had ever dreamed of.

SUN GOING DOWN...

He stocked up. Made sure he scowled and muttered under his breath so he'd fit right in with most of the people who came into the shop like the world owed them for bad luck... a twist of Fate...for being angry...or maybe just being dumbfuck stupid. Everybody looking for something to set things right, once and for all.

He handed over his Visa card, shovelled all the stuff on the counter into his backpack and headed back out into the sunset with a small curl of computer paper that he crumpled up and left on the sidewalk for someone else to total up the cost of the night's festivities.

Night's festivities he thought, laughing to himself. *Maybe just for me...*

A luxury of words. He turned left and went walking into the wind. Trembling. Suddenly he knew that nothing would be festive ever again.

All the other times at this time of year since the surgeon had told him he needed to keep exercising so the bypasses wouldn't go flat he'd just put his head down in the wind, kept on going, pretending not to remember how the corkscrew in his chest had made him fall down on his knees and beg for the pain to stop...beg for someone kind... soft...safe...at the end of those walks... somebody to hold him up and lay him down and make up for all the warm that had never happened.

Years and years and years ago...a different lifetime... they'd never found his father. He'd made too many pieces, scattered them in so many places where the Humpty Dumpty puzzle was just too far-flung to ever be put back together again...

So he walked...head down in the comfortable agony of his blind inexplicable rage...the hope that it would stop soon...the vacuum he had not been able to escape no matter what he did or how hard he had tried to ignore the emptiness that lurked on the edges of his existence...

Once upon a time he had dreamed of being in love forever. A life of doing whatever it took during the week, with the nightly and weekend reward of loving arms. Peace. Somebody who would love him in spite of all the damage.

So now he just walked, deeper into the dark, as the city became shadows and the neon became eyes that opened on the End of Days.

It had been in the back of his mind for such a long time, hiding, the whispered promise always there...so he knew exactly what to do in order to get to where he wanted to be...high above the city...looking down... snapping black steel Lego-bits into what he knew was wrong and empty.

He wept as he looked down through the gun sights of his shiny new assault rifle.

He wept because nobody had ever noticed all the damage in his heart; that there had never been the least hope that something or someone could have come between him and what was in the wind. He wept because he'd never once even dreamed of ever hurting another human being once his father was gone...but even then *the voices* hadn't stopped and it was like he was someone else, totally different from whoever he had been the moment before he had become what he was tonight.

He took a deep breath and begged forgiveness from a bullshit god.

Tonight...a lot of fuckin' people were gonna die and he had no idea why it was he had to be the one to do it...

COMFORTABLY NUMB

I'm not going to cry.

She kept repeating it to herself, like a mantra, hoping that if she said it enough times it would work. She could feel something much worse, like a volcano, inside her. Tears were nothing compared to the feeling that she was filling up with something so horrible that it would tear her apart if she acknowledged it; that if she began to cry she would begin to howl, and after that...she couldn't imagine it...the violence...the blind rage that had been hiding...waiting to come out.

She closed the image file on the desktop monitor in front of her. Martinique, less than a year ago. White sand castles and sunshine. Lazy intoxication and lovemaking late at night once the girls were in bed. Now a different lifetime. A different life. No longer hers at all. She shut the computer down and closed her eyes, wishing she could simply stop and somehow...disappear. Not be herself anymore.

I'm not going to cry.

But some kind of sound must have escaped. She heard Daphne's claws clicking across the tile floor in the kitchen. When she opened her eyes the Corgi was camped on the rag rug at her feet, looking up at her with unnerving doggy concern.

"It's okay, Daffy," she said slowly...softly...carefully. "You don't have to worry. I promise."

Daphne's new expression was one of complete skepticism. The day before it would have made her laugh. Today she didn't dare. She looked away, just far enough to see her perfectly manicured fingers clawed on perfectly brand-new denim-clad knees, nails in perfect ovals, polished to a glistening all-natural healthy-looking perfection.

"I'm not going to cry, Daffy," she said aloud, and stood up...but so suddenly the Corgi jumped up along with her...startled...worried again...following her into the TV room where the pompous idiot with the beard was silently informing her of *What we know*...for the twentieth time in the last hour, in what would have been his pompous idiot newsman voice if she had turned the volume up...

"*...And we've just received word...McDonalds has announced a new crispy octopus sandwich, with only four calories and no fucking cholesterol...*"

...As the tape at the bottom of the screen scrolled news of mayhem and disaster in between winning lottery numbers and pre-season baseball scores from Florida.

She picked up the remote and clicked the *Off* button, watched the 72-inch screen go blank, turned, and through the archway caught the reflection of a stranger in the mirror on the other side of the entry hall. She whispered her mantra one last time and fast-balled the remote into the reflection, felt vicious pleasure as the stranger disintegrated into a hundred shards of herself, all over the antique desk and the marble floor of the *foyer*.

She heard a car pull into the driveway, recognised the sound of the Beamer's engine. Daffy was gone, scared off by the smash of the mirror. She took a couple of steps forward, just far enough so she could see and be seen by him when he came through the front door....heard him pounding up the walk...stood quietly...waiting...

He was wide-eyed and frantic, his tie rucked off to one side suddenly quiet when he saw her, closing the heavy oak door behind him his eyes never leaving hers...

"Char...thank God," he breathed.

Charlotte nodded. Stood silently. Waiting. She could hear her heart beating beneath her breasts, measured like thunderous armour, protecting her from the thing snarling inside.

"Yes, Kevin," she said. "Thank God."

"You're all right."

"Of course I'm all right."

"What are you doing here? I went t'the school. Libby Dandridge said you'd been there, but then you'd gone home."

Charlotte nodded.

"I did. I was there."

"They said he was Hispanic."

"Yes. They said he'd escaped from one of our concentration camps. Went looking for his four-year old daughter."

She looked at him as if seeing him for the very first time, so smooth and so handsome and so upwardly mobile, the perfect Ivy League husband to give her a beautiful home and beautiful children and a life utterly free from care or worry. Except for today, because Reality had come calling, invaded their perfect little world, and he still didn't have a clue.

"Concentration camps?" he said. "What are you talking about?"

"I packed your bag for you this morning. Your big weekend, isn't it? Golf in New Jersey with all your friends...and him..."

He looked at her like she was crazy.

"Charlotte I'm not playing golf this weekend."

She smiled.

"Of course you are, Kevin," she said. "Why on earth not? This is a golden opportunity. Do you think *he's* going to call it off?"

Kevin noticed the splinters of broken mirror all over the floor, looked up at her, waiting for some kind of explanation. Charlotte smiled.

"They wouldn't let anyone in, Kevin," she said, "so I just came home..."

"But the girls are all right."

"Of course they are," she said, and even though there was a tape loop in the back of her head telling her she wasn't going to cry she could feel tears welling up in her eyes.

"They're someplace where no one will ever hurt them ever again..."

"They're upstairs."

"No."

"Charlotte where are they? Why aren't you with them?"

She smiled and felt the rage churning up through her guts.

"D'you really think I'd be here if Molly and Cassandra were alive? D'you think I'd've let anyone keep me away from my babies if they were alive... hurt...terrified? Are you a fucking idiot, Kevin? They're dead, you sonofabitch. They're dead because you and that turtle-faced piece of shit you work for have stood in the way of every effort anyone has ever made to keep this from happening over and over and over, and still all you motherfuckers ever have to offer are your thoughts and your prayers so the bastards who make the guns can keep on making them. You're like hookers in three-piece suits, except whores have more integrity."

She walked towards him...slowly...never felt the shards of glass in her bare feet...never looked at the smears of blood on the white marble tiles...picked up her purse...called for Daphne...scooped her up before she could cross the wasteland of broken mirror.

"Move your damned car, Kevin," she said. "When you've got all your thoughts and prayers sorted out you can send some to me at my sister's house. I carried my little girls inside me for nine months. I brought them into the light. I fed them and bathed them, changed their diapers and kept them safe while they taught me all over again what it was like to be innocent and happy. But I'm not putting them in the ground, Kevin. You and those heartless greedy bastards masquerading as our leaders are the ones who killed them, so you can do it...and between now and then...go fuck yourself. Fuck all of you."

FORTY YEARS AND FIFTEEN MINUTES

She recognised him in a heartbeat, had wondered all along if he would be there, even if he'd not been on the list...never forgotten...she'd gone round the room twice before she found him, realised it was where she should have looked for him in the first place... well out of the way...by himself...buried in a corner...

She walked across the banquet room slowly, afraid he would look her way, afraid he wouldn't; that she would call his name and he'd turn, not recognise her...or worse...

"Toby," she said...softly...in the exact moment he turned in her direction and saw her, his eyes going wide and she could feel herself trying not to cry, and read something on his face that made her want to die at his feet and run for her life, all at the same time...

She whispered "Toby," again, reached across the last few breaths between them. "You came..." she said, and he nodded, barely moving his head staring at her, swallowing hard.

All the other guys were wearing suits, sports jackets and ties, creased trousers and polished shoes. Showing off success with shiny new clothes to offset all the time gone by. Toby was in his jeans, a chambray shirt frayed at the collar and the cuffs, his boots scuffed and cracked as if it was yesterday. Four decades gone and all the years had simply ignored him...never even dreamed of touching him...except that he really didn't look anything like the boy she'd known anywhere but deep down inside his eyes.

He swallowed again and his answering whisper was so low and hoarse that she could barely hear him, or make out the sounds that were her name he said:

"Cory."

And she nodded and put her arms around him, could feel the back of his shirt wet with perspiration, tasted the familiar acrid smell of him, where they'd sat together at a single lab desk through two years of high school homerooms.

"Oh...Toby..." she said his name a third time, and then over and over again because she couldn't think of anything else to say that would be relevant to the strange violent crash in her heart and the wave of sadness making it so hard to breathe.

"Here I am," he said.

"Why didn't you write to me...or call...?"

She felt him shrug, and then pull away from her embrace, looking down at his feet...she expected him to kick at the polished wooden floor as if it were dirt under the bare toes of an eight-year old, but he took another step back from her and sighed...

"You stopped being Cory Sanchez."

"Oh please Toby don't," she said. "I couldn't stop living. You disappeared. You never said anything. You just took off. One morning I went looking for you and you were gone."

He put his head down.

"I know, Cor," he said. "I wasn't blaming you. It's all on me, I know that."

She couldn't stop herself there was still something so sweet and so helpless in his face and looking at him brought back a flood of memories...being adrift together...hanging on to each other in the face of too much...something...Life...

She put her head down on his shoulder and wept.

"Cory don't cry...please don't cry...I just wanted t'see you...one more time. I don't care about anything in between. Don't cry, fuck please don't cry..."

She couldn't stop. It was more than two years since Sean had paid in full for all the Marlboros...years and years of giving him what was left after Toby had gone. It wasn't that she hadn't loved him, only that she had never given him what he deserved for loving her. Because she never forgot Toby.

"I knew you would come," she admitted to him and herself. "I knew you would be here. Somehow I knew. There's an suitcase in my car and I left a note for the kids. I never stopped missing you....so badly...there were nights when Sean was inside me and I couldn't think of anything or anyone but you..."

Gently ever so gently he put his hands on her shoulders and moved her just far enough so they could look in each other's eyes...see the tears running down each other's faces...

"Don't, Cory," he whispered. "Don't even think about it. You can't go with me now, like I couldn't go with you then."

She reached up with both hands winding themselves into the grey and gold curls that streamed down either side of his face.

"I can go anywhere, Toby."

"Not anymore," he said, shaking his head. "Not anymore..."

There was a sound from somewhere outside their misery...something he seemed to know was coming as he looked past her...clenched his hands on her shoulders...let go...stepped away...

"They're here," he said, and for a moment he was again the beautiful boy she had known-loved-died-a-hundred-times-for when she was sixteen years old.

"They're gonna take me back. I'm never gonna see you again..."

She said "Toby...?"

"I got totally fucked up and I killed someone, Cory. It was a long time ago when I knew I wasn't good enough for you. I got drunk and I was angry. I knew I could never come back..."

She turned. Saw half a dozen black suits running towards her she realised his hands were gone from her shoulders and she felt adrift in some horrible soundless storm.

They ran past her...following Toby's (bread-crumb?) trail out some other exit from where the class of 1979 celebrated having survived so well.

MICHAEL SUMMERLEIGH

She heard three gunshots...tried to remember him begging her not to cry.

HAUNTED

Somebody fumbled with the zipper of his windbreaker and said *Just hold on, mister, we got help on the way*, and Ellis nodded dumbly, having heard the words before, long ago, in a dark desolate place where the stars were like no other stars he'd ever seen and the night screamed at you with crimson streaks of tracer fire, echoed to the thunder of invisible artillery, whispered with the promise of Death hot on your heels on noiseless cat feet.

He opened his eyes—a distraction from the pain that had begun to creep through the numbness in his body—and remembered the few short steps he had taken, the sudden squeal of tires on slick pavement. There had been a brief blinding glare of headlights and then a sickening thud...a crazy pin-wheeling parody of flight...and now he could almost see himself sprawled in the middle of Fifth Avenue, almost feel the splinters of bone jutting into the cold air where his left leg was bent beneath him.

There was a salty copper tang in his nostrils and he knew he was bleeding; that the ragged flutters of snow falling down around him like tiny pieces of broken moonlight were being swallowed up by blood-red going to black on the pavement. He knew that Shelley was at home with a casserole ready to come out of the oven, but tonight supper was going to have to wait. Tonight the whole world was going to have to wait as far as he was concerned, at least until he knew whether or not Death was going to pass him by on the early evening run.

"Mister can you hear me?" asked the voice that had spoken earlier.

The sound cut through the clamour of rush-hour traffic noise, brought him abruptly back into awareness of his immediate surroundings, the circle of faces looming over him, all staring down at him waiting to see Death. He once had heard someone say there were people who showed up at the scenes of accidents and disasters, the same people every time, no matter where they occurred or who were the victims. Ellis knew them all intimately, had seen them countless times in that other place, drinking tragedy with their eyes. Now they were drinking him...again...feverish with thirst...feasting on the pain as shocked nerve-endings and bruised torn tissue succumbed to the reality of a cab running a red light...the telescoping of Time outward until Ellis had been able to count the number of his heartbeats as the taxi went sideways across the intersection...brakes shrieking...and the yellow enamelled fender rushing closer and closer in slow motion to where he was in mid-stride...

Marty Paulsen whispered, "Can you see anything?"

Ellis cursed as his right foot slipped in the muck along the bank of the stream and jammed the rifle butt up into his ribs. He found a new foothold, levered himself slowly up to where he could peer through the tangle of tree-roots directly in front of his face.

"Brown," he said coldly. " I can see Brown, Marty. There's a big fucking hole where his legs used t'be and I don't think he's ever gonna see his mama in Richmond ever again."

Another shell, like the one that had killed the guy from Virginia, came ripping out of the darkness and wiped him entirely out of existence, showering Ellis and his buddy with more muck and filth and whatever else it had torn loose from the rice field. Paulsen began to make meaningless sounds in his throat.

"I fuckin' hate this place, El," he whispered at last. "I really do hate this place."

Something in his voice made Ellis want to turn to him, look him straight in the eyes where he hunkered down beside him, and pat him on the shoulder...do something... anything...to cut through the stench of fear that hung around him now, just waiting to infect anyone close by.

"You sure as shit ain't alone on that score, Marty," he said softly, without looking at him, because after a while you learned never to focus all your senses on any one thing, especially a friend. Friends didn't rise up out of nowhere to stick a bayonet in your guts. They didn't hide from you, so you let the small sounds they made, or their smell, let you know where they were while the rest of you kept alert for the non-friends...the ones who would *do you harm...with a knife-blade or a bullet looking for your name to wear...*

"Don't try to move," said the voice beside him. "Looks like your leg's busted pretty bad and if you move it'll make it worse. I'm gonna lift your head now, okay...put my coat under you for a pillow. Just take it easy..."

Yeah I'll do that Ellis thought. He opened his eyes again—not remembering when he had closed them—and stared up from the bottom of a concrete-and-steel canyon, beyond the glare of the streetlights bouncing off glass into the black night sky where the ragged flutters of snow were growing bigger...growing into thick heavy flakes dancing down to sting his face with cold...like a shroud. Someone covered him with a blanket or another coat and he could feel Marty Paulsen's fear churning up out of his belly.

Don't cover my face he begged silently. *I'm not dead yet don't cover my fucking face...*

He remembered the rice field in front of them had been a place of shifting dark and shadow, ever-changing in the glare of exploding rockets, the sluggish rain of flares that arc-ed into the sky and fell like Christmas ornaments on a sagging tree. He remembered his last Christmas with Shelley, her parents gone out for some last-minute shopping, and the two of them naked beneath the tree, their bodies twined like magic in the winking lights, silvered with tinsel, gifting themselves on each other.

"I'm not gonna die," he had promised, but the urgency of her hands dragging him deeper and deeper inside her told him it was a fragile promise at best; that they wouldn't be so frantic if suddenly in all the delirious joy of fucking for the very first time there wasn't some hint, some faint whiff of Death creeping closer, informing him that the surge of his pride and patriotism would prove to be an unreliable armour at best.

Paulsen screamed as the darkness behind them thrashed into movement and Ellis whirled, sliding down the bank of the stream into the water, bringing his rifle up to centre on the shadow plunging towards them.

"El for Christ's sake it's me!" hissed a terror-filled voice, and a pair of staring eyes went fire-engine red in reflection of the shell that screamed over them, exploded into the rice field.

"For fuck sakes don't ever do that again, Peterson!" he said, hearing himself shake every word loose from his tongue. "Not ever a—"

"I'm sorry Ellis, I couldn't...I heard that shell comin' in and I didn't think..."

He turned back to the rice field, not wanting to hear his apology, not wanting to see his fear, or let either of them know how close he had come to blowing Peterson's guts out his asshole.

"Where's everyone else?" whispered Paulsen, already knowing.

"They're dead," said Peterson. "Sarge... McCormick...Ryerson..."

Ellis nodded and Paulsen started crying, a choking sound that wove in and out of the rattle of weapon-fire echoing around them. When he looked out past the splintered trees on the edge of the field he saw shadows moving, away from them, joining other shadows on the far edge of the field...not-friends...as another rocket sliced through the night and thundered into the stream less than a hundred yards away.

"We can't stay here," he said, not looking at Marty or Peterson, not caring if they were listening or not. "They're gonna blow this place to shit and then come back lookin' for us...."

He began to crawl along the muddy bank of the stream, heard the whoosh of warm wet displaced air gone to furnace flamethrower heat and then the whole fucking field erupting like a Fourth of July in Hell. He crawled faster...

"I'm not gonna die," he told himself. "No fucking way..."

But now all the numbness was draining out of him and he could feel the shuddering stabs of pain that came from his leg, and the harsh grating sound that came out of his chest every time he tried to draw a breath into his lungs.

"There's an ambulance on the way, buddy," said the voice at his side. "Just relax now you're not gonna die."

You got that right, pal he swore to himself. *No goddam VC's gonna take me out. No way!*

He tried to get up, felt the numb in his broken left arm dissolve into agony as hands held him down, gently lowered him back to the pavement. He heard horns blaring, the wail of a distant siren; the stink of gasoline and burnt human flesh...

"Ellis you mustn't move," said a different voice, quieter than the first. "Just be still until help gets here and don't make it worse by moving around..."

Oh Christ how can it be worse than this? he asked himself, moving in a crouch through the undergrowth. *I can't see a fucking thing and all I can smell is my own sweat and Marty where he pissed his pants...*

"Stay close t'me," he whispered hoarsely. "Don't let me be alone. Shelley's got supper on the table by now."

Suddenly he was cold and wet... and the darkness in front of him kept shifting into shapes of deeper darkness that danced and disintegrated, became empty darkness all over again. He stopped, listened for any other sounds lurking behind the weapons-fire, the sound of his breathing, the two men behind him...

He knew his life depended on keeping his thoughts clear and his senses alert. The tension was almost not quite unbearable he trembled and had to force himself to stop.

Paulsen and Peterson were like leeches behind him, so close he could feel them a breath's-length from his ass, sending shivers up and down his spine he took three quick steps, just to get some distance between them and him...heard Marty Paulsen go frantic... following him...and a branch snapping under his boot.

"Oh God Ellis...!"

He threw himself forward, burying himself in the muck as an automatic rifle stuttered and Marty screamed again without any words. The moving shadows came back again but now he could see one of them was Marty jerking back and forth as muzzle-flashes from a dozen yards away spit bullets into his body, held him doll-like in the air until the VC stopped firing and he collapsed into the mud.

Peterson said, "They're all around us. Jesus fuckin' Christ they're all around us."

Ellis inched himself away from Paulsen's body and kept on going.

You can make all the noise you want to, Peterson he told him silently but I'm not gonna make another sound. Thanks to dumb-ass Marty they know we're out here, so I'm just gonna be real quiet until they go away...

"I'm gonna be real quiet..."

"That's right, Ellis," said the quiet voice. "Real quiet. That's good. That's perfect. You're doing fine. It won't be much longer."

His eyelids fluttered open, searching for the voice, but all he could see were the faces that had come to watch him die.

"Don't leave me," he said.

"Not going to happen, Ellis. I'm here..."

And he began to breathe more easily, reassured, feeling the tension and the fear start to drain away in the cool resolve to wait...patiently...where Death couldn't find him... where they would not even know he was alive to be hunted...

"El where are you?" Peterson whimpered. "Ellis they're comin' this way for God's sake would you say somethin' please don't let me be the only one out here!"

He heard Peterson stagger to his feet, begin to run towards him even as he backed away into the jungle all the while listening to the quiet voice whispering to him to be real quiet so the VC wouldn't know he was there as the dark became filled with an excited Babel of voices and bursts of flame from a half dozen rifles all of them aimed at Peterson doing the same stupid dance as piss-pants Marty, his body shredding in a hail of gunfire.

You can't run or even hide now, Ellis, not if you want to keep your promise to Shelley you've got to figure out some other way...

And now the voice sounded very much like his own thoughts—or maybe it was just his thoughts sounding very much like the voice—as he backed further and further away from the corpses of Paulsen and Peterson, deeper into the undergrowth, wriggling along on his belly like a snake, racing to outflank the knot of VC growing tighter...crowing over the bodies of their two kills...and then...moving on...

Your knife, Ellis, use your fucking knife...

He let five of them go by...waited breathlessly... knowing there was one more...one more moving past him on noiseless cat feet...inches away from his nose...and the faint glimmer of a smile as he left his rifle on the ground and rose up behind them...no longer hunted...

"Okay mister can you hear me? The ambulance is here. Don't move just let them lift you...that's it...relax you're doin' great..."

Everything's gonna be fine *he grinned, and eight inches of tempered blued steel glinted dully in darkness unseen by the moving shadow in front of him. He snaked his left hand forward to cover its mouth...smother the cry of warning as he brought the chin up and the steel in one smooth stroke across the unprotected throat. He knelt with the collapsing body in his arms felt the sleeve of his tunic grow heavy with a carotid flood, stalking forward again, finding that the ritual now was practised, sure-handed and deadly. The second one went down without a sound, drowning in his own blood as the next one turned...*

I'm not the one gonna die...

Ellis leapt towards him, this time closing a hand around the windpipe...choking the warning cry into silence...burying his knife in the abdomen and ripping upwards... grinning into the unseen face rigid with fear and that voice...that strange voice always whispering that everything would be fine so long as he was quiet and dealt Death swiftly...with a smile...not realising there were seven instead of six until a short burst of gunfire raked across his left shoulder and spun him around into a second spurt of fire that threw him backwards...away from the hunt...falling endlessly...

"We're almost there now, pal," someone told him over the wail of a siren and the slash of tires rushing him through the night. "Just hang on a little bit longer..."

Ellis remembered how the dawn somehow had found its way through the dark, brought light into the nightmare of slowly sinking into the muck and the slime and the blood oozing out of his body. How the VC had found him but left him for dead... so careless...

"Fuck he's still alive...!"

"Well get someone down here before he stops bein' alive!"

"One more minute, buddy, and we'll have you inside."

I'm not gonna die he kept telling himself. *I promised Shelley. I'll be quiet and still forever if I have to, but I'm not gonna die...*

He sensed bright lights through his closed eyelids, a flurry of activity around him as he was juggled carefully from the ambulance gurney onto another, heard a multitude of voices crowding into his ears and felt the close presence of Death...and dying...

But not me he thought confidently. *I'm not finished yet. I promised...*

"What happened?"

"The Cong hit him broadside and knocked him half a friggin' block down Fifth Avenue."

"Anybody with him? Has he said anything? Help me cut him out of his clothes he looks like half the bones in his body are broken..."

"There was one guy at the scene. Not a lot of people that hour of the night, but he didn't hear him say anything holy shit! look at the scars on him! He looks like he's been in a war..."

"Check his pockets for ID he's gotta be a Nam vet. Pam, get him on an IV stat he's in shock."

Ellis smiled to himself, knowing what was going to happen next because he'd been through it all before, in a dark desolate place where the stars were like no stars he'd ever seen and the night screamed with crimson arrows of tracer fire...

"I'm not gonna die," he said.

"You're damn straight, pal...Ellis...hang in there..."

Yeah...I'm gonna do that...

And Ellis knew it was the truth. Prayed it would be the Truth. He was going to be all right. Again. It wasn't his time. He'd done it before and he could do it this time. They couldn't kill him. They couldn't touch him...not anymore...not ever...

Please...

PAST DUE

Somebody came through the door of the Rose & Crown and a slash of sunset snuck in with, knocked him blind for almost a minute, so he didn't actually see her walking up to his table. The effect was like she had materialised out of thin air. A bit of magic. He smiled into his bourbon, pleased with the thought, and she said:

"Hi. There's lots of empty tables but you're here by yourself and so am I and..."

She shrugged in silhouette, and as his eyes came back to where he could use them again she made a wry smile that was charming and somehow very childlike. Like maybe she should be scuffing at some dirt under her bare feet. He took half an instant to think about it, then said:

"Please..." and nodded to the empty chair beside him, half-standing as he reached to pull it out from under the table for her.

Her strapless cocktail dress was clingy, hugged her up close in all the right places, some dark stretchy fabric that was as elegant and sexy as the smooth dip and swivel that sat her down beside him. She plunked a tall drink glass on the table and held out her hand.

"I'm Carly Atkinson," she said. "Carla really, but my friends call me Carly."

"Then I'm pleased t'be a friend," he said, taking her hand and making sure it was something that came close to being a real handshake. In the meanwhile, before they both let go, he met her gaze in the half-light, saw a glint of green-gold in the shiny eyes, and then registered the cool almost ivory feel of her hand before she drew it away.

He sensed a seduction in production and realised she'd already won him, that he didn't really care if she was a working girl. The shadows in his corner of the local tavern hid a multitude of sins, his own as well as hers, if she had any. He liked her. Immediately. And mostly he was just all of a sudden happy for her company.

"Travis," he said. "Travis Harker. Do you come here often?"

And he started laughing, and so did she, because they both got the joke immediately and he knew damn well she'd never been in the R&C before and she knew he knew.

"Hundreds of times," she said. "How strange we've never met."

"Life is full of stuff like that," he said.

"You can say *that* again."

"Must I?"

Her laughter gave way to giggles as she shook her head. An errant ray of light from somewhere struck a deep gingery colour from her hair that wasn't copper but wasn't carrot either. It framed her face like she'd washed it and then just shook it out rather than bother with a brush or a comb. She reminded him of Pamela Rodgers, one of the adorable Rowan & Martin Laugh-In girls from the

Seventies. He'd lusted after her from the moment she appeared on the show,

"So here we are," he said, and that hot meltdown feeling came rolling out of his past like a little locomotive on a short run to Heaven.

"Yeah. Here we are. *Now* whatta we do?"

It was his turn to shrug and kick dirt. He felt like a schoolboy and the warmth of it, the thrill of something sweet...imminent...becoming possible...becoming almost...something...flooded through him. He said:

"I have no idea, Carly. You ever just sit down with somebody and feel so good with them just being close by? Not saying anything at all, but all of a sudden so very comfortable...so stupid happy all at once for no particular reason?"

She nodded and smiled again, but then looked down into her lap and started twisting her fingers together,

"You looked like a nice guy. Not hunting...or anything else like..." she whispered.

The Rose & Crown was always busy on Friday nights, the go-to neighbourhood tavern for pub food and drinks and weekend party kick-offs. In the time it had taken for them to get where they were together the level of noise and conversation should have become intrusive, but it wasn't. Somehow the overhead was still just background music; the level of volume in the clatter of glasses and the babble of voices muted, like sounds from a room on the other side of a closed door.

"Lonely," he said.

She looked up. "Yeah. Guys that sit alone in bars like this are lonely...or looking for fun."

"I'm not lonely," he said. "And I'm good with fun, but not the way you meant."

"I knew that! I could tell. That's why I came over."

"Company."

"Yeah. Exactly."

"I'm glad you did," he said. "I live around the corner so I come here a lot, but tonight it was because I've been used to being around people all day long and last week that stopped."

Her eyes widened a bit to let him know she was asking how come.

"I retired," he said.

"Are you rich?"

"Enough t"buy you another drink if you want one when you finish that one, but no...not really..."

"So how d'you get to retire?"

"Well I'm tired of being an accountant for forty years and I turned sixty-five last month."

"No. Way."

Two sentences. He felt flattered.

"Way," he said. "Wanna see my driver's license?"

"You can't be! Sixty-five. You?"

He nodded.

"Travis I thought you might be fifty."

"I'm thinking you might be maybe twenty-five if you were havin' a bad day, but that means I should've been at your high school graduation...the proud parent..."

They weren't even pretending to play games. It was like they'd been something to each other forever.

"Who's your favourite movie star?" she asked, leaning forward, a challenge of some sort.

"Don't really have any...but I like Helen Mirren... Scarlett Johansson...and Adele Exarchopoulos...from France..."

She thought them over, then tilted her head to ask *Why...?*

"They're all three gorgeous and they always say what they mean."

She got quiet. Lifted her glass up and sipped at something clear and bubbly that came to him as citrus and maybe vodka. He said:

"What about you?"

She shook her head. "I don't have any favourites, but I don't go t'the movies so much."

"I haven't gone in forever. Most of it's crap...with more violence than I need in my life once I've gotten past the news feeds on my computer."

"Are you gonna have another drink?"

"Not if you're not havin' one...and maybe wouldn't mind walkin' around for a while. It was looking like a magical night when I came in here and I guess I was right."

He'd never even noticed the small clutch purse or fringed shawl, but the shy smile came back and continued to shine as he handed her back up onto her strappy open-toed heels. She put her arm around his waist before they got to the door, had to go sideways to get back out onto the street. Travis was almost certain he was gonna get lucky, but there was this really odd hope that there would be hours and hours of something else in between before it happened.

Out on the street Carly was soft and warm up against him and her almost-but-not-quite-coppery hair up near his nose smelled like some exotic tropical flower. They walked up to the park and found a horse-drawn carriage waiting for them; Travis got lost in the silence when her heels stopped clicking on the pavement. There had been an instant just before he handed her up into the *caleche* when the horse dipped his head down against hers and he saw her eyes close in something that could have been ecstasy...

He told the driver to take them into the park and then just wander, looked up at Carly who smiled, nodded in agreement. After that they both let the quiet close in on them, the clip-clop of the horse's hooves, the sound of traffic, the breath of wind whispering in the treetops...all fading away to leave them in silent shifting shadows every time the carriage passed beneath a streetlamp. She curled up against him again and he put an arm around her as she whispered:

"Oh, sir, this is so wonderful."

She shivered against him, made a sound that could have been quiet laughter, or a *frisson* of infinite sorrow. When another streetlamp cast light down on them her face was upturned to him, her eyes glistening.

"Take me home with you," she whispered. "I want to be someplace safe that belongs to you. I want to belong to you, even if it's just a dream."

She wriggled closer, his arm dropping down to the curve of her hip, a soft radiant invitation of warmth beneath the fabric of her evening dress he felt the thin brocaded length of the thong she wore beneath it, traced it with his fingers, down to the swell of her behind. His turn to shiver.

He said her name very softly. She sighed so very gently. Travis closed his eyes...

In the darkness she breathed *Oh!*...over and over again every time he moved....slowly... deeper inside her...almost sorrowfully...as if the pure sensation was too exquisite to be borne. She broke his heart with her total surrender to his invasion of her body...almost but not quite sent him reeling into something not at all gentle or kind or in any way having anything to do with anyone but himself and the feeling of himself growing longer and harder inside her...something dreadful and cruel and primitive...an invitation to an ancient dance of violence...

He stopped.

In the night outside his bedroom window, neon and starlight made half-formed images that crept through the wicker window shades...painted her with mystery and desire and a wordless wish for something more gentle than the snarling orgasm between his legs that was howling for release.

He fell down beside her still inside her, with the reality of her lovely behind against his belly and his head in the rain-forest luxury of her hair.

UNTIL THE END OF THE WORLD

Sunlight. Little bits and stabs of it sneaking past the edges of his bedroom blinds he opened his eyes...closed them again feeling something warm and breathing beside him...remembered...her name...Carly...and hours long into the night reaching out for her...the rush of her warmth into his arms and the seemingly endless lovemaking all blurred into a bright morning...complete physical exhaustion masquerading as total Peace.

He felt the sunlight sneaking through the bedroom blinds and when he opened his eyes a second time she was there...curled up in a little ball against his stomach with her spiky ginger-copper crown of hair more spiky than ever and the bumps in her spine like kisses on the underside of the satiny skin of her back.

He moved slowly so he wouldn't wake her...wide awake now himself...thinking a thought from the night before...

Breakfast. Breakfast just him and Carly in the little windowed alcove off his kitchen. The breathtaking gift of scrambling eggs for somebody...making toast... browning up home-fries...finally...after so long...for somebody else not Travis Harker...

She seemed so small...that childlike thing all over again belied by the underside of a breast he had come to know and love in the space of hours. Where the bedsheet had come away from her behind there was the scent of matted cinnamon-coloured hair salty-sweet and desperate against his lips in the hours before light had come back into the world. And now, the curiously arousing image of her thumb in her mouth...her face smooth with sleep...marred only by thin streaks of mascara where tears had loosed them from her eyes.

She seemed so small. Fragile. He thought of breakfast again. Waking this lovely creature guised in the form of a woman who had appeared like magic in his life he thought:

I'm gonna shower and then bring her breakfast in bed.

He didn't hear her follow him into the bathroom. Had no idea she was there until the shower curtain slid back and he saw a glint of steel for an instant before the big carving knife from his kitchen slid into his stomach and they were naked again eye-to-eye but now he could see the tears in her eyes and that kind of pain was worse than the one in his belly.

"I'm so sorry, Travis," she sobbed. "Why couldn't you be like the rest of them?"

"...The President of the United States fucked me when I was twelve years old. They told him I was fifteen. And the fat movie pig from California...and the television preacher..."

She was staring straight at him now but she wasn't seeing him at all. Carly was back into the nightmare of being barely anything at all with brand new tits, and parents who didn't give a fuck what happened to her. She clutched a bath towel to cover herself and tears as clear as diamonds fell down over her face.

"We weren't allowed to cry. We weren't allowed to say *Please stop it hurts...* and some of them wouldn't let us go or wash ourselves until we swallowed..."

Travis felt his legs turning into jelly beneath him, sank down into the deep claw-foot tub too scared to look at the handle of the knife in his belly or the look in the eyes of a little girl named Carly Atkinson. The shower–head above him was miles away.

"They said he killed himself...the one who was always there smiling...promising everything if we promised to be good...and now he's dead and nobody cares about us anymore...nobody wants to know what it was like to be so scared...to have to listen to fat hairy ugly men tell us we were being so good while they were fucking us..."

Travis said:

"Carly...?"

"Why couldn't you be like them?"

"Don't do this anymore, Carly. Don't let them ruin your whole life."

She looked down at him, tears streaming down her beautiful face.

"I'm so sorry, Travis. I didn't mean to hurt you."

"I know, honey," he said...slowly...because all of a sudden the knife in his gut had begun to be painful and he noticed the black Hitchcock ribbons of blood meandering away down the drain of the bathtub...

She bent to reach for the knife and he put his hand out to stop her.

"No don't, Carly," he said. "Leave it be. If you take it out I'll bleed faster and I need to say stuff to you and you gotta listen, okay?"

She nodded. The bath towel fell away from her and even though he knew there wasn't that much more breath left in him he gave most of it away just looking at her.

"First thing you have to do is put some kitchen gloves on," he said. "Right there, under the sink, okay?

"Then you have to go everywhere you touched anything and wipe it clean. And after you do that I want you to take all the sheets and pillow cases on the bed and put them in a plastic bag..."

"Travis..." she whispered, reaching down to him.

"Carly please just listen..."

She nodded again. Stood up beside the tub.

"Let me be the last one, Carly. Can you promise to try to let me be the last one?"

"Okay. I'll try. I promise."

"Don't hurt anymore. I'm taking all of that away now."

She started crying.

"Do you love me, Travis?"

"I love you more than anything else in the world, Carly. I'm sorry they hurt you, but you haveta start doing all the things I just said...and then...this is important...

"When everything is wiped clean and you've got all the bedsheets and stuff in that plastic bag, I want you to get dressed and listen at the door to make sure there's no one in the hallway. When it's quiet, put one glove back on and open the door...go to where there's an *Exit* sign at the end of the hallway and take the stairs all the way down to the basement. Can you do that?"

Carly nodded again.

"Okay good girl..."

He stopped, took a deep breath in concert with the lance of fire in his stomach.

"When you get to the bottom of the stairs open the door and turn left. There's another door at the end of that hallway. That one opens onto the alley behind this building and even though it says it's a fire exit and an alarm will go off if you open it, it's been busted for six months so just go ahead but make sure nobody sees you leaving...

"You gonna do that?"

Carly nodded. Travis felt Death creeping up on him.

"Go, sweetheart. Start now. Hurry, but be careful. And I'm gonna be the last one, right?"

Carly nodded.

"I love you."

Carly nodded.

And then she went away. For a while he could hear her doing all the things he'd told her to do. Then he heard the door of his apartment close quietly, and after that there was nothing, just the sound of the shower raining down on him, washing away the last of his life.

Travis gave the last few moments of it to his own tears. Breakfast would have been so nice.

A SONG FOR CATHERINE

1.

"...You're really gonna do this?"

"It's already done, Roger. I've had enough and I'm getting out. I found a place up northwest of Kingston and I'm going..."

Ellie sat on the couch with a glass of chardonnay and looked a bit stunned, at this point stunned enough to let her husband deal with something I'd been mulling over for weeks.

"You're still rebounding, Mac...grieving...you gotta give it some time. It's only been six months...and now this...?"

"You grieve for dead people, Roger. Lisa's not dead. I just stopped living with her."

"After forty years?"

"Yeah...well...shit happens, and some of ours caught up with us...in addition to the fact that I don't want any witnesses to me drinking myself into the ground... certainly not Lisa. She hasn't done anything to deserve that."

I refilled his highball with some Glenfiddich, turned away and slapped a line of packing tape across the top of my last box of books...

"What the fuck are you going t'do there, Mac? It's out in the middle of nowhere. You're gonna play piano concertos for the fucking cows?"

...Turned back to him.

"I'm gonna try t'find a way to play for anyone who will listen, Roger. It's been twenty years since my *triumph* at Massey Hall. It took me almost forty years to get there... and then I got torn apart for anything I did after. I don't wanna deal with that shit anymore."

I wasn't really angry. My idea of "creativity" had taken me far beyond the boundaries of traditionally accepted classical. It had never been an issue about traditional; I had never stopped adoring Beethoven, Lizst, Chopin, Mozart and Rachmaninoff; I'd simply stopped trying to add to musical constructs that had been perfected long before I'd ever been born. And I'd paid for it...in spades...

"Lisa wants you to come home, Mac," Ellie said.

"Ellie, she's your best friend, and she's been my wife for almost as long as the two of you have been pals...but where *she* is isn't home for me anymore. It's over. Maybe she can explain it to you, but it's not my place to try to do it now.

"Now I just want out of here. I wanna start over where I don't have to hear that little sigh of disapproval, or see the look on her face every time I crack the seal on another bottle of whiskey; where if I'm gonna be alone, at least I'm not being reminded of it daily by how we've failed each other..."

2.

So I left the big city. Getting the piano up the narrow stairway into the loft above the general store was an exercise in modern miracle; but an hour later my Broadfoot & Sons small parlour grand out of London circa 1870 was in the front room with all its legs back on and only a couple of strings in need of re-tuning...

That was late summer. In the fall something bad started to happen to the world. In early winter it got ugly...crisis...an intro to Armageddon without benefit of rockets or guided missiles, fire or brimstone...just a wee little thing called a virus that nobody could stop.

One afternoon I got a call from Ellie.

"He's got it, Mac," she said in tears. "Oh my God they took Roger to the hospital this morning and he's in a coma...on a ventilator...and Lisa's sick too..."

I said I would be there by suppertime but she shouted at me.

"No Mac you can't...I shouldn't have called like this you can't come back here it's not safe. I'm so sorry I just didn't know what else to do..."

Within a week Ellie got infected as well.

Inside of three weeks I lost her and Roger *and* Lisa. I looked at my piano, sat down on the polished walnut bench, put my head down on the ivory keys...real ones from when it was all right to slaughter elephants...

By that time I'd been on my own long enough that I'd run out of tears and gone a bit numb. Luckily I had plenty of whiskey to stay that way...

3.

It was never a challenge to do the self-isolation thing. About a week after I moved in everything went into pandemic mode; most of the local businesses were trendy little boutique affairs offering local crafts, artisan-baked goods, bistro-style lunches on the banks of the small but enthusiastic river that ran through the village. When the influx of weekenders from town slowed and then stopped, they all closed down to nothing but special orders for the locals. The general store continued to do a brisk, one-customer-at-a-time trade, but even that was seriously constrained by plastic sheeting and the shimmer of Plexiglas shields in sunlight filtered through plate glass.

And everyone seemed to take the entire affair seriously. Even though we never did have a "case" of our own, all of my new neighbours would remain strangers for months to come, faceless behind masks hastily ordered from Amazon—homemade when the suppliers all ran out of stock—or scarves that came up to eye level. As the cool weather deepened into real winter I watched it all from my windows, caught up on my reading, glared at my piano, and drank a lot more single malt than was good for me.

Every now and again I'd drive the hour into town to a real grocery store. Then I'd stand in the line-ups waiting for a shopping cart to roll out before I could roll mine in, stock up on whatever, and see the real face of what had visited itself upon the earth...the terror that stalked some of the people I encountered, the stark staring fear mirrored in their eyes.

I never really considered the possibility of catchiing the virus myself. Subconsciously I knew that someday I would have to do the grieving that Roger had talked about, but for the time being I couldn't find whatever was necessary to fuel it, so I just floated along, spent my days comfortably fuzzy on single malt...waiting for spring... something...

4.

In early April I got restless. The weather stopped being blizzardy and I started walking. I Googled maps of the area and charted myself four- and five-mile loops for the sunny days when there was no wind-chill to ambush you once you were outdoors. It kept me from hitting the liquor cabinet too early in the day, and provided much-needed exercise for my lungs, the intake of fresh air that might be crucial to the survival of a high-risk oldster like myself if I ever met up with Mr Covid-19...

I wasn't alone. As winter drew back from our pleasant refuge halfway to the back of beyond, my neighbours began to reappear; though still hidden behind our face-masks and scarves, the muffled greetings we exchanged whilst trudging along or sidling past one another were welcomed by all...sometimes even filled with amusement at the lengths we would go to in order to keep that six-foot social distance intact. One afternoon a couple approached me on a rather narrow little hiking trail out in the woods; with nowhere to go I waved hello and half-flung myself into a stubborn patch of snow so they could stay on the path. I could hear them laughing and calling out *Thank you!* long after we'd passed from each other's sight.

And Life in the village seemed to get better, a bit more relaxed, even though I'm sure we all were watching the same newscasts on the television, receiving the same news feeds on our computers. The world outside our little bubble was falling apart.Thousands of people were dying. Nobody knew how to stop the virus. The big industrials, the 1%ers and the governments that catered to them, had been too busy raking in profits to even consider spending any of it on a failsafe system to safeguard our health, but now they were paying the price. We the people who provided the blood sweat and tears that made them their fortunes were staying at home, desperately trying to survive with relief packages that were, from the very start, too little too late.

But we were mostly okay. The snow disappeared. Frost no longer etched itself onto windshields overnight. Mornings began to be bright and cheery, and windows began to open to let the sunshine in and all the stale winter air out...

And maybe it was the walking, that little bit of exercise, that did the trick for me, but I stopped scowling at the Broadfoot, and one evening actually found myself noodling through some Vivaldi. It felt good. I could feel myself smile, and it was almost like I'd forgotten how for the longest time, but not anymore.

In the merry month of May as it got warmer and warmer I started walking every day, and in the evenings I decided I would play Beethoven...one piano sonata at a time...until I'd run through all thirty-two of them and maybe jump-started my own creativity.

5.

Before that happened I got a phone call. Through a staticky connection that faded in and out as I tried to find better cell reception in the far corners of my loft, I recognised my attorney who also had been my agent in better days.

"...I wanted to give you some space," he said. "Some time to get settled...some time for you and Lisa to decide what you wanted to do."

"Kind of late for that now, Stuart," I told him.

"Yeah...I know," he said by way of an apology. "She said you both didn't want to start any kind of divorce proceedings, had decided to just let thing go for now...and then..."

"And then," I said. "Listen...Stuart...just sell everything, okay? Whatever you can get for the house...furnishings...I don't care I've got enough to get by on here... more than enough actually, so just make sure you get your cut and then we'll talk about donating the rest of it."

He sounded sceptical.

"Are you okay?"

"I'm fine, Stuart, thanks for asking. Just take care of yourself, stay healthy, and let me know how things are going whenever you think I need to know..."

He was quiet for a minute or so. I could make out the vague sound of papers being shuffled, maybe some notes being written down on a scratch pad. Finally he said:

"There's something else, though..."

"What's that, Stuart?"

"Lisa left a note on that little writing desk in her sewing room, before she went into hospital. It had your name on the envelope. I sent it up by courier this morning..."

When it arrived I read it two or three times. That was when I finally started grieving.

UNTIL THE END OF THE WORLD

6.

I didn't want to have to deal with people. Anyone. For a week I never even left my loft above the general store. I phoned up the liquor store around the corner, gave them a credit car number and asked if they could just leave the case of Scotch at the bottom of the stairs. In the city I would've been laughed at; out here in our little village the manager said *Sure no problem* and my medication arrived about ten minutes later.

A couple of weeks later I sobered up and started walking again, because it was the only thing I could do mindlessly...just plot a course and go...come back in an hour...an hour and a half later...

When the second wave of the virus exploded in the States, all of us country bumpkins just kept on with what we'd been doing all along. The problem was all of us were out walking; it cost nothing, kept us reasonably healthy and mostly sane; when I figured out most of us were out in early morning or late afternoon in order to avoid the burgeoning heat of summer, I started my wanders around noon when the sun was all the way fired up and turning backroads dusty, or into slightly spongy tar-and-chip.

One of my loops took me past flooded farmland and swamp, alive with invisible frogs making clacky croaking sounds like *claves* or *guiros*; birdsong that began long before sunrise. Seemingly overnight the hawthorn trees had burst into white flower; trillium peeking up out of the ground in pink, white and purply red; lilacs clouding air gone sweet with their lavender and purple clusters; and just as suddenly everything was green, vibrating with the explosion of Life, as if to make up for all of the death-dealing of a virus winter.

I met her my second or third day out. It was early June. Summer had taken its own sweet time to get here, but now it had arrived with a vengeance. By mid-day the temps were decidedly toasty. I stripped down to shorts and a t-shirt and rarely encountered a soul, but that afternoon, less than a kilometre from the village on a wooded trail that ran off from Adair Road, I saw her coming towards me.

She looked to be about my age, maybe a bit younger...petite was the word that used to describe someone of her less than middling stature...but slender...grey hair long past her shoulders that the light breeze lifted up around her face. In spite of the heat she wore some faded blue jeans over her hiking boots, and a long-sleeved blousy white dress shirt neatly cuffed at her wrists. I figured the black flies and mosquitoes found her irresistible; they tended to ignore me, likely from some insectoid antipathy to single malt Scotch.

As she got closer I saw sleepy brown eyes in a startlingly smooth oval face, her age showing only in some faint lines at the corners of her eyes and mouth. I inched a bit farther off the path as we approached each other, nodded and smiled a bit as she passed me, and then turned on the off chance she would do more than simply nod in reply. But she kept on walking, never looked back, and soon she was gone, lost in the shadows of the overhanging trees, her footfalls fading away in the distance

7.

UNTIL THE END OF THE WORLD

After that day I bumped into her pretty regularly, maybe three and four times a week when the weather made walking imperative. Unlike most of the people I encountered (and like me) she never wore a mask to hide her face, so I began to notice more and more things about her; that her eyes weren't so much sleepy as distracted, as if she were somewhere else and seeing things no one else could see. And her skin was pale when you considered that we often met on some of the paved and dirt roads outside the village that were open to the sun and the sky. As time went by I realised she was still quite pretty; that age had done good things to her, and I found myself attracted to that quiet beauty, and the "mystery" of her silence.

The fact was that I was lonely. When all was said and done I'd finally absorbed the sad reality that Lisa and my best friends were gone, and what was left of my life could only be what I chose to make of it; that after just nodding politely to each other from opposite sides of the road, I wanted to know more about her, hear the sound of her voice...

One afternoon without even thinking I did my usual nod-and-smile thing, and then started back-pedalling slowly, hoping for some conversation. I said *Hi* and waited to see what would happen.

She stopped. Turned to look at me, surprised I think, to have been addressed at all.

She said *Hello* in a way that it was almost a question—*Why on earth would you say hello to me?*

I introduced myself and she said "I'm Catherine"... cautiously...

"Pleased t'meet you," I said. "Nice t'know I've got a little bit of company out here in the crazy part of the day."

Suddenly she seemed about as sad as a soul could be.

"I like walking," she said, "but not with too many people around. I used t'be different, but times change, and I guess I've gone and changed along with them."

I stopped walking backwards and went towards her, stopped a little bit more than the requisite two metres away, but close enough to appreciate the soft brown in her eyes, the refuge of her rueful-gone-sad smile.

"Me too," I said.

"You're new here."

I nodded. "Moved into the village at the beginning of all this...above the general store?"

She nodded back. "Word gets around. I've lived almost my entire life here so..."

"You're in on all the news."

"You mean the gossip."

Her smile got a little bit less cautious and sad.

"Yes."

"So...? What's the poop on me?"

"You're a musician...from the city...almost famous even..."

"I had my fifteen minutes," I said, trying to be modest about it. "Since then it's been ...well...I guess the truth is that I ran away from what came after."

She went back to being more sad than anything else; her eyes got a bit unfocused with looking backwards into her past.

"My husband was a musician. He played the piano, and very much admired your concerto. I remember him shaking his head, and saying the critics were right to rave about it; but I think he knew the direction you were going, and that you'd have to pay for it someday."

She started to move away...stopped...

"It's been nice talking with you," she said. "I hope you'll find some peace here..."

I watched her for a while, a small figure in denim and a dress shirt that probably had belonged to her husband... two or three sizes too large for her...

8.

That night I remembered Beethoven, and the thought that he would be a good way to bring the music back into my life in such wise that it demanded no more of me than to somehow pay homage to his genius. I flung open the windows at the front of my loft as the sun went down and the heat of the day went away...lit two tall candlesticks that stood on the Broadfoot...sat down... closed my eyes...let the *allegro* carry me...into the *adagio*...the unspoken nods to Josef Haydn...of a sudden the music familiar all over again, like old friend come to call, or a beloved book grown dusty on the shelf for far too long.

When the last thunderous echoes of the prophetic *prestissimo* faded away I sat quietly, breathing in air gone cool in the night...opened my eyes to the mystical dancing of my two candles...and felt something like *peace* steal over me for the first time in as long as I could remember. I poured a brandy instead of Scotch, stood at one of my windows...and saw her standing across the street, a shadow in front of the shuttered bakery storefront.

I raised a hand, felt my candlelight transforming it into a silhouette that was answered by her own shadowed response. She turned and walked away into the night.

9.

I never again met her on the backroads, but for the rest of June well into July, night after night as I wandered my way through *le Pathetique*...the *Waldstein*...the *Appassionata* and the *Hammerklavier*...when I would come away from the piano and breathe in the night air through my windows, I would see her standing across the street, if only for a moment before she would turn and walk away.

I began to play in such a way that I recognised as I had never played before...for my audience of one...with some strange furious passion that often left me in tears, somehow channelling the tragedy and the triumph that made Beethoven so important to me...all the while knowing she was out there...listening...a small quiet creature named Catherine with sad brown eyes...

10.

By August, the worst of our thralldom to the plague seemed to be over. It raged on in the south, the States become victim to the incompetence and ignorance of the heartless thing they had elected to lead them. In our village though, Life began to blossom again in spite of the drought-like heat. Faces that for the better part of a year had been only eyes over top of cloth masks now grew noses and mouths that spoke clearly, and laughed, and my neighbours stopped being strangers.

UNTIL THE END OF THE WORLD

After the sonatas I went on to anything at all I could play without benefit of orchestral accompaniment, and still I played for the small figure who would stand in streetlight shadow, and then walk slowly away into the night. Sometimes I thought I could see her nod in response to my wave; sometimes I wanted nothing more than to rush the length of my loft and down the back stairs into the street. But I knew she would never be there waiting; that whatever it was we had been for each other through the evenings when I learned to play music again, it would never see daylight, or anything that could translate into our village's return to "normal".

I woke up one Sunday morning and walked across the open space called Five Corners, where two county highways and three local streets met in the centre of the village. I was looking for some sourdough bread to go with breakfast...walked into the bakery to the sound of some bells jangling over the door. The youngish man at the counter looked up and grinned *Good morning*...gave me what he called a long overdue welcome...

"...We heard you'd moved in over the general store," he said. "I'm Devon Craig..."

We shook hands. Ohmygod it was the most strange of all sensations after months and months of *social distancing*. I got a wee bit crazy and bought two fresh-out-of-the oven loaves with the traditional criss-cross crust. Paid with a ten-dollar bill that might have been anywhere before it landed in my wallet. He didn't seem to care. We had survived and now it was time for life to be lived again.

"Devon," I said. "I have an odd question. You live over your shop, don't you?"

He nodded. "Yeah. Me and Jen and my son, Terry..."

"Who's the woman who comes to stand in front every night...just to one side of your windows? She said her name was Catherine..."

He looked at me strangely.

"Catherine."

"Yeah. I spoke to her once when I was out walking. She said her name was Catherine. Small. Grey-haired with sad brown eyes. Whenever I'd see her she was wearing old jeans and a big white dress shirt I figured must belong to her husband?"

Devon gave me another strange look, cocked his head to one side, took off a long white apron and came round the counter. I followed him, to some photographs that hung up along one wall, over one of three tables in the shop that were there for sit-down customers...pastry and desserts...

"You saw *her*?" he asked, pointing to one photograph.

And I nodded.

"Yes. And him, the man beside her? I know him too. Alasdair Craig. I saw him perform in Toronto three maybe four times..."

Devon said, "They were my grandparents."

"Alasdair Craig died in Toronto during the SARS epidemic."

Devon nodded, said "But you saw *her*."

"This summer out walking. Many times. And every night when I played Beethoven she stood outside your shop and listened."

Devon sat down at one of his tables, looked up at me.

"My grandma died two years ago," he said. "There've been a couple of people in the village who said they'd seen her out walking, but I...I..."

He stopped. Just looked at me and at the photograph on the wall...and me...and then the photograph...

11.

That night I began writing music again. A week later, at the end of August, I opened my windows and played something I had titled "Beethoven's 33rd Piano Sonata... for Catherine"

She stood outside the bakery and listened. Stepped into the light. Waved and smiled. I never saw her again.

SANCTUARY

Perhaps it made sense in the movies where just about everything usually ended up as a fucked-up mirror of real life, but he'd never truly understood why a naked sweaty woman in his bed after the fact would feel the need to rustle up a bedsheet between her boobs and him. He took a small amount of satisfaction in that she still was having a bit of trouble getting both eyes to focus on him at the same time, but he was puzzled just the same. He imagined there was a good reason for it, but so far no one had ever been able to explain it to him.

"You said were gonna fuck me," she said, reaching back down under the sheet to where she could wrap one hand around him.

"No…" Garrett said softly. "Actually it was you making all the promises, sweetheart. I went along with it hoping we could both get lucky."

"Well now I feel badly…y'know…"

He shook his head, reached past her to the table beside his bed and one-handed uncorked the bottle of Jim Beam…poured half a tumbler full and became philosophical with her reflection in the glass and the bourbon inside it.

"It's the way it is. As long as you had a good time then I did too...but why d'you do that?"

"Do what?"

"With the sheet," he said, because suddenly it seemed like this might be a good time to try to solve the mystery. "It's not like I didn't get a good hard look at your front in all of this...and pretty cosy with them in the bargain."

He nodded towards the bottle. "You can help yourself," he said, "or there's Buds and Rolling Rocks in the refrigerator if you'd prefer a beer."

She took the glass from him, sipped cautiously, made a face like she'd been poisoned, and then seemed to consider his question...tilted her head to one side and look puzzled.

"I have no idea," she said. "Maybe girls just get taught this default modesty thing...like, y'know...oh my god that wave just carried off my bikini top now what the fuck do I do?"

He started laughing, retrieved his glass and put his other hand alongside her face.

"You're a real beauty," he said, and tried to say it like he wasn't old enough to be her grandfather. "What's your name?"

"Melanie."

"Like the First Lady."

"No way! She gives hookers a bad name! Anyone who would spread her legs for that fat pig for any reason has to be either digging for gold or just plain stupid."

The face she made just then was worse than the one where she'd been poisoned.

"My parents had hippies for parents. Somehow I got named for a singer...from the Sixties..."

He nodded. "I had a crush on that one," he said. "She sort of disappeared from the mainstream in the 70s and I worried about her for a couple of years until I found out that her producer was also her husband and they'd pretty much decided t'go indie when she became less than the rage."

Melanie took another stab at the bourbon, with the same results.

"Everybody in my family took a joint and a book of matches to every Crosby Stills Nash and Young reunion concert," she said. "It made 'em feel like maybe they were still in the vanguard of the *revolution*. It's so pathetic..."

There was an infinity of scorn in her words. The beautiful unlined face became a little bit less beautiful with some contempt thrown into the mix. He rescued his bourbon, took a long swallow.

"What are we listening to?" she asked.

"Classic old blues song. *Dust My Broom*...black dude named Robert Johnson wrote it back in the *Nineteen* Twenties. The band doin' this cover is Canned Heat."

In response to her look of total WTF he said:

"The Woodstock movie. At the very beginning. *Goin' on up the country, baby don'tcha wanna go...* Same guys. *Canned heat* was what the old bluesmen called Sterno...the stuff you use for fondues and keeping shit hot on your buffet table? The old guys used t'drink that shit for the alcohol content, which is probably why so many of 'em was Blind Willie this and Blind Willie that...

He digressed a bit. "I was at the first CSN gig in Chicago...followed them back t'the mudfest at Yasgur's Farm."

"Really? Woodstock. Like the movie?"

"Not *like* the movie. *The* movie...and the weekend that went with it. Yeah, really..."

"How old *are* you?"

"Sixty-eight last winter."

"Holy shit what the fuck am I doin' in bed with you?"

Garrett grinned. "I'm askin' myself the same question, though not with any kind of regrets."

"You don't look that old at all. And you're still pretty hot..."

"Well I am...that old...and only lukewarm at best..."

"So what's wrong with your dick?"

"You mean besides the obvious?"

"He *seemed* ready t"go."

Garrett stopped grinning, but tried for some humour anyway.

"Melanie, I've got my good days and I've got my bad days. *He* is a bit unreliable in that regard. Long time ago I lost my temper in a place where I shouldn't've... said some stuff I should've left unsaid and pissed off this asshole in the process...got a two-by-four in the balls for my trouble and a less-than-satisfactory love life in the aftermath..."

Her soft suddenly very sympathetic doe-like brown eyes asked a question.

"Whoever the hell he was, now *he's* mostly blind in his left eye, a lot uglier than before he met me, and, hopefully, if I hit him hard enough that last time, he can't fuck either. We really went at each other."

She said "Wow."

He said "Damn straight wow," and reached for the bourbon bottle again.

"You're down here with your girlfriends."

She grinned wickedly.

"My hippy dippy mom and dad sprung for an early graduation present."

"Did you hold out for that snappy thing on wheels parked out by the road, too?"

She looked proud, and forgot to hold the bedsheet up in front of the perfect pair of half-tanned C-cups that didn't require them in the first place. He said:

"Good for you, honey. Where's all the boyfriends?"

"Back home where they belong."

"Lucky me."

"Grady's dick can't do half what you can with your fingers and your tongue."

"I'm a lot older. Maybe he'll learn."

"I doubt it."

"Too fuckin' bad for him then. Can we see what happens if I put my tongue up your pretty little ass?"

―――

The next morning at the restaurant he made breakfast on-the-house for her and her girlfriends. Sat them down at the best terrace table with the rising sun at their backs, where they could watch the pelicans gliding in off the Gulf without worrying about them shitting on their omelettes.

UNTIL THE END OF THE WORLD

Between mouthfuls Melanie likely was regaling them with some kind of rundown on their night together. He waved from the kitchen and they all giggled and waved back with big shiny cheerleader smiles, and he made a point of being too busy to check in on them...see what they had planned...the chance he might be expected to do encores of some sort with Melanie or her pals. After the breakfast rush he helped the wait staff clean tables, pitched his apron back into the kitchen and went down to the water for coffee and a cigarette.

"Y'all sure do like 'em young."

Brenda was there on the dock before him, with her own smoke and coffee.

"I like 'em when there's little or no chance I'm ever gonna see them again."

"Well *that's* one hell of an attitude."

It didn't matter anymore if sometimes he couldn't fuck them. They didn't expect all that much from him anyway, so mostly he could get away with being a pleasant but in no way threatening bit of danger and strange to tell about when they got home from wherever it was they were on holiday from.

Brenda had risen to long-time resident status, after almost twenty years as much a fixture in the joint as the owner himself. He guessed he had maybe fifteen years on her, but not from appearances. She still looked pretty good in ragged hip-huggers and tattered thrift-shop dress shirts knotted up under her breasts.

She flung a heavy fall of dark silver-shot curls back over one shoulder and tapped cigarette ash into the water. He knew if she looked up at him there'd be anger in her grey eyes...and something else...

"You all're a real sonofabitch sometimes, y'know that?"

Definitely anger and something else...

"Yeah. I know," he said softly, wishing there was something he could say, wondering if it would make a difference; or if he decided to get honest, if there was any difference at all between her and all the Melanies who'd shared his bed in the time since he'd shown up in Santuario.

She flicked her cigarette into the water and started back up the rickety wooden stairs to the restaurant. He watched her, the shimmy of her hips under the threadbare denim...a patch on her right cheek that read *You Can Kiss It Here*...pretty much exactly where he'd start if somehow he could dredge up courage enough to get into the honesty thing...with her...or himself...

It didn't matter to him if there were times he couldn"t fuck the young ones. He tried telling himself that and knew it was a lie. And then there was also how he wished Brenda didn't give a shit...

By lunchtime the Midwest honeys-on-holiday all had moved on to younger thrills, Ms Melanie included. She waved at him and tilted her head at the All-American preppie guy sitting beside her and shrugged apologetically. He shook his head and gave her a thumbs up, a conjure that was equal parts relief and disappointment. She'd been a lot of fun to play with, with a lot more on the ball than your average Midwest blondie with the imminence of yet one more bachelor's degree in business admin. She'd been fifty pages into his copy of *Life: The Movie* when he got out of his eco-friendly rooftop-cistern shower and told her he was already late for his breakfast shift at the restaurant. She asked if she could stick around a little longer to look at his books. He told her not to worry about locking any doors and slogged out to the lean-to where he parked the rattletrap Sportster that had brought him to the tiny resort town on the west side of the Everglades.

Brenda made a point of keeping clear of him and he felt badly about it, but not bad enough to try to patch up whatever he'd managed to fuck up the day before. He recognised the all too familiar duck-and-cover pattern in his behaviour, and all the rationalisations that followed. She needed to understand…stop expecting stuff that wasn't gonna happen.

With the lunch crowd gone he made himself a New Orleans-style *po' boy* with leftover shreds of crab and shrimp on crunchy bread, poured himself a beer to go with and had a couple of smokes before he fired up the Harley and headed down 41 to where an unpaved road wandered off to his place on one of the nameless spits of sand and coral on the far side of Marco Island.

He left the bike in the lean-to, kicked off his boots and started walking to the water, closed his eyes as he felt the sand sliding under his feet, between his toes…the luxury of dappled sunlight shimmering through the palm tree towers overhead…moments of heat and coolth… breezes sneaking through the saw-grass...the croak of unseen amphibians on the make...

He could do it blindfolded and shit-faced drunk...had done it a hundred times...

His *place* was a mere resemblance of what other people might consider a home—to all outward appearances a small half-circle of inter-connected ramshackle shelters incapable of sheltering anyone from anything in the way of wet, warm or whatever. He knew that the less-than-moisture-proof room where all the books and vinyl lived would go down in the first serious storm to find it, but as time went by he realised that the rippling pages of his signed first edition of *All the President's Men* didn't really have any more to offer him than the thrift store copy in paper covers he'd bought for fifty cents; that his once-mint vinyl copy of *Ptarmigan* from 1973 still made exquisite music, but the sleeve just wasn't what it used to be.

After a while he began to view all his possessions, no matter how much value he or the world had attached to them in the past, with a casual disdain; after all, they were a perfect reflection of his own slow disintegration. How expect them to survive his neglect for their welfare, when he paid no attention to his own.

He dumped a six-pack of Budweiser cans into a small ice-filled cooler and sat in the little paved courtyard he had laid down in front of his door...watched the sun going down on the Gulf as the colony of neon-green geckos that lived under the concrete slab of *the library* scurried around snatching bugs out of the air. One of them, the one he'd named Green George the Gecko—after an agonising hour trying to find the *right* name—came to perch on the arm of his Adirondack chair, giving him funny gecko eyeballs from one side of his head and then the other. Garrett had mostly given up garlic and onions. Now the lizards were his friends.

"You guys have got it made," he said, with no rancour at all. "Look at ya. Free rent. Free food. Girl geckos fallin' all over you. Livin' the dream..."

He shook his head and emptied his Budweiser, reached slowly past Green George to get another one out of the cooler.

"Lemme ask you something," he said, squinting philosophically into the sun as he popped the tab. "What happens when you little fuckers get brokedown old and decrepit? Do all the little girl geckos stop comin' round? Or do you have to keep on knockin' yourselves out to keep 'em happy...t' keep yourself from freakin' out over bein' all brokedown old and decrepit in the first place?"

Green George wasn't in the mood for conversation. For two years he'd listened to Garrett, ignored him, went off to talk with his own—chirps, whistles and squeaks that no doubt made all the sense in the world to neon-green lizards but meant nothing at all to him. Green George had remained unshakably inscrutable, and today being no different from any other day, he flicked his long tongue out for a sand-fly and then scampered.

MICHAEL SUMMERLEIGH

Garrett watched the sun dissolve into the sea, made sure the battery connects to the solar panels had soaked up their daytime usual, went inside with the Buds, rolled himself a joint and blistered his mouldering AR speakers with a vinyl copy of *Led Zeppelin II*...

He didn't remember actually going out, thought he knew Santuario fairly well after two years...but he didn't this know part of it, or recognise the sagging docks or the maze of alleys between the ramshackle warehouses leaning precariously out over the water. And there was the issue of just where his drinking buddies had buggered off to, though he couldn't for the life of him remember who they were...or where he'd parked the Harley...

He started walking away from the water, not feeling at all like he'd overdone anything alcoholic or otherwise, but still cocooned in a strange unsettling sense of total disassociation; that nothing was as it appeared to be even though intrinsically recognisable.

He forced himself to walk slowly, fought the urge to run to the next corner—find some landmark or signpost to tell him where the fuck he was—even though it was the only thing he wanted to do. In the end it didn't matter where he turned in any direction, or that there was no other soul out in the night who could point him where he wanted to go.

And yet...in spite of all the surreality of being utterly *lost*...when he woke up covered in sweat staring wide-eyed at moonlight-spawned shadows shifting across the ceiling of his bedroom, there was no sense of relief...no lifting of the weight that was crushing him down. No *It was only a dream...* He could hear the geckos skittering around all over the place going about their gecko business, but when the sun stabbed a first pinpoint of light across his spit of sand and coral, he was wide awake and still trying to backtrack his way through the stark suffocating terror of it.

He couldn't remember pulling *Zeppelin II* off the turntable, or switching off the stereo.

He couldn't remember the first time he had dreamt the dream...only that it seemed to have been there... always waiting for him...for as long as he'd been alive...

He was up then just before the dawn, out in the slow surf casting for whatever aspired to be lunch at the restaurant that day. He rented his small corner of the universe from his boss, but pretty much got his digs rent-free by providing the kitchen with fresh catch and making home improvements; what little else he needed in the way of food, smoke, beer and bourbon got covered by his hourly on the grille. Seeing as he had no desire to see much of "civilisation" ever again, the Harley didn't eat enough gas to make any impact at all. When he got to the restaurant, Bernie the owner looked anxious.

"What the fuck did you do?"

Garrett said *Huh?* and waited for illumination.

"Brenda, for fuck sakes!"

He made noises that indicated he had no idea what his boss/landlord was talking about.

"She phoned me this morning and said she needed to take some time; that she was gonna spend a few days with her sister over in Homestead. Now I'm short-handed in the middle of spring fuckin' break..."

"How the hell does her taking off have anything t'do with me?"

Bernie gave him a look, the one most often referred to as *withering*, wherein it was understood that there was an obvious answer, and then all the other answers that ranged from patently foolish to just plain bullshit.

"Bernie, look, she doesn't approve of me. What the fuck am I supposed t'do, join the priesthood? Then she'd be on my case for maybe fucking little boys out back."

"You don't have t'piss her off that much."

"Bernie, I got lucky with a twenty-year old—"

"Again."

"So what!"

"So she's maybe got a thing for you and you could pay some attention. Meanwhile, now I'm scared shitless some night when me and Naomi are goin' at it I'm gonna say her name out loud."

"Naomi?"

"Brenda, you asshole."

"You've got a hard-on for Brenda?"

Bernie looked disgusted. "No, of course not," he said. "There *is* this other woman been comin' in here lately...but now that Brenda's all pissed off at you I'm thinkin' about her a lot...worryin' about her, y'know..."

They both started to laugh.

UNTIL THE END OF THE WORLD

"Bernie, my case of development is so fucking arrested it's a wonder I'm not doin' time in Leavenworth. Besides, Brenda and I have some very serious conflicts of outlook and interest. If I slept with her and she thought I meant it, it would only lead to worse things than her takin' off for a few days over spring break...like me having to listen to her twang at me while we fucked each other."

His boss looked at him, shook his head and sighed.

"You're a pig, Garrett. Go make breakfasts," he said. "All that red snapper you brought in looks good, like it'll go for lunch *and* dinner."

He made breakfasts. In between, he shelled crabs, boiled potatoes, and turned week-old stale bread into a seasoned shake'n'bake for the crab cakes they served to the Miami-Dade crowd on weekends. In amongst all of that he thought about Brenda, and what kind of sugar she kept neatly packaged away in her ragged jeans and cotton dress shirts; or if there was any way he might be able to stomach the insipid Nashville crap she listened to whilst at the same time struggling with his on-again-off-again hard-on.

Pretty girls mostly went on to be beautiful or handsome as they got older; he thought of Brenda as *salt of the earth*, whatever that meant—with an asshole for an ex-husband if you listened to her stories—but a good heart in spite of some of the strange ideas she carried around with regard to what was right and proper in the world. She just didn't make a dent in whatever was dogging him. Nobody did. Another Robert Johnson song *via* Canned Heat...hellhounds baying for the blood of his soul...

But he'd gone as far as he cared to go. Santuario was an unlikely destination. People mostly ended up there by accident, whether they arrived and then decided to stay, or were on their way to the Keys and had gotten lost along the way. A long time gone in 1521, a bunch of renegade *conquistadores* went AWOL on Ponce de Leon and disappeared into the cypress swamps until the native population—the Calusa tribe—got pissed off at his attempts to appropriate their land, and delivered him a mortal wound in one last pitched battle before sending him back to Puerto Rico to die.

After that, the *renegados* crept out of the swamps, creaking along in their rusty armour and soggy damp-mouldy everything-else, and flung themselves upon the mercy of the tribe. Amongst those who fancied themselves experts on the subject of Santuario's history, the story ran that big chief whoever-at-the-time basically looked at these poor schmucks and said *Fuck it! you can stay, but only if our women will speak for you.* So off came the armour and all the damp-mouldy shit that passed for clothing in those days and, happily, most of the guys measured up.

At lunch Melanie cornered him, looking contrite and holding out a brown paper bag from Gulf Coast Liquors.

"It was scary truth stuff," she said, ponying up the bag with his copy of *Life: The Movie* inside. "I wanted to finish it, but you took off so I didn't get t'ask if it was okay if I borrowed it."

Garrett nodded, tucked the bag off in a corner where all the grease and shit coming off his grille wouldn't do it any more damage than his everyday neglect.

"I mean…it's pretty obvious that *news* isn't really news anymore…but the bullshit started a lot farther back than I ever imagined, and while it was pretty uncomfortable t'read about *how* it happened, this guy Gabler setting it all out in logical progressions was pretty amazing, even if it makes most of us out t'be fucking idiots. I guess it's kinda sad we're all so bored with our everyday lives that we'll do just about anything for our fifteen minutes of celebrity…soak this crap up…demand it…pearls of wish fulfillment straight out of God's asshole.

"Anyway…thanks…"

It hung in the air and she went back to the table where she and her mates and the preppie boys were having the lunch he'd cooked for them. She was wearing short-shorts, beach sandals and an emerald green halter top that reminded him of Green George the Gecko…that made her hair shine like Spanish gold when she stepped back into the sunlight.

He flipped crab cakes out of the fryer, gave them a quick run over the grille to crisp them up a bit more while he prepped a table's-worth of plates with mushrooms and rice, a wasabi-based drizzle and some homemade cole slaw…

"Naomi says come to dinner…"

Bernie snuck up on him as he was shelling clams for the night cook. Garrett snickered without looking at him.

"No she didn't. You have a guilty conscience about some shit or another and you want me there t'provide distraction."

"You're a pig."

"But I'm right...right?"

Bernie was heard to sigh largely. Garrett said:

"Whatever the fuck you're feeling guilty about probably doesn't require the level of self-flagellation you've got in mind. Besides...Naomi doesn't deserve to have me inflicted upon her no matter what it is *you've* done...*and*...I don't wanna be embarrassed when I show up for supper un-announced."

Garrett turned around. For a couple of seconds Bernie's eyes bugged out like a five-year old being caught in some innocent transgression that was bigger in his mind than it would ever have been in the mind of a real adult.

"I have no idea why I even hired you," said Bernie.

"Temporary insanity," offered Garrett. "And maybe self-preservation...like you were lookin' for somebody to protect you from yourself when you looked at somethin' sweet and wanted a taste in spite of the fact you fucking adore your wife."

"You don't have that problem."

"Fuck no. I know I'm a sonofabitch. I don't need to look for reasons to feel good about myself because I already know it's a waste of time."

He and Bernie were of a height and weight. Garrett was grey and Bernie was only just starting in on grey, with at least a couple of generations between them. Garrett had a moment of thought being amazed that Bernie's upbringing on Long Island in New York still moved him to the tides of some weird-ass ancient sense of propriety where you got to feel like a bastard even if all you might have done was think about being one.

"Go home," he said. "Naomi's got a great rack and she must be all sorts of fun to hug so just do that before you even open your mouth and leave me the fuck out of it please. Whatever it is you thought about doin'—with whoever it was you thought about doin' it with—doesn't fucking count because you didn't fucking do it and you'd be a fucking idiot if you did. Hell, if it wasn't for the fact that I respect you as much as I do, I'd go for Naomi myself."

Bernie blinked. Garrett grinned.

"I know," he said. "I'm a pig. Go home, Bernie, just go home…"

He walked a couple of blocks inland to the *Mapa del Tesoro*, nursed a beer and a Beam and ate bar-top peanuts from a basket, throwing the shells down onto the wooden floor while the sun went down where he couldn't see it. There were nights when it was all so commonplace you never noticed all there was to be noticed, but tonight he could taste the saltwater spice in the air, lift up his head and catch the perfume of the bougainvillea, the hibiscus and magnolia, close his eyes and pretend all was well in his world.

At some point he lost count of how many times he'd raised up his hand to Bayardo tending bar...could feel his head sinking closer and closer to the scarred varnish... and couldn't put two thoughts together long enough to figure out why he just wanted to lie down and die and never have to face the prospect of seeing himself in the mirror when he remembered to shave every three or four days. His train of thought stayed on the rails just long enough for him to acknowledge that likelier than not he was going to spend his night in the sand at the bottom of the rickety stairs behind the restaurant.

There wasn't much light left outside when somebody called his name, bellied up to the bar next to him and started in on a whole bunch of things he couldn't care less about... until whoever it was started talking about Brenda...

"...Heard she took off on you, Garrett...

"Always wanted t'fuck that girl...

"So what's she like with the lights out...them great fuckin' tits wiggle themselves flat out when she's on her back...?"

Garrett woke up...sort of...just slow enough and then fast enough so when he did come off his bar-stool and swung on whoever it was dumbfuck stupid enough to make a comment like that there was no way the asshole saw it coming...

It took six guys to pull him off. Bayardo had heard some of it...tried to be sympathetic...but told him not to come back. Two years in residence was obviously not long enough to win you a *Get Out of Jail Free* card when it came down to inflicting damage on a handful of locals.

UNTIL THE END OF THE WORLD

He woke up in one of the alleys he'd visited in his dreams, drenched to the skin by a downpour he never even felt...got to his feet and staggered off into the unknown, though suddenly, even though it was pitch black middle of the night dark there were millions of stars in the sky blinking on and off, and a gibbous moon with light enough to show him the way back to the Sportster where he'd d stashed it behind the restaurant that morning.

There was a sense of relief that he was still attached to Reality—that the dream was still no more than just a dream—and a bleary awareness that trying to get himself home would be stupid. He stumbled down the stairway to the beach and went back to sleep...

...Got woke up by Ramon who stumbled over him in the pre-dawn half-light and cursed as his cigarette flew into the Gulf.

"Buenos fuckin' dias, Garrett, qué coño estás haciendo aquí?"

"What's it look like, Ramon?" he said, getting himself to where he could at least get upright on his knees.

"It looks like you got the shit kicked out of you, *hermano*."

Garrett nodded cautiously.

"Given how goddamn crappy I feel, I'd say your assessment of my physical condition is pretty fuckin' accurate, buddy."

Ramon laughed.

"You poor bastard. Go home."

Garrett laughed, but it cost him.

"I told Bernie t'do that last night. He's got his dick up after...I dunno... somebody...but he's got the guilt thing workin' on him before he even starts."

Ramon laughed again, lit another cigarette and went serious.

"I can drive you home if you don' wanna get on the bike, man."

Garrett put a hand down in the sand and lurched up onto his feet.

"*Gracias, hermano*, but I might as well just stay here. I'm doing breakfast again."

"Not today, asshole. *I'm* doin' breakfast. This is your day off."

Garrett wagged his head.

"No shit. Really?"

"Yeah, really," sighed Ramon. "I know you're not gonna take a ride home; you want a coffee before you get on that piece of shit Harley?"

Garrett hung his head.

"Yeah. Thanks, buddy..."

Ramon walked him up the stairs, one arm up around his ribs to make sure he didn't fall backwards and break his neck. He went through three coffees before getting up onto his feet stopped being a invitation to call 9-1-1.

Then he chugged home on the Sportster. Half asleep. Went to bed. Woke up late in the afternoon and broke open a new bottle of bourbon before going out to shoot the shit with Green George.

A couple of hours later nothing much had changed for him. He had this vague sense of something he once might have called *shame* over what had happened in the last twenty-four hours, but he kept on pouring bourbon and Green George kept on with his lizardy pretense of paying attention while the palmetto bugs whacked themselves stupid against the screens behind him...

Garrett came to his crossroads...

He got up out of his chair...wandered down to the edge of the water and spent an hour just watching the sun sink down into the other side of the world...turned to look back at what was behind him and figured it would be a fair trade.

He stripped off his shorts and t-shirt, left them in the sand and started backing away, listening to the soft whisper of the surf as it began to wash up on his heels and over his ankles he turned back into the sunset, blood-red and gold painting the Gulf from the horizon to his feet...the sound of the gulls wheeling above him their shrill cries fading in his ears...now only listening to the sound of his heart beating faster...

He began to walk into the painted stream. The water was *so* warm...enfolding him...he imagined it was like being born...the Beginning...felt the sand sliding away beneath his feet...so tired now...one last glimpse back at the world going dark behind him...tasting the salt in the air burning away into aether he whispered some grateful encouragement to himself...glad to have finally found the courage...made the decision... that the whole damn thing was finally going to be over....

The Gulf lapped up around him, reaching higher and higher with each step until he didn't have to move at all, the offshore undercurrents now doing all the work all he had to do was close his eyes and the earth would crawl out from under him one last time...one...last...time...

"Hey!"

He felt like he was waking up from his nightmare...turned...saw someone on the beach waving to him...suddenly so much farther away than he imagined it would be in so short a time there was an instant of panic as he hung between the Now and the absence of Tomorrow—the old familiar world full of all his failures and the death of Hope, and the one where there was no promise of anything except an end to all of it...

She called out to him again.

He flattened himself on the tide, swam slowly back to shore, felt the earth rising up to take him back. He slogged his way through the shallows, uncaring that he was naked against the sunset.

"What were you doing out there?"

He couldn't speak. That part of him had not yet returned to the world.

"We're driving back home tomorrow. I'm gonna be graduating in June...but when it's done I wanna come back here...to you."

The thought was unheard of. Staggering. A lifetime ago there'd been someone, but a lifetime ago he'd been a bigger asshole than he was now and when she had walked away he knew she was never coming back, and after a while he'd stopped caring because it was the only way to deal with the reality of her leaving—that he'd engineered the whole thing, gave her every reason, because that was what you did when someone thought better of you than you did yourself.

"Why the hell would you want that?" he said. "There's fuck-all here besides mythology, hurricanes, bird shit and broken people..."

"Well why're *you* here?"

He fell on his knees in the sand and shook his head.

"This was about as far as I could go without a passport."

She was right there in front of him now, so close he could smell the sunscreen and sweat on her skin and the salt water in her hair, and see the sunset glinting off the new bronze on her knees.

"I wanna come back," she whispered, so soft he almost couldn't hear her, but he had to look up to see what was happening because there was a storm of something in the way she'd said it. "I wanna read all your books. I wanna listen to Canned Heat. I wanna stick around long enough to catch you on all of your good days, and make it okay for you t'stop running..."

It took him a minute or so to process the immensity of the implications...and then another one to realise something had cut loose from inside of him and fled away from the quiet ferocity in her voice. She fell down on her knees beside him, reaching for his hands.

"I wanna come back," she said a third time. "I want you to be here when I do. I need you to promise me you'll be here."

Garrett could feel the crashing in his heart ebb away, the pace of his headlong flight from the world slow down to a crawl...and then stop...

He said "Okay..." and she put her arms around him and kissed him where his throat lay bared on her shoulder.

DIANE

He woke up in a cheap motel, for a minute or two not at all sure where he was, until he remembered the web feed he'd kept alive for the better part of ten years...the sudden horrible tightness in his chest...and then the frantic thrashing around in his closet... finding the passport...finding Grafton on a Google map...again...and then throwing some stuff into an overnight bag and simply driving...Customs a blur...some child in a uniform...

"...*Why* am I visiting the United States? Because I feel like it. Because I was born here and I can come back any time I want to for no reason at all."

"Sir if you're going to be combative I'm going to have to ask you—"

"I'm not being combative. I'm an American citizen with a valid American passport, and it doesn't matter why I'm visiting the States because legally you can't deny me entry to the country where I was born. I don't need a reason to be doing this. If you have reason to believe I may be involved in something illegal, then just have me detained over there where you've parked your car...but otherwise please just let me get on with my day I've got a long drive in front of me..."

And then hours and hours on the interstates south from the border...and then the motel...where he realised he was only half an hour from where he needed to be the next day...and...finally...someplace where he could just sit down in a corner and weep.

He didn't own a suit or a sports jacket. Any time in the past when they had been at all necessary he'd found one in the same thrift stores he'd found his jeans and denim shirts...and once worn they went back into the donation bins...

His boots were over thirty years old and ready to finally fall apart the same way he was falling apart...old enough to feel it...more than old enough to not give a shit anymore...

He got out of bed and flung the sheet and comforter back in the general direction of the pillow...got dressed... left his room key on the night-stand... shouldered his pack and stepped out into a spectacular sunny day in early summer. There was a magnolia tree at the end of the parking lot of the motel...and lilacs going mad with purple and pink and lavender and smelling so good it was insult to the hurt in his heart.

Not for the first time he heard the faint echo of a beautiful girl's laughter.

He unlocked his car and rolled down the windows... put his head down where there was no chance of anybody seeing him and wept some more.

UNTIL THE END OF THE WORLD

After a while he double-checked the time and the GPS app on his phone...made sure he knew where was going and pulled slowly out of the motel parking lot on his way to get there. Kept to secondary roads because the traffic on the major highways was more than he wanted to deal with.

When he got to the cemetery he had to ask three people for directions to where it was he wanted to go...got there and realised there was an hour time difference...he was more than two hours early instead of just one, and nothing nowhere but a hole in the ground... waiting...

He didn't know anyone, didn't recognise anyone except maybe one face he had known a long time ago...her younger sister. He stayed well back from the empty place in the ground...sank down beneath an ancient oak tree three feet around lifting its leaves up into the light for another year. He couldn't seem to keep himself from crying; anytime there was time to stop and think *she* would creep up behind him and tear another hole in his heart...

Dozens of people began to arrive, milling around on the hillside like lost sheep... everyone dressed in black like they'd forgotten an entire life had been lived and now more than ever was in need of celebration.

And because he'd all but stalked her once he realised he could find out small things about her, he recognised *him* when he finally did arrive...the long black limousine trailing in his wake... and the box...the place where they were going to shut her away into the dark forever.

MICHAEL SUMMERLEIGH

It didn't take very long. He couldn't even hear anything that was said. Imagined all the words had been spoken at a service before anyone had even found their way into the cemetery. He stood up and let the wide brim of an ancient Stetson keep the sun from his eyes and the last of his tears from witness.

When it was over, he edged closer, waiting for the stragglers to go away so he could say goodbye. Someone had set a small photograph on the small bump in the earth that was left. He knelt and felt his heart stop, reached for it without thinking...

"What the fuck d'you think you're doing? Who the fuck are you anyway?"

He stood up. The other *he* was there in front of him...bigger...wider than he'd ever imagined he would be. Maybe if he'd been the one to live with the life that was gone he would've been bigger too...the luxury of loving...

He took a step backward. Outweighed by fifty sixty pounds. The face was something new; he realised he'd never actually known what he looked like. He said:

"I knew her. A long time ago."

This much larger presence got even much larger. He backed away some more, still with the small square of Kodachrome paper in his hand.

"Please...can I keep this?" he asked. "You must have dozens...hundreds of them just like it..."

"Who the fuck are you?"

He closed his eyes and took in a deep breath. Let it out slowly.

"I'm Matthew," he whispered.

"Matthew."

"Yes."

"I don't know any Matthews."

"We never met. Spoke only once...on the telephone...for all of maybe half a minute...fifty years ago..."

The shaven head tilted to one side, eyes locked with his and staying there. He could see him thinking.

"You're David," he said. "You took her away from me. I saw her one last time...the summer before she told you she was pregnant..."

David's eyes went wide and he took a step forward, his hands curling into fists.

"Why the fuck are you here?"

He swallowed down on his sorrow; his grief belonged to the girl they were burying.

"You think because she left me I stopped loving her? When all the shit I've done to myself and anyone I've ever known stops howling itself in my head, I still can hear her laughing...I can still see her smile...I can still feel her fingers touching my face...

"She never had my baby. It never even occurred to me that it might be mine. Only that she couldn't have a child without being married and you never stepped up to fix it...so I did..."

"Motherfucker."

"Sure. Whatever works for you. I just couldn't let her leave without saying goodbye. Please let me keep this."

Matthew offered the photograph back to him.

"I didn't come here to give you any more grief than you've got. As long as you loved her...adored her every fucking minute of every fucking day. As long as you gave her everything she ever wanted and made her laugh...never made her cry."

David stopped looking like he wanted to tear his head off. Nodded down at the photograph.

"She was wearin' that the day I met her. It was her favourite. She wore it to shreds."

"I'm gonna go," Matthew said.

David swallowed a couple of times.

"No one of *us* is perfect," said Matthew. "I could never have been what she needed or wanted. But I loved her because *she was perfect* and she was the first girl who ever loved me back."

He walked to his car and looked for an interstate to take him back to Canada... found his eyes drawn over and over again to the four-inch square of Kodak paper propped up on the dashboard...the photograph of her wearing the long flowery hippie-*chic* dress he'd given her on her nineteenth birthday.

CHELSEA

Part One - CHELSEA MOURNING

1.

He walked every day. Had to. His doctor said.

"You're gonna die if you don't, Charlie, so bundle up in the winter and strip down in the summer, but don't stop walking because it's the only way your heart is gonna keep ticking. And stop drinking for god's sakes! I know you have no idea how t'deal with the world, but there are people out there who love you, Charlie, and they're happy to drink *with* you but not one of them is booking passage on the same Titanic you're on, so can you please cut yourself some slack and spare us a fucking funeral!"

So he walked. Every day. Down Riverside Drive and up West End Avenue from wherever he happened to turn left to go home...rain or shine...no icebergs but always the threat of one looming up somewhere in the vast frozen Atlantic Ocean of his life...

He wasn't writing anymore, had not been able to put a sentence much less a paragraph together since the day he'd walked out of the hospital...months ago...still sleepless and haunted by the latest four-hour sojourn to black empty nothingness while the surgeons bought him some time...

Chelsea was a name he learned later, but on the day he met her she was hunched over the passenger door of a late-model Lexus, armed with a coat hanger and an attitude, trying desperately to fuck her life up a little bit more than it had been when she woke up that morning.

He said, "Stop it. C'mon I'm standing right here. Whatever it is you were hoping to accomplish without witnesses is now a memory."

She said, "Piss off old man or I'll kick your ass."

And he said, "Knock yourself out, little girl, I been waiting a long time for an offer like that."

She stepped away from the car, threw down the coat hanger and took his breath away. There wasn't enough mascara in the world to darken the blue sky in her eyes... nowhere near enough black hair dye to disguise the pale Spanish galleon gold in her roots, or lip gloss in any colour that could cover the pout and the glory of her mouth.

Charlie remembered growing up thinking Marilyn Monroe had been too heartbreakingly delicious to be human. This one made Marilyn seem ordinary.

She flipped him the finger and said "Fuck you..." before she walked away... chains and dirty denim and a threadbare patch on her ass showing pale flesh that flexed with muscle every other step...

He saw her again about a week later, on Broadway near the Barnes & Noble...hanging with her friends. He recognised her from a block away and for a second or two he was certain she had seen him.

And it went on like that for most of the summer. Granted the extent of his grazing ground was limited by the shortcomings of his damaged heart muscles, but suddenly it seemed like she was pretty much everywhere; that they were a pair of pinballs from two separate games bouncing up against one another constantly. She became a regular background cast member in the ongoing soft-soap opera of Charlie's life, and when he thought about her—which was way too often, and with a clarity of detail he normally reserved for the ravenously emancipated heroines in his novels—it was with such a hurricane of conflicting emotions that he usually had to find a place to sit down until the storm clouds had gone.

2.

One day in October the three-plus blocks to the park turned out to be a bit more than he'd bargained for, so he camped on a bench on the West Drive...watched the leaves dancing across Strawberry Fields...turned his face up to the sun let his nose catch the crisp musty smell of them...and saw her out of the corner of his eye. The same tattered black jeans, a hoodie sweatshirt under the same tattered black denim jacket. She had her spiky-haired head down and seemed intent on rushing headlong into some new disaster. He said *Hi* and as her head snapped up he saw recognition in the impossible blue eyes. She stopped three or four paces away facing him, hands in the pockets of her jeans...

"What the fuck d'*you* want...and why're you following me everywhere I fuckin' go there you are..."

"I'm not following you," he said, shaking his head. "We just seem to be ending up in all the same places."

"Bullshit."

"No, it's not bullshit. Besides...I could never keep up with you. You move too fast."

"You're not that old. You're like maybe fifty or something..."

"Tell that to my heart."

He tapped his chest where his heart was and felt it bump and flutter as a gust of wind ruffled her hair, rippled it like a wheat field in midnight. She tilted her head and sunlight caught something silver dangling from her left ear.

"What're you staring at?"

He didn't realise he"d been staring...or that it would be so obvious...

"You. It's rude and insulting and you're young and very pretty and most men just can't not stare...no matter how old they are. I'm sorry."

She seemed unfamiliar with apologies...or honest lechery...

"Is your heart really fucked up?"

"In spades."

"And they can't fix it?"

"Not any more...not without some serious shit that would just as likely kill me as cure me."

"Well that sucks."

Charlie nodded. "It surely does. Worse than that...I have to depend on blind chance to keep bumping into you."

Something hard and cold and empty swept over her face...

"Now you're gonna offer me a joint," she said softly. "Maybe invite me home t'see your fuckin' etchings...?"

She whispered the words venomously. Angrily. He shook his head.

"No...why would...hey! you think I'm hitting on you? I may not be that old, but I'm old enough not to be an idiot."

"So what is this...and *bumping into me*...what's that supposed t'mean?"

Charlie listened to her throwing his own words back at him, forcing him to take stock of what he actually had *said*, not words on a page to create a frame of mind or emotion for one of his characters

He said, "I like looking at you..."

Very slowly...

"You're a fuckin' sicko—!"

"Let me finish sorting this out okay...?"

She folded her arms across her chest...not defensively...waiting for him... scornful as he went searching for what he wanted to say...carefully... He realised he was desperate not to offend her.

"Y'know how you are when you listen to music that you really like...you turn it up...or play the song over and over again? It makes you feel good...delights you...you want to keep on feeling that way...

"I don't participate that much anymore...not physically...so my sense of smell... eyesight...hearing...I soak up pleasure through them..."

"So what you're saying is you're not gettin' laid and you wanna watch?"

She sneered at him, which suddenly was perfectly acceptable because it wasn't what he was saying at all.

"What I'm saying is that I think you're lovely, okay. My heart almost stopped when you looked up at me from that Lexus, and from that moment on I kept seeing your face in my mind...kept trying to soak up everything about it that I found so lovely...like just now when you curled your lip at me for being a pervert. It was wonderful. It added a new totally different dimension of *loveliness* to your face."

He saw a change in the loveliness...a slight softening of the attitude...like the words had sunk in and somehow had managed to convey to her the essence of *fascination*...his own...anyone's...as if he had somehow described something she herself knew very well.

"My name is Charlie," he said, holding out his right hand. "Charlie Stinson."

He watched himself become someone else in her eyes...cautiously weighed and measured...in some mysterious way grudgingly accepted. And then she said:

"I'm Chelsea..."

In a different tone of voice than before she reached to shake his hand, still keeping a bit of distance between them. He asked her if she was hungry because he was starving and she showed him how beautiful she could be when she was caught off-guard so casually and puzzled in the bargain.

"Are you asking me out on a date?"

Charlie hazarded a grin. "Hell no. I'm forty-seven years old..."

And a theatrical sigh.

UNTIL THE END OF THE WORLD

"Thirty years too old to be asking you out on a date."
"Thirty-*two* years too old," she corrected him.
"You're fift—"
"Yeah," she said. "So just behave yourself, okay."

It took a while to get there. She constantly had to stop and wait for him, or backtrack a dozen paces whenever she forgot.

"Don't be racin' any fuckin' turtles, Charlie."

Eventually they stopped in front of the Arte Café on 73rd where Charlie had been a regular since his first best-seller. She said she didn't have any money for a place like that; he told her not to worry he had plenty and dinner was on him. Then they went inside and he said hello to everybody and watched their eyes follow the fifteen-year old Goth girl to his table beside the fireplace, stripping off her jacket and hoodie along the way and plunking herself into a chair as if the ragged Metallica t-shirt she had on under them was an ATM or Alex Wang. Charlie followed her following the hostess and would happily have done that for the rest of the evening.

"They know you here," she said, looking around as if they'd landed on an alien planet.

"I live close by. The food's pretty good and there's usually somebody around can take me home if I have too much to drink."

He ordered his usual Maker's Mark neat with water on the side. Chelsea ordered a Coke, glared at him when he winced.

"What?!?!"

"That stuff is no good for you."

"Oh like whatever it was you ordered is?"

The firelight danced across her face, turned her bronze and gold while the warmth baked the chill out of their bones and crept into the way her voice sounded when she spoke to him.

She smiled...pretending to be at ease...dazzling... Charlie sipped his bourbon and felt sleepy...happy... bathed in the heat and soaking up the luxury of nearness to her... drinking in the way she drank Coca Cola through a straw...how her blue eyes blazed green in yellow firelight...

"Shouldn't you call somebody...let them know you're—"

"Havin' supper with my grandfather?" she said not unkindly, and then all the warmth fled from her. "I don't go home if I don't have to."

Charlie didn't say anything. A lot of it was selfish. He didn't want to piss her off by pushing...prying into things she didn't want to talk about; but suddenly she seemed vulnerable where before she'd had the armour of her attitude, and like everything else about her it was another facet of what she was and he knew he was hopelessly infatuated; that she could blow her nose into no-name toilet paper and he would hang on every moment of it and then go out and buy the toilet paper in case she ran out.

He said, "Okay let's have dinner then. Anything you want is okay."

"What've they got?"

"That's what the menu is for," nodding towards hers.

She picked up the parchment folder...opened it...

"What is this...Italian...can I have pizza?"

"Sure...whattaya want on it...?"

"Pepperoni and onions and mushrooms."

"Done."

He ordered a large pizza with pepperoni and onions and mushrooms along with some deep-fried mozzarella sticks and a dinner-size salad for himself.

"That's all you're gonna have?"

"I might have another couple of these," he said, nodding at his whisky glass. "Is it all right if I steal some of your stuff?"

"Shit...you can have whatever you want, Charlie, it's your fuckin' money."

As it turned out, Charlie mostly just drank bourbon... picked at his salad and watched her eat...gently disengaging slices of pepperoni with (surprisingly clean) fingernails devoid of any kind of polish. She left the mushrooms and onions to be neatly disposed of with the rest of the pizza...knife and fork cutting small mouthfuls she ate two slices and trimmed the crusts...

"I feed the pigeons...can I have the rest of this t'take with me?"

He nodded. She excused herself to go to the restroom while his salad and the pizza got boxed up...took her jacket with her and was gone just long enough for him to start conjuring images of her sneaking out a back window never to be seen again. He was waiting for the credit card tab when she came back, picked up her pizza box and said:

"I gotta take off, Charlie. Thanks for supper I'll see ya okay..."

And she was gone before he had a chance to make a fool of himself with stupid questions like *When will I see you again?* or *Have you got someplace to stay tonight?* He signed his card receipt and nearly missed the folded rectangle of almost-card stock paper she had left on her chair...ragged along one edge...torn from a small spiral notebook. He checked the perspective on it and realised the pencil sketch had been drawn from the door of the restroom...

He thought the person she had drawn looked old and a little bit lost...paid cash for another bourbon and took a cab home.

3.

"You didn't tell me you were famous..."

She scared the crap out of him, roaring up behind him on Broadway just round the corner from Beacon Wines & Spirits. He almost dropped his brand new bottle of Maker's Mark. She was wearing the same sloppy denim gear from dinner three days before... somehow still managed to seem fresh and bouncy attractive even with the safety-pin that had replaced the silver dangle in her left ear.

"Jesus don't do that!"

"I forgot. I'm sorry," she said, falling into slow motion beside him.

"I write cheesy soft-porn romances disguised as contemporary thrillers. That's not famous...it's something else..."

"Well known then. You got a whole shelf t'yerself at the B&N."

"That's because I live in the neighbourhood. Other stores hide my books in the back."

"I read a little bit from one of 'em...you got a thing for boomers, dontcha?"

"Baby-boomers?"

"No, Charlie...big zzz-oomers..."

She wiggled her front at him and grinned. He could feel himself going red.

"So I'm an American male, Chelsea...sue me..."

"How are ya?"

"Same as most days, thanks for asking...and thank you for the drawing. You didn't tell me you were an artist."

"I just doodle. It gives me somethin' t'do in class..."

"Then you doodle pretty damn good. I thought it was somebody else until it occurred t'me it was so much me that I didn't recognise myself. Are you feelin' okay today?"

"Huh?"

"I haven't heard too many four-letter words yet. I thought you might be under the weather."

"Fuck you, Charlie."

"That's better."

He smiled just in case it had been a serious *fuck you*...to let her know he was just teasing...astonished to find himself trying to be charming. They walked most of a block in the silence of traffic noise...other people having conversations in passing...occasional blindness when the afternoon sun ducked past a building on the west side of the street and smacked them in the eyes.

"What're you doin' today?"

"Just walking, Chelsea...couple of times a day..."

"Takin' a break from the boomers," she said knowingly...jammed her hands into the front pockets of her jeans...sideways glancing to see if he'd risen to the bait.

Charlie shook his head. "I been takin' a break for almost a year now," he said coldly. "People say major surgery of any kind is a big thing...a game-changer...I guess they're right. I was sort of hoping I'd've gotten used to it by now."

He held up four fingers in answer to her unspoken how many times. She said *Shit* under her breath, hop-skipped into slower slow-motion beside him.

"Charlie, could we get somethin' to eat? We don't haveta go to a real restaurant or anything..."

It became a ritual. Early on he entertained the almost-certainty she was sponging off him. Early on he knew he didn't care; that if she wanted to play him he was more than willing to be played.

As time went by he became familiar with her moods and habits whenever she was with him—the quirks of behaviour that made her physical beauty truly interesting...the times when she was troubled by something and would get angry over what he felt was not even the slightest of provocation...glower at him from across the table...

And the other times when she forgot to put the chip on her shoulder and allowed herself to be a fifteen-year old—enthusiastic and inquisitive. They'd walk outdoors if it wasn't too cold...go to an afternoon movie...sit somewhere for snacks she'd trot out a small sketchbook and he'd sit quietly, amazed that she required only a few pencil strokes to capture the essence of a winter sparrow feasting on a cast-off McDonalds french fry...the momentary scowl of someone across the room that seemed to encompass the entirety of a personality... He watched her...drank in every nuance of what she said and what she did and realised that for him, the only unrest in what passed as their *relationship* was the feeling that she was like a chapter in someone else's fictional account of his life; that her visits always had to end, and there was always a distinct hole in the plot until the next time she appeared in the story-line.

It changed on the day he found the photographs. Spring and a new summer had been in their own way...for him...idyllic...the happiest days of his life. They went to the zoo and commiserated on how fucked up the world must be if the only way you could keep animals alive was to put them in prison. Went to art galleries. The Museum of Natural History where they were seconds away from calling 911 for him after she looked up at the T-Rex skeleton and totally deadpan said *Holy shit he was a big motherfucker!* with the entirety of a second grade class from a Catholic school standing nearby...nuns included...

They had breakfast for supper at the diner in the Beacon Hotel, and she asked him if she could crash at his place...if he had room. She took off her jacket and one of her sketchbooks fell out onto his living room floor...and a handful of photographs fell out of the sketchbook. As he knelt to pick them up he felt his heart doing things it shouldn't do...

"Chelsea...what are these...?"

And she looked at him...horrified...and then like it was something she had to be ashamed of...and she screamed at him...

"Whattayou think they are, Charlie? They're photographs. I was ten years old when my mother disappeared and right after that my father started fucking me and he took pictures so I could show 'em t'my fucking grandchildren. I stole them why the fuck are you lookin' at my stuff anyway just because you're lettin' me crash here doesn't mean you get t'do that..."

She flung the sketchbook and photographs at him...stormed across his living room and spent five minutes cursing and crying as she undid the deadbolts and stumbled herself out past the door.

She was gone for two month's-worth of the most miserable chapters in the story of his life...

4.

...Until he found her again, one day in October standing in front of a bench on the West Drive in Central Park watching leaves dance across Strawberry Fields he said:

"Hi, Chelsea."

She looked up at him and took his breath away all over again said:

"Hi, Charlie."

"I think I have t'sit down?"

UNTIL THE END OF THE WORLD

"I think you fuckin' better, Buckwheat. You look like shit."

"Well if it's any consolation to you, I feel like shit too."

"Are we guilt-tripping now?"

"No. I worried about you. And I missed you...."

"I've had some strange stuff goin' on in my life, Charlie. You wouldn't happen t'know about any of it, wouldya...?"

He was cold. Felt like he had shrunk in on himself half size normal there on the bench beside her.

"I gave those photographs to a friend of mine, Chelsea. I told him I needed to have something fixed and I really didn't give a fuck how it got done. And I then gave him a pile of money t'make sure it did...

He'd seen *startled* on her face before...but not that kind of startled...

"My friend made copies of the photographs and they went to a friend of one of his friends...someone you'll never meet and who will never meet you...and this guy somehow managed to bump into the sonofabitch in the photographs...showed him the copies...explained to him that if he ever had anything to do with the little girl in those photographs ever again...*ever again*...then he could expect some serious shit to enter his life and probably end it for him...

"It's also possible that this guy...this friend of a friend of my friend...may have beaten the crap out of this sonofabitch...just t'make sure he was paying attention..."

A gust of wind swirled around them...leaves crackled between them trying to escape the wind...and she turned to look at him sitting beside her...

"Why're you crying, Charlie?"

"I don't know," he said. "Paradise Lost...?"

She put her hands down between her knees, stared at her feet. He realised she had always worn sneakers ...black...low-slung...hardly anything that qualified at all as footwear and probably cost a half million dollars a pair if you bought them new.

"That would be the reason he was dumpin' painkillers...and why he threw my ass out and told me never t'come back..."

She stared out into the sunset beyond the Strawberry Fields...out past Columbus Av and Amsterdam and the West Side Drive...the Hudson River and the Palisades... whispered:

"Imagine."

And he hugged himself harder trying to do just that...

"I've read shit...he was like a real nut case sometimes..."

Charlie nodded. "I guess we all got baggage."

She said, "Yeah...but if we all imagined at the same time and suddenly the world was fuckin' rosy...who would be the crazy people then, Charlie...?"

He said, "That's probably the best goddamn question I've heard in all the years since that asshole shot him... "

"I gotta sort things out."

"Will you promise t'be careful...and not do anything really stupid...?"

"I promise, Charlie."

"Okay then."

He pulled a small notebook from the inner pocket of his coat and wrote an address on one of the blank pages.

"This is where I live. The doorman's name is Jeremiah Stokes. He's a good gentle man, and if you show him this piece of paper and tell him I gave it to you he'll make sure you get upstairs off the street."

She looked at it for a second...folded it up... scrunched it into one of the front pockets of her jeans... the black ones...a year more threadbare than when he'd first met her...

"'Kay thanks, Charlie. I'll find you again soon. I promise that too..."

She kissed him fast on the cheek and he almost froze to death watching where she'd run away north on West Drive...long after the sun had gone down...

5.

A week later he got home from a sit-down with his pissed-off-as-usual cardiologist and she was sitting on the floor in the hallway in front of his door, surrounded by a small mountain of boxes and sketchbooks and a gym bag full of clothing. She wouldn't look at him... mumbled hello...ruefully asked if she could borrow twenty dollars so she could give it back to the doorman.

"...I didn't know the cab would be so expensive. I was out on the sidewalk with this guy givin' me all sorts of shit ready t'call the cops on me. Mister Stokes came out t'see what was goin' on and I showed him that piece of paper you gave me. He just paid the guy, apologised for the misunderstanding and said he should've been outside when I arrived. And then he helped me bring all my shit up here..."

Charlie smiled, went through the process of unlocking his door, took off his coat, poured a bourbon and watched as she moved all her stuff in from the hallway. She sat down on the sofa across from him in the big overstuffed armchair, looked down at five twenties and a set of keys on the coffee table and whispered something that might have been *Thank you Charlie*. He said:

"Tonight you gotta sleep on that couch, but tomorrow I'll get somebody in to air out the extra bedroom for you. It's the first door on the left and it's got its own bathroom. If you need or want anything just tell me, okay? And don't ever think like you're taking advantage of me because I know you won't...or that you're gonna owe me, because *that* is bullshit.

"If it's what you want, you live here now. This is your place too. Just promise me you'll finish school the best you can...and don't let your weird friends fuck with my record collection. Have we got a deal?"

She nodded.

"Are you hungry?"

"Charlie, I'm fuckin' starvin'..."

She looked up and smiled like a ten-year old. Sunshine on a cloudy day...

6.

He didn't have another doctor's appointment for four weeks so he made mac & cheese with bacon *and* all-beef Kosher hot dogs for dinner. She said it was one of her favourites when she was a kid, but she had to have milk with it so he sent her down to the West Side Market on Broadway with instructions to put whatever she bought on his account.

UNTIL THE END OF THE WORLD

After dinner she tried green tea and he had bourbon and he played old Joni Mitchell records for her...some Styx and Neil Young before the grunge...and later on, Beethoven...the Ninth...and Chelsea had never heard anything but snatches of it before. In the middle of the *Ode to Joy* she suddenly curled up on the couch and started sobbing...put her hands out front of her to warn him away when he instinctively stood up...

When it was over there wasn't enough silence to hold them.

He got sheets and pillows for her while she took a shower...turned his head away when she came out of the bathroom in a long t-shirt...toweling her hair he noticed there wasn't as much black as there used to be...went down the hallway to his bedroom and stared at nothing until he saw the sliver of light in the hallway go dark... got out of bed and padded back into the living room... stood over her for a while listening to his heart pound and her breathing. Watching her sleep he leaned over... kissed her forehead...said *G'night Chelsea* and went back to bed...

He stared up at the ceiling and imagined the digital clock ticking away seconds and minutes of his life until he started to drowse...drifting off into sleep he thought he heard his door open felt another presence in the room...his bedsheets moving over him...then her hands...it had been so long...and it was so wrong he said:

"Chelsea..."

And she said "Shut up Charlie," so very gently. "You just shut the fuck up..." before she put her arms around his hips and her head down...

MICHAEL SUMMERLEIGH

He slept in...forgot his life had been radically altered...remembered...looked around his bedroom and listened...put on some pyjama bottoms and went exploring...found a note beside the sink...

I had t'go to school...the muffins didn't turn out so good...see ya later...

With a heart at the end...

He found things that resembled blueberry muffins in the trash bin...

He started taking his walks early in the day so he would be home when she got home...

found out what she liked to eat and started learning how to cook other stuff... real food... instead of going out for dinner all the time, though mondo mac & cheese was once a month no fail...

Every now and again she would give him advance notice of a punker invasion... friends coming to visit. He gave her lots of her own space until she insisted on inviting him into it, introducing some of her friends who turned out not to be too much of a trial except for the times when they ragged him over some of the albums in his collection.

"...Karen Carpenter...?!?!?!?!"

Charlie told that one to *Fuck off she was a damn good drummer and good at what she was doing at least you could tell if it was good or bad, as opposed to whatever it is the drummer in Drunk Pussy Hotpants thinks he's doing...*

UNTIL THE END OF THE WORLD

Chelsea laughed herself sick.

He kissed her forehead goodnight almost every night...

※

...And after a while stopped feeling guilty. He loved her. Would do anything for her.

Her bedroom began to resemble his idea of what a teenage girl's bedroom ought to look like, with some of the dark stuff giving way to teddy bears as she got comfortable...walls covered in posters...her pencil sketches and then water-colours. As *they* got comfortable with what they had she could spend hours looking at his books...making fun of the ones he had written and feeling bad after...asking which ones were really worth her time to read, she trusted his judgments entirely...

On the weekends she rambled...partied with her friends...brought them home... or not...

School nights after homework and dinner they watched videos...classic movies... listened to his records. He never stopped being totally hypnotized by the play of her emotions...how they became more and more spontaneous as her daily life became less and less threatening—an easy routine that took what had gone on before and gradually let it become transformed into a something with blurry edges.

In the dark he tried not to think too much... rationalised as much of it as he could on any given day. She didn't seem to mind. He finally stopped staring into nothingness for most of the night...got to rest...sleep...dream...

7.

Their winter was warm and Christmas was merry and bright. He bought her a giant set of Rapidograph drawing pens, woolen everythings in rainbow colours, and though he knew he would miss her old black jeans for one specific reason he bought her new ones anyway.

As she stopped being wary of her own laughter it became a soundtrack to his waking hours whether she was home or not.

He started drinking a little bit more wine instead of bourbon... a little bit more water instead of wine...

On her seventeenth birthday in April he had another one of his wonderful sessions with the cardiologist scheduled...primed himself to accept another hour of excoriation even though he'd tried to behave himself...

He asked her what she wanted to do and she said he wanted to go back to the place where they had started... would be there keeping the chairs warm for him after his duel with the doctor...

And she was. The hostess at the Arte Café said there was *someone* waiting for him at his table...surrounded by the dozens of red, white and yellow roses he'd had delivered...

"I missed your sweet sixteen party..." he said...

...To someone who stood up when she caught sight of him...looked embarrassed...apologised for spending so much on a dress...and sandals...someone whose hair was miraculously free of black or purple or green...who cried when he said *Happy Birthday*...and had no idea she was the most magical creature ever to walk through their doors...

No idea she was the most magical creature to ever walk into his life...

A couple of months later his share of the magic ran out.

8.

"Hi. I missed it, didn't I...?"

"It's okay, Charlie. I'm pretty sure the doctor's gonna give you a note."

"I wanted t'be there."

"I know. But it's still okay and it was nothin' special... except for when the principal had t'tell everyone I got an honours degree. That was pretty fuckin' good."

She grinned down at him and he gave her a tired grin back, trying to figure out a way to tell her how proud he was of her. She pulled up a chair and sat beside the bed... took in the IV lines and the monitors...suddenly for the first time in a long time uncomfortable...

"You look nice...didja get some pictures for me?"

She nodded. "But I didn't brush my hair until after... made good and sure it looked like a bird had crapped in it and that they all knew I had my chains and shit on under the gown..."

"Well you wouldn't want 'em t'think you were totally reformed..."

"Fuck no!"

"Well...I like your hair without all the different colours and stuff..."

"Thank you, Charlie," she said, putting her head down. He thought he saw tears in her eyes. "I talked t'the nurse...she said it's bad."

"It is, honey. I don't feel very well at all."

She was quiet for a few minutes and he didn't have the energy to do more than just watch her...still breath-taking just breathing. He remembered the day they had met in the park and the couple of hours having dinner when it was all he could do not to stare at her. Two years had transformed her into something even more exquisite.

"Charlie, if I ask you somethin' will you promise t'give me an honest answer?"

Lost in daydreaming and sedatives he wasn't paying close attention.

"Charlie...?"

And now he could see that she was crying for real.

"What is it, Chelsea...honest...yeah of course I will..."

She said "Charlie how come you never wanted t'fuck me?"

And all the cobwebs went away; he knew his heart was betraying him...that if she looked up at one of the monitors she would know it too. He took three deep breaths that filled his lungs and made his chest ache.

"Chelsea, what makes you think I never wanted t'make love t'you?"

She looked up and it hurt worse...tears running down her face through streaks of mascara that didn't do anything but make her beautifully grief-stricken.

"You always locked your fuckin' bedroom door."

"No I didn—"

"Yes you *did* Charlie you said you wouldn't lie!"

He closed his eyes, couldn't bear to see her suffering because of him.

UNTIL THE END OF THE WORLD

"That first night you let me stay at your place...I knew what you were doin' I was sure you'd been playin' me, Charlie, I just knew it. I was lyin' there waitin' and sure as shit a half hour later I heard your bedroom door open and you came right up beside me thinkin' I was asleep...

"I was so scared I couldn't fuckin' move and I knew nothin' was really any different with you than it had been anywhere else so I just lay there and said *Fuck it* to myself *what's one more cock up my snatch*...

"So I could feel you standing there...breathin' the way you do when you're upset or whatever...and then you leaned over and kissed me on the forehead and said *G'night Chelsea* and went back into your bedroom and locked the door..."

She was bent over his hand where it lay on the sheet he could feel the back of it getting wet as she sobbed and choked on her tears. He turned his hand over and she put her cheek against it.

"I don't remember my father ever kissing me like that, Charlie...or saying g'night to me ever...not even before he started using me, Charlie, I...I wanted t'be with you so badly after that I woulda done anything..."

He took his hand away from her face...put it on her head for the first time felt the reality of how soft her spun gold waves and curls could be...stroked her head gently...

"I didn't wanna be one more cock up your snatch, Chelsea. I'd done that for years. I didn't want to be somebody just adding to what'd already been done t'you."

"You would never have been like any of the others..."

"But it might have felt exactly the same...and you didn't need another pair of hands being laid on you like that...neither did I..."

She picked her head up...not understanding. He reached for a Kleenex from his bedside table...started making the mascara tracks even worse he handed it to her... nodded toward the mirror over the sink in his bathroom. Talked her there and back again...

"I spent the first twenty years of my so-called adult life doing every stupid thing I could think of, and a ton of stuff other people thought up for me. Charlie Stinson was a legend on Long Island. He could drink more than anybody else...smoke more...drug and dance more. He just looked at the girls and the women and they stripped down for him anytime anywhere he fucked everything that moved and had a swell time doing it...

"I was thirty-three years old when this book I'd written on a bet became a best-seller. My first book-signing tour was four months long and I went t'over fifty cities in North America. My second one was two weeks long...three cities...and it almost killed me. That was when I had my first heart attack..."

She came back from the bathroom...no more mascara...no make-up at all... Charlie had rarely seen her like that before it still didn't matter nothing mattered if it was Chelsea...

"When the doctors were done putting their heads together it was determined that Charles Stinson the New York Times best-selling author had in the course of his carousing and hell-raising thoroughly fucked the way his heart did business. And my life just stopped. I couldn't do anything anymore. Almost a year just so I could walk to the corner and back...

"So living in my head, and what I could put on paper, became my reality. I lived in my books. I watched the world going by and rearranged what I saw to suit myself and my devoted but mostly tasteless readers...

"And then one day I see this girl doing a piss-poor job of trying to jack a Lexus in broad daylight and she's fifteen years old and she's the most beautiful female animal I've ever laid eyes on...every movement...every breath she takes...every inch of her from top to bottom is what every male from age eight to eighty wishes would walk into his life...

"But all I can do...all I've done for fourteen years...is look...so now I have t'wait for her to cross my path again so this lovely gorgeous stunning creature can light up my retinas all over again..."

There was mascara on his hand and fingers. She reached for it...wiped them clean...didn't let go.

"I love you, Charlie. You taught me how to trust somebody. I wanted...wished you woulda let me give you somethin' back..."

He lifted their two hands together and kissed hers.

"You did," he whispered. "Every night. I locked my door and through the magic of my steamy Harlequin romance imagination you ended up in my bed anyway. Where Charles Stinson was living his life you gave Charlie the one thing he needed more than anything else...the chance to grow up and really love somebody... without all the bullshit and the terror and only a little bit of guilt for *wishing* I could have you...imagining what it might be like. But you put your life in his hands...and then you let him live up to all of the expectations you should have had from when you were a little girl..."

"What am I gonna do, Charlie?"

"You're gonna find somebody to love you with passion and kindness, Chelsea... someone who's gonna turn the garbage in your life into what it should have been all along...something deep and earth-shaking and joyous...and after that...well...*whatever you wanna do*. I'll come along as far as I can, but thanks t'you I've gone as far as I need t'go...Shit! I remembered something just before you came in...you gotta do me a favour what time is it anyway..."

"I don't know three o'clock maybe..."

"I was supposed t'be home today...meeting somebody there..."

"Can't you call them?

"I don't have my phone."

"You can use mine."

"Will you go...just let him in and let him do what he needs t'do?

"Okay sure...can I come back after?"

Charlie nodded and squeezed her hand. "That would be so swell..."

9.

She ran most of the way...dodged traffic...Jeremiah Stokes saw her coming from across the street.

"...Afternoon, miss."

"Hello, Mister Stokes."

"There's somebody here waitin' t'see you."

"I can open the damn door myself y'know."

Mister Stokes said, "I know that...but I gets paid to open that damn door so I do it...'specially for you.... Have you been to see him, miss?"

Chelsea nodded.

"Not so good, is it?"

"Not so good at all. It sucks, Mister Stokes..."

"Well...I'll do some prayin' for him then... That gentleman is waitin' in the office I'll let him know you're here..."

She nodded again and went to wait for the ancient elevator...heard someone coming up behind her as the cab clanged and banged and opened up in front of her she turned...took in a suit and a briefcase and a guy that looked like the grey-haired dude in *The Young & the Clueless.* She saw his eyes go wide for a fraction of a second before he said:

"You're...Chelsea...?"

She said, "I'm Chelsea. Who the fuck are you?"

"I'm Charlie's friend...Jeff...we went to grade school together in Oceanside... Long Island...he asked me t'meet you here..."

He held the elevator door...followed her...hit the button for the fifth floor...

"Charlie..." he said, smiling and shaking his head. "Always with the surprises."

"What about Charlie and the surprises?"

"I've sort of known about you for what...six eight months now? You answered the phone a few times so word got round there was somebody else here besides Charlie. Those of us who know him well, we all got curious. When he asked me I said sure I'll meet Chelsea at your place. I thought you'd be a little bit older, is all..."

"Surprise then."

"He's not gonna make it this time."

"I fucking know that will you stop fuckin' acting like we're pals or something. I have no idea who the fuck you are!"

She slammed her hands against the walls...turned away from him...the elevator shuddered to a stop and the door creaked open. He held it again until she was in the hallway...stood well away from her as she turned her keys in all three locks opening the door he followed her into Charlie's place.

"Okay. I'm sorry. I've got a totally different set of reference points about Charlie and his life...and why I'm here. It never occurred to me that most of my assumptions could have no possible relevance for you."

She flung her shoulder bag onto the couch...lost in late afternoon sunlight curling around the curtained windows...stealing across the spines of shelved books... framed posters and prints on the walls...the couch where she had slept in this place for the first time...

"He asked me to have you sign some papers, Chelsea. I'm his friend. I'm also his lawyer. Up until last year, in the last fifteen years I've spent a lot of time here...which now seems to be one of only a few things we really have in common...so I'm gonna make myself at home and pour myself a big glass of something and see if we can do this for Charlie without dying ourselves."

Jeff took off his jacket and undid cufflinks and rolled his shirt sleeves up on his forearms and poured himself a big glass of whisky while she watched him...began to realise that whatever it was that was making her heart hurt so much was something else they shared...began to feel numb with impending loss...could feel it hear it coming like a freight train.

Jeff swallowed three fingers of single malt and poured three more...opened his briefcase and started laying out a dozen paper-clipped files dotted with sticky Sign-Here-Post-It notes on the dining room table. She watched stabs of sunlight twinkling with dust motes slowly dying...signed everywhere he pointed...on the dotted line she watched him countersign each one when there weren't anymore he said:

"Y'know Stokes downstairs...Charlie paid for his daughter t'go to college...and when his wife got sick and the HMO ducked through a loophole and wouldn't pay for her surgery or homecare Charlie covered that too. Charlie took care of everybody he loved... all the time...

"He has dozens maybe hundreds of friends...some of them are the biggest assholes in the world, but they've all known all along that if it comes down to rocks and hard places Charlie will always be there to stand up and take care of them..."

She looked at him. Sat down on the couch hugging herself suddenly afraid of what was going on she said:

"He set this up..."

And the cold got deeper.

"...Jeff...what is all of this...what'd we just do...?"

For an instant, Jeff looked back at her without comprehension.

"He didn't tell you."

"Tell me what?"

He cupped his whisky glass in both hands, took a deep breath and let it out.

"The last time Charlie got a market appraisal for this apartment it came in at just over eight-point-five million dollars. Last year his royalties on all seven of his books totaled over two million worldwide. For the last two months we've been in a bidding war for the sale of film rights for one of them, and there's also all the money that's been invested in the last fourteen years. All together we're looking at something between thirty and forty million dollars..."

She stared at him. There was nothing in the world that could darken the blue sky in her eyes...nothing that could dim the light that wove itself through the pale spun gold of her hair, or lip-gloss in any colour that could cover the pout and the glory of her mouth.

"A month ago he told me you'd gotten an acceptance from the Arts program at Cooper Union so I hope you'll forgive me for contacting them...for letting them know you *will* be there in September...and then beating them over the head with an endowment that will not happen unless every penny of your tuition for as long as you want to be there is covered by a scholarship.

UNTIL THE END OF THE WORLD

"So now...whoever the hell you are after all...Chelsea...now you are the one who I hope will understand what he's done because even if you're not someone he shared with me...I do know that my best friend...Charlie...stopped being lonely after he met you.

"You've already got keys and now *all* of it belongs to you," he said softly. "I'm beginning to understand why...and that Charlie's last gift to me was to be the one who gets to help you see your way through it. Christ! My daughter is your age. When my wife gets a look at you she's gonna shit herself..."

He stood up. Gathered up signed papers...his suit jacket...

"I gotta go. My card's there next to your copies from now on you call me any time for any reason...."

At the door he stopped and swore softly.

"I forgot something. This..."

Reached into his briefcase, walked back into the room and laid a standard size manila envelope on the table.

"It's his original print-out for a short story...the only one he ever wrote...the only thing he's written in the last two years. I'm not supposed t'sell it until after he's gone...but it's funny because when we were growing up he had this big big thing for Joni Mitchell. There was this one record he used t'play all the time...it was a gatefold... y'know what they are...? Inside, Joni was standing on a cliff overlooking the ocean buck naked. He was in love with her like you wouldn't believe..."

She said, "*For The Roses*. Charlie played it for me all the time..."

"That's the one. I thought this story was just...like an *hommage* to his teenage lust for Joni Mitchell. Now I know better..."

After he was gone Chelsea sat watching the dust motes settle and disappear. She poured herself a glass of the sweet white zin that Charlie had convinced her had to be better for her than fucking Coca Cola. She gathered up all her papers but didn't have the courage to look at the story inside the manila envelope.

When the telephone rang and the nurse she'd met that afternoon asked for her by name she listened quietly...hung up the phone...picked up her shoulder bag and went back to the hospital to kiss him goodbye.

Part Two - CHELSEA IN TWILIGHT

1.

They stood on the hillside in ragged little tatters of snow...late November...overhead clouds grey and heavy with an early surge of winter. In the wind that whistled through the trees and thrashed October leaves against gravestones, piled them against the walls of family mausoleums, she stood beside his oldest friend and cried for when he had sat quietly watching her...never asking more of her than to simply be herself...to somehow stop being angry and afraid...be who she would have been if not for someone else's sick baggage.

Jeff said, "He's in good company. This place is famous. Duke Ellington's buried here...Joe Oliver...Guggenheims...Hammersteins...Lionel Hampton...Otto

Preminger… La Guardia…Countee Cullen…hundreds of famous people…"

"Charlie's here," she said. "I don't give a fuck about the rest of them. I miss him. I miss the feeling of somebody looking past my ass and my tits…looking into my heart and caring about me…

"That was my Charlie…"

She turned away from the little chunk of granite in the ground that told where they had put the last of her Charlie, started walking back down the hill towards the Lincoln SUV below. Inside, out of the wind, she stopped crying. His best friend had a thought cross his mind that she was something uncanny…to be crushed by grief and still be blindingly beautiful. His best friend had lived with this…

"Listen…" he said, "don't be angry okay…"

She turned on him…knowing…dead certain…

"Never! Not fucking once! You tell all his good good friends for me, okay? You ask those fuckers if they really thought he would start where my father left off…"

"I didn't know, Chelsea. I'm sorry."

"Sure you are, Jeffrey. But how would your sorry hold up if I hit on you? Would you say no…or would you make excuses…blame me…go crying to your wife *I couldn't help it she was beggin' for it…*

"Fuck you! Fuck all of you! Charlie was supposed t'be the wildest fucking wild man of your whole crew and he was the only one who knew what was real. He admitted he wanted to fuck me…and I would've spread my legs for him in a heartbeat…but he never asked because he had balls and he was thinking about what *I* wanted and what *I* needed...not like the rest of you fuckin' pussies..."

He drove her back to West End Avenue in silence, watched her hug the doorman and go upstairs to his best friend's apartment.

Chelsea played Beethoven on his stereo and cried some more.

2.

Winter closed in on her. In the summer...in the wake of his death...she had fled back to her friends, but no one of them was going on to college or university. They were still on the street, no longer in sync with any of the things that had begun to matter to her. In September she had school, the challenge of taking her natural talents as an artist to somewhere above and beyond what she had done before, but it meant traveling a length of Manhattan where she came into contact with people...men...who only saw her in passing and somehow believed that whistles....looks that stripped her bare of clothing... were things she would appreciate...

Christmas without him...after one Christmas with him...was more loneliness than she could bear, and not even the quiet kindness of Jeremiah Stokes and his family during the holidays could fix it. In January, before she even went back to school for second semester, she called a telephone number on a business card.

"Good morning," said Jeff, picking up after his receptionist. "How are you?"

"Are you thinkin' with your brain today?"

She heard him suck in a long breath.

"I'm trying harder not to be an idiot, if that's what you're asking."

"It's a start," she said coldly.

"What can I do for you, Chelsea? Is there anything you need...?"

She took a deep breath and tried not to be angry.

"I get the bank thing...goin' t'the bank when I need money. How come I don't get any bills for electricity or what...taxes...stuff like that...?"

"I look after it for you. All the bills come to me. That's why if you need anything...something not everyday...you call me... "

"Well I need t'do it myself. Some of it, anyway. So I can get a clue...some small sense of responsibility. I mean, how am I supposed to know I'm buying a dangerous amount of fuckin' Twinkies if I never see a bill...?"

She heard him laugh even though he tried not to.

"Valid point. Okay...I can do that...we'll work something out with one of my people here, to set it up and walk you through whatever you need or want to know."

"That would be good. Thanks...and I wanna learn how t'drive next summer too..."

"Anything else?"

She didn't answer right away. The part of her that still lived with memories from before Charlie cringed; the part that ached for him and what he had wanted for her needed to go somewhere. She looked around the apartment...at his books and the records and all the trappings of what was supposed to have been a peaceful transition into young adulthood. All of it had been part of his gift to her, but all of it just served to remind her all the time that he was gone.

"I need t'talk somebody, Jeff," she said quietly. "I feel like I'm stuck someplace where I don't even know which direction can get me out..."

He said he knew a couple of people...asked if she had a preference to male or female... would work something out and get back to her.

"When d'you want to start this, Chelsea?" he asked.

She said "Yesterday."

Said goodbye...walked down the hall into the bathroom and took off all her clothes...looked at herself in the full-length mirror on the back of the door...saw someone on the outside who should have been a Playboy Playmate of the Year but on the inside felt a lot like Charlie had looked, sitting in the Arte Café waiting for her to come back to the table...

Lost and lonely...

3.

Early Saturday morning she walked crosstown and south to Grand Central...caught a train into Westchester... watched the city at 125th Street begin to give way to open space...snow...the Hudson a mosaic of grey water and grey ice that sparked silver fire whenever the sun showed through the clouds...the Palisades across the river...

She realised she had never been north of the Bronx... only recognised the station-names...Hastings... Dobbs Ferry...Ossining...

She stepped out onto the platform looking for a face she'd never seen before and heard her named being called...a tallish slim woman in a red-plaid lumberjack and jeans...tall boots to her knees...short shagged pepper-and-salt hair and the same startled look in her grey eyes that she'd seen in Jeff's six months before...the one that said *Wow!* before she introduced herself...held out her hand...

"Chelsea. Hi. I'm Doreen Patterson. Dory...forgive me for staring."

"I'm the fucking poster child for Total Strangers Who Stare," she said. "I'll get over it if you will."

Doreen Patterson pressed her lips together and nodded.

"Fair enough. Are you hungry? My place is just a couple of minutes over the line in Chappaqua but we can stop if you want something to eat?"

Chelsea shook her head said thanks she was good...followed her off the platform and across the parking to a plum-coloured Escalade.

"Do all of Charlie"s friends drive expensive cars?"

"How d'you know I was one of Charlie"s friends?"

"Jeff knows you and Charlie would've gone for you. You're still pretty hot...and you're in a lot of his old photographs."

Patterson didn't say anything, unlocked the car, took them out along the Pleasantville Road and then left onto Chappaqua Road...east over countryside showing houses well off the beaten path through the dense woods. Ten minutes later they turned right onto a long paved drive that wound into the trees. Chelsea closed her eyes, still feeling stared at by strangers...

It was barely noon but she asked for a glass of wine... asked for the some of the sweet stuff she was used to...accepted a Chablis and decided it was okay.

They sat on fat chaise cushions in a glassed solarium at the back of a small Tudor cottage—dark wooden beams and diamond-paned windows...some floors tiled in slate and others bare wood covered in rag rugs... furniture and fixtures totally upscale and modern but fitting right in anyway.

They sipped wine for a little while. She was grateful for the time, fascinated by the way she could be inside and look up at the sky at the same time...watch the play of light and dark across the sky and the way it fell down across the trees making shadow places in the pines... etching the deciduous ones like the old bones she had seen with Charlie in the museum.

"Jeff tells me you're an artist...a good one."

Chelsea came back. Doreen Patterson's stare wasn't as obvious anymore... nowhere near as warm as Charlie's...nowhere anyplace near as cold as the men who tried to see through her clothes. Doreen Patterson didn't want anything from her...already had what she needed...

"Did he tell you my father fucked me but Charlie didn't?"

Patterson nodded.

"I needed to get an idea of why you wanted to see me so he mentioned it. He didn't intend it as a violation of your privacy, just felt it was something I should know ahead of time…"

"Did you ever fuck Charlie?"

Doreen Patterson blinked.

"I was looking for something more than he was willing to give…at the time…"

"That's not an answer!"

Suddenly she was as angry as she'd ever been…had seen this woman flinch and had felt a glow of satisfaction.

"Chelsea I want to help you."

"Why?

"Because you asked for help…and you were important to him."

"So now I'm the fucking mascot for the Charlie Stinson Fan Club?"

"No…not at all…"

"Did you fuck him?"

Dory nodded slowly and Chelsea started crying all over again.

⁂

"…I'm going to ask you lots of questions. Some of them are going to sound stupid. Some of them you may not want to answer right away…or at all…

"I'm good with whatever I can do to make this work for you, and starting an hour ago nobody but you and me will know what goes on here. I promise…"

The afternoon had grown dark…snow beginning to cover the flagstones of the terrace on the other side of the glass…shifting and swirling across the sky to fill the shadow pines with ghost corpses. Chelsea was drowsy with more wine and warmth, desperate enough to be trusting Dory Patterson without consciously having made the decision to do so.

"Why was it so important for you to know?"

Chelsea knew what she was talking about, curled herself up on the chaise and turned on her side to look at her...

"It was the only thing I had that I could give back to him and he never took it...he said he didn't wanna be like everybody else...like my father..."

"Why do you think he said that?"

"I don't know."

"Chelsea, let me tell you more about Charlie, okay?" She poured more wine for herself. "When I knew him we were both still really just kids, and we had baggage just like everybody else. He tried to bury his by being plain outrageous crazy...lookin' for love in all the wrong places and cutting a pretty wide path through the female population. In a lot of ways he was a real bastard, but he never ever really intended anybody any harm...

"And then he got sick. Did he tell you how it happened...?"

Chelsea nodded.

"Nobody is not changed by stuff like that...and as time went by I could see that even writing those dumb-ass books there was something else going on in his head; that something about the way Charlie had looked at the world was undergoing a huge transformation and it wasn't just because he couldn't party anymore."

"He was alone," Chelsea said. "The first day we talked to each other he tried to explain why he couldn't stop staring at me. It was like...you have this spectacular set of tits and a great ass and you have a beautiful face and it's so easy to just look at you and pretend...

"But then he started talkin' about this weird stuff... that he liked watching me because ...I don't know...I never really understood what he was saying... but in one way I understood perfectly...like when I would see something that I wanted t'draw... whatever it was that made me *want* t'draw...I don't know...a fuckin' squirrel...it went beyond just what was on the outside...

"Sometimes I wish I could kill the assholes on the street who think it's okay to look at me and pretend they can do whatever they want to me. When Charlie looked at me it was warm...and safe...and there was love in it...he made me happy t'be just what I was...he never asked me t'be anything but what I wanted t'be..."

"But you felt badly that he wouldn't sleep with you."

"Yeah. And it wasn't fair. He said he dreamed about me...about us bein' together...

"I used t'wake up in the middle of the night and think about him...how nice it would be if he would just put his arms around me and hold me..."

"Which is what you wished your real father would have had done."

She could feel her breathing stop...knew that she was the one staring now...

straight out into nothing...

"It's nowhere near as simple as that, Chelsea. I'd be really surprised if that one little thing *fixes* everything... but I think the two of you found each other at just the right time.

"Charlie had discovered a different way to deal with the way he viewed himself and the world. Somehow...maybe because he honestly felt crazy-ass physical sex was all over for him...he got to look at you as something much more intrinsically beautiful than just a pair of boobs...and when the two of you started to inter-relate his attitude began to change the way you viewed yourself...

"For however long it was, you were just a sex toy for your father. Then Charlie comes along and he's attracted to you for the all the same reasons, but because of...I don't know...whatever...the way he related to you was something entirely different.

"He didn't want to be your father. Knowing Charlie I'm pretty sure it would not have hurt his feelings at all to have been your lover...except for the part where you were fifteen...but he wanted to be something good for you more than he wanted anything else. He'd learned a different appreciation for what you were on the outside...and it led him away from just observing you...objectifying you...to where he could appreciate what you were on the inside as well."

"He said I didn't need another pair of hands bein' put on me that way...that he didn't need it either..."

"He was right, Chelsea. I'm having trouble describing the distinction I think he made in his own head, but whatever it was it was right for both of you...the balance between physical love and the concept of attraction...and something else that had nothing to do with physical at all."

Chelsea sat up...asked for another glass of wine...watched the afternoon get longer and the snow outside get deeper.

"I'm really lost without him," she said to the trees. "I don't know how or what t'feel anymore...what t'say or do with anybody..."

4.

"...Where did it start, Chelsea? Can you talk about it?"

She nodded asked for more wine. She knew she was getting shit-faced but it was the only way she could say anything...everything...hope it would stop hurting...

"One day when I was ten years old I came home from school and my mom wasn't there. I guess she just got tired of my father beating the crap out of her every time he got drunk. She never came home and I never saw her again."

"Did he hit you?"

"As far back as I can remember...but it stopped on the day I stopped crying whenever he fucked me."

"Why?"

"I have no idea."

"No...I meant why did you stop crying?"

"Because it made him angry and then he'd hit me."

"Anything else?"

"I went somewhere else. I stopped listening to his bullshit about how my mom never did right by him but I was a good girl and I loved him and blah blah blah...

"Everything would stop. Somewhere else there was this whisper about how good I was and how good I was making him feel and I just turned it off and sang *Somewhere Over the Fuckin' Rainbow* to myself until he was finished. When I knew he was asleep I went t'the bathroom and washed myself...brushed my teeth...spit into the toilet and pissed on it before I flushed..."

"...Would you like to stay? That snow is looking pretty determined to go most of the night."

"Can I? I didn't bring anything."

"Henry...my husband... is away on business for the weekend. I wasn't planning on it, but I was hoping that we'd get along okay...that you'd consider staying overnight. Jeff and I talked for quite a while and he said if I was patient we'd probably end up liking each other..."

"Patient."

"Yeah...he said you had a few quirks. Would poached salmon with wild rice and vegetables to go over be okay with you?"

"I could force myself."

"We're gonna need more wine though..."

"Did you really steal the salmon?"

"...Whenever Charlie asked me if I was hungry I'd say *Charlie I'm fuckin' starving* and he would grin like I'd just made his day by being hungry. After a while I started doin' shit I knew he liked me t'do...like peeling pepperoni slices off the pizza with my fingernails an—"

She stopped... looked at Dory looking at her.

"What?"

"Did you hear what you just said? You started doing things because you knew he liked it when you did them. You wanted to please him..."

"Well sure I did."

"Did you get rewarded for pleasing him?"

"Charlie bought me stuff all the time."

"Do you think he wouldn't have bought you stuff all the time if you stopped picking up those pepperoni slices?"

"Fuck no of course not. I told him he didn't have t'do any of that. He said when I got stuff I really liked it was a different look on my face than just bein' regular happy."

"So he wasn't asking for anything from you...and even though it's something you probably did all the time to try and get your father to stop using you for sex, you didn't have that problem with Charlie. So what d'you think was going on...?"

Chelsea shook her head, shrugged.

"Is it possible that both of you were reacting like... regular human beings maybe... trying to give some happiness to each other...?"

"I don't know...maybe...me for Charlie...definitely..."

She pushed herself away from the table and made happy after-dinner noises... another couple of glasses of wine drowsy...but suddenly not hurting so much ...

"That was really good."

"Not really fucking good?"

"That too."

"Thank you," said Dory. "I'm a pretty good cook. Henry loves my cooking. Henry says he loves my cooking too much."

"Was that him in the photograph in the kitchen?"

She nodded. Chelsea watched her face warm up and start to shine.

"That's the way I got with Charlie."

"What way?"

"Don't fuckin' pretend you don't know, Dory. Not with something like that. We're supposed t'be feminist all-business-can-do-anything women but if we love somebody they make it out like we're bein' pussies..."

"Are you okay?"

"I'm better...I just hate being in that apartment without him being there too."

Dory collected dishes, put them in the sink and moved them into the living room where she put a pile of logs in the fireplace and Chelsea on one end of a big couch where she was in no danger of sliding off. She held out her glass but Dory shook her head.

"Take a break, little girl," Dory said, wriggling down into the other end. "What I was talking about before was just that Charlie was very good at making you feel good. He knew what t'say and when t'say it. Most of the time you knew it was a good measure of bullshit, but he was charming and while he always seemed to get what he wanted he somehow never let you feel like you were being short-changed."

"Charlie never bullshitted me."

"Honey I do believe he never did. That's why I'm shaking my head a little. Somehow the two of you managed to have a relationship that was normal if you ignored the fact that you were fifteen and he was forty-something. She laughed. "At its heart it resembled something more like what two eight-nine-ten-year olds would do…assuming sex didn't get in the way …which it didn't seem to do…"

"So…?"

"So what you're missing is the next logical step, Chelsea. Where the two of you get older and simply pleasing each other begins to include the possibility of physical intimacy, as well as everything else you shared before. By social standards you should have been with child services and Charlie should have been in jail…but instead, the two of you are having this lovely charming innocent healing romance…you…and Charlie… of all the people in the world…"

"Whattaya mean Charlie of all people…?"

"The Charlie I knew wasn't quite like that. I'm starting to wonder if Jeff didn't have some ulterior motives in asking me to talk to you. Funny though…in one sense… back there at the train station…you were really close on the mark…about there being a Charlie Stinson Fan Club. He made big big dents in everyone who knew him. Big good dents and big bad dents. I'm thinking maybe Jeff figured I was ready for some shop time to finally bang out mine with you."

"You loved him a lot."

"I did, Chelsea. I think I loved him for all of the reasons he gave you to love him...only I never saw much of them."

"How's Henry with that?"

"Henry thought Charlie was an asshole but he loved him anyway. We all did. It was almost impossible not to love Charlie. We were this big raise-a-lotta-hell-together family...incestuous...it was crazy...and Charlie was so desperate for love that in his own way he gave it away hoping to get more..."

Dory's face got soft and dreamy with looking backward...Chelsea saw the corners of her eyes go shiny...

"We looked out for each other."

"Charlie was always lookin' out for me. He was so scared I'd end up someplace where I would get hurt again."

"That was him too."

Dory sighed. Stretched for the bottle of Chablis she'd just opened for herself. Tipped it in the direction of Chelsea's glass. Firelight turned it into liquid fire pouring into the crystal wineglasses...pine logs spat spice and warmth...

"I'm breaking so many fucking rules," she said, swirling the wine in her glass, looking down into the little golden whirlpools. "I was so fucked up for so long...before and after Charlie...and here I am trying to play psychologist for you...the one who pretty much got what I wanted from him...and you really are the most beautiful girl I've ever seen in my life... and I'm really happy he did something good for you..."

5.

"Dory I can't figure out why it's so fucked up."

"Are we gonna try and unravel it all out tonight?"

Chelsea shrugged. "I spend a lot of time starin' up at the ceiling. All I know is that if some of them would just say *Hi* instead of whistling or telling me where they wanna stick their dicks I could be a lot friendlier."

Dory wagged her head. "It's pretty amazing what they think will get them into our panties."

"That's for sure! I was goin' up Fifth Avenue and this well-dressed guy in a suit sees me...starts walkin' a little bit sideways so I won't see the hard-on in his shorts...and he starts in with how would I like to have lunch with him and he's a big-shot in some modeling agency and he can guarantee a girl like me could be famous inside of a year."

"I sense a train wreck," Dory said.

Chelsea grinned. "I asked whattaya mean a girl like me, and I can see him trying to figure out a polite way t' tell me I have humungous tits. Instead he says something about being smart and sexy and oh my and I just started laughing..."

"I'm sure that went over well."

"No...I shouldn't've laughed...but he asks me what I'm laughin' at so I just say I'm eighteen years old and I'm a student doing exactly what I wanna do...

"And he says well wouldn't it be better if I was doin' that with a place of my own and a six-figure bank account. So I tell him I've already got eight rooms on the upper West Side, eight figures in the bank, and one asshole in my jeans is more than enough but thanks for tryin' t'be so fuckin' altruistic t'poor little ole me."

Dory smiled into her glass. "So you didn't end up as friends."

"Not unless calling somebody a wise-ass cunt is the new way to make the little girls swoon..."

"You hurt his feelings. Took a chunk out of his assessment of himself in the role of the manly male benefactor."

"Damn straight yes I guess...and I almost felt bad about it because he was one of the nicer ones."

"That's too bad," Dory sighed. "Charlie's a tough act t'follow..."

Chelsea stared into the fire, said "Yeah...so now I get t'choose exactly whatever it is I want whenever it comes along and I'd still rather be out on the street bumpin' into Charlie in the park. Why're they such assholes, Dory?"

"I think they're scared more than anything, honey. There's all sorts of theories, but mostly I think it's because they're scared, and Western culture has never managed to get comfortable with sex. Too much religion to get in the way. Too much capitalism. Too much bullshit to cover up the insecurities we ladle out to our children...

"When I was your age I'd agonise over a pimple or if I was carrying two pounds more than would comfortably fit into my bathing suit."

Chelsea said, "It's like it's still this big dark stupid secret. I mean you can turn on a computer and watch people doin' it for hours, but Janet Jackson pops a boob at the Super Bowl and suddenly the whole fuckin' world is ready to collapse from the shock."

UNTIL THE END OF THE WORLD

Dory nodded."We program our girls and women to believe that what's between their legs is a precious commodity to be protected and bartered in a cold marketplace... and then all our little boys get taught it's something they have to steal...or trick us into giving away...

"For too many of them it becomes this guilt-ridden game that's not a game at all. Honest sexual urges end up being sublimated...turned into something to be ashamed of. Even regular sex... never mind the adventurous stuff...is something they're not allowed to expect or ask for; then a sense of frustration gets built into the equation and next thing you know a misplaced and totally unnecessary *anger* has replaced simple desire as the foundation of interplay between men and women. Aggression instead of passion."

"It sucks."

"It does."

"How'd you and Henry get together?"

Doreen started to glow from the inside again...

"One of our beach parties...dozens of us just hanging out...bonfires...lots of beer and stuff... Henry wasn't really part of our crowd but I'd seen him a few times usually on the edges being quiet...not so crazy as the rest of us...

"One night after being especially stupid I sort of staggered out into his part of the solar system and threw up in the sand. He waited until I was all done and offered me his towel...asked me if I was okay...just kept me company until the world stopped spinning so much and we talked for a little while before I passed out.

"In the morning in among all the casualties I was in this comfortable little hollow in the sand with his blanket on top of me and him sitting there waiting for me to wake up."

Chelsea realised she was smiling. "That sounds really romantical..."

"It was. Romantical and sweet. All the stuff that Charlie was at his very best...but slower and less bullshit. Henry was my grown-up teddy bear Casanova..."

6.

Chelsea made breakfast in the morning. Toast. Bacon. Scrambled eggs. Dory sat in the breakfast nook sipping coffee watching her, and she felt an almost ghostlike presence that gave her goose bumps...then a rush of warmth as she turned to the older woman... puzzled for a moment before she recognized the feeling, and something unspoken passed between them. They smiled in the same instant.

"I got an email from Henry this morning. He's got a 4.35 flight into LaGuardia and I told him I wanted to drive into the city to pick him up...that I'd met someone special I wanted him to meet. You could come with... have supper with us...meet my teddy bear..."

Chelsea smiled again.

"It's so strange, Dory," she said.

"What's so strange?"

"Everything. Nothing at all."

"Fuckin' amazing?" offered Doreen.

"Yeah."

They ate breakfast, washed dishes, went outdoors to dig themselves out of a two-foot snowfall. Chelsea was introduced to the snow-blower and took a faceful of snow before Dory showed her how to rotate the thrower to follow the prevailing wind that wound its way up the driveway. A snowman in front of the garage followed. Then a snowball fight...then back indoors for showers and an hysterically successful attempt at *Benny & Joon* grilled cheese sandwiches after dusting off Dory's not-used-in-a-decade steam iron.

"D'you have nightmares, Chelsea? Anything that keeps rearing up inside your head to remind you...?"

She thought about it...shook her head...

"Not really."

"You said you went somewhere else...sang to yourself...were you ever scared?"

Again she shook her head no. "Only at first. Then I knew what was happening... what he was doing...and I knew it had nothing t'do with me."

"But you were ashamed when Charlie found out."

Revelatory...Chelsea went blank...then slowly said, "I was..."

"D'you know why? Deep down maybe felt what your father was doing to you was something you should accept and offer gladly...but someone else finding out made it shameful...?"

Chelsea felt numb sitting beside the fireplace...

"No."

"Because you didn't fight back...or stopped fighting back?"

"No."

"So why...why was Charlie finding out so horrible?"

...Felt numbness giving way to the same sense of shame...

"Because...I knew it was wrong...and I was afraid Charlie would stop caring about me....that I would lose him and have nowhere t'go...have nobody t'care about me."

"But it wasn't your fault, Chelsea. You never encouraged your father. This was something that was done *to* you...not something you participated in. Accepting his guilt as your own was something he forced on you...making you feel as if it was your duty to make up for the failure of *his* relationship with your mother.

"You have no blame in this, honey. Parents are supposed to take care of their children, not use them to fill up the holes in their own souls. Your mother abandoned you because she saw it as the only way *she* could escape an abusive relationship...and then your father made you pay the price for having driven her away himself."

She started crying. Helplessly. Sat in front of the fire and felt tears pouring down her face and raining down on her heart. Fell into Dory Patterson's arms when she came off the couch to hold her.

"Chelsea, you're going to be okay, I promise. It might take a while but you're going to be fine. We never ever forget what they did to us, but if we can hang on...hang in...find the right people to help us...we can live past it..."

She looked up. Felt Dory's hands in her hair smoothing it away from her face.

"For me it was my uncle. My mother's brother. It was only for a summer when I was thirteen but it was more than enough to fuck up the next fifteen years of my life.

And then one morning I woke up on the beach and found Henry watching over me.

"Charlie started the same thing for you...and while he still might have a pretty precarious balance sheet when it comes to Heaven or Hell, right now he's probably sitting on a cloud he intends to move someday soon so you can have some sunshine in your life. You just have to believe in your right to be there when it shows up..."

7.

Chelsea borrowed a clean t-shirt and they needlessly wintered up for what had turned into a mild almost spring-like afternoon...some of Dory's promised sunshine...the sound of snow-melt in the gutters...the intimation of small rivers running beneath white-carpeted fields and sleepy field mice moving unseen through snow caverns. They piled into the Escalade and Dory took them onto the Hutchinson River Parkway heading south to the city.

At the 678 interchange she said, "I think I should warn you though...Henry could be the president of your Total Strangers Who Stare club. He's polite and he tries to be discreet but he's got that same *fascination* thing you said Charlie tried to explain to you. He was pretty shy compared to the rest of us so he spent a lot of time watching too.

"Anyway...please don't be offended he doesn't mean t'be rude. The funny part is that I think he thinks I don't notice...like all the extra hugs and smooches I get afterward come out of nowhere..."

Chelsea smiled. "He sounds like he might be okay."

Dory said, "You'll like him. I hope so..."

They traveled in silence for a while, Chelsea watching Westchester County float by in the almost totally-silent cocoon of the Escalade's interior.

"You guys don't have any kids, do you?"

Dory shook her head. "Thanks to my uncle, no. We thought about adopting so many times, but it just didn't seem to be a comfortable fit...and then Henry's work took off and I started grad school..."

"Jeff told me you teach psych at Purchase."

"And I've been teaching a course at NYU. His daughter Caroline is in the psych program there... somebody else you should meet. You guys are taking your classes in the same neighbourhood..."

"What's Henry do?"

Dory took time out to navigate them onto the Whitestone Bridge, sunlight bouncing off ice-floes in the East River, Long Island materialising out of snow-glare and afternoon haze.

"He and Jeff look after your money," she said.

"Charlie's money..."

"*Your* money, Chelsea," said Dory forcefully. "Charlie had his faults but being a cheapskate wasn't one of them. We all got more than our share from him. Those of us who really cared about him would never dream of begrudging you something he gave willingly."

"So Henry's..."

"A suit," Dory laughed. "He's even got a politically correct briefcase to carry all the paperwork pertaining to all your politically correct investments. He doesn't deal with anything that's not eco-friendly, self-sustaining and green."

They exited onto the Grand Central Parkway and minutes later pulled into the short-term parking at LaGuardia. In front of the terminal Dory turned to her and fluffed her hair, marched them arm-in-arm inside... sipped hot chocolates...people-watched and were watched in turn until the arrival of Henry's flight was announced. Chelsea recognized a feeling of warmth...felt it in Doreen Patterson's smile...her touch...the way she seemed to be so pleased to be there in her company...

It almost felt like being with Charlie.

When Henry appeared through the checkpoint at the arrival gate, Dory bounced a couple of times and waved at him; Chelsea walked right up to him and took the briefcase out of his left hand, offering him her right she said:

"Hi Henry I'm Chelsea and Dory says it's okay if you stare at me."

Grinned impudently. Watched the neatly-bearded face grow a couple of shades more ruddy than it had been a moment before. Decided she would like him just fine.

8.

They had dinner at the Palm Court in the Plaza Hotel, Henry taking a smiling Buddha-like satisfaction in showing them off in way-less-than-elegant dinner attire. Chelsea sensed a quiet rebel inside the three-piece suit.

"You have t'let me pay," she insisted. "It would make Charlie smile. We useta walk down here t'talk to the horses...and besides, if Jeff sees it on my credit card bill then he gets t'find out he finally did something right without me having to tell him he's not as big an asshole as I thought he was."

Henry snorted into his cognac. Dory tried not to laugh. Chelsea realised she wasn't near as lonely as she'd felt on Friday.

When Henry pulled the Caddy up in front of Charlie's place Dory got out to walk Chelsea inside...waved to Stokes who let them open the door on their own and won a stuck out tongue from Chelsea for his trouble.

"Henry's hooked," said Dory. "He wants to know if you're going to issue fan club badges or membership cards. And he's volunteered t'be acting president."

"So that means lots of hugs and good lovin' for you tonight?"

"Got all my fingers crossed," she laughed, and then, seeing a small cloud pass over the sky blue eyes, "Just be patient, Chelsea. I promised. Remember that. We've still lots of ground to cover so you call me any time day or night for any reason at all...okay?"

Chelsea swallowed and nodded. "Can I come up t'visit too?"

"All you have t'do is tell me you're on your way."

Chelsea nodded again and Dory leaned into her...kissed her forehead.

"G'night, sweetheart, I'll talk to you soon."

She watched her walk back to the car, slide in beside Henry...wave...and drive away. A voice behind her said,

"They good people...and it's good t'have you home, Miss Chelsea."

She turned to Jeremiah Stokes, said "Thank you Mister Stokes it's really nice t'*be* home..."

Part Three - CHELSEA RISING

1.

She visited Charlie just about every week without fail. Took the subway uptown to Woodlawn station and got lost trying to find him on her own the first few times....then began to appreciate the hike into the heart of the cemetery...away from the noise and the smell of diesel...the crowded sidewalks. When the weather was nice she stayed for hours... thinking out loud...telling him about stuff...sketching the seasons as they moved around him...

Sometimes Jeff would spend an hour with her. Sometimes his daughter Carrie would come along to visit her "Uncle Charlie" and camp out for lunch...or Dory at least once a month to just stand in the quiet with her... dole out Kleenex whenever necessary...

At home she moved out of her bedroom and into his. Laid awake...slept... dreamed...or maybe he really did lean over her in the darkness...somehow manage to whisper goodnight...kiss her forehead. When it came to Charlie, after the initial crushing sense of loss, she seemed to always feel his presence nearby...a tiny bit of warmth left over from the shower of it he had shown her in life. It kept her going whenever she was tired or discouraged, or desperately in need of something to fill up the empty places in his bed...

Her old room became the studio...the place where all the emotions she was trying to learn about came out on rectangles of canvas...pages stripped from sketch pads...scraps of cloth...anything that came to hand that would provide her with a spontaneous look into her own soul. She wandered into the outpouring of her talent and with school...Dory...her visits to Charlie...started to find her way back into the world on terms she could accept...

Well into her junior year at CU she began a series of paintings...talked the concept over with her instructors and convinced them the experiment was worthy of consideration as the determinant of her final grade for the year. She didn't need their grades...or even a degree...but it was part of the challenge she had set herself and the promise she had made Charlie...

She spent almost six weeks on a four-by-six-foot canvas....received incredulous looks from everyone who saw the finished product...the almost featureless dark mass of colour sprawled almost haphazardly over twenty-four square feet of space...then invited them all to Charlie's apartment to show them what they were really looking at...

Dory saw it the next day. Chelsea explained where it had come from:

"...I was listening to one of Charlie's records... Crosby Stills and Nash...the first one where they're sitting on this broken down old couch in front of a broken down old house...

"Did you know the photographer wasn't happy with the pictures so they went back the next day to shoot some more and the house was gone? In the space of twenty-four hours they just leveled it...tore it down...!

"Anyway...there's this song about the darkest hour bein' the one right before dawn...and then I thought about how people can be looking at the exact same thing but still see something totally different...and how environment can alter perception to make that sort of thing happen."

Dory wandered down to the end of the hallway where Chelsea had hung the painting... came back shaking her head...

Chelsea said, "Okay...now go back to about ten feet away and lean against the wall to your right...tell me when you're ready."

Dory called out and Chelsea swept the drapes away from the big picture window in the living room....heard something along the lines of *Holy shit!* whispered along the shaft of light that bounced down the hall. Wide-eyed Dory came back to the living room.

Chelsea grinned.

"It's you."

Chelsea nodded. "I called it *Reaching for Daylight* and painted it so the only way you could see what was really there was if you had the right kind of light on it."

"So that faint outline in the dark is your doorway... with just a hint of light in it...and the other one to the left of it is you...your hand...reaching..."

Chelsea nodded again.

"D'you like it?"

Dory got thoughtful. "I don't know if *like* is applicable, honey. But it's amazing. Like *trompe l"oeil* makes you think you're seeing something real...."

"Sort of, yeah. I just wondered what would happen if a specific setting was necessary in order to gain the desired effect. I mean...Art is supposed t'be an integral part of Life, right?"

"So how'd you do with your professors?"

Chelsea shrugged. "Still waiting t'find out. Mostly I think they think I'm trying to sneak a sludge painting past them."

"But you've seen that first glimmer of light on your horizon."

Chelsea nodded. "I think so..."

2.

On her twenty-first birthday Dory came into the city for lunch and to spend the afternoon.

"How're you doing, honey?"

"Okay. Mostly great except for the parts that aren't... but I'm working on them. How're you guys doing?"

"We're doin' good," Dory said. "Henry's been acting a bit strange lately, but I'm not complaining because he's being really funny and really sweet...like something's up and he's trying like hell t'make sure I don't find out."

Chelsea sipped water, hitched back in her chair a little bit as the waiter brought their lunch...Caesar salads and bruschetta.

"Wow," she said.

"Looks good," Dory said.

"It does…but I was talkin' about my knees. I'm not used t'lookin' at them."

"You've been wearing dresses a lot lately."

"Well I'm always scrubby at school…"

"Nobody here is complaining," Dory said softly. She dipped her head over each shoulder at the rest of their company on the café's terrace. "That one's a beauty… showin' off the boom-boom just right…"

Chelsea blew a Marilyn kiss across the table and Dory's smile melted into something that was half astonishment and half unabashed pleasure.

"Look at you, Chelsea girl…accepting a compliment without one swear word…"

"Oh bullshit."

"Really."

"You said I should stop being angry about guys drooling on their shoes…and just because some of 'em are jerks isn't gonna stop me from bein' a girl."

"So…?"

Chelsea chewed thoughtfully on salad greens, a small slice of grilled chicken.

"Well you were right," she said. "I was gettin' pissed off because I was scared… and so I wouldn't have t'deal with the everyday reality that most of the boys were gonna be boys…that the only thought left in their brains after all the blood went south was the one where they got into my pants. Getting angry all the time just made sure nobody got too close."

"And now…?"

"Now it's not so bad," she said, waving her fork in the general direction of somewhere else. "I really have absolutely no desire to punch that douche-bag over by the railing for trying to look up my dress."

"Oh Chelsea that's wonderful!"

"Anger management, Dory," she said, spearing another sliver of chicken. "The key to male-female relations. Can we have wine?"

They spent most of the afternoon window-shopping... strolling south on Fifth... reveling in the warm... Chelsea's newfound sense of balance in perfect harmony with Manhattan making its first big wake-up stretch out of winter...

"So you're graduating...June..."

"Yep."

"Excited?"

"Not so much. I mean...I'm gonna keep doing what I'm doing and havin' a degree really doesn't change that at all...but there's other stuff..."

"Oh...?"

"I'm savin' it, Dory..."

"Now you're keeping secrets."

Chelsea nodded. "Yep. Secrets. Tough."

They stopped on the sidewalk under the arch in Washington Square, Dory suddenly serious as she reached out to brush blonde curls out of Chelsea's face.

"I hate to admit this but I owe Jeff forever for putting you in my life."

Chelsea stepped into her arms. "Me too but we can't ever tell him..."

They hung onto each other for a while. Chelsea noticed them being noticed by a pair of city guys doing clean-up in the park...said:

"Oh for god sakes she's my mom you assholes..."

And smiled sweetly as they walked past them with a switch of her hips...turned to Dory...

"See? Not one drop of blood," she said proudly.

Dory said, "That's my girl."

3.

"...I should be going, honey. I can still catch a train and get home before Henry."

Chelsea shook her head.

"No you have t'come with me. Henry's not goin' home tonight because I said we were gonna have supper at my place."

Dory cocked her head to one side.

"Secrets."

Chelsea nodded. "But I wanted t'talk t'you about other stuff first okay?"

"So we'll go home and cook and talk?"

"That's the plan."

"You're a pretty devious little creature, Sunshine."

"But now you're my mom so you have t'love me anyway."

Dory shook her head in resignation and hailed a cab.

4.

They sliced and diced and chopped things up in Charlie's kitchen...boogied to an original vinyl Chicago

Transit Authority on Charlie's stereo...changed into comfortable casual and cracked another bottle of red wine. Dory harboured suspicions when it became apparent that five pounds of veal was destined to be the centrepiece of their meal for three but said nothing...just waited for Chelsea to come round to where she needed to be for conversation...

"What was it like with you and Henry ...the first time...is it okay if I ask?"

Dory nodded over fresh egg batter and breading for the veal...took her time answering...

"I was scared to death. Before Henry I'd just been fucking. Trying t'pretend it was normal everyday stuff. Suddenly it was something else...and just as suddenly I stopped being afraid. The look in his eyes...I knew it would be all right...and afterwards I cried for an hour... scared him pretty badly but it was because I was...I don't know... stupid happy...free...

"Henry was just being Henry...but fucked up Doreen had decided to step off into the deep end of the pool. Once and for all I decided I wasn't going to let my fucked up uncle fuck up my life anymore."

"It was nice?"

"Chelsea it was the most beautiful feeling in the world...to be able to trust somebody that much... finally..."

"Charlie told me it should be that way," she said wistfully. "I wish he was here..."

"What's been goin' on, honey? Have you been...shit! Listen to me trying to sugar coat this... Have you been trying things on?"

Chelsea nodded...shrugged...

"The first time was over a year ago...right after my painting...this guy in one of my classes. We got t'talking and he was pretty talented y'know...and a little bit hunky... so we finish up and stop for a coffee and then he asks me if I wanna go back to his place so we get up and get our coats on and he stops in the bathroom before we head out...then walk down to a loft on Christopher he shares with a bunch of guys...

"I'm really nervous so I ask him for a glass of wine and he says all he's got is beer...and since because of you I'm now a snobby West Side bitch, I think to myself *Oh swell it's fifteen degrees outside and I'm gonna get smoochie over an ice-cold fuckin' Coors Light woo hoo...*

"So I hear him poppin' tabs in the kitchen and after a while he walks out with two poured glasses and that's when it hits me...the extra long trip to the men's room... walking into this loft he shares with three other guys and nobody's home but there's leftover supper on the table...

"I told him I liked havin' a slice of lemon or lime in my beer and when he went back into the kitchen to look for it I switched glasses. Then I just waited until he got really dozy... pulled out my Xacto knife 'cause I'd been cuttin' mattes that afternoon..."

"Chelsea...!"

"It's okay, Dory, I didn't do anything but scare him. I guess I just wasn't payin' attention ...and it's not like I was expecting Prince fuckin' Charming to sweep me off my feet when I'm scared shitless of bein' swept in the first place. I just told him he had been doin' all right until he started treating me like a fuck-toy in the bottom of a Cracker Jack box...asked him how many people knew he was plannin' on havin' some fun with Chelsea tonight? He couldn't talk but he didn't have to. I told him there was no way I was gonna let him do his shit on somebody else...then I called a cab and went home."

"Oh honey..."

Chelsea shrugged "It worked out fine. I called Jeff. He came over and we told the police what happened. Whatever they decided t'do, Kurt was gone inside of a week... back to Bumfuck Acres...or wherever.... anyway...I made Jeff promise not t'say anything t'you."

"We curse a lot more when we talk about stuff like this."

"That's because we're being defensive."

"Y'know you really do scare me sometimes, sweetheart."

"Dory, I may be a blondie but I got a lot of smart people lookin' after me..."

They moved on to the pasta sauce.

"Anybody else since then?"

"Two other guys," she said almost miserably. "They were okay I guess....tryin' really hard not t'be jerks...and I think I even came once...but there wasn't any real sparkage... not like what you said with Henry..."

"Chelsea it doesn't have t'be that way *all* the time...even with me and Henry...just liking the guy is okay. And...it's also supposed t'be fun..."

"I know that," she said, making a face. "I guess I keep thinking about what it would have been like with Charlie...somebody who really cares..."

"Well...eventually you'll find out..."

"You keep saying that."

"It's true, honey, just give it time. You're lucky enough that there's always gonna be a line-up so just wait it out and be careful..."

Dory spooned sauce at her. Chelsea tasted and pointed at oregano.

"Okay now?"

"The sauce or me?"

"Yes. Any other secrets you wanna spill?"

"Tons...but only one for right now can we leave this stuff for a little bit?"

They moved into the living room and Dory picked an old live jazzy Ten Years After album out of Charlie's collection, turned the volume down so they could talk.

"He never got sucked into the CD thing," she said. "Never wanted to leave the vinyl behind...stubborn... holding on to all the things that made him happy when he was a kid..."

Alvin Lee got grooved and the keyboard player comped. They plonked onto the couch and poured wine...

"Happy Birthday, Chelsea. I didn't buy you anything 'cause I know you really don't need or care about the stuff...but I guess that's just one of the reasons I love you, Chelsea girl. If you're giving anything away on your birthday can I have a corner of your heart... ?"

"You've already been there a while, Dory..."

"I'm gonna ask Jeff and Henry to sell this place...or whatever they think is best maybe just hang on to it for anybody that needs a place t'stay. I don't know. It's nice when you and Henry come into the city and it's nice when Carrie comes over...or my friends... but it's too big...it's too empty without Charlie. I don't wanna live with his ghost anymore. After I graduate I wanna go someplace where I can just have good memories of him, not sad ones..."

"Where do you wanna go, Chelse? You can live pretty much anywhere you want to."

"I wanna live close t'you and Henry...in the country where it's quiet. I like the chipmunks and finding foxes when I walk ...will you help find a place...like yours... maybe a little smaller...?"

Dory nodded. "Honey you know I will..."

"Is it okay?"

"It's better than okay, honey. It would be the best thing ever happened t'me since Henry and what you said five minutes ago."

Chelsea beamed...bounced...

"We gotta get going then, Dory. Henry's not the only one comin' t'supper..."

5.

Turned out it wasn't just Henry by a long shot. The downstairs intercom keep buzzing and Chelsea just kept hitting the entry lock. First up was Jeremiah Stokes and his wife Corinna. Then their doctor daughter Nkechi, teacher-husband James and their little girl Keesha. Carrie

Forbes followed, in company with her parents, (no longer an asshole) lawyer Jeff and her mom Sandi. Henry was the last to arrive, wearing an air of smugness that only Chelsea knew would be short-lived.

They got stupid on veal marsala and salad and pasta and wine. Chelsea looked down the long dining room table at faces belonging to people who had become her family...the very best of the people who had loved her Charlie for a dozen different reasons...who had welcomed her into the Charlie Stinson Fan Club...taken her heart off the street and set in firmly in a place where she could grow and be safe and be loved. Keesha said *Happy Birthday* in four-year old and gave her a slinky little brown Beanie-Baby ferret. Chelsea wasn't the only one who cried.

After all the ice cream and birthday cake, coffee and after-dinner sweets, liquid and otherwise, she got serious.

"I guess you guys are supposed t'give me gifts on my birthday. Thing is, you've been giving me gifts for over four years now...two years before that when you gave me Charlie without even knowing it...a chance for me to be...I don't know...normal..."

She laughed. Looked at all of them laughing back because normal didn't really apply where Charlie was concerned. In some way she realised he had managed to add something special to all of their lives....his own brand of magic...

"Anyway...I'm gonna spring surprises on all of you instead...starting with what I told Dory before you guys got here, because nobody else knows about that yet...that I wanna move t'the country after I graduate...be neighbours with her and Henry...

"So that means him and Jeff have t'decide what's best for this place...where Charlie took me in and saved me from heaven knows what. We should figure out whether to hang on to it for whatever, or sell it...

"...Because what nobody knows but me is that last month I sold three paintings for a lot of money...way more than they were worth...and one of the people who bought a painting is a professor at a university in Austria who wants me to visit his house in Vienna this summer and paint a mural in his living room...or whatever they call them there....and also teach a short summer seminar about my *Reaching for Daylight* series...

"Which means maybe I can make a living doing what I love t'do...and I don't really need all the money that Charlie gave me..."

Keesha was bored. Came to sit in her lap and put her finger in what was left of Chelsea's chocolate ice cream.

"So now everybody gets the surprise where I ask Jeff and Henry to find a way to give it all away."

She wiped chocolate off Keesha's nose so she wouldn't have to look at them having heart attacks.

"I'd like for them to find someplace upstate...a big house...with some land around it and room for more stuff t'be built...and to turn everything into somewhere that girls like me can be safe...where they can get away...have people who care looking after them... learn stuff...away from the cities...so they never have t'beg anyone for what they should have at least had a chance t'get on their own...

"The best part is that if you all think that's a good idea...then I'd love for Dory to have that place t'do for others what she did for me...and Carrie t'be there with her... Nkechi t'keep us all healthy and James to keep the education thing going...Corinna and me can do all the cooking and Jeremiah can teach everyone how open doors *all by themselves*..."

Jeff said, "That's a tall order...and a lot of money, Chelsea. It can be done, but are you sure?"

She nodded. "Totally," she said. "I think if we do this Charlie will be really proud of all of us...and that makes me dead sure...

"And also....because it's gonna be such a big freakin' job all of us should go to Europe this summer for a vacation before we start."

6.

It was all too perfect. The cool breeze of new summer running through the elm that stood over Charlie's little headstone; the butterfly that winked gold and black on the daisies she'd laid across it. Not that it would have mattered, but she checked to see if there was anybody nearby before she laid a blanket down over top of him and curled up on it... dozed for a while running through the last six years of her life.

"So we're all goin' tomorrow, Charlie," she said. "Big adventures. Stuff t'do. I wish you were here..."

Anybody watching would have seen a stunningly beautiful young blonde woman who had survived a slice of hell crying...and then smiling...and champing at the bit to get on with things. She kissed the polished granite once...

"Thanks Charlie," she said. "Thank you so much. You really are gonna be a tough fuckin' act t'follow."

7.

The professor who had purchased *Reaching for a Miracle* for his wife...commissioned the mural...would sit with her...spend an hour or two a day talking with her as she worked after her morning class...chalking outlines... examining the possibilities of light and shadow and what she might do with the image of his dream. Sometimes his wife would play the piano...Beethoven sonatas...

One afternoon one week into the gig in Vienna she got a chance to breathe...could feel the city waiting for her out beyond the bounds of her ridiculously luxurious accommodations...

She went walking...found a small cafe high up overlooking the river...sat on a terrace watching barges go by...gulls scavenging along the banks...hints of music and traffic and languages she didn't understand...and a sort-of-maybe uncomfortable feeling that had become a companion almost from the day she arrived.

She looked around, trying to find whatever it was that was that was monkey-wrenching her peace of mind...scoured her surroundings three times before she figured it out....stood up quickly... defensively...forced herself to relax...move closer because she was scared...

"You're in my seminar," she said quietly. "You're the guy from England..."

"I am."

"What're you starin' at...?"

She looked down into a pair of eyes she almost recognised. An instant of dismay. A flicker of something that approximated fear...and then something else...

"Same as in class. You. I'm staring at you."

"Well I'm the fucking poster child for that shit so maybe you can tell me why or just quit starin'...it's rude..."

"Some of the reasons are pretty obvious...."

She curled her lip in disgust and started to walk away.

"...And then there's this other thing I can't describe."

She stopped...came back to the table and pulled the chair opposite out from under...sat down...draped one leg over the other...folded her hands in her lap...waited...

"When I was a growing up my mother was big on Fifties and Sixties American pop music. She loved this one song and thought the guy who sang the song was cute. My father thought it was tripe and the guy was a blithering idiot, but he liked my mother well enough that he learned all the words to the song and whenever he'd been a jerk—which was quite often if you listen to my mother tell the stories—or was hoping to get lucky... he'd sing this song to her...and that's the best I can do to describe that other thing."

"The story?"

"The song."

"Which was...?"

"*Poetry in Motion*."

Chelsea smiled.

"You're pretty fuckin' smooth."

"Well it's true."

"Then tell me what's a best-case scenario for you tonight. Where're you goin'?"

"I was hoping I could go home with you, or you would go home with me."

"Just like that?"

"Pretty much."

"And what d'you figure's gonna happen after that?"

"I have no idea. I'm good with anything."

Chelsea looked at the eyes again…and the face…

"You remind of somebody I once knew," she said. "You remind me of somebody I loved…somebody I still love…who loved me back and never ever asked for anything in return…except maybe poetry."

"I'm getting a little bit lost here…"

"That's okay. What I'm saying is whatever happens you have an awful lot to live up to…just to walk through my door. I'm never gonna settle for less, and if we do this more then once I'm just warning you…the minute you stop lookin' at me the way you are now I'll throw your ass out in the street."

The eyes and the face grew thoughtful, but only for moment.

"I'm good with that too."

"What about when I'm hundred years old and all wrinkly?"

"You'll probably have the most beautiful wrinkles on the planet."

Chelsea stared at him staring at her.

"Y'know that guy I said you remind me of? He saved my life…or maybe he just gave it back to me so I could do something with it...but he wrote me a story too. He gave me a happy ending..."

She reached across the table and took his hand... turned it over and liked the way he let her do it...patient...trusting...edging towards something without knowing what it might be. She got the feeling that Charlie was somewhere close by waiting to kiss her goodnight.

The English guy asked if he was in her story and she smiled, told him there was really only one way to find out.

THE YOUNG GIRL & THE SEA

She was neither plain nor lovely, only exquisite in the way she moved through a world that seemed to exist as an adornment to her soul. When she was born in the small place without a name on the coast of New Brunswick, her parents named her Athena Rose, because they themselves were newly come to Canada from a placed called Kasos, and roses were the first flowers to flourish in the garden her mother had planted in that first summer in their new home beside the Bay of Fundy.

As she grew older she seemed as pleased to be alone with herself as with any of her playmates. Like them, she bopped to Miley and Beyonce, but loved Haley Reinhart for her smile, and the deep throaty warbles that made her heart sing. She worshiped the memory of Stan Rogers, whom she discovered at the age of twelve on one of her infrequent visits to St John with her parents, and was astonished at how the traditional Persian music of Azam Ali bore resemblance to the sounds she heard when her father would take his bouzouki out of the hall closet, and she could watch her mother fall in love all over again.

When she was small she scared the daylights out of them...wandering off before she could even properly walk...but it was only a few weeks before they realised she was drawn to the ocean...the ebb and flow of the tides...and when they found her with her little diapered rump in the sand, it was always just close enough to the water that the white foam would tickle her toes without ever threatening to carry her away.

"Athena," her mother would say. "You cannot do this. You are making us crazy."

Athena, being inarticulate at the time, said nothing, but obviously understood enough to moderate her meandering just that little bit to spare her parents the trauma of maybe finding her soggy dead, permanently asleep, and/or just food for the fishes.

As she grew it became easier. And more difficult.

Athena was ethereal. More often than not unshakably at peace with the world around her. For that reason other children were drawn to her. When she grew older it was the boys who came calling with stupid empty helpless longing in their eyes. Her mother and father, who were mere mortals, nevertheless began to understand something out of the ordinary had occurred; that what their love had created was a child who more than likely belonged in the canon of their cultural mythology...a creature only half of this world and half of some other place where all the questions ever asked were answered, all the secrets ever hidden were revealed, and all the pain and misery of the mortal plane were dissolved in the placid peaceful gaze of a mysterious other-worldly thing in the guise of a young girl.

Athena Rose.

1.

She was sitting by the window in her history class, staring out past the headland where the sky seemed to merge with the horizon a million miles out to sea, an indiscriminate haze washed in early morning sunlight that shimmered in the first warm days of summer. The hum of what went on in the interests of higher education surrounded her, but she sat in her own sleepy silence, pondering upon the mystery of what might or might not be out past that horizon.

Behind her sat a boy named Andrew, who had followed her around like all the other boys, and won a large portion of her heart by actually coming up to her one day in the hall...between classes...and even though it was painfully obvious he was scared to death, when he told her she was the most beautiful girl in the world—that he loved her and would love her forever—she was humbled by the fact that anyone could feel that way about her, and thought he must be the most courageous of all boys to have risked her derision or contempt with such an admission.

"Well it's true," he'd said, and she could see he was forcing himself to look into her eyes, not look away, in spite of his terror and the possibility of being summarily dismissed... rejected...humiliated by so much honesty.

She had taken one of his hands and pressed it to her cheek, and she'd cried a little bit too, because even then she knew how little it was that she lived in the world, and she felt that his declaration somehow was magical and sad and could never be appreciated enough...

"Athena..." he said, whispering...reaching to touch her shoulder. She came back to the classroom in time to hear their teacher repeat his question to her.

"That was the end of the Hundred Years' War," she said. "After Castillon, the only English on French soil were in Calais, until later that year...1453...when Charles VII drove them out of Aquitaine and Normandy for good."

She heard Andrew's sigh of relief as he leaned back in his chair, gazed earnestly at their teacher, who, in spite of all prior experience, still half-expected her to be caught totally unawares by his questions even as he secretly hoped it would never happen. The sorcery that was Athena Rose knew no bounds; if there were spells extant to counteract it, they were yet to be discovered by anyone who knew her.

After school she was embarrassed, thanked Andrew for waking her up from daydreams. He just shrugged, reached out and almost touched her face before he remembered. She reached out for him instead...hugged him...put her head on his shoulder...felt his heart pounding through his ribs against her chest. For a moment she believed she could stay that way forever; that something in her soul had broken wide to receive the quiet intensity of his feelings for her and she could, after all, surrender herself to them without qualm or regret... and then the sadness and the longing came back... whatever it was struggling inside her taking hold once again...

"Andy let's go swimming," she said, wanting to run away, and wanting to keep him close by all at the same time.

"It's too late today," he said, "and the water's gonna be really cold."

"Let's go swimming anyway," she said brightly. "We can bike home fast to get our bathing suits...or we could just go..."

She wasn't teasing him, even when she saw his eyes go wide with the second thought of what she'd said.

"You're my best friend," she laughed, as if that was a perfectly reasonable explanation.

He blushed, and she laughed again, but again took his hands in her own and kissed them, never letting her eyes stray from his.

"You really *are* my best friend, y'know," she said, and this time Andrew laughed with a vast sense of relief, and a flush of warmth running through him that had nothing to do with embarrassment.

Half an hour later they were slogging through the sand, hand in hand, sneakers and sandals left beside their bicycles where the tree-line came down to the shore. Halfway to the water he stopped, turned to face her.

"Are we really goin' in?" he asked, trying not to be overly unenthusiastic, even though he knew that he'd never be able to say no to her...about anything...ever again...

Athena looked over his shoulder, where the half-tides of the afternoon whispered and waited, gathering their strength for the evening. She shook her head, drew him down onto the sand. They sat shoulder to shoulder.

"It's not the same as in the morning," she said wistfully.

"Like how not?" he asked.

She shrugged, shivered once, snuggled up closer to him. He put one arm around her.

"I dunno. In the afternoon it's like all the magic that started the day is getting used up so night-time can come along. It's different..."

As was the case with so much of what she said, Andrew was never quite sure he was anywhere near understanding her, but such was the luxury and magnitude of his devotion, that even her most casual pronouncements to him carried the weight of divine prophecy and cosmic law.

He took advantage of her more-often-than-not cryptic words by pretending to give them thought, ponder over them, when in fact most of him was brainlessly joyously jumping up and down (but in a metaphorical sense) with the simple pleasure of having a goodly portion of his new best friend all willowy and warm up against him.

"What's out there, Andy?" she whispered.

"A lot of water," he said, and she giggled against his chest.

"What else?"

"Fish."

"You're not being very helpful."

Chastened, he ran down every last thing he could think of that might swim, float or lurk in the depths of the deep blue sea. He finished with:

"Oil slicks and plastic garbage too, but I don't think that's what you were askin' about."

She was still giggling. After a while she became quiet.

"What about magic stuff?" she said. "Silkies..."

Being a child of the Modern Age, Andrew had no idea what silkies might be.

"Shame on you, Scottish boy," she said. "Silkies. The seal people that live in the sea. Sometimes they're called selchies. And sometimes, for Love, they come to live on the land, shed their seal-skins so they can be human...but if they lose their skins they can never go back to live in the ocean again, so they hide them carefully."

"Where's yours then, Thena?" he asked. "So I can keep it safe for you."

She put her arms around his waist and said nothing. When the sun had disappeared behind the trees at their back they bicycled home; he waited until she waved at him from her door, stood in the falling-down dark for another ten minutes before he felt he had acceptably fulfilled his role as her protector.

2.

"...Andrew is very attentive," said her mother. "Your father is concerned."

A week had gone by and he'd called their house twice, asking for her. Both times her mother had answered the telephone, listened intently and even engaged in conversation while Athena stood by with her mouth open and her eyes growing bigger and bigger with each passing moment.

"He is very polite. Also he loves you very much."

"He said so, Mom, but I'm not old enough. Am I?"

"You are more than old enough, Athena, because I see that you love him too."

She was sitting at the kitchen table eating corn flakes with milk and brown sugar and bright yellow raisins. Her mother was rinsing monster big eggplants and zucchini, preparatory to turning them into *moussaka* for dinner, with four kinds of grated cheese on top. When she was finished rinsing she turned away from the sink and looked at Athena with a monster big cleaver in one hand. Athena paused with a spoonful of corn flakes halfway to her mouth. She seemed puzzled.

"I guess I do like him...a lot," she said quietly, as if surprised.

"And...?" Mom asked pointedly. The cleaver in her hand served to punctuate the question in a manner that was unmistakable.

"I'm not even fifteen years old yet," Athena said. "I'm not sure."

"There are some things you should be sure about, Athena...and careful also..."

Athena nodded, her eyes going slow and faraway, softening as though they had lit upon the answer to one of her mysteries.

"I don't think that's what's up with me and Andy," she said.

For the time being that seemed to be something along the lines of an answer that was acceptable to both of them. Athena finished her breakfast and went outside, still pondering over the question. Sex with Andy. Wow. She remembered how good it felt sitting in the sand with his arm around her, but decided without truly knowing how or why, that very soon her faith in what they shared would prove itself to be better than sex, even if she didn't really know if sex would be good.

She walked through their village, out into the blaze of morning, past the empty docks waiting for the return of the fishing boats that had been gone since before dawn, past the sheds and warehouses and the little tavern on the edge of their civilisation. She knew he would already be wherever she was going, and when she got there, he was.

She said, "Hi. I think my mom asked me if I was gonna have sex with you."

Andrew's eyes bugged out and he swallowed two or three times before he sank down onto the sand and did his best not to throw up.

"What'd you say?" was all he could manage.

She sat down beside him and put her head on his shoulder.

"I told her I didn't think it was such a good idea for us."

Andrew gave that some thought, not daring to look down at her.

"Thena," he said, "am I really your best friend? I mean *really*...where we can say anything and know it's just gonna be for the two of us?"

She nodded where she was, whispered Y*es you are...for always*...and he took a while to let that unnecessary assurance sink in...came to a decision.

"I'm pretty sure I'm gay, Thena," he said.

"Me too," she said slowly.

"You're gay too?"

"No, silly. I mean I'm *also* pretty sure you're gay...I think..."

He said, "Oh"...and then "Is that all right?"

She wriggled herself around to where she could straddle his hips and look down at him, into the beautiful childlike trust in his eyes, and the shared sense of exile from everything around them that might be construed as normal. She said:

"It means we can do anything we want, Andy, and be whoever we want or need to be for each other, with nothing to get in the way."

"I wasn't lying...about being in love with you forever."

"I know."

She smiled into his worried face and couldn't remember ever being so happy...twisted around a little bit so both of them could look out into the distance, where the sun climbing up into the sky slowly dissolved the shimmer and softness of the mist that had lain like a lover's hand on the ocean.

"It's different in the morning," she said, with the gentle arrogance of dead certainty. "It's magical...so we can be like this, you and me."

For a moment they were quiet, then she said, "Close your eyes, Andy. Pretend I'm a boy..."

She kissed him for a long time, aching with the knowledge of his love. When it got too breathless, Andy wept into the front of her t-shirt.

3.

"...My dad wants me to help him on the boat," she said, reaching for his hand.

They sat together on a rock totally surrounded by the roar and thunder of the tide rolling into the bay, moonlight pouring down in luminous rivers across the water, striking silver sparks on the whitecaps.

"I qualified for the advanced marine biology summer program at UNB in St John. I can come home on the weekends."

She pretended to be heartbroken.

"You're gonna find some wonderful cute guy and forget about me."

He said: "I hope so. The first part, anyway."

"You better let me meet him before you do anything silly."

"Silly like what, Thena?"

She laughed. "I dunno. Before you get so happy you forget about me."

"I love you, Thena. I'm never gonna stop...I'm never gonna forget you."

"Date night every Friday Saturday you and me right here?"

"Can I bring him with, if...?"

Athena smiled in the moonlight.

4.

It was lonely during the week, but it was wonderful too, being with her father in the dark every morning, already on the water as the new-rising sun turned the world into gold and quicksilver. She never noticed the diesel fumes or the rumble of the twin engines beneath her feet; her father took them into the unknown, one strong brown hand on the wheel of his fishing trawler, his other arm over her shoulders. If not for Andy being away in St John, she couldn't imagine anything more that would have added to the adventure, the sense of expectation and discovery.

"Tell me about your friend," said Pyrrhos Psaras, when they were five miles out, the anchor down, and the nets in their wake settling into the slow rise and fall of the ocean's breath. He was broad and stocky, olive-skinned by birth, gone dusky with days in the sun. His dark eyes, lit upon his only child, the one he knew to be miraculous, were concerned but not overly so, as he had spoken with her mother.

"Tell me about mermaids," she said, smiling.

He smiled back. There was a hint of sunrise on the horizon that somehow made it dazzlingly white in the half light. He, like anyone else who knew his daughter, also knew that one must wait upon the pleasure of deity come into the world disguised as children.

"I have never seen one, Athena," he said.

"But they live here," she insisted, sweeping one hand before them, out over the water. "Surely, Papa..."

"Not even once, my love," he said softly, "but perhaps I have not been so vigilant as I could have been. Sometimes it is an expectation of what should be that can make it real?"

She pressed up against him, listened to his heart beating through the linen of his shirt.

"Now you're teasing me, Papa," she pouted.

"I would never," he said, ducking down to kiss the top of her head. "It is my experience that when we least expect the existence or the occurrence of anything, it can only become part of the world if we become aware of its reality.

From today I promise I will look for your mermaids...and this summer we will look together."

She nodded against his chest.

"Andy is my brother," she said. "He holds my heart and keeps it safe for me until I'm ready to give it away, knowing he will always be have his place there too, with you and Mama."

And like everyone else who encountered the creature that walked in the guise of his daughter, Pyrrhos Psaras, if not able to thoroughly understand her words, recognised the truth in them.

They watched the sunrise in silence, and the gentle gathering storm of glistening mist that fuelled her longing for the magic hidden there.

5.

At a moment she could not place in the quiet stream of that summer, about the time she turned fifteen, Athena decided the mystery was too much to be ignored. Rationally and logically she knew that no matter how far she and her father crept out into the early morning ocean, with a sunrise would come the shimmering curtain of light before them, and what lay beyond it—other than the obvious—would never reveal itself to her without some effort. She remembered an old kayak in the boathouse where her father berthed their fishing boat; in between their time snorkelling together in the tide-pools and shallows round the village, she and Andy spent weekends fixing it up...

6.

"...Papa, why did you and Mama come here?" she asked...late one morning...when all the mists and magic had gone for the day. "What's it like in Greece? Why did you leave?"

Pyrrhos seemed startled by her questions, and was quiet for a long time, though he made certain that she knew he was looking for answers to them, not just ignoring her when his gaze became thoughtful and faraway. The fact of it all was that neither he nor Athena's mother had ever really given it any thought at all. He said:

"Someday we will go back and you will see," he said with a smile, "but why did we leave...?" He shook his head a bit and the gaze he levelled at his daughter was one of amazement, that she somehow had managed to burrow into the heart of something they had never even considered. Her big dark eyes asked him again.

"I don't know, my love," he said. "Now I must ask your mother to see if she knows...but one day it seemed that it was the most right and proper thing for us to do, so we packed what bits and pieces of our lives that were important...and we booked passage on a ship...and then we were here."

This seemed to make perfect sense to her. The day had become overcast, but her smile was a sunshine of perfect understanding.

"...Is it all like this, Papa?" she asked.

He turned away from the winch on the starboard nets and came to sit beside his daughter in the stern, watching the rise and fall of the ocean, and the world breathing far below.

"Athena," he said, "when your mother and I came to this place, we were not suffering. We were not starving or in flight or in fear for our lives, but the ship that carried us here from Greece also was the place where you were conceived...on a day when so suddenly the ocean was like a small lake that mirrored the clouds and the blue sky and made a magic so strong that for us we could not resist it...

"That night we stood like those two in that old movie and watched the moon spill itself down over the water...so different from the home we had left in Kasos...and in one moment both of us knew our journey would end with all the things we hoped for in our dreams, and that night in November our celebration made you...who came along nine months and two weeks later ...

"But the ocean between here and Kasos...it is as you see it now, Athena, endlessly deep and dark, full of kindness and cruelty, life and death. It is a mystery."

She said "But that's the whole world, Papa," and let herself be rocked by the boat and the waves and the strong arms of her father.

"Yes."

"How will I find the answers that are right for me?" she whispered.

His arms tightened around her, both of them lost in something unspoken but understood nevertheless.

"You will know them, Athena. They are the ones that have no doubts hiding behind them. And I think once you have found them you will see how they were always there in front of you, just waiting for you to look up and see them..."

7.

UNTIL THE END OF THE WORLD

July and August grew warm and bright on the bay. Athena and Andrew patched up the ancient kayak and spoke of everything except the day when it would be sea-worthy again, when they both knew she would venture into the mystery; that when it happened it would be only Athena who would go, and he, for no other reason than the will of a girl whom he loved, could only wait for her...and pray that what was out there would not be so unkind as to take her away from him forever.

8.

"...I should go with you," he said. "We could both fit."

"I have to go by myself, Andy," she said. "It's my problem. Maybe I *am* a silkie! Besides, when I get to where I'm going I think you're gonna be there..."

"I don't see how that's possible."

"I can't see what's out there waiting for me, but I know *something* is there. Everything. All the possibilities in the universe. And you could be there too. You could."

"How will I know? My eyes don't see the things the way yours do."

She knew that was true; that Andrew's devotion to her was blind; that he would do anything she asked of him, without question, and for that very reason she knew he might have to pay some dreadful price for not understanding the *something* even if she didn't understand it fully herself. *She* had faith in who she was, but all he had was his faith in her.

The last of the outgoing tide licked at their bare feet, drawing the sand out from under them as it foamed up around their ankles. Farther along up the beach sea gulls squabbled over the bones of something washed up on the sand; the light wind off the ocean was cool and crisp with salt and promise. Andrew's eyes glistened and she put her head on his shoulder so she wouldn't see him cry.

"I'm so sorry, Andy," she whispered. "I'm so sorry I wish I was different from being so different. I'm gonna look for you...and tomorrow will always be the day when I see you again."

She kissed his cheek and pushed him gently away.

Wherever it was she was going, whatever it was she was hoping to find, she prayed it would be the answer to the question of *Who is Athena Rose?* and the mystery of herself would fall away and no longer require revelation. All that was required now was a first cautious step into the Otherwhen, and thereafter she trusted that her feet would find the path of their own accord.

She watched him trudge back across the sand, could see him struggling not to look back at her over his shoulder...was grateful to him even as she again marvelled at his courage, and the instinct that told him if he were to look back at her then she *would* stay... and that he would become the architect of her unhappiness for the rest of their lives.

When he had disappeared up among the rocks, when she no longer could hear him climbing back up to the headland, she turned and dragged the kayak down into the surf, zipped up her wetsuit, strapped herself in and laced herself into the collar. She looked out into the sunrise, where the sky seemed to merge with the horizon a million miles out to sea, where an indiscriminate haze shimmered in the last warm day of summer.

She began to paddle out into the ocean...out where she hoped her answers were waiting...

9.

Andrew watched her until the sunrise got lost in the haze; then the shimmer swallowed her and she was gone. For a moment he wanted to fall down on his knees and weep for the loss of her, until he remembered...and then he was certain she would be back... because she was who she was...just because...Athena Rose...

He went home and told his parents they would be camping on their rock that night...the all-night affair of their summer where the tide made them prisoners of the torrent that filled the bay.

He packed up water and all sorts of useless garbage energy food...a sleeping bag...a million-kilowatt light thing...

10.

Hours and hours later she rested, her paddle cross-wise on the oiled leather collar of the kayak, half-asleep in the haze crowding round her, gently rising and falling on the barely discernible swells. The warmth of the sun seemed magnified through the mist, lulling her into a peaceful communion with the unseen everything around her. She had a funny feeling, that grew and grew until it was not so much *funny* as it was overwhelmingly humbling, something so strange and wonderful that she could not describe it in words or even begin to think of it in terms that were of relevance to her smallness in the universe.

She thought *Wow!* to herself...smiled to think back to the other *Wow!* that had been about having sex with Andy. And then somehow she found herself on the *other side* of where she had been...where everything *looked* exactly as it had been a moment ago, but now seemed to be entirely different. She talked to Andy because he was the keeper of all her secrets...

"I know you're here," she said. "I know because you would never let me go so far away from you that I couldn't share..."

The sun was invisible, hidden in the shimmer of a noontide that should have been filled with blinding light and the endless expanse of the north Atlantic sweeping to every horizon; yet Athena sensed she somehow had travelled to somewhere well beyond the mundane and the ordinary, and in that moment the haze began to melt away.

It was nothing like being out on the fishing boat with her father. This time the growing immensity of the ocean took her breath away. In every direction no matter which way she turned the distance became greater and greater. A vast silence seemed to envelop her, as if the ocean itself, having spoken to her for the entirety of her lifetime, now declined to say anything at all, rather than distract her from its majesty and power.

"I'm so small," she whispered. The thought was oddly comforting, made her smile, made her feel like a weight of some impenetrable responsibility had been lifted away from her shoulders. "Not even special except for the people who love me...just me...this once alone in the middle of my world..."

UNTIL THE END OF THE WORLD

She couldn't say how long she sat as if drugged, gently rising and falling on gentle swells as the day grew warm and then blazingly hot she let her hands fall to either side of her craft, into a rippling mirror of a sky gone sorcerous with impossible blue, and clouds that swirled and danced above and below, with the world in between.

She thought out loud *This is where I began!* and unzipped her wetsuit, slipped out of her panties and into goggles and flippers, with a hundred feet of yellow nylon boat cord attached to one ankle and the prow of her kayak.

Below the surface the day seemed to reach down forever in one long unending curtain of light, showing darkness only when the ocean grew too deep, but everything within her gaze now bathed in the warmth, schools of cod and young salmon darting round her she felt she could live there forever, her lungs filled with air that would last lifetimes and more. She bumped noses with a cranky-looking bluefish and had to rush to the surface so she could laugh out loud...

Found herself surrounded by sea-birds, bobbing like little feathered bathtub toys on the water—huffy-looking gannets, dusky-headed guillemots, kittiwakes and murres, Iceland gulls arrowing and wheeling overhead...a small gang of puffins, smiling with big white faces and clunky colourful bills as they came closer to look at her...unafraid... curious...

This is where I began! she thought again, feeling the world now swirling and dancing up around her, a sarabande of release, an elegant *pas de deux*...all around her, a mantle over her shoulders, a lover's caress between her thighs, a kiss and a smile, welcoming her back from the world into which she had been born.

She started to cry. Helplessly. Paddled her way through the silly smiling puffins and back to her kayak...sobbing with joy...

11.

Andrew sat on their rock with his knees up under his chin, feeling the sun slipping away behind him. When nightfall came he sipped some water from a canteen and ate a few handfuls of trail mix, draped a woollen blanket around his shoulders. Beneath him he could feel the stone beginning to vibrate as the tide marshalled its voice and began to roar back into the bay. With moonrise he saw thousands of his Athenas coming back to him... until he fell asleep swearing he would never sleep until she was holding on to him and they were safe again... together...

12.

Athena had fallen asleep hours before, exhausted, drained by the sun and sea and the certainty of her nebulously newfound understanding of her place in the world. She sensed that she had returned from the Otherwhen, suddenly; then became aware of the ocean beneath her and the soundless but unmistakeable surge of it moving back in the direction from whence she had come.

Athena had forgotten about the tide, or simply not gone far enough to escape its own need to return to the nightlong shelter of the bay. The kayak seemed to rise of its own accord as she tried to slip back into her wetsuit, wincing with sunburn in tender places gone neglected through sleep. Her paddle on its tether trailed along in

UNTIL THE END OF THE WORLD

her wake and suddenly she was alone again...riding on something altogether different from what it had been that morning...through the magic of the day...

The soundless thing roared beneath her, spun her around and turned her over in the water, now lit only by the first shards of moonrise at her back. She struggled underwater, unsure of whether or not she should cling to the kayak at all now, or trust to weather the tide on her own. She felt the kayak slipping away from her...into the dark... struggled to regain the surface even as she could feel the inexorable pull downward...the dark and cruel face of her mysterious destiny.

In the last light from above she saw the shadows racing, coming for her from below...

13.

Andrew awoke in first dawnlight...desolate with guilt for having slept...desolate with the emptiness of Athena not being there. He chewed on granola bars that tasted like dust; drank more water from his canteen and felt sick with loss.

He remembered the bay thundering around him like so many other nights before when she had been there with him, but now it was like dying of thirst in the desert with his only companion the horrifying thought that he had lost his best friend; that he would have to find someone else to hold his secret...until he could find the courage to hold it in his own hands before offering it up to strangers.

He gathered up the bits and pieces of his fortress of devotion, climbed down the landward face of their castle, head down, weeping as he slogged his way back through the sand he heard a voice calling his name...turned...saw her running long-legged in sunlight, her hair streaming along in her wake...

She arrived breathless. Smiling.

"Thena you don't have any clothes on," he said, and he couldn't stop staring at her.

"You're my best friend," she grinned, as if that explained everything.

"You're way prettier than Bo Derek...or that Botticelli painting," he said.

She gratefully let him wrap her up in his blanket, for no reason she could put into words feeling at peace for the first time since her little girl thoughts had moved her apart from the world. She told him what had happened.

"I didn't see any silkies, but then a bunch of dolphins came to save me," she said.

"Were you afraid?"

"Nope."

"Not even a little?"

"Just a little bit," she admitted...then...

"But now I'm home and here you are," she said quietly, hugging him closer, stunned with the implication of the words. "It was just like my father said...all I had to do was look up and see how it was for real..."

He said, "I love you, Thena."

She said, "I love you too, Andy...forever...we're gonna make magic...you and me..."

"Thena, did dolphins really save you?"

She nodded and wriggled around to where he could put his arm around her shoulders.

UNTIL THE END OF THE WORLD

Andy said, "Wow..."

DREAMING OF DAMASCUS

1.

She stood bundled up and shapeless in a down-filled nylon winter coat that went past her knees, tucked a heavy tangle of coarse black hair back under her collar. The Atlantic surged and roared in front of her, grey and endless through the haze of wind-whipped falling snow, tendrils of foam crawling across the sand to swirl around the toes of her boots.

Three thousand miles away was a narrow channel streaming past a massive rock, and then the deep blue Mediterranean, ancient and deceptively benevolent. East of Cyprus, where it rose up from edge of the Aegean in the early morning mist, was the place where she had been born, though the only images in her mind were of violence and blood and sorrow, the faces of two strangers, tearful with the imminence of loss...terrified...

The memories were almost twenty-two years old, so far removed from Long Island and the life she had lived that often, *before* she had found the Truth, there had been days when she looked at herself in the mirror and inwardly wondered who it was inhabiting her body.

"I'm certainly not this Francesca person," she had whispered then...to herself...to no one. "Once upon a time,

I was someone else. Now it seems I'm stuck with being this strange Francesca, for the most part the reasonably-attractive-but-unquestionably-adopted daughter of Salvatore di Cenza and his lovely wife, Gabriella...but before that—"

From far away she heard Raymond in the car, impatient now...the horn cutting through the shrill of wind every few minutes, each time distracting her from her thoughts so she had to "begin again"...conjure up the fading memories from scratch...

God but he's such an asshole sometimes, she thought, and the image of his face rose up before her. One more distraction, and the small twinge of annoyance and contempt...and the shaking of her head when she realised she had managed to put up with him for almost a year. She turned and slogged her way back across the sand to the parking lot, kicking up surface splinters of ice and bits of garbage left over from the summer. She slipped back into the passenger seat of his Mazda and was assaulted by the heater going full blast. The heat brought back more shards of memory, but these were even more terrifying than the ones rattling around in her head because she had no reference points to deal with them, no assurance that the disjointed images and nightmares even belonged to her.

"Why is it that whenever you have t'do something you don't necessarily understand you always get impatient and pissy?"

He looked at her as if he hadn't the faintest idea of what she was talking about, and another realisation formed in her mind, one that didn't bode at all well for the future of their relationship.

"I just don't get why you do this," he said irritably. "This is like the millionth time you've dragged me out here..."

"You didn't mind it so much during the summer, when you thought there was chance I wanted to fuck you in behind the dunes."

"That's not true—"

"Of course it is," she said quietly. She didn't care enough to tell him he was a lousy lay; that he was so wrought up in recreating scenarios from his online porn life that she all too often felt like a paper bag over her head would have been inappropriate only when it came to oral sex.

"What d'you do out there?"

For a moment she wondered if he actually *did* care.

"You wouldn't understand," she said, afraid that he might.

"You could try me," he said coldly. "I may not be the brightest bulb in the chandelier, but I can make sense of simple things when someone takes the time and effort to explain them to me."

She put her mittened hands to her face, trying to put some warm in her cheeks that was less brutal than the roil of the Mazda's heater.

"Ray, I'm just a fantasy for you," she said, trying not to sound insulted... disappointed that he was incapable of escaping from the prison of his own upbringing.

"What's that supposed t'mean?"

UNTIL THE END OF THE WORLD

"What it means is that it's like when you were a kid you mainlined some alternate universe out of the Arabian Nights, and every Technicolor Aladdin movie you could lay your hands on, and now—"

"*And now* what...?"

"And now..." she began, but stopped when she remembered the time when he wanted her to dress up like Barbara Eden from that old sitcom, but only so he could undress her and—

"Nothing," she said. "Can you please just drop me off..."

"I thought we were meeting up with Blake and Bonnie for supper."

"I'll call her."

"So we're not going."

She dropped her hands into her lap and looked at him, said nothing for almost a minute while she watched him get uncomfortable with actually having to look at her.

"No we're not."

She could hear him becoming angry now, the way his breathing started to hitch in his throat, his hand going tight on the hand brake between them.

"I'm sorry, Ray," she said softly, still looking him square in the eyes. "I don't want t'do this anymore."

"Do what, Fran?"

"Us," she said, deciding in that moment. "I don't want t'see you anymore. It's not working...*we* are not working..."

It took five minutes for her cell phone to cut through the crappy weather enough to call a cab. She watched him drive off with no sense of abandonment, or even anger that it was going to cost her a bundle for the cab-ride home. All she felt was relief that he was gone.

2.

"...We can still go out," Bonnie said. "Blake likes you, and even if he didn't he knows better than to get between me and my best friend. How'd Raymond take it."

Fran felt it was inappropriate to be overly emotional one way or the other.

"You know how he is. If he doesn't think things are the way he thinks they should be he gets cranky. This time he got pissy, kicked me out of the car and drove away."

"The prick!"

"No, Bonz. I don't blame him, not at all. For a little bit I even thought he might really give a shit, but it was true what I said to him—I'm just one of his fantasies—and I couldn't think of a better way to cut him loose. As far as that goes, maybe I just wanted some payback for being a cartoon in his life…"

"Are you okay?"

"I'm as okay as I need t'be for now…"

"Come t'dinner with us."

"I'm gonna walk Missy and then take a bath. Is it okay if I decide after?"

Bonnie snickered. "No. Fran, you have t'tell me now or it's all over."

"What's all over?"

"I have no idea. Call me when you're all over wrinkly?"

"…'Kay…gimme an hour or so?"

"You got it."

"You're the best, Bonzo."

"So I've been told, but you know Blake...he's so easy t'please..."

She dressed carefully—slinky in black and black nylons, a pair of matching sling-backs for when they got to the restaurant—but with some accommodation for the weather turning downright nasty as the afternoon had worn on. Missy hadn't liked the idea of getting all snowed on or having to plant her butt somewhere cold and wet, so she'd done her business in record time before high-tailing it back to the apartment. Half an hour in a steaming tub with her in tail-wagging attendance had evened out all the bumps from before. Now she was curled around her feet as she sat in front of her dressing table, doing things with kohl and henna and mascara, with a touch of something to give some definition to her cheekbones. Dutiful Blake climbed the two sets of stairs to collect her, made appreciative whistling noises as she slipped into her coat and he made a big deal out of helping her on with her boots.

"Don't tell Bonnie," he said. "You know how she gets."

"I know how she gets when you try t'pretend you're not lookin' at the competition," she said pointedly. "Really, Blake, you don't have t'be a saint around either one of us, just so you show respect, y'know...like not drooling when you see something tasty that's not on a plate."

He thought about that for few moments.

"The two of you are fuckin' scary, y'know that?" he said with a grin. "And that dress is really hot on you. The mostly total absence of colour in your *ensemble* makes you look like a Harry Clarke drawing, but more dangerous. And that red lipstick... woof...that's killer..."

"Woof? What's that?"

Blake shrugged. Fran sighed.

"You ever go *woof* to Bonnie?"

"All the time."

"And how does that work for you?"

"You know..."

"Well honestly I *don't* know, Blake, and I really don't *wanna* know...but the compliment is duly noted and appreciated, if not totally understood," she said, shaking her head. She wasn't familiar with Harry Clarke. "You realise you can't put anything over on her, right?"

"Oh yeah," he said in a hurry.

She wished she could find someone...anyone...with anything that even remotely resembled his utter shamelessness and unflinching honesty. She was still shaking her head and smiling for no particular reason when he scratched Missy between the ears and then bowed her out her own door...

"You are such a sleaze-bag," she said, with not even a hint of unkindness.

3.

Bonnie was concerned but trying not to intrude.

"You're pretty quiet tonight, Francesca," she observed airily. "I guess breaking up, even with assholes, is unsettling?"

Fran came back to Earth.

"What about assholes...?" she said.

"I was just making an observation," said Bonnie, pouring more house red for both of them. "That *breaking up* business, even when it's dumping an asshole like Raymond, can be unsettling. I of course know nothing of such things..."

Blake sauntered back from the men's room in time to be his usual self, expressing great interest when he heard the word *asshole* in the all-over-the-map possibilities of Fran's observation.

"It' not what you think, Blake," said Bonnie. "And don't be gettin' your hopes up. Franny dumped Raymond this afternoon."

He gave it a moment or two of thought.

"Oh...*that* kind of asshole," he said. "Well it's about time, Franny. Even I thought he was a dickhead, and that's saying a lot."

Fran looked at Bonnie and Bonnie looked at Fran, and they all laughed....and then Fran thought maybe it was time; that ten-plus years was long enough to keep a secret from anyone, even your best friend.

Being regulars, they were in a coveted corner booth three sizes too big for just the three of them, cosy and golden in the warm glow of the fire blazing away at a ten-foot remove. Fran had only pushed her dinner around some, unconsciously thinking that the *pollo al Marsala e pasta all'nuovo* probably would be good for breakfast the next morning, but consciously a bit more concerned with *how to begin*...

Blake emptied the rest of the carafe of wine into his glass and sat back with a self-satisfied air, revelling in the furtive/envious glances of other male patrons who thought he was going home to a girl-sandwich under the sheets. Bonnie said:

"Look at him, wouldja? It doesn't matter that he may not even get lucky at all tonight... just so it *looks* like he might get lucky..."

Fran said, "Don't be mean to him, Bonzo. He's a nice guy. I like him. I wish I had one like him. Blake, d'you have any brothers? Shit, I'd maybe even go for a sister if she was anything like you."

Blake had three of each.

"Sorry," he grinned, "but if you clear it with Bonnie maybe I can make room for you."

Doing her best to convey a totally unconvincing disgust, Bonnie said, "You are such a sleaze-bag."

Blake looked proud. She who was not Francesca Maria di Cenza decided there and now was as good a right time as any...

"...My real name is Nadra al-Hamoud," she said quietly.

Miraculously, Francesca found herself alone in the little row house in Brooklyn. She'd turned twelve years old a month before. Somehow that had meant something to her parents; that maybe she was old enough not *to need a sitter anymore. Through the big picture window in the living room, she waved and watched them drive off to deal with a family crisis—the tragic incarceration of an older cousin for trying to sell amphetamines to an undercover cop. She liked Gino. He'd always been good to her, once he realised she sympathised with his inexplicable* alienation *from the traditions and rituals of* la famiglia...*but he wasn't very bright and his taste in music sucked even though he was really cute. Francesca knelt down to scoop up the rescue puppy her parents had gotten her for her birthday.*

Missy. All maybe twenty pounds of her, though if you looked at her paws you knew she was gonna be one big mother of a doggie someday she said:

"C'mere girl...c'mon...gimme a hug..."

And it wasn't until Missy was delightedly squirming around in her arms like a total idiot that the thought came to her; that the house she lived in was almost bursting with something that needed to be brought into the light; that in her heart she knew she had only been waiting for the right moment...

⊙≫

"...When they were gone a couple of minutes I knew I wouldn't have a better chance; that they'd be gone for hours and poor fuckin' Gino was gonna catch a boatload of shit once they got him bailed out.

"Missy quieted down and after she ponked out on my bed I started looking...not even knowing what I was looking for, but knowing there was *something* and I needed t'find it; that the face of the person I looked at whenever I washed my face or brushed my teeth belonged to someone I'd never met."

⊙≫

She started in her parents' bedroom and less than an hour later found the heavy steel cashbox doing duty as a repository for the chronicle of their lives together. She sifted through dozens of old photographs of family members she'd never known and who meant nothing to her, nothing more than faded faces to finally match names she'd heard in snatches of conversation during more felicitous gatherings than the one Sal and Gabby were at now. In amongst the photographs were old receipts and warranty cards for appliances they no longer owned; in amongst those she found a marriage license and birth certificates and her adoption papers. Sal and Gabby had never mentioned adoption to her. She heard a small whine of unhappy in the hallway...

"Maybe they were waiting until I was older," she observed to her dog.

Missy appeared in the doorway, gave her a heart-rendingly soulful look of total adoration and complete incomprehension and put her chin down on her big puppy paws. Francesca looked at the folder for twenty minutes before she found the courage to actually look at the papers inside...

"...So that's when I found out I was really Nadra al-Hamoud," she said, "that my real parents were Badriyah and Rafiq al-Hamoud, and we lived in Syria until they were killed right before my second birthday..."

"They never told you?" asked Blake. "That seems pretty weird. I mean, they're nice people."

"They would have t'be," said Bonnie. "They like *you* in spite of your sordid past and rather pathetic present."

UNTIL THE END OF THE WORLD

Blake was being uncommonly serious. Fran...*Nadra*...found herself surprised that he was dealing with her revelation like someone who was making a rather large effort to understand its implications.

"I wondered about that for a long time," she said. "Even now, after another twelve years, I can come up with only one reasonable explanation, but it wasn't something that occurred t'me until a few years later..."

She sat on the floor at the foot of her adoptive *parents' bed and didn't realise she was crying until she had to wipe her eyes in order to read. Missy got worried and launched herself off the bed onto the floor beside her, licking at her hands and then her face. She couldn't decide if she was glad or sad to find out...finally...for sure...something she'd always known.*

Badriyah and Rafiq...her mother and father...had been executed within weeks of the date on her adoption papers. They had been nationally known in Syria... activists... protesting the slow takeover of the Assad family that would eventually place Bashar al-Assad in complete control of the country where she had been born.

"*He had them shot, and then left them for the crows...*" *she whispered...*

She was twelve-years old and a large portion of her childhood fled away in mindless grief. Missy made more unhappy noises.

"...After that I spent a lot of time at the library," she said. "Hours squinting over old microfilm and digital files, trying to find out what had happened."

Blake and Bonnie had lapsed into an uncomfortable silence, not really certain what they should say, or if they should say anything at all. Another carafe of house red was called for, delivered, glasses filled and emptied and filled again.

"In the adoption stuff, my parents... my real parents...insisted that no matter who it was took me in that I was never to be told the truth; that if Assad ever found out I existed, never mind that I was still alive and well somewhere else, he wouldn't rest until I got to join them as food for the crows...

"My real mom and dad were so adamantly...loudly... rightfully...opposed to anything the Assads did that even I was surprised when I found they had a place in Syria's history that had survived in spite of him."

"You've been carrying that for...what...ten years?" asked Bonnie.

"Twelve, and I'm sorry," she said. "I should've told you guys."

"Not necessarily," replied Blake "Your parents thought it would be dangerous for anyone to know who you really were. That would include your friends too, if this Assad guy was anywhere near being the bastard you make him out t'be."

"You haven't heard anything about him?" she asked, once again surprised by Blake, but looking at both of them, trying not to sound incredulous...or critical.

Bonnie said, "Of course we know the name..."

"But we're Americans, Franny," added Blake. "We don't need t'know shit about anything anywhere as long as we go t'work every day, tell anyone who'll listen that we're good Christians, shop at WalMart, and pretend that we believe we're living in a democracy."

Everyone laughed quietly, though it was a bit on the uncomfortable side.

Fran/Nadra said, "Blake I think I may have been judging you unfairly."

He grinned wickedly and shook his head.

"No, Franny, I'm a sleaze-bag all right, but it doesn't mean I'm a total half-wit. What are you gonna do now... about Sal and Gabby, I mean?"

She emptied her glass and demanded another refill.

"I've been tryin' t'figure that out for more than ten years and I still don't know," she said.

4.

Missy lurched across the living room as she came through her door. She was getting creaky, and in amongst all the other crap that of late seemed to be clogging up her life, Francesca sensed a looming crisis where her doggie was concerned. She still "smiled" at her in her own loving-but-distinctly-Alsatian way, yet she knew Missy was beginning to hurt, badly, and soon she would have to begin trying to deal with life without her. She struggled out of her boots and coat and knelt on the floor to wrap her arms around the dog, crying because she was mostly drunk and an intimation of Death suddenly had intruded upon their quiet world when she'd only just truly dealt with Death that was already old in spite of being anything but forgotten.

"You don't care who I am," she whispered into the heavy ruff on Missy's shoulders. "As long as whoever I am comes home at night and smells like the person you've always known, it's okay. Oh baby I wish it was that simple for me."

She struggled out of her dress...wrapped herself around her puppy and hung on until they fell asleep together on the living room rug...

5.

In the morning she called Gabriella.

"Hi Mom. *Come va?*"

"*Buongiorno, dulcezza, sto bene. E così bello sentire la tua voce. Va tutto bene?*"

"I'm okay...I was wondering if I could come by this morning?"

"*Cosa chiedi? Questa è ancora casa tua.* Why are you asking you don't have to ask to come home. Your father has gone out for the newspaper and *foccacia* at Benedetto's, but he should be back soon. Francesca, come have breakfast with us..."

She closed her eyes. Being two people in one body had finally become painful.

"'Kay...I'll get breakfast for Missy and come over...."

She kicked the skim of snow from her boots on the brickwork and pushed through the kitchen door on the driveway side of their semi-detached. Gabriella rushed to hug her, with a spate of *italiano* to let her know she had been missed...*Why don't you visit more often? It's so good to see you, my baby...*

For a moment in her foster-mother's arms she resisted the all-encompassing love and flow of affection. A moment later she realised that the sham of it all only made it that much more precious to her; that having had *the Truth* cast her adrift for half her lifetime only made her need for it and something warm apart from it that much more desperate. She began to cry. Gabriella stood back from her at arm's-length, her hands on her daughter's shoulders. She looked terrified. Her father left off reading his newspaper, jarred coffee onto the scarred surface of the old wooden table as he rose to join his wife. Francesca struggled to say what she felt.

"I'm not angry. I'm just scared. Suddenly after all this time it's frightening. Why didn't you ever tell me?"

Salvatore and Gabriella looked at each other. Nadra knew they knew exactly what she was talking about, but after all this time had stopped thinking they would ever have to explain. It only made her feel worse.

"Fr—" said Gabriella..

"Nadra," said Salvatore.

Now both of them were crying.

"Nadra," said Gabriella. "They said we should never tell you; that we could never tell anyone. How long have you known...?"

She could see agony in her eyes, and then Salvatore put his arms around his wife and suddenly there was this horrific feeling that she no longer belonged to them, though she knew he had never intended it to make her feel that way.

"The night Gino got arrested. I never felt right...not because of anything you ever did...or said...but I used t'look in the mirror and wonder how I was yours when I didn't even feel like I belonged to myself. That night while you were gone I went looking..."

6.

Missy was dead when she got home.

For the longest time she never even wondered why there were no yips of welcome or tail-wagging as she came through the door of her apartment. She had gotten lost going through all the tears and guilt and inexplicable heartbreak of breakfast...

"...Francesca...Nadra..."

Gabriella had been almost frenzied with terror; Salvatore had been out of his depth, but had known enough to hang on to her. They'd stood together in the middle of the kitchen and looked at her like she was some strange creature from another planet, yet desperately clinging to the memories of the baby they had brought home over twenty years before.

"..They said we couldn't tell you..."

"But now....more than ever...they died so long ago and he's still there..."

"That's why," said her father, *who was only her adoptive father...only...*

Eventually they went into the living room and sat on a sofa that had belonged to Gabriella's grandmother, modern-and-tacky Italiana...a big-screen LG on one wall and lace doilies on the end-tables...

She wandered into her bedroom and thought Missy was just sleeping, the way she always did in wintertime, when the afternoon sun shone so brightly you thought it had to be warm outside until you got there and froze your nose in minutes.

She stood at the foot of her bed, afraid to move, until she forced herself to reach out, bury her hands in the thick fur. She was still warm, like she had warded off Death just long enough for her to spare her human the trauma of witnessing her slowly slipping away.

Some horrible sound of grief came from someone else in the room. There had been no resolution with *Sal and Gabby,* only a sense of numb despair that something had come and gone without any of them being any the wiser. And now she was alone all over again...

Salvatore spent three hours breaking through the frozen earth in the small back yard of their house, helped her wrap Missy up in her favourite blanket with her favourite stuffies tucked alongside...and a pair of old cotton panties she once had gotten her head tangled up in when she was a puppy. There was a photograph somewhere...

She stood at the kitchen window, watching as he gently lowered her down into the dark.

Gabriella stood beside her, saying nothing, afraid to even touch her daughter. In the space of twenty-four hours, they had become not so much strangers as two people suddenly separated by an unimaginable distance.

"Come stay with us for a while..."

She shook her head. Her mother's voice became strained, hoarse with misery.

"Fran...Nadra...it doesn't matter to me or your father. You don't have to do or say anything if you don't want to. You don't have to sit down with us for meals, you don't even have to pretend whatever it is you think would be necessary right now in order to spare *our* feelings. Just don't go back to your apartment and be alone there..."

One day Gino came to visit her. Being in prison for over four years had not been kind to him. Deep down he was still pretty dopey, but that sweet stupid air of innocence was long gone and its absence had etched itself into the essence of who he was, put lines on his pretty face, and occasionally showed itself as a blank-eyed stare of terror when he thought no one was watching. For all the years after getting out he'd done grunt work at his father's produce shop, never seeming to care whenever he met up with everyone who had known him before.

"Sal and Gabby sent you."

He shook his head. "No. They told me, about Missy and...you know...but I came because you were always good t'me when the rest of the world was too fuckin' ready t'write me off. You always came t'see me...brought me stuff..."

UNTIL THE END OF THE WORLD

The guards at the prison always had some sort of snide smiling comment ready when Gino's *little girlfriend* came to visit him. Bonnie finally got round to tell her what *that* was all about. She went anyway.

Now she looked at his old/young face, that always looked tired and scared and out of place, and began to understand how your life could be totally fucked up by just about anything, if it showed up at the wrong time and the wrong place.

"Are you okay, Franny...Nadra...?"

She wanted to scream at him *Please just fucking stop making me into two people!* but couldn't bring herself to inflict that kind of cruelty on him. She sensed Gino had been walking a narrow path every bit as long as the one she had come to know; that his sense of who he was... who he might be...who he might have become...was a constant source of misery to him every bit as much as it had become for her.

She asked him, "How are *you*, Gino?" and inexplicably his big stupid beautiful dark eyes started to glisten with tears.

"I don't know, Franny," he said, looking away from her. "Sometimes...sometimes I just don't wanna have anything t'do with anybody...t'run the fuck away and never have anything t'do with anyone who ever knew me...and then I get scared and talk myself into staying where I am, because I got nowhere else t'go."

"And nobody will let you forget."

He nodded. "And nobody will let me forget."

"I need some o' that myself. Forgetting..."

Later, she took comfort in the thought that he wasn't really her cousin; that even if what had made them get naked together in her bed was a desperate but necessary comfort in the wasteland of their lives...that at least now they both truly were set apart from *la famiglia*...

7.

Bonnie said, "You look like shit."

She said, "Prob'ly because I feel like shit?"

"What can I do t'help?"

She sighed. It had been months. Winter was gone and Summer was making everything into steamy bright gold and endless cerulean blue and she kept thinking she needed to go see Gino and leave flowers for him... flowers for Missy...something...

She looked up at her friend and asked her if she would take her out to the ocean. When they got there, for the first time since any of her friends had learned *the Truth*, she took someone with her...out to the edge of her world to where she could stare out at an imagined image of something she'd never known.

"...I used to do this for hours..."

"I drove you out a bunch of times."

"I always thought about what my life would have been like if two strangers with no future had not sent me away."

"The strangers who took you in love you. Whenever I used t'get so pissy with my folks I'd end up at your house and Sal and Gabby would just make everything so good that all the shit would float away...

"What are you lookin' for, girlfriend?"

UNTIL THE END OF THE WORLD

She looked at Bonnie and shrugged, turned to look at the dreams of cotton clouds coming apart on the horizon, leagues and leagues of ocean...to Gibraltar...the Meditterannean...Cyprus and the Aegean....a place she'd never even known...and two faces fading into a chapter in a history book that likely would never be written.

"Will Blake let you have an evening without him?"

Bonnie grinned her evil grin. "Sure he will. I'll promise him something will make him piss his pants and he'll spend a week waiting for it t'happen."

"You shouldn't be so mean to him."

"He knows, honey. He loves me...fuck if I know why...but he also knows that no matter how much shit I throw his way, I love his dumbfuck ass until Doomsday."

"You don't think maybe there's somebody better out there?"

"Fuck no! Ain't nobody better than that shameless sleaze-bag of a boy."

⁂

That night they went dancing...without Blake. They got hot and sweaty and took a perverse delight in what most of the male patrons of the club seemed to perceive as a pair of lezzies on the town. Bonnie went to the loo to pee and fix her make-up. She sat staring at nothing... listening to Roxy Music...

Someone not Bonnie sat down in her chair.

"Can I buy you a drink?" he said.

"No thank you. I've got one."

"For after?"

She looked away at nothingness.

"My name's Tony. I'm Italian."

"No shit."

"It's obvious, I know."

She took a deep breath, looked into some dark eyes that made her ache for an anchor in her past.

"Me too." she said. "My name's Francesca..."

HEART'S-EASE

Once upon a time I fucked anything that moved.

Next day in the morning I went on my way so the next night I could do it all over again.

Endlessly, it seemed. There was never anyone waiting for me at home because I hadn't had one in a long time.

So here I was dancing the same old dance, and the long blonde curtain of her hair came down over my face where she couldn't see me being disgusted with myself.

I said, "They're not real, are they...?" because all too often on bad days it's easier to punish someone else for your own shortcomings.

She started to cry. For a moment I couldn't figure out why. I'd found her a couple of blocks down from the Port Authority on Eighth Avenue, hoping for someone who could give me a memory worth keeping in my head. And I looked into her brown eyes and realised she was about as damaged as anyone I'd ever met. Damaged as much as me. Probably more so. And it didn't matter if her tits were all silicone and saline, I recognised the hurt in her eyes and that it was the same as the hurt in my heart only worse. I'd ponied up a C note on the off chance she could give me back whatever it was I'd lost, and instead found myself fucking someone who needed some kindness even more than I did.

I said: "I'm sorry. Really. Please don't cry I'm just a drunk and an asshole and I...I'm angry as hell but not at you...please..."

She was so used to being naked under unshaded 100-watt bulbs she stood up and didn't even take the sheet with her.

"You're a sonofabitch," she said. "I did all kinds of stuff for you I don't do for anybody..."

"I'm sorry, Melinda."

"My name's not Melinda you bastard it's Polly. Like a fucking parrot. A cracker named Polly from a cracker town in Tennessee, fucking people like you..."

I didn't say anything. Whatever came into my head would have come out like some stupid platitude, words that would only convince her I was all the things she said and thought I was. I didn't want to be just one more fuck in her life. I couldn't tell you why, but suddenly it was important to me that she should know that; that I had never meant to make her feel bad.

She got up and stood naked in a corner of a shithole hotel room, with her back to me, her hair with brown roots that trailed down her back to an ass that once upon a time must have wiggled its way into the dreams of dozens of her male high school friends...a little bit more weight to what might once have been killer cheerleader thighs...

"Come back to bed," I said. "Please. I told you. I'm a shithead, but I didn't mean to hurt you."

UNTIL THE END OF THE WORLD

She turned around. Now I could see the long scars where some hack had given her the boobs of her dreams; still ache for the sweet little triangular promise of light brown hair between her thighs. She wiped her eyes with the back of her hands, inhaled some snot back up through her nose. She was used to being used. I didn't think she was more than twenty-two or three years old and I couldn't even remember what had been in my head when I was that young, only that it was wrong for her to be so broken.

"Come back to bed," I said again, and she did... crawled back under the flimsy threadbare sheet and curled up in my arms, pressed up against me where her body heat started me back on the road to wanting to fuck her again. She pulled away from me but I wouldn't let her go.

"No more," I said softly. "That's not me talkin' to you now...just ignore it..."

She looked up at me...tired brown eyes and runny mascara...mirrors begging for a place to not be afraid... and I nodded, reached over her shoulder to turn out the lamp on the flimsy cheap pressboard nightstand.

She said, "Is it okay if I go t'sleep for a little while?"

I didn't say anything, just inched her closer up against me and kissed the top of her head. Sleep sounded like a really good idea...

We both woke up a few hours later, still nothing but dark and neon lights out on 9th

Avenue. She said:

"Is your name really Richard?"

"Yeah," I said, still dopey with sleep. "You can call me Dick...short for dickhead."

It was almost...*luxurious*...feeling her next to me, somebody that young her skin all smooth and you could still find all the muscles underneath. I ran my hand down between her dearly-bought boobs and made circles... gently... in the hair on her pussy.

"You wanna go again?"

"No, Polly...more than anything I wanna pretend we've been in love forever and me putting my hands in places they don't belong is because we've been together for long enough that it's okay t'do it."

She took my hand and put two fingers inside her.

"Go slow and soft," she said. "I wanna pretend too."

A few minutes later I could feel her starting to come around my fingers, hugged her closer and then waited until her shivers stopped.

"Okay?" I asked.

She nodded against my chest and we went back to sleep, a few more hours of quiet before the world woke up around us again.

She'd been watching me sleep. Only for a couple of minutes, she said. I kissed each one of the scars hiding under her breasts and she started crying again.

"Don't," she said. "He told me if my tits were bigger I could make a lot more money."

I said: "I've been faking everything since I was ten years old."

And then: "Sixty-two," because there was that question on her lips.

"My grandfather is that old," she said.

"Lovely," I said. "Is he gonna mind much that after all the other stuff we did we just decided sleep was something we both needed?"

She shook her head answering no question at all...looked away and for no reason I could imagine dragged the sheet up between us, so I couldn't see her naked anymore.

"I gotta charge you for a whole night," she said.

"I'm okay with that," I said. "Just not if you give it all to whoever it was thought your tits needed to be bigger."

She shrugged and forgot to hold the sheet up in front of them.

"I can't do that," she said.

"Sure you can," I said. "Starting today it's all different."

"Sure like how?" she wanted to know.

It was my turn to shrug, because I didn't have any answers. I was just trying to be upbeat for her, leave her with something more than the desperation that had brought us together.

"You're not such a dickhead," she said.

"Oh yes I am, Polly," I said, wishing it were otherwise; that I wasn't so old, and that me and a Times Square hooker had met before our lives had turned to shit. "You wanna get some breakfast?"

She smiled. It was the first time I'd seen her smile. It seemed like something she kept hidden away so it wouldn't get spoiled. We got dressed slowly. Before we stepped out into the hallway of the shithole hotel and shocked the crap out of a dozen crazed cockroaches, she stood up tippy-toe on her platform shoes and kissed me on the lips. It felt like more love than I'd known in a million years.

She ate enough for three of us. Big glasses of milk with pancakes and eggs and bacon and home fries and it made me feel so old to see her being so young. At some point she forgot who she had become and who I was and she asked me what we were gonna do for the rest of the day. I said we could do anything at all, but I think maybe she understood that I was just being overly optimistic; that it was wishful thinking from a long long time ago.

He was out on the street looking for her when we walked past the Port Authority. I could hear the catch in her voice, feel the return of fear when she saw him and he saw her.

I opened up my wallet and pulled out the handful of hundreds still there...some twenties...a ten and two singles...handed them to her.

"Just keep walking, Polly," I said to her. "Don't stop. Go wherever you wanna go."

He put himself in front of us, said something to her and then I put myself between them, said "Keep walking, Polly," again, before I turned back to him and said, "She doesn't belong to you anymore. You can make an issue out of it, but it wouldn't be the smartest thing you'd ever done."

I took one last look at her looking back at me and nodded for her to keep going. He decided to make an issue out of it after all, and I didn't care what he was bringing to our pathetic little street-fight. All I needed to know was that he wouldn't be sucking the life out of any more lives after I got finished with him.

That I was finally going to do something useful.

L'OMBRE DE RIEN (The Shadow of Nothing)

I'd just gotten home. Taken off early on a Friday in anticipation of a celebration. My birthday. I cranked up an old CD...a live Fleetwood Mac album I'd inherited from my mom...*The Dance*...the first two tracks like open wounds in a lover's heart. The silence before the third track—Christie McVie wanting somebody *Everywhere*—held a knocking on my door I'd not heard...

It wasn't so much that he had changed physically. It was more the look about him when I opened the door, and thought twice because he seemed the same, yet the spirit... whatever it was that had animated his face three years ago...had changed in such a way that for an instant I felt it couldn't possibly be the same person.. And then there was the mistaken belief he was still in Paris...or somewhere...with the girl he'd taken away from me.

"*Bonjour*, Brooke," he said softly.

The same voice, and the same charming smile to go with, though now it seemed wholly contrived and *broken*. I was too stunned with surprise to do what I had wanted to do for most of those three years. Instead I said:

"*Bonjour*, shithead," quietly, and tried to slam the door in his face...

UNTIL THE END OF THE WORLD

That didn't happen. His hand reached round the door before I could manage it, so it was just his fingertips and the voice and the fact that no matter how pissed off I'd been or had so suddenly become, I still wasn't up to flattening his fingers in my doorframe. So then there we were sitting in my living room and I'd made a pot of coffee and while I still wanted to beat the crap out of him, I guess I'd resigned myself to whatever strange reality had come to visit me.

"…I've left her," he said at length. I knew he always took his coffee with cream or milk with sugar so I'd poured it black to the brim because I knew he hated it that way, and would have to drink some of it in order to get the milk and sugar to fit.

"You left her," I said, getting angry all over again. "Really. You left her and now here you are just to let me know. Why is that, Etienne? What happened, did you get her pregnant and a baby was too much for someone who was only interested in fucking her?"

He seemed surprised, like I'd discovered a secret he'd spent a lifetime trying to keep hidden.

"Is that why you slept with me? So you could get close enough to sleaze your way into Maia's bed…our bed…?"

"You are unkind," he said, making a wounded face. "It was not just me…and there was no baby…"

"Stop, Etienne," I said. "I really don't care one way or the other. She *said* she wanted us t'have babies, and I happily would have given her up to anyone but you to have them as long as she stayed with me."

He made some open-handed Gallic gestures that seemed to say *Why am I to blame for that?* and I thought about killing him all over again.

"I loved her, Etienne," I said to him. "Mostly I still do...but back then you knew that all along and you still did your irresistible French whatever, sleazed *me* into bed and then stole *her* away from me.

"Why are you here?"

The look on his face was so pathetic, but so transparent that simply murdering him would not have been enough.

⁂

We had met in Paris. For my last year of university I had come to the Sorbonne from Boston on an exchange programme. Maia had come from Mauritius, a tiny island that was slowly sinking into the Indian Ocean, and she was so exquisite there was nothing alive that could have passed her by without wanting to get to know her in every way imaginable.

I'd never even thought about my sexuality...assumed I was whatever I was supposed to be when it came to wanting bedmates and getting wet over them. And then there was Maia, and I wanted nothing ever again but for her to rock me to sleep every night, but only after hours of...well...up until then I never wanted anything or anyone as much as I wanted her. From the moment I saw her. And then I made the mistake of letting her let Etienne into our lives...

UNTIL THE END OF THE WORLD

"...Bonjour, ladies, comment se fait-il que deux si belles femmes s'assoient sans compagnie?"

We were sitting side by side on the patio of *le Café des Quatre Vents*, listening to the river whisper below us, ignoring the rest of the world. It was springtime in Paris, our first together, and standing on the flagstones beside our table he certainly was handsome and dashing and *oh si francais,* but I said:

"We are our own company, *merci,*" and turned away from him...turned back to Maia, who reached for my hand though her eyes never left him.

When he sat down across from us without benefit of an invitation, her hand clutched at mine and I could feel her pulse jumping against my fingers. I knew right away she was intensely attracted to him. Maia loved pretty things, and Etienne was very pretty on that lovely spring day in Paris.

He grimaced over two small mouthfuls of black coffee, reached for the cream and sugar.

Watching the minor discomfort I'd caused him made me feel small...ashamed...as if I somehow were doing Maia a disservice...trivialising what we'd had...

Somehow he managed to *attach* himself to us. Most nights we became a threesome out on the town. If Maia and I went dancing at *La Maison des Rêves*, Etienne would suddenly be there beside us; if we went to dinner at *le Chat Noir*, magically he would appear at the next table...and during the day, when we would meet for lunch or simply walk between classes, Etienne would be walking as well...close by... *Quelle coïncidence!* he would say *What a coincidence!*...and all three of us knew it was no coincidence at all.

Maia was fascinated by him, with his glittering smile, his brash disregard of convention, his naked adoration for both of us. I could see it in her eyes.

Have I told you about Maia's eyes? They weren't a pale brown so much as twin lamps of some strange golden colour...amber...sun-drenched honey...and they shone from a face of such shattering innocence and beauty that you couldn't look away even though the rest of her clamoured for attention...

She would bask in it, as if somehow she always knew the instant when total strangers would turn their heads and look after her as she passed them by on the street. I think her people came from somewhere in Southeast Asia, though she never spoke of her parents or her past at all. She was flawless though, from her toes to the roots of the shimmering black hair that fell past her tiny waist...and her skin was a strange and magical pearlescent grey, that shone with inner light, glowed from within, smooth as silk...

I thought of her as being some alien creature from another world, and never once felt anything but pride at her being with me, or jealous when she would acknowledge the admiration of others with a smile or a wave. For a brief while, until Etienne came along, she seemed impervious to anything more than that, happy to be with me, and I, like everyone else, knelt to her perfection, went breathless when she would lie naked beside me at night...

But Etienne was different, and whatever it was that made him so was enough to draw more than a casual wave or smile from Maia. As time went by I grew to resent him horribly, and once even fought with Maia when she spoke of him too often.

"I followed her," he said, almost childishly. If I'd been inclined to look at him more closely I think I might have noticed there were tears in his eyes.

"I thought you said you'd left her, Etienne."

He seemed surprised...again... and then realised it had been less than a two or three minutes since his bullshit lie and the truth.

"I followed her," he said...again..."She met someone else, someone from California who said he could make her famous..."

"So why are you here in Boston, Etienne, or did you decide to drop in just to annoy me?"

His hands shook when he tried to take another swallow of his coffee. Looking at him I realised what little composure he had mustered in order to knock on my door, sit in my living room, was rapidly coming apart. The look in his dark eyes was frightening, made even more so because I'd seen it before...in my own mirror...on the day after Maia had left me for him, and just about every day thereafter for the better part of a year. It was the look of someone hunted...or haunted...or simply a soul whose world had come apart at the seams. I suddenly realised that Etienne somehow had loved her every bit as much I had; that he had come to me in desperation—the only other soul he knew who would understand the shattering nature of her desertion.

Once upon a time when he had been so dashing and so confident, this sudden display of vulnerability would have been irresistible, something that would have had me all over him in *mother mode*, and then likely naked in a frantic sympathy fuck to take his mind off the pain...but in the wake of Maia's departure I'd become a lot more cautious so I just sat on the other end of my couch and watched him dissolve, at the same time feeling a distinct sense of superiority that I had never let anyone see *me* cry.

"...She has a Facebook page," he said a bit later. "Tik-Tok...Instagram...all of them. Dozens of photographs and selfies. Hundreds of guys *following* her, waiting for a special word from her lips, a smile or a little secret to be shared. She even did a video for this fellow from California, but you never see her face...you don't have to...you know it is her..."

I'd seen all of it, knew exactly what he was talking about, even the video. Though I had never consciously formed the thought, I'd known it was just a matter of time before Maia upped the ante in order to maintain her ascendency in the hearts and minds and shorts of her admirers. And it was the nature of our infatuation to seek her out wherever she was, no matter what she was doing...even if it was fucking someone else.

It had taken me most of three years to acknowledge she was gone, that I would never see her again in any way except the way she presented herself to her loyal followers all over the world. That I was one of them—though now a *silent* spectator out of pride and some nebulous form of self-preservation—was my dark secret. I began to feel an uncomfortable empathy with Etienne in spite of the fact that he had been the cause of my desolation, recognising it now was something we shared...something I realised he was hoping would win him *more* than a sympathy fuck from me

"You can't stay here," I said. Coldly. "I have a roommate."

"It would only be for a few days," he said cautiously, casting his line in the water again.

"Until you get a place of your own," I said, not trying to hide my sarcasm. He did another turnabout and I began to get angry again.

"No...no...I cannot stay," he said, smiling apologetically and taking shelter in the Gallic shrug that had been *si charmant* in Paris. "I must go back to France... "

"Well I hope you have a nice trip," I said...and then Tasha bumped through the door, behind two grocery bags containing the sumptuous meal she had promised me for my birthday.

Etienne stood up in a hurry—embarrassed though I couldn't figure out why—murmured a pleasantry without waiting for an introduction, and took off. She followed him with her eyes until the door to our flat closed behind him, then looked a big question at me.

"Just somebody I knew in Paris," I said. "He had a few hours layover on his way back…"

That lie became pretty obvious the next day, when I got back from a quick foray to the *patisserie* for fresh-baked *croissants* and our weekly infusion of near-deadly espresso-to-go. Etienne was waiting for me halfway down the block from our apartment building.

"Why are you still here? Where did you stay last night?"

"I need to talk with you, Brooke," he said, dishevelled and looking like he'd had maybe an hour's-worth of sleep.

I shook my head *No* and edged past him on the sidewalk. "I've got breakfast, it's getting cold. and I don't have anything else t'say t'you."

"Please," he begged, ignoring my questions, following me until I was almost to the door of my building. I turned on him, angrily.

"Just go away, Etienne. There's no point to any of this."

I made the mistake of looking at our living room window three storeys up, saw Tasha looking down at me with a big frown on her face. For no reason I could think of I felt guilty, and must have shown it, because she shook her head in disgust and turned away.

"I am not leaving until you talk to me," he said stubbornly.

"Then you're gonna be here a while," I snapped over my shoulder, juggling breakfast, fumbling for keys, letting myself into the *foyer* of the building. I snuck a look back at him, a fun-house caricature of himself through the ancient glass panels of the entrance door.

Tasha was still padding around in her undies, but most of her smiley-smile from the night before was gone.

"He's been outside waiting for you," she said, with no inflection in her voice at all. "I saw him right after you left. Did you sleep with him in Paris? I thought you were gay..."

The espresso and *croissants* got cold as I spent the better part of the next hour trying to explain. I'd never said anything to Tasha about Etienne *or* Maia. Now she wanted to know what was going on, and I couldn't come up with anything that wouldn't have been just me digging myself deeper into a hole.

"I thought you were gay," she said again.

"Maybe only half," I said, looking away from her.

"What's that supposed t'mean, Brooke?" she asked, very quietly, to let me know she was furious with me.

"It means I've slept with men and women," I said. "Etienne was one of them..."

And then I told her a bare-bones about Paris...and Maia...and she listened quietly, saying nothing, even when I was finished, until the silence between us got so heavy I could feel it crawling up over my shoulders and dragging me down into that horrible place where you know you're standing in the waiting room for Misery, with no appointment and no way of knowing what you were in for.

"I never lied t'you, Tasha," I said.

"You never told me all of the truth either," she snapped, and went into her bedroom, came out dressed and on her way out the door without even looking at me. In the street I saw her shove her way past Etienne who was keeping his promise not to leave until we'd spoken, and glared up at me before stalking away.

Tasha was working her way through the ashes of an abusive straight relationship that had put her in hospital two years before we met. She never really talked about it, but from some of what she did say I got the feeling that in her experience, an awful lot of women went gay in self-defense...hoping for some empathy...something...a respite from the unhealthy aggression our *culture* seemed to have made factory-issue in too many men.

I didn't...couldn't tell her everything...that I was on the run from Maia...that I'd been wounded as badly by her as any boy I'd ever known. Things in my mind became quite clear in the dead of night when I'd stare up into the dark and try to figure out what the fuck was going on; but in the morning most of the crystal-clear revelations had wandered off into the sunrise, and I was left on my own again, trying to be true to myself and to Tasha. When she looked at me with her withering contempt—for never being able to fully commit to the level of her own alienation—it was because my own sense of Maia's betrayal somehow had alienated me from both sides of what she now perceived as *the conflict*.

UNTIL THE END OF THE WORLD

But I could never meet her gaze in those moments of confrontation, or shrug off her obvious disappointment...

It went on like that for more than two weeks, day after day of her stony silence, and Etienne, always somewhere...waiting for me...looking worse than the day before... wild-eyed with whatever was making him as crazy as he was making me. One day he was there as I was leaving work, waiting between me and the bus-stop. I got so pissed off, so angry, and so tired of his constant *unwelcome* presence in my life, that I gave up, called myself every last thing I could think of that should have warned me off what I did...and then I did it anyway...

I let him crowd me into a corner of the shop that was deafening with trendy conversation and drowning in the aroma of trendy Starbucks crap masquerading as coffee. I looked down into the steaming mug of whatever it was he had gotten me, looked up at him—bleary-eyed and unshaven and definitely in need of some personal hygiene—and just raised my eyebrows.

"Thank you for doing this," he whispered.

"Just tell me what *this* is, Etienne," I said, "and let me get back to the shit you've made of my life."

"I did not intend for it to become this way."

"Well what *did* you intend, Etienne?"

He wouldn't look at me, checked out the steam rising up off his own mug.

"*Je ne c'est pas*," he whispered. "I don't know. I saw the two of you and I was jealous."

"Jealous? Of what?"

"Whatever it was between you...the way you looked at her...the way she would turn to you and reach for your face...like some ancient princess...regal...bestowing a blessing... granting some impossible request..."

That was when I began to understand; that somehow Etienne had read into my soul just by observing Maia and I dancing through our brief life together.

"I am very sorry. That is what I wanted to say to you."

I hate Starbucks coffee—no matter what they do to it it's not very good to start with, so it's like tarting up something of no real value and being able to sell it because you have a good press agent—the heart and soul of American capitalism. I sipped some of it anyway, and felt the Revelation that escaped me each morning suddenly become something real and capable of existing in daylight. It didn't make me feel any better to know that Etienne was drowning in the absence of something he had wanted so badly; it didn't give me any sense of payback for what he'd done, but it made me aware of the distinct possibility that under a different set of circumstances I might have acted in exactly the same way.

"I keep trying to telling myself she is not worth it."

In my newly-acquired wisdom I shuddered and reached for his hand, could feel him trembling with exhaustion and the absence of Hope.

"Oh she's worth it, Etienne," I said softly, "but only if you you're willing to accept day-old bread for your devotion. Maia's probably got her own story to tell, but she's not someone who has anything to give away beyond what you can see of her."

"What are you saying?"

"What I'm saying, Etienne, is that suddenly I see that Maia is like some kind of emotional vampire. She doesn't mean t'be that way...I can't allow myself to think it's something she does with premeditation...but she *requires* adoration...she needs to be worshipped... and can only respond to it by demanding more. On the outside she's perfect; inside she's like a black hole in a universe of broken people..."

"How do you live without her, knowing that she will fuck for anyone who will kneel at her feet ...?"

Unspoken was the fact that now, with the Internet, there were thousands who would kill to be able kneel at her feet with the even the merest prospect of a fuck in the offing. Etienne had lost all sense of himself...wept openly...in a Starbucks, of all places... oblivious to everyone around us...his breach of all that was trendy and cool in the temple of crappy coffee and great hype.

I stood up, brushed his cheek with my hand, no longer angry with him. No longer blaming him for stealing my illusion of Paradise away.

"I've stumbled away from all of it," I said. "I've let her take away all my good sense in exchange for an empty promise of something that never existed between us in the first place. Go home, Etienne...call me if you want to...whenever...we've got something to share now, for better or worse..."

When *I* got home Tasha was sitting on the sofa, looking like she'd been waiting for me. There was a suitcase by the door. She said she was sorry...

"I can't do this with you," she said. "I've got my own fucking baggage to carry and I won't...I can't...carry the weight of yours with this woman as well. I'll come back for the rest of my stuff when you're not here..."

When the cab outside honked for her, she kissed me goodbye on the forehead. She never looked back. She picked up her suitcase, opened the door and was gone.

I watched sunset creep through the windows...make empty shadows on the walls...

When there was no more light I realised that I had been dreaming for a very long time; that what I had imagined to be the loss of the most precious thing in my life had been, in fact, every bit as much of a dream as I had ever imagined to be mine. A shadow of something that probably had never been real to anyone but me...now just an empty shadow holding nothing at all.

The next day I went looking for a life in the real world.

Milton Keynes UK
Ingram Content Group UK Ltd.
UKHW022001131124
451149UK00013B/974